Letter from a Dead Man

A Jessica Minton Mystery
Book 2

Sharon Healy-Yang

TPP
Relax. Read. Repeat.

LETTER FROM A DEAD MAN (A Jessica Minton Mystery, Book 2)
By Sharon Healy-Yang
Published by TouchPoint Press
Brookland, Arkansas
www.touchpointpress.com

First Edition

ISBN: 978-1-946920-24-9

Editor: Kimberly Coghlan
Cover Design: Sharon Yang (concept); De-Ping Yang (compilation)

Library of Congress Cataloging-in-Publication Data
Healy-Yang, Sharon, author.
Letter from a dead man / Sharon Healy-Yang.
Series: A Jessica Minton Mystery
Description: Trade paperback edition | Jonesboro, AR: TouchPoint Press, 2017.
Identifiers: ISBN 978-1- 946920-24- 9
Subjects: LCSH Sisters-- Fiction. | Family-- Fiction. | New York (N.Y)-- Fiction. | New York (N.Y.)-- History-- 20th century-- Fiction. | New York (N.Y.)-- Social life and customs-- 20th century-- Fiction. | Mystery fiction. | Historical fiction. | BISAC FICTION / Mystery | FICTION / Historical.
Classification: LCC PS3608 .E237 L48 2017 | DDC 813.6-- dc23

Printed In The United States Of America

For my friend, Phil Burns

I owe a lot of thanks for help along the way with this novel. First, I want to thank the people at TouchPoint for continuing to give me the opportunity to bring you Jessica's adventures. I'm especially thankful that they respect my creativity and work, allowing me to follow my own drummer. They don't try to make me cookie-cutter my writing into what some people think are the popular trends. I'm particularly appreciative of Sheri Williams for her encouragement and good nature. I also had a wonderful time working with my editor Kim Coghlan. We really click. It's great to have someone who not only knows her writing, but respects a writer's prerogatives – and she enjoys my work, too! I bet she's as great a teacher as she is an editor.

Before *Dead Man* ever made it to TouchPoint, there were lots of people who helped me, sometimes by holding my feet to the fire to eliminate inconsistencies as well as clunky wording. So thanks to Ruth Haber, Amber Vayo, Judy Jeon-Chapman, Kathy Healey, and Sonia Cintron-Marrerra. I hope I haven't left anyone out! I also want to thank folks at the Worcester State University Library who aided me with some of my research, when it came to dealing with the Microfiche Machine (love that *NY Times*!): Pam McKay, Kate Zebrowski, Matt Bejume, and Linda Donohue. I'd also like to say thanks to the new friends whom I've made through Sisters in Crime-New England, who have given me advice, encouragement, and support: Leslie Wheeler, Arlene Kay, Lisa Lieberman, Connie Johnson Hambley, Gina Fava, and Judy Travis Copeck. Also, technical advising as to what Dusty was really thinking came from Rosalind and Natasha Yang. Then there are the friends who loved *Bait and Switch* so much, they pressed me to get a wiggle on and get out this sequel: Barbara Werblin, Monica Salca, Mary Kramer, Lisa McCarthey, Diane Jepson, Phil Burns, Ginger Vaughan, Angela Weisel, and ESPECIALLY Tricia LeBreton. I know that I must have left out good friends, and I'm sorry. Just know that I tremendously value your encouragement and support. You guys will be happy to know that I have more plans for Jessica's further adventures. How does the title *Always Play the Dark Horse* strike you?

Finally, my greatest thanks go to De-Ping Yang. He's given me every kind of support you can imagine: from designing the cover to reading the novel to going on NYC expeditions to help me enact the escape from the subway scene to just being my best bud. I love you very much, Yang.

Chapter One

April 28, 1945

Moonlight streamed across the nightmare-tortured bedclothes and Jessica Minton, her face buried in trembling hands. Waves of bitter helplessness peaked and ebbed with her furiously thundering heart. Dark, damp hair clung to the back of her neck. Again, she'd had the dream about James being captured and tortured by Nazis, while she was unable to save him. Jessica expelled a tremendous sigh before sinking back on the bed. But the sigh hadn't carried away her terrible inner ache. She switched on the bedside lamp.

"Aow?" Dusty's head poked out from under the desk.

"I guess I let out quite a holler, didn't I, pet?"

Dusty snaked herself out, considered a moment, then trotted across the room for a graceful leap onto the foot of the bed. She gave Jessica her best Lauren Bacall glance of sophisticated inquiry.

"Nightmare, pal, nightmare. C'm'ere, buddy. I could use a little feline sympathy!"

Dusty sauntered over to Jessica's beckoning fingers. Despite figuring that Dusty was interpreting the signal as a call to food, Jessica accepted the feline camaraderie. Dusty's warmth and furry softness were potent anodynes for the chronic torment of not knowing–and having no way to find out.

"How about a little tuna for you and a cup of tea for me?"

At those words, Dusty dashed to the doorway, coyly arching her back and blinking before Jessica could throw a robe over her nightgown.

After navigating the short hallway leading to the kitchen, Jessica had no concern about flipping on the kitchen lights. Her apartment was well below the fifteen-story blackout requirement. Zombielike, with an occasional preoccupied thrust of tangled hair from her face, she went through the motions: feed the cat, put the water on for tea, get out cup and saucer, flick on the radio. At least the silence wouldn't be measured out by the tick of the wall clock and the hum of the refrigerator. All the while, Jess couldn't keep her worries about James Crawford out of her head. No news is good news. Ha! Not with him incommunicado in the middle of a damned war.

Something brushed against Jessica's leg, and Dusty was suddenly seated primly on the kitchen chair next to her. The slightest of smiles turned up Jessica's mouth, and she rubbed her companion's neck.

The cat gave Jessica's hand a reassuring, towel-rough lick, then stretched her neck back into her human comrade's massaging fingers. Jess paused, shrugged at Dusty's annoyance at the interruption of being petted, then sighed, "War news, war news, but no James news."

Shouldn't she have heard from him? The war was almost over in Europe. That was when he went silent. What did it mean? The pictures in today's paper of congressmen touring German prison camps came to mind. She'd actually scanned those atrophied faces, those wasted bodies, looking for James. And she'd practically salivated over some general's congressional testimony that many people thought dead were actually prisoners. But he was talking about American soldiers. He wasn't talking about spies—spies they shot.

Flipping up her tail, Dusty disappeared under the table at the teakettle's sudden screaming. Jessica trudged across the white linoleum floor to the stove, its surface gleaming white like the cabinets' paint. Everything was clean. Damn clean. A person had to break up the time somehow when her career dried up.

Jessica turned down the gas, lifted the kettle off the burner with a potholder, and returned to the table. Of course she was antsy–an out-of-work actress could do nothing *but* brood. Her active imagination needed the discipline of a role; otherwise, it would be off like Busher showing her heels to whatever field of runners they threw at her. Even when she was working, imagination had lured her into James's bait and switch caper almost two years ago.

But more than an over stimulated imagination had brought them together–and kept them together since. Too bad that togetherness was only in spirit now. She hadn't seen James for about nine months, and here it was April 27th, 1945, one a.m. Make that April 28th, then. He had gotten word to her at first. But in early spring, just after the Allies had repelled the Germans' breakout–nothing.

James was undercover. That's all! It wasn't as if he could just drop a nickel and have the overseas operator connect them. She'd have known, somehow, if he were ... not coming back. It had just been a bad three months, a killer three months, what with one play closing and another dead before it even opened. Then to top it all off, Roosevelt had just died. If all that weren't bad enough, the rationing was getting more complicated every day.

Well, all this Hamlet-caliber brooding wasn't going to end the war, bring James home, or untangle rationing restrictions, let alone resurrect Roosevelt.

So Jessica forced her thoughts into more comforting channels as she poured boiling water into the teacup. Mmm, tea leaves steeping gave off a homey and relaxing scent. Frank Sinatra was lazing through "Be Careful It's My Heart" with Jimmy Dorsey on WABC. Absently swirling her tea bag by its string, Jessica admitted that she had much less to fret over than many people. She wasn't in the South Pacific where victories were marked in yards not miles. She wasn't a kid or an old lady hiding in the rubble of Berlin. She wasn't the victim of a German concentration camp. She was just like millions of mothers, sweethearts, wives, and sisters, all waiting for their families to be whole again when their loved ones came home. It was tough, but you could do it.

Her glance fell on the front section of the newspaper on her table, the headline about the United Nations opening in San Francisco. Already they were squabbling over who should be permanent head. But there was hope, wasn't there? Forty-six nations had signed on the dotted line. If they, no *we*, could all act together, head aggression off at the pass, maybe we would never have to do *this* again. James could return, just like thousands of other guys. Jess liked what Truman had said in his opening address: "If we do not want to die together in war, we must learn to live together in peace."

So she *shouldn't* be afraid to hope. A girl couldn't let a bad couple of months throw her. She had so much going for her: her home, her friends, the cat. And her friend Vic, the radio soundman, was trying to help her get work.

Jess continued picking through the newspaper for something distracting. Oops! *Get that tea bag out or the brew will be strong enough to stroll off on its own!* Now, where was she? Sports? Nope. With the ban on horseracing, nothing interested her there. Fortunately, last season had been exciting enough for two years. Hadn't it been the cat's meow to witness the first recorded triple dead heat? Brownie, Wait a Bit, and one of her favorites, Bossuet. Too bad she couldn't get James anywhere near the track. Who'd expect a man who was able to stay cool while keeping a jump ahead of Nazis to be afraid of horses? Swell, back to James and the Nazis, again. Jess tried to kid herself out of her fears by thinking that the Nazis might try to make James talk by forcing him to pet Percherons. No dice.

Entertainment. Great. Another reminder of how a juicy part in *Ill Met by Moonlight* had gone south with a rocky New Haven tryout and an all-too-brief run here in the city. And things had only gotten worse when Jess's shot at another successful run at the Cherry Street Theatre literally went up in smoke, thanks to an embezzling backer with an arsonist friend.

There was still radio. Her agent was dead set against her moving in that direction. To him, it was a step down for a theatre actress, but what about Paul Stewart and Joseph Cotton and Agnes Moorehead? Then there was Don Ameche. He started in radio, moved on to being a film star, and still had *The Bickersons* on the radio, without losing a jot of his movie-star status. Of course, she didn't have Orson Welles or a successful movie career to back her up.

The telephone chimed into her thoughts. Jess knew who it was. Not ready to deal with the caller, she didn't move. But the phone was brassily insistent. Well, better to face the music now.

"Hello there, Jessica," the voice of her sister, Elizabeth Minton, arched over the wire.

"How did you know I'd be up, Liz?"

Jessica leaned into the wall near the door, where she'd had a kitchen phone installed some time ago.

"Just had a feeling. You know my 'feelings.' Couldn't sleep, kiddo?"

"I ... well, I guess I have a lot on my mind."

All that uncertainty and tension shot through the wire, despite Jessica's best efforts. Would Liz really want to know her sister had been fretting over the man who helped send her husband, ex-husband now, up the river?

"Nothing from your agent about a new play?"

"Wrong time of the season, Liz."

"How about the radio work?"

"I'm working at it. It's good money, and there are lots of jobs; the catch is that lots of good, experienced actors and actresses are already filling them. Breaking in is murder. You can audition, but the competition is just about impossible for a new kid on the block like me."

"You have all that experience in the theatre."

"But nothing in radio. It's a whole different acting animal. In fact some theatre actors are at a real disadvantage because they're used to having long rehearsal stretches or have gotten out of practice doing a solid cold reading, you know where you're handed a script and have to hit the part running. That's what Vic has been telling me."

"The guy who's been helping you? Sound man or something?"

"Correct on both counts, Liz. In fact, he's been great, showing me how to act to the mike, get in synch with the sound effects. He and his girlfriend have even been doing readings with me. He's a grand coach. I wouldn't be surprised if he didn't become a director someday."

"Ambitious sort, isn't he?"

"That's the beauty of radio. Once you're in, you have so many chances to learn and branch out. The trick is getting in."

"So nothing definite, yet."

"No. Not yet."

"Mmm. Well, Jess, I might be able to scratch your back, if you'll scratch mine."

"We're speaking metaphorically, right?"

"Wise guy. Now Listen. You know I've been trying to convince Evan we should launch an evening-wear line?"

"Sure, Liz. But how do I fit in?"

"Jess, I want this to go over big. It's our shot to break out of the $16.95 dress game. We needed some real flair to put this over with the upscale crowd. *You* will be our main model. Think Chili Williams with class instead of the polka dots."

"Me? Liz, what do I know about modeling?"

"You can walk across a stage without tripping–when you're in character..."

"Thanks a heap."

"Besides, I've been thinking. If you can re-train yourself for radio, you can re-train yourself to be a professional clotheshorse. Think about it. You're an actress from the stage. People respect you, and you look darned good in some of our gladrags." A pause and then, "It's up to you, Jess, but you'd be perfect–plus, this would keep you busy. And of course we can afford *you*."

"Gee thanks. You really know how to flatter a girl. But, Liz, won't the other girls mind my snapping up this sweet gig?"

"Don't worry. There's plenty to keep them busy, and they know we're looking to bring in someone with an outside name."

"It's about time you admitted your kid sister has star quality."

"Don't kill it, Jess. What do you say? Are you in? You could start work on Monday. We need some promotional shots. Since the photographer's in the same suite as our business offices, we can go in together. Better limit yourself to salads for lunch, though, if you're going to keep your girlish figure. What do you say?"

What *should* she say? What she knew about modeling could dance on the head of a pin and still leave room for a couple of chorus lines of angels.

"Listen, Jess, I've seen your portfolio. You already know how to pose for a photographer. If the radio work comes through, we can schedule the photo sessions around it. I'll let you show off the new creation you inspired at the fashion awards dinner coming up. What do you say?"

"I ... yeah. Okay. You have yourself a deal, Liz. It's about time I got back to work. This will be an enormous help."

"I know you've a lot on your mind. It's tough to be waiting."

"Even if I'm waiting for a guy who brought you so much grief?" Jessica ventured.

"You're my sister, Jess," Liz reassured her. "That's what I know. Anyway, what guy? I meant you were waiting for the tracks to re-open."

"Okay, Liz. I'll probably live to regret saying this, but you're a good scout."

"Skip it, kid. Pick you up at seven on Monday."

"Great. And, Liz, thanks."

"That's okay. Now, go get some sleep. I don't want you accessorizing our outfits with crow's feet and blue circles under your eyes. Just remember, people who are a pain in the patoot always turn up. See you Monday."

"'Night, Liz."

Dusty regarded her human roommate with quiet satisfaction.

"I suppose you had her call?" Jessica smiled at her be-furred comrade. Still reflecting on her sister's call, Jess didn't even mist up when, over the radio, the ultra-romantic "It's Been a Long, Long Time" flowed out of Harry James's liquid trumpet. Maybe she'd hear from James before the Kentucky Derby, now that it had been moved back to June. And this job would give her a grand chance to keep an eye on Liz's business partner, Evan Blair.

Chapter Two

April 29, 1945

Sunday-morning light gleamed through two walls of plate-glass into the bustle of a chinging cash register, clinking plates, and the buzz and rumble of diners slurping, eating, and conversing while crammed into red leather booths or against one another at the sweeping counter. Waitresses, over-laden with orders, maneuvered amongst tables jammed with customers. The relentlessly sizzling grill flavored the air with scents of bacon, sausage, eggs, hash, and pancakes.

A tall, slender young woman, blonde hair regally swept off her broad, curved forehead, scanned the restaurant and mentally demanded: *Where the heck are the others? I can't hold down this booth by myself forever. And what's this scoop of Jessica's?*

The mass of people waiting at the door reluctantly bulged, and out erupted a young, dark-haired woman in a robin's egg blue suit. The blonde woman smiled. *Great! There's Jess!*

Jessica Minton caught Iris Rossetti's megawatt smile and impatient beckoning. She threaded her way through the currents of waitresses and customers to reach her friend. Sliding slid into the seat across from Iris, she grinned, "That coffee smells heavenly! My java addiction is kicking in!"

"Best coffee on the East Side!" Iris declared, allowing herself the luxury of a rationed sip.

"I'll say," Jessica laughed. "Most places just let the grounds wave to the hot water as it goes by."

A waitress slapped down a menu on the placemat in front of Jessica and automatically quizzed, "Coffee?"

"Certainly. Thanks."

It was all Jessica could do not to crack up at Iris's glaring curiosity while the waitress poured. Her friend did not handle suspense well. At last, they were alone, or as alone as they could be in this din. Perching her hands on the edge of the table, leaning forward, Iris urged, "Well ... ?"

"Mmm?" Jessica teased innocently, pretending to peruse the menu.

"Don't get cute with me, Jessica Theresa Minton. What's your scoop? Patton call and invite you to rumba with him in Berlin? Give out!"

Jess smiled sweetly, "We don't have a full house yet, Iris. Let's wait for Lois. I want to tell you both at the same time."

Iris snorted in frustration, a ladylike snort, but still a snort.

"It's not *that* hot, Iris. Calm down. Anyway, how's your play?"

"Never mind my play, you stinker. Well, actually, okay, let's mind the play. Great. We're still running strong. You know how I *love* to do comedy. Sometimes I think what happened to the Cherry Theatre was the luckiest misfortune. Otherwise, I never would have been free for this job..." Then, remembering her friend's situation, Iris blurted, "Ooh, sorry, Jess. I didn't mean ... well, you know..."

Behind her coffee mug, Jessica smiled mischievously, "Maybe we won't have to avoid the subject of gainful employment much longer."

Iris brightened, "A job? Where? The radio? Your friend came through for you? You squared it with your agent? C'mon, pal, spill the beans! Maybe this is better than what I thought at first."

Jess relaxed against the red leather seat, warmed by her chum's enthusiasm for her prospective good fortune. Half the fun of good news was sharing it with your friends. She chuckled, "What *did* you think at first?"

"Why that your James, that teacher at Washington Irving University, came back. You were getting mar ... Oh, I did it again! Sorry, Jess. You still haven't heard from him?"

"No."

Her voice was not harsh or angry but still betrayed powerful emotion held in check.

Iris bit her lower lip before venturing, "Still having nightmares?"

Jess responded with an expression of wry resignation.

"Do you think something is wrong, Jess?"

"Like ... ?"

"Well, you only went out with him for November, December, and January, not long after your brother-in-law and Liz broke up. Then you two have only been in touch through the mail. I hate to say it, but do you think he's lost interest?"

Jessica disagreed, almost amused, "Oh, Iris, I'm not worried that he's given me the gate. I've been afraid that James might have been killed–in a blitz or something."

"Of course I know there's a war on," Iris rolled her eyes.

Jess couldn't exactly tell Iris the whole story about James's endeavors for the Allies, so she only said, "I know he hasn't lost interest, Iris. I'd been hearing from him pretty regularly until just this spring. You know lovers aren't exactly top priority in the mails right now. Anyway, he's written when he could."

"But not lately."

"No, not lately."

Jessica's long red nail traced the rim of her white diner mug.

"I'm sorry, Jess," Iris was genuinely regretful. "I'm not trying to make you miserable. I just don't want to see anyone hurt you. It would be such a shame for the guy you started seeing after you broke up with Larry to give you the air."

Jess tapped the mug a little impatiently. Even if *she* knew the truth, she didn't enjoy hearing James slammed when it was so unjust. Regardless, she couldn't exactly explain to Iris that the chap that they once "happened" to bump into on the steps of the Public Library had earlier involved her in a spy plot to snare a quisling. Or that this new beau was not a visiting professor at Washington Irving University but an agent on loan from England training American agents to work with the French Resistance. She and James had been allowed to see each other only because his superiors had decided he needed the cover of having a girlfriend to make him seem like an average Joe.

Still, what would Jessica have given for someone to whom she could confide about her fears? Unfortunately, none of the people in her life who were hep to the facts about James were in any frame of mind to offer her sympathy. So, Jessica kept her fears to herself and took another sip of coffee.

Those reflections flashed by before Iris eased the conversation to safe ground with, "So, Jess, I can't believe I was the first one here, and Lois Wong is going to be the last."

"Maybe the train was late. Remember, she was visiting her mom in Boston."

"Mmm," Iris agreed, flagging down the waitress for a refill, continuing as she splashed cream and sugar into her mug, "That girl is so good to her mother. She's always taken darned good care of her."

"Hasn't Lois always carried a heavy burden for the whole family?" Jess mused sympathetically.

"I'll say," Iris nodded decisively. "What a raw deal they had. The scandal with her brother and the jade, and then his ... you know ... suicide. Her dad just died out of despair at losing the son and everything else. Poor Lois had to give up her dream of running her own gallery because of the scandal and her trying to pay back something of what her family owed to the jeweler who owned the jade."

"I know," Jess agreed sadly. "It was a downright sin. Lois so loved the art world, and they just wrote her off. You wouldn't think that three little two-inch squares of jade could cause so much heartache. The fact that they were Ming dynasty and had poetry intricately carved on them only upped the value. Liquidating her family's cherished heirlooms put a big dent in the debt, but Lois still had to work herself like crazy for years."

"It still burns me up, Jess, every time I think about how people turned their backs on her. There was no proof *she'd* done anything wrong, but she couldn't get decent work anywhere. The best she could do was as a cleaning girl at one of those agencies."

"Where she worked her way up from being a maid to *running* the company," Jessica smiled. "Our Lois is indomitable."

"Sure, but even if she does handle some of the big residential hotels, it's still a grind," Iris shook her head. "You know as well as I do, even though Lois tries not to let on, it still eats at her–like she thinks she still has to reclaim her family honor. Do you think it's a Chinese thing?"

Jess shrugged and remarked, "Well, Tom Tulliver did the same thing in *The Mill on the Floss*, and he wasn't exactly Chinese–and, unlike Lois, he was a little stinker at times."

"Hmph." Iris took another shot of coffee. "Professor Minton. You can have the long hair stuff. I'll take Kathleen Winsor–and the guy who wrote *Leave Her to Heaven*."

"Tsk, Tsk, Iris. Such low-brow reading for a girl who played Celia to my Rosalind."

"That's different. Good comedy is good comedy, no matter when it was written." Then Iris caught sight of someone familiar picking her way politely but determinedly through the crowded diner. Iris pronounced, "It's about time."

Jess followed her friend's gaze and smiled to see a thirtyish woman in a wine-colored, nipped-waist suit, her dark hair pulled off her face, except for bangs curving precisely across her brow. A pertly angled dark beret lent her dash.

"Don't look so impatient," Lois Wong teased Iris as she slipped in next to Jessica, "I overslept–and the train was late."

"My mother always said that any time someone had more than one good excuse, get suspicious. Maybe there's a mysterious man in the picture," Iris conjectured knowingly.

Lois eyed her friend skeptically before remarking, "If I could find a man who could sweep me off my feet, I'd put him to work sweeping apartments at the Ballard Arms. We've got this wolf of a tenant who can't keep his hands off our girls. I've been thinking of requiring our maids to be either in Golden Gloves or on a track team before I let them clean there."

"How about I require we order before I pass out from hunger?" Jess changed the subject.

Before too long, Lois was contemplating the best way to attack her cream cheese and lox on a bagel without anything slathering her slender, manicured fingers. Meanwhile, Jessica started digging merrily into steak and eggs, only to pause and tempt her companions with, "You know, girls, this may be my last hurrah for a big meal, since my new job requires me to stay on the trim side."

Iris leaned forward to demand, "That's the news? That's what you had me on tenterhooks over?" Her eyes narrowed, "So, it can't be radio if you have to *look* slim. What *is* it?"

"Maybe I should rent a horse and take a few turns around Central Park to work off a few pounds. What do you think, Lois?" Jess impishly ignored Iris.

"I think that after this breakfast, *you* should carry the horse around a few turns," Lois deadpanned.

"Oh, come on, you two! What's the job, Jess?" Iris insisted.

"Okay, Iris, although I'm afraid it's not all *that* exciting," Jessica allowed. "I'm going to work for Liz, as a model. She thought my name might give their new line a little 'oomph.'"

"So, what exactly will you be doing, Anne Sheridan?" Lois inquired.

Iris cut in, "Never mind that, Lois." Turning to Jessica, she demanded, "Do you get to keep any of the clothes?"

Jessica shook her head. "No, Iris. Liz just thought that even a minor celebrity might add a little pizzazz to her line. She asked me to do some photo layouts and wear some of their numbers on the town: the Stork Club, El Morocco. Liz even believes she can charm us into 21 and get us seated somewhere to be seen. Not in the back, you know 'Siberia,' where they put all the nobodies. She has it in her head that if we go where people with prestige and money see us, they'll be captivated by the elegance of her designs, especially at this fashion awards dinner that's right around the corner."

Iris crinkled her brow and puzzled, "I know she'd be with Larry, but who would you go with?"

"She'd like to pair me with her partner, Evan Blair," Jess answered, almost pulling off sounding neutral.

Lois's expression told Jessica that she hadn't been fooled. However, before Lois could comment, Iris switched the topic: "So when are Liz and Larry going to get married, anyway? You don't mind my asking, do you, Jess?"

Jessica shook her head before answering, "Don't jump the gun, Iris. The divorce was only recently final. Liz doesn't leap into the big decisions."

"Except for the partnership with Evan Blair," Lois stated.

Jessica would only admit, "I know she was desperate for an investor to get the firm off the ground. He had the money, and other investors really wanted to see a man at the helm with her, but..."

"But what?" Iris queried a little too eagerly.

Jessica frowned, struggling to convert instinctive doubts into convincing reasons. Finally, she answered, "I just wish he were a little shorter on charm and longer on substance."

"Does he charm your sister?" Lois asked thoughtfully.

With a shrug, Jessica answered, "You know Liz. She *thinks* she can handle anyone–even after her marriage. I have to admit she does have a finger on every aspect of the business, though. The books say she's doing pretty well. No evidence of Blair dipping where he shouldn't. And the bookkeeper is 100% on the square. I guess I shouldn't worry."

"How do you know that the *bookkeeper's* kosher?" Iris proposed significantly.

"She comes through our lawyers, Bushey, Baggott, and Greene. After all these years as our family lawyers, believe me, they've proven they're on the level. Anyway, it's not the money going out I'm worried about. It's where that first stake of Evan Blair's came from."

"Elizabeth met him out of town, didn't she?" Lois recalled.

"On a vacation out West," Jessica concurred. "He had a small dress company out in San José, which I later found out he won gambling."

"And Liz went in with him, knowing that?" Lois wasn't exactly amazed, but Pearl Harbor hadn't amazed her, either.

"Well," Jessica allowed herself a swallow of coffee before continuing, "He'd won the company several years back. According to Liz, he'd been running it quietly, successfully, no high-rolling, for some time. He told her he'd been aching to get back to his home turf in the East–though I never could figure out exactly where that was. Anyway, he told her he loved putting his money on what *he* saw as a sure thing, especially when everyone else thought it was a long shot. Her designs and business head were just the kind of bet he thought he could score big on. So he liquidated the company out West to back Liz here in New York."

"Did she buy that?" Lois was skeptical.

"She bought the backing, Lois. And I have to admit, I haven't seen any double-dealing. Neither has Larry. It's just that nobody knows anything about him before the dress company in San José."

"What I've always wondered," Iris chimed in, "is why *Larry* never helped stake Liz."

"Larry's last name isn't Rockefeller," Jessica pointed out, mildly amused. "He wouldn't have that kind of cash lying around."

"I suppose, Jess. I just remember that Larry wasn't that crazy about you having a career when he wanted to marry *you*," Iris pointed out. "He can't be all that thrilled about Liz owning her own business."

Lois added, "If Evan Blair is as charming as Jess describes him, I imagine Larry isn't crazy about Liz's business for more than one reason."

"You two!" Jessica shook her head in mock disapproval. "You've been listening to too many soap operas."

"Jess, you have to admit that a guy getting dumped by one sister, moving on to the next one after she divorces a no-good husband, then maybe losing her to a mysterious business partner is a little juicy," Iris countered.

"Speaking of juicy, get a load of that *grande dame*," Lois interrupted, nodding out the window. "I could tell you a tale or two about her."

They hadn't noticed the Rolls pull up across the street before. Now they saw the majestic blonde, her upsweep tucked under the cocoa globe of a hat that matched the capacious sleeves complimenting the chocolate brown dress sheathing her curvaceous figure. A chronically growling black Scottie strained at its leash, color-coordinated with the woman's hat. A tall man in a dark trench coat and fedora waited to escort her, his eyes hard and shrewd in his Roman-nosed face.

"Who's *that*?" Iris broke the silence.

"Isn't she Mrs. Wilmington Tewkesbury, Lois?" Jessica queried. "You know something about her, right?"

"Her and Fala's evil twin there. Look! He almost got that priest right in the ankle!" Iris gasped.

"That poor dog," Lois said sympathetically. "He used to belong to one of Tewkesbury's business partners. That man and dog adored each other. Would you believe that when she drove the man broke, she seized even the pup as an asset? Blue-blood Scotties are worth a fortune. The owner passed away, and the dog's been a miserable creature since."

"Liz always used to say there are no bad dogs, only bad owners," Jess considered. "That woman sounds dreadful! Poor puppy."

"You know it, Jessica! She married rich, and she wants everyone who didn't to know it–tastefully but decidedly," Lois agreed. "My old connections tell me she hits every gallery in town trying to find a new discovery. But God help her discoveries. She makes pets out of them then crushes their talent. Then it's toss them into the trash bin and on to the next victim."

"I guess there aren't enough flies out there for her to de-wing," Jessica concluded.

"There's also the way she treats the 'peons.' Not a pretty picture, but I suppose she has a lot of pressure on her. It's terribly tiring spending all that money, being a patroness of the arts, and pronouncing all the big words correctly," Lois continued. "Look, there they go into Sergei's gallery."

Jessica nodded toward the lady's knight-in-a-trench-coat and quipped, "He looks like the type to be into art. Methinks the lady's past is showing."

"He looks a little like Lloyd Nolan to me," Iris decided.

"I heard his name's Eddie Kubek," Lois said, "and you're on the money, Jess. *He's* definitely *not* from the right side of the tracks."

A little man, nearly bald and with a mustache that swept dramatically upward on either side of his nose, greeted the odd couple at the door before they all disappeared into the gallery.

"So, do you think that's her real hair?" Iris dished.

Lois and Jessica cracked up, with Lois qualifying, "Color or quantity?"

Nudging the creamer toward her friends, Jess mischievously inquired, "Perhaps you'd like a little cream to go with those catty comments?"

"Oops, excuse us Saint Jessica," Iris retorted, with mock contrition.

"Actually," Jessica began, growing serious, "I'd like to know a bit more about that woman, for my sister's sake. Elizabeth met her at a fashion soirée not long ago. Madame Tewkesbury was interested in some of Liz's designs. She seems to have put a bee in Liz's bonnet about going upscale. Lois, maybe you could give me an idea of what Liz would be getting herself into with that gal."

"Liz could take her. They're both cut from the same cloth in many ways," Lois reflected. "This one's probably tougher, but your sister's smarter. It wouldn't be a picnic, though."

Iris advised impishly, "Just have Blair run interference with that pooch."

"Oh well," Jessica rolled her eyes, "that's another story entirely. Evan Blair does not want Liz to pursue the Tewkesbury deal. He thinks she's biting off more than she can chew. He wants to keep the business low profile for now."

"His objections hit a sour note to your ear?" Lois queried.

Jess shrugged. "He might have a point. It's just that people in business usually *want* to be noticed, to have a chance to sell more. Starting tomorrow, though, I'll have opportunity to get a better feel for the situation."

Jessica would have been much happier if she hadn't then noticed that the song coming over the diner radio was some gal boogieing through "And Her Tears Flowed like Wine."

Chapter Three

Monday, April 30, 1945

Although Elizabeth Minton's office was hardly the Rosalind Russell executive model, it was still a nice slice of real estate. The walls were papered a light golden brown, picking up the sunlight through the window on the wall behind her desk. Opposite the window, a door led to the reception room. Flanking that wall were file cabinets and comfortable but businesslike chairs, ready to be drawn up to Liz's desk for conferences. A large, blond-wood credenza filled the wall space between the dressing-room door and the window–Liz's one indulgence since going into business.

Businesswoman chic in her emerald pinstriped suit, Liz glanced quickly at the door on her right: Evan's office. Time to get in there and go over sales figures with him. Mighty healthy ones at that!

Hesitating, Liz looked to the dressing room on her left. Jessica was in there. She really wished they could share a heart-to-heart about Larry. Jess was not alone, however, and Elizabeth was not about to cry on her kid sister's shoulder in front of the help. Maybe "cry" wasn't the right word–"snarl" much better conveyed her present feelings about Larry Sanders. Damn, why couldn't Larry understand how good she was at her work? It really killed her to admit that she was finally walking a mile in her sister's spectator pumps on the subject of work and marriage with Larry Sanders, especially since she'd given Jess such a hard time about not appreciating him when they had been a couple.

The tall, brunette woman sauntered over to an easel displaying a sketch of a new concoction of eveningwear she'd designed. Well, she and Larry had both been working hard: she in establishing her business and Larry in wartime civil service. The war's headlong rush toward its brutal closure certainly hadn't made his life easier. And Larry was still smarting over being moved out of a job dealing with sensitive information after his involvement in the debacle with her ex-husband, aka the Nazi spy. Larry had been cleared, but his superiors had felt more comfortable transferring a living reminder of their security slip-up out of their sight, even if it meant an unjustified demotion. Tough luck for Larry, but no hard feelings, right?

Dead wrong. Though Larry wasn't one to complain to his superiors, Elizabeth sensed his simmering resentment. Her success must have been particularly galling to him when he felt betrayed and demeaned in his career.

Elizabeth forced her attention back to her desk between her and the window and gave a determined tap to the black metal hood of her Underwood. *Snap out of it, kiddo*! Some verbal jousting with Evan ought to perk her up. It usually did! She might even finally persuade him to let her go after Mrs. Wilmington Tewkesbury's endorsement. Evan always seemed to find some way to weasel out of discussing that subject, but she'd pin him down sooner or later. The challenge was half the fun!

Liz Minton snatched up a folder from her desk and with take-charge strides crossed the room. A sharp rap on his door, and she bore down on Evan Blair.

Behind a desk strewn with paperwork, Evan Blair smiled over one of those volumes on code that so fascinated him. Even when he was sitting down, his height was apparent. The sun glinted off the red in his golden brown hair, and a trim mustache added dash to his features. He rose slightly at Liz's entrance.

"Look over the sales reports yet?" she queried.

"No, Elizabeth." He settled back in his chair, arms stretching back to cradle his head in clasped hands. "I'm afraid I've been playing hooky. Just couldn't get in the mood. Thought I'd indulge myself in reading up on Wheaton's cipher disk."

"Oh you and your darned codes."

"Cipher, Liz, cipher," he corrected her with mock disapproval.

"Cipher, code. What's the diff?"

"Remember, Liz, I told you: a code uses symbolic figures or a special grouping of letters to replace words or groups of words; a cipher replaces individual letters with..." his voice trailed off into silent amusement as Liz raised a hand to cover her feigned yawn.

Liz glanced down at the models' proofs scattered over her partner's book, then observed, "Hmm. It looks to me like the figures you're checking out aren't in the least 'symbolic.'"

"Now, Liz," Blair began, dropping his hands in mock protest to his chest, "I'm wounded that you don't trust me."

"Oh, sure I trust you, but only because you have to go through my office to get to the models' changing room."

"Ah, but our lovely secretary is working merely a few paces beyond the door," he returned, his eyes as puckish as his smile.

"Maybe I'll have to do something about that. Let Ginger go and replace her with Wallace Beery or Victor McLaughlin."

"You wouldn't settle for Marie Dressler or Marjorie Main, now would you, Liz?"

"Would you?"

"No, I suppose not," Blair conceded. "They aren't exactly the loveliest figures on the silver screen. However, I must credit your sister with ample charm. I had a chat with her earlier today. Lovely young woman."

"She has a lovely right hook for wolves," Liz smiled, coming around to his side of the desk and picking up his appointment book. "She also has a fellow."

"Now, Duchess, I'm just trying to make you jealous."

"I'm green with envy," Liz deadpanned, before returning to his appointments.

"I can see. Notice anything interesting in there?"

Liz snapped the book shut in her hand and answered, "I see you have been busy. I guess I can allow you a little recreation. But I'll just..." she deftly drew away from Blair a proof of Jessica in a bathing suit, "remove a little of the temptation."

"My care-worn mother and my parish priest bless those grey hairs on your head."

One hand started instinctively to check Blair's assertion before Liz caught herself and countered, "Wise guy. If there's any gray up there, *you* gave it to me."

"If you'd only leave Sanders and fly with me..."

"Then I'd have more white on top than Pike's Peak. So, what about these sales figures? When can we talk?"

"Well," a cock of his head and a quick sigh, "I'm pretty much booked for the rest of the day. Let me take them home with me, think about them over night. You said before that you had some additional notes for me..."

Liz tapped the folder she'd placed on his desk.

"Madam Efficiency," Evan smiled at her, "this business is in the palm of your hand. All you needed of me was a stake."

"How could I carry on without your wit and charm," Liz cracked over her shoulder, heading for the door.

"Now, can Sanders offer you so much urbanity?"

"That," Liz paused in the doorway, "*and* a British accent. Sorry to break your heart, Evan. Oh, I almost forgot–we need to talk about Alanna Tewkesbury..."

Evan Blair's eyes shifted just a tad too quickly to his engagement book, but his brush-off was perfectly causal. "Certainly, certainly, Liz. First things first, though."

As he buzzed Ginger to check on his next appointment, Liz raised an eyebrow but said nothing, for once. Let him think he'd stonewalled her; it would put him off guard. Besides, once he took a good look at those figures, he wouldn't have any excuse for not wanting to expand. She shut the door behind her.

Tuesday: May 1, 1945

Elizabeth closed her book of accounts, concluding it was time to close up shop. Larry was picking her up at 7:00 for dinner. But there was one more item of business to handle.

Kicking off her comfy slippers, Liz pulled on her sling backs, then slipped into her fitted suit jacket, the color of pale violets. The mirror on the inside of the closet door gave ample assistance as she deftly secured the matching pancake hat just so with a hatpin. Tucking the tulle veil from her chapeau into her jacket, Liz was ready for action. A quick glance at her watch and she calculated she had exactly the right amount of time to go to work on Evan Blair before Larry arrived to pick her up.

Blair had his hat on, seemingly ready to go, but he stood staring out his window at the late afternoon sunglow on the street below. Liz couldn't help hesitating at the sag in his shoulders. He hadn't even heard her open the door. Where did he go nights, anyway? She knew his address but had certainly never been there, to a bachelor's digs. It also was *not* in her neck of the New York woods. Surely, though, their profits were sufficient for him to do better than that. A peculiar situation, to her mind. She did not, however, have time to worry about Evan Blair's housing situation.

"Penny for your thoughts, Evan?"

He barely glanced at her in acknowledgment. As she came to stand next to him, Liz realized her partner was watching someone or something several stories below. A glance downwards revealed Jessica and Lois talking as they sauntered off.

"That woman with your sister, she's quite striking." Evan Blair's forehead wrinkled reflectively. "It's rather peculiar, but ... well, she seems somewhat familiar."

"Becoming an Orientalist now, Evan?" Liz teased, turning to him. "You've already cornered the European market. Now you want to branch out?"

Rather than responding to Liz's humor, Blair mused, "Even from up here, I can see she looks so weary."

Liz followed Evan's gaze and explained, "If anyone has a right to be that way, it's Lois." She recounted her friend's painful story, finishing, "When the jade never showed up again, some people actually thought that Lois and her mother might have been holding on to it till the heat died down. I guess people eventually figured out they were way off the beam, but it was too late for Lois. It's a wonder she's not a bitter woman."

"She's not?" Evan faced Liz with his question.

"Well, not as bitter as she has a right to be."

"Mmm," Evan considered, turning back to the women below. He was quiet before concluding, "Sounds like a pretty tough break. I guess life can be packed with unexpected consequences."

Abruptly, Evan went around his desk and sank into the client's chair, the silver cigarette case there his objective.

"Cigarette, Elizabeth?"

"Sure. It's that time of day." Liz hesitated before warning, "Just don't tell my sister. She thinks I'm giving them up."

Coming over and selecting a cigarette, Elizabeth leaned forward for Blair to light it. She straightened, inhaled, then released a casual stream of smoke before pointing out, "You were quite the good boy, Mr. Blair, getting those sales reports back to me this morning. I'm impressed."

Evan smiled, "When I put my mind to it, I'm sheer devotion to duty. By the by, I like your projections for the autumn line, based on past sales and present economic indicators. *You* are a lady who does her homework."

Liz nodded her thank-you, then, after a reflective exhale of smoke, added, "I'm also a lady who wants to make some money."

"We're doing that–thanks to your designs, budgeting, and, I might add, appropriate schmoozing."

"You think so?"

"I know so, Duchess," Evan assured her. "Look at the figures. We may not be deep in the black, but we're coming along splendidly. Thanks to you, Elizabeth Minton, I'm maturing into a man who enjoys a slowly but steadily increasing income. I've backed a class-A winner in you."

"Confidence in me, huh?"

"The highest, Duchess."

"Trust me with your life, Evan?"

"I almost have. You haven't steered me wrong."

"Great, because I have more plans, Evan. I know a way to greatly expand our market without a crippling expenditure of capital."

"This doesn't have anything to do with Alanna Tewkesbury, does it?" Blair was not exactly angry, more wryly exasperated–and maybe a tad wary.

"Now, Evan, relax. She's not Eva Braun..."

"According to whom?" he countered skeptically.

"According to me, for one ... and our lawyers, Bushey, Baggot, and Greene, for three," asserted Elizabeth.

"Liz, did it ever occur to you that I have a few friends and associates with whom I can consult as well?"

"You certainly keep them under your hat," she remarked.

"That's why I wear such a large size." Evan could see Liz start to fume, so he conciliated, "Look, Elizabeth, I do know this woman well..."

"You? How could you? She doesn't know you–said she'd never heard your name before. I tried to find a picture to show her. Maybe I should have sketched you. That's an idea. What? Why are you looking jumpy?"

"Because I can't get a word in edgewise," Evan hastily replied. "At any rate, I meant to say that I don't *know* her but that I know *of* her from mutual acquaintances. I don't like what I hear. She has a nasty habit of taking over then hanging her partners out to dry. I didn't help you build this business up so that woman could crush it ... and you."

"I think we're *both* smarter and stronger than that, Evan."

"Perhaps, Liz, but I'm not in the mood to spend the rest of my life in *battles royales* with Mrs. Tewkesbury. Anyway, we're doing all right as it is. What's your rush?"

"My rush?" Taking another drag on the cigarette, Liz debated how much she wanted to share her worries with Evan. An exhalation and she had it figured. "Evan, you put up a lot of your own money. Lots more than I could scrape together, but what I put in *cost* me much more. I borrowed from friends and family. I won't feel right until I've squared my debts with everyone, especially my sister. She's been out of work, and I've tied up a lot of her savings. We are giving her some return; she's not exactly standing in a bread line, but her luck has been pretty bad lately. I'm the big sister. I have to look out for her."

Admitting all that hadn't been Liz's plan, and she flushed a little.

Evan nodded, looking away, thinking. At last, he said, "Liz, I understand. Unfortunately, I know too well that the Tewkesbury woman is not the answer. You might not end up with *any* profits if you let her in. You've read about her art partnerships, haven't you?"

"But my lawyers suggested..."

"Liz, your firm is good, but we both know that this woman can afford to buy and sell all of us. Her husband's lawyers have scored before the Supreme Court. Give it a rest, Elizabeth."

Frustrated, Liz bounced the hand holding her cigarette off her hip before finally giving in, "Yes, all right. All right, Evan. It's tough, though."

"I know, Duchess, I know."

Liz gave her partner a sharp look and grumbled, "But why do you have to be so darned right? There are times when I could just kill you."

"That's a nice thing for me to walk in on," quipped Ginger, the secretary.

"You heard it, Ginger. I have a witness should foul play occur," laughed Evan.

"I didn't hear a knock," Liz observed, feigning ominousness.

"Probably because you were too busy listening to yourself orate," Evan teased.

"Very funny."

"Okay, Miss Minton," Ginger began in business mode. "The reason I came in was to tell you that Mr. Sanders is waiting for you in your office. He asked me not to bother you, but I know how he gets if he has to wait long for you two to finish up."

"Thanks, kiddo. You're a life saver," Liz grinned.

After Ginger left, Evan inquired, "How *does* Mr. Saunders get when we talk too long? The green-eyed monster hath possession of his soul? Kindly never lend *me* a hankie."

"Huh?"

"*Othello*."

"Oh, you and your long-hair stuff. You ought to get together with my sister. She loves all that poetry jazz. Say, that reminds me; who's the lucky bachelorette you're taking to the Awards dinner?"

"Ah, Liz, whom could I take to compete with you?"

"What about Jessica?" Liz brightly suggested.

Evan blinked. "Jessica? I thought I was supposed to keep my wolfish ways far from baby sister."

"I'll be there to chaperone, with Larry. And this will be a great opportunity to show off 'Spring Fantasy in Lavender' !"

Evan shook his head, "Liz, you never cease to amaze me."

Liz thought, *Brother, you don't know the half of it*; but she said, "It's a date, then?"

"I thought your sister was not overly fond of me. Doesn't she see me as the wheeler-dealer blackguard sort?"

"I'll work on her. Besides, it's just for the awards dinner. We'll all leave from here."

"Don't you trust me to pick her up at her apartment?" His tone was pure mock-innocence.

"It'll be much easier to dress her here. But, come to think of it, no, I don't trust you."

"To be honest, Liz, I wasn't all that certain I would go."

"Not go!" Liz exploded. "Listen here, rube, this is an important event. It's going to look mighty funny if only one partner shows up, especially since some of our business associates will be there. I need you to keep up the connections. No, you've backed out of these things too often."

"Okay, okay, Duchess. I guess one night isn't going to kill me," he surrendered. "At least you can't spring Madame Tewkesbury on me. She and her dear spouse are planning a trip to Virginia Beach."

"Fine. I've got to run. Larry will shoot me."

"I've no doubt that you would shoot back," Blair returned dryly.

"Ha, ha," Liz cracked. Stubbing out her cigarette in the ashtray next to her, she added, "I'll talk to Jess tomorrow and let you know in the evening. Got to run."

Elizabeth left Evan Blair shaking his head, unable to see her canary-consuming grin. Plan A, the direct approach had failed, but Plan B, the sneaky one, had worked like a charm. Evan might be under the impression that Mrs. Tewkesbury was headed out of town, but Liz knew that she *would* be at the awards. After all, *her* hairdresser had the lowdown from the grand lady's hairdresser, and Liz knew that no woman could get away with lying to the woman who coiffured her. They saw to the roots of everything, so to speak. Oh, she just cracked herself up!

Chapter Four

Saturday, May 5, 1945

The immense foyer of the New York Public Library might have been called cavernous, except that the term seemed inappropriate for a space that gleamed so white, marble reflecting Saturday sunshine. Descending the stairs to the mezzanine was a young woman, dressed smartly in a short, nipped waist, cheerfully yellow jacket over a black jersey, complimented by a chocolate skirt. Black-gloved hands swung a clutch bag hefty enough to fell an elephant, should the need arise. Flowing from under a yellow turban, her dark hair bounced along her shoulders as she almost bounced down the marble steps. Just out of a weekly session where she and her friend Rose Nyquist got city kids fired up about drama and lit, Jessica Minton marveled at how working with other people on something she adored could "accentuate the positive" for her.

How could you be blue after opening up new vistas for these kids? Jess easily understood how Rose could spend her life teaching, how James had found his cover as a teacher a refuge from his grim responsibilities. And it had been outside this library, on the terrace near the stone lions guarding its entrance, that she'd told him about her temptation to teach, before the acting bug had nipped her. Today, memory of her "chance meeting" with James there didn't wound her with longing for their time together. On such a beautiful morning, a lover only wanted to savor memories and kindle them into hope.

Jessica smiled at the attendant by the door, then paused at the brass carvings on the enormous wooden doors opening onto the stone landing outside. One of those carvings was an intricate image of Pan. How appropriate: a pastoral god seeing her off after she'd been having fun with a pastoral play. And Pan played the woodwinds. Maybe her James wasn't a god, but he did have the same musical bent. Hmm, would she consider James just as frisky as Pan?

Playfully tapping Pan's nose, Jess teased, "Just because my name's not Syrinx, doesn't mean I'm not a lady. But I won't blame a guy for asking."

"Asking what?" interrupted a familiar masculine voice behind her. "Or is it out of line for a chap to intrude on a private conversation between a lady and building decorations?"

Jessica didn't turn around immediately. She hadn't heard that voice very often of late, even if it did belong to the man dating her sister. It wasn't easy being around a fellow you'd let go for another guy, especially when the new guy had been trying to put the first one away for espionage. Of course Larry Sanders was much too much the gentleman to let on exactly how hurt he'd been, but she'd sensed it. And some of the awkwardness sprang from her guilt.

But Larry's appealingly sardonic grin left Jessica feeling downright silly at her disquiet. She pleasantly greeted the handsome, dark-haired man, "What brings you to this neck of the woods?"

"Can't a fellow take advantage of a world-class library and look for a book?"

"I always thought of you as more the buying than the borrowing type," Jessica kidded.

Unexpectedly, Larry's smile faded. He studied Jess before confessing, "Maybe a chap needs to borrow a little advice."

That was a switch! Larry wanted *her* advice? Surprised, Jess asked, "You're sure I'm the girl you want to talk to?"

Larry faced her steadily to reply, "Yes. *You* know your sister best." He put a hand on her elbow and suggested, "This is far too public for a discussion of this nature, Jessica. There's a place around the corner, in the Bryant Hotel on 40th. Let's go there, have a drink, and talk."

Jessica wavered. After all that had happened between them, she owed Larry. Still, she could be getting into the middle of an emotional mess that would set all three of them at odds. Temporizing, Jess said, "You know, Larry, I'm supposed to meet Elizabeth in a half hour for lunch."

"Half an hour regular time or half an hour Elizabeth time, Jessica?"

"Okay. Point taken. But are you sure that you want to talk to *me*, Larry? You trust my judgment?"

"Is there anyone else to whom I can talk?"

The quiet sadness of Larry's question hit a soft spot in Jessica's heart, and she agreed, "Okay, Larry, I'll do what I can."

Shortly later, they were seated in the lounge of the Bryant, and Larry still wasn't explaining. He'd maintained the same strained silence the whole time he'd politely hustled her down 5th Avenue and into this building. Jessica was not pleased that she'd have to get the ball rolling. Slowly removing her gloves, she screwed her courage to the sticking place and then prompted, "Larry, it's going to be hard for me to give you any advice on Liz if you don't tell me what the problem is."

Larry emerged from his preoccupation to question carefully, "Liz hasn't said anything to you?"

"Not a word, though I have a feeling there's *something* she wants to let out. It's not like Liz to keep things to bottled up. And it's not like *you* to be so mysterious, Larry. You're both getting me worried. How long have you two been on the outs?"

"Something happened Thursday."

"Thursday? Elizabeth didn't say anything yesterday, but I didn't see much of her, either. For heaven's sake, what *did* you *do*?"

His smile slightly bitter, Larry remarked, "A little louder next time, Jessica. I think two or three people in the Village may not have heard you."

"Never mind the smart remarks, mister. If you want help with your problem, come clean with me now," Jessica chided Larry.

She knew trouble was afoot when Larry didn't get his back up at her fresh tone; instead, he sighed, "I'm afraid I've really put my foot in it this time."

Concerned for her sister, Jessica questioned uneasily, "Larry, what happened Thursday night?"

"Evan Blair happened."

Of course, that's when the waiter arrived.

Jessica barely managed to contain her frustration. Larry didn't seem terribly pleased at the interruption, either, hurriedly requiring a scotch and soda and scarcely allowing her time to order a coffee.

As soon as the waiter left, Jess leapt in: "Larry, last I heard, you and Liz had a great evening planned. How did Even Blair manage to SNAFU everything?"

"Thereby hangs a tale."

"Go on," Jessica urged skeptically.

As he remembered, Larry's features disquietingly twisted into those of an infuriated Heathcliff. But he took hold of himself to continue more calmly, "It started out grand. We saw a play and laughed more than we had in weeks. Later, we went to dinner at the Skylight with another couple. It was superb."

The light of that reminiscence dimmed under his lowering recollection of the rest of the evening.

"Enter Evan Blair, twirling his mustache?" Jessica tried to lighten the mood.

"We'd just returned from a fox trot to 'Why Can't You Behave'–one of Liz's favorites. I should have seen the handwriting on the wall." A sigh, another swig of scotch, and Larry resumed, "I'm sure you can guess who was waiting for us at the table."

"I think I can."

"I'll give Liz credit," Larry allowed. "She did not seem pleased to see him. Just when I thought I'd gotten her away from that miserable job, made her happy, relaxed..."

"Back to the main tale, Ishmael."

Larry cocked an eyebrow at the Melville reference, then went on, "I, of course, was polite–even though Blair was flip. Flip enough to annoy Liz and Jack and Lillian. Then, he started flirting with your sister."

"How did Liz take that?"

"Don't you mean how did *I* take it?"

"Nope." Jessica shook her head, took a sip of coffee, and continued, "I know you both too well. If she'd ignored him, you'd have been irritated, but nothing fatal. If she kidded back, however, innocently..."

"She should have cold-shouldered him."

Larry was adamant.

So Jessica was careful not to sound dismissive when she responded, "That's it, then? You two had a dust up over Evan Blair's flirtatiousness? Larry, you remember they do work together. She can't be rude to him, even if he does get a little out of line. And he flirts with everyone; no one takes it seriously. Anyway, Larry, you know you're the one she loves. Is that the problem, then? Liz is mad at you for not trusting her? Did you say something to her?"

An awkward pause, then Larry admitted, "It's not so much what I said as what I did."

Lifting the coffee cup for another sip, thinking this would be easier to mend than she'd anticipated, Jessica asked, "So, what did you do?"

"Socked Blair."

The only reason Jessica managed to avoid a spit take was that she hadn't gotten any coffee into her mouth. As it was, her cup clattered and splashed back into the saucer.

"What?" she hissed, remembering to keep her voice down.

"Didn't think I had it in me, did you?" Larry queried wryly.

Jessica didn't bring up the veiled anger she'd seen in his eyes at his near arrest for espionage. She did, indeed, think that, given the right circumstances, Larry had it in him.

Instead, Jessica pointed out, "No wonder, Liz is mad at you, Larry. Will she ever be able to get into the Skylight room again?"

"Well, *she* will."

"What a consolation, Joe Louis. Maybe you're forgetting that she has to work with the guy you socked."

"I didn't hit him out of jealousy, Jessica—not entirely," Larry protested. "It wasn't until he made her cry."

"That stinker!"

"Bit of a change of attitude you're sporting, isn't it?"

Jessica deliberately ignored Larry's slightly superior smile and demanded, "What did he say that made her cry?"

"It had something to do with an awards dinner. She needed him to attend due to some special plans of hers. He was trying to back out and not being terribly decent about it. I think he'd had a few. He tried to make Liz feel guilty about the money he'd put into the business, so she hadn't any right to ask more of him. I tried to get him to leave. He made some crack about Liz and me, and that's when I let my fist do the talking for me."

"Well, not that I condone violence, but certainly Liz could forgive you under the circumstances," Jessica reasoned.

"There were a few extra circumstances that she appreciated more."

"Such as ... ?"

"I'm rather afraid when I hit Mr. Blair, I didn't consider trajectory, the law of gravity, and the laws of etiquette."

"Translation, Einstein?"

"Blair sailed over the balustrade and landed on the table of the party of Mr. and Mrs. Blessington-Cure," Larry elaborated sheepishly.

"You know you might still be able to get in on that pesky mess in the Pacific," Jess suggested. "It'd be a lot safer than facing Liz—not that I can blame her."

"You're not being very helpful, Jessica."

"I can't work miracles, Larry," she returned. "You know, for a smart guy, sometimes you're such a dope."

"I beg your pardon, Jessica. If I wanted to be insulted..."

"Look, Larry, it all comes down to this: you let that weasel make a monkey out of you."

"I thought your sister was the mixer of metaphors."

"You're missing the point! Liz chose you after all that agony over Peter. She has absolutely no interest in anyone else in the romantic department. Don't let this smooth operator push your buttons," Jessica warned Larry.

"I can't help it, Jessica. If I lose Liz ... I just keep thinking she was such a blessing after you and I ... turned out to be a wash. She's everything I want: smart, funny, level-headed, responsible. I don't want another love to blow up in my face."

A sharp "Ah" escaped Jessica at this unintended reminder of how badly she had let him down when they'd been a couple.

Larry's expression revealed that he only now realized the full effect of his words. Yet Jessica noticed that he didn't attempt to salve her feelings any too quickly. Did a part of him want her to think about the damage she'd done him?

At last, he said "Water under the bridge is not something I worry about. I do need your help with Liz, Jessica."

"Well, yes. I want to see both of you happy. What do you want, Larry?" Jessica asked earnestly.

"Jess, you're seeing Liz today for lunch. Would you sound her out? Help me determine the best way to make it up to her?"

"I could try, sure. But you should know Liz well enough by now. She needs time to cool down. Of course some gifts wouldn't hurt, either. Don't forget that chocolates are much higher on her list than flowers. And admitting you were wrong goes a long way with my sister."

"Do you think I was wrong?" Larry was touchingly penitent.

"To slug the guy, yes," Jess decided. "But, frankly, I don't trust Blair, no matter what Liz says. It's not so much the romantic angle as the fact that I don't know where his money came from."

"If your sister would just settle down, she wouldn't have to worry about money. I can support her," Larry contended.

"Look, Larry, you know that *I'm* the wrong person to try that argument on. Besides, after all the widows I've seen this war produce, I would never tell a woman to give up having something to fall back on or to just expect a man to take care of her. You also keep forgetting that Liz loves what she does. You've got to respect that if the two of you are going to get along."

"I guess I'd better," Larry ruefully agreed. "The only female Minton left for me to date, after Liz and you, is Dusty."

Jessica's relief that Larry could joke about their breakup sent her chuckling more than either of them would have expected.

"It's good to see you laugh like that, Jessica. I haven't seen that in you in quite some time. Everything all right?"

Was that a reference to James? Jess decided to play it nonchalant, answering, "Not bad, Larry. There's a good chance I'll be doing radio work soon, and..."

"And what about my successor? "

Jess wasn't pleased with the slightly antagonistic turn Larry's wording had brought to their conversation. Nevertheless, she calmly answered, "You know I'm not allowed to say anything about James's missions. But I made the right choice, Larry."

"Even if he's not around?"

"You don't know that." She wasn't about to let even the usually tight-lipped Larry know what James's status was. "But what *I* know is that if you want to make things work with Liz, you'd better hop to some bridge mending. I'll talk to Liz at lunch and let you know what she's thinking. Just give her time to cool down, today, anyway." A glance at her watch and "Oh for Pete's sakes look at the time! I've got to get a move on."

Jessica was on her feet, advising, "Just keep a level head, Larry. Don't let Evan Blair manipulate you. Liz is yours to keep or lose, so get a grip on that temper. If they ever find Blair floating face down in the East River with a knife in his back, you don't want to be the one the cops come looking for. That would really put the kibosh on your chances with Liz."

"I'll try only to look daggers, not use them," Larry smiled. "And, Jessica, thank you."

The look accompanying those last words went a long way to soothing the prickliness Larry's allusions to James had provoked.

Almost twenty minutes later, Jessica skidded to a stop in front of della Mirandola's Restaurant on Village Ave, not terribly far from her own digs. Although she hadn't much excuse for being late, Jessica wasn't too worried. On Liz time, she was only five minutes behind. So, what kind of mood would her sister be in after Thursday's rhubarb? Weepy? Spitting fire? Dare she even bring up the fight before Liz had cooled down? She'd better come up with something. After all the grief she and James Crawford had caused Larry and Liz, she felt an enormous responsibility to help them stay together.

Della Mirandola's was a typical Italian restaurant: checkered tablecloths, Chianti-bottle candleholders, earthy hued walls, photos of pre-war Italy–but the food, ah, the food was typical only of heaven. Liz *would* have to decide on having lunch here while Jess had to eat like a model.

"Signorina Minton, so nice to see you again. My favorite honorary Italiana. With that sunshine in your jacket, you dress like spring. Just like your sister."

Jessica broke into a smile at the effusions of Alfonso della Mirandola, the sixty-something proprietor. James had introduced her to this eatery some time ago; and, when he had to go away, she'd still come, sometimes by herself, sometimes with Liz. Signor and Signora della Mirandola had practically adopted them.

"So, Signor della Mirandola, you're saying my sister is here, already?"

"She's here and she's waiting for you. That's a switch, eh? Anyway, she looks like she's got some kind of a bee in her bonnet, and a nice little bonnet it is."

Jessica couldn't quite squelch her trepidation. "She's in a mood, then?"

"Not a mood exactly. She just has something on her mind, I think. Is there something wrong? Something Signora della Mirandola and me can help you with?"

"No, not at all. We're just fine. It's just that Liz being on time is quite a shock. How often does that happen?" Jessica tried to joke away her nerves.

Della Mirandola gave Jess the reassurance of his smile and invited, "Come on now. I'll take you to your sister. She's out in the garden."

"Wonderful. We love to sit out by the arbor," Jess answered. "Now that it's warming up that would be swell."

As they moved through the rear of the restaurant, Jessica thought, *Bee in her bonnet, huh?* Maybe she wouldn't have to worry about curbing her appetite because dealing with Liz would send that appetite south, but fast.

The garden terrace was at the rear of the restaurant, down a flight of wrought-iron steps. Della Mirandolla led Jess across flagged stones, to the left, towards a table at which she saw a familiar brunette upsweep rising just above a menu. Jessica steadied herself. *Here goes!*

"Signorina Minton, I bring you your sister. Ah, and I see that you need more bread sticks."

The menu was lowered, and Jessica was surprised by Liz's cheery greeting, "So there you are, kiddo! I thought I might have to start gnawing the table leg soon. What took you so long?"

"I, ah, met a friend, at the library. I, um, couldn't get away."

Not the best save in the world. Nevertheless, Jessica wasn't about to say anything concerning Larry until she figured out why Liz was acting perky enough to make Shirley Temple look like a Bassett Hound.

"You're certainly in a good mood," Jess observed, sounding reasonably nonchalant as she sat down and once again pulled off those black gloves.

"Why not, kid? Everything's coming up roses."

This time Jessica didn't bother trying to keep the confusion out of her face. Still, all she said was, "Is it?"

"Sure. We've received a stack of new orders, from some of the better stores no less! And I've finally managed to get Evan to come to the awards dinner with us. Once some of those potential investors see a man running the business with me, they'll be a lot more interested."

"Evan? You want Evan Blair to go? After Thursday night ... ooops."

Liz tilted her head, smiled suspiciously, then inquired, "Thursday night? Exactly what *did* you hear about Thursday, little sister? Hmm, the friend who made you late, that wouldn't have been Larry Sanders?"

Short of a case of national security, Jessica once again realized that she never had been adept at keeping secrets from Elizabeth. Oh well, in for a penny in for a pound.

"Okay, Liz, Larry stopped me outside the library today and wanted to talk about Thursday. The poor guy's a wreck. He's afraid he might lose you. He told me the whole story: and, if you ask me, that Evan Blair is a fourteen-karat heel. I don't blame Larry for decking him. Well, maybe not in front of all those people. But that Blair, what a nerve, making you cry!"

"I wasn't crying, Jessica. I was laughing."

"Laugh ... laughing?"

"You know," Liz demonstrated, putting a napkin up to her face to cover a laugh, "like this–and then, you know how I tear up when something's really a hoot."

"But Larry said..."

"Kiddo, Larry really shouldn't have even a little to drink on a work night, when he's tired. I think his judgment was a smidge impaired–and he is jealous."

"But Larry said that Blair made you feel guilty about owing money and all," Jessica protested, confused.

"Jess, I know when to feel guilty and when not to. Evan was so absurd, trying to manipulate me, and I thought he was a dope for needling Larry. I thought Larry would see through him and laugh along with me, but before I knew it, Evan was airborne. What I'd like to know is why can't Larry see I'm not in the least interested in Evan. And why can't he understand that Evan doesn't mean half of what he says?"

"He's just afraid of, well, I guess a repeat performance of what happened with me. I let him down..."

"I'm not you, Jessica," Liz pointed out. "Anyway, you did give it your best shot. Don't blame yourself. It wasn't your fault that the two of you weren't right for each other, then someone who was right (even if I don't particularly like him) came along."

"That's the problem," Jessica warned. "Maybe Larry's afraid Evan is another James Crawford."

"Really, Jessica, Larry ought to give me credit for better sense than that!"

"Get on with your sweet talk, Liz," Jessica deadpanned.

"That's not how I meant it, kid. Even if I don't like Crawford, I know he doesn't have the same questionable past as Evan. How could Larry really think I'd throw over a sweet, dependable guy like him for the likes of Mr. Blair?"

"Liz, Larry's feeling pretty darned insecure. You need to reassure him," Jessica explained.

"Ah, I guess I have been putting him on the back burner a bit for my work, lately," Liz allowed. "The poor guy must think he's stuck with another gal who'll put her career before marriage. I wish I could make him understand that after what Peter did to me, I just can't bring myself to be completely dependent on another man. Without some insurance, happily ever after is just a phrase to me."

The two sisters lapsed into a glum, silent stare at the checked tablecloth. Jessica spoke first, apologizing, "Sorry I crushed your earlier ebullience."

Liz shook her head and smiled, "It's oke, sis. But would you mind eighty-sixing the over-the-top vocabulary?"

"I wish I could make it up to you–the crushing not the vocabulary. I'm proud of that."

"Well, actually there is something you can do," Liz began impishly.

"Why am I afraid to ask what?" came Jess's suspicious query.

"Remember I told you about the awards Saturday night, that I'd persuaded Evan to go?"

"Won't you need a referee if he and Larry are both there?" Jessica queried. "Oh, hold on. I don't like that gleam in your eyes, Elizabeth Pamela Minton."

"You did say that you wanted to help, and, if you go as Evan's date, you can keep him distracted, out of Larry's hair," Liz reasonably insisted.

"Distracted? With what? A flaming torch?"

"No, but *you* get to wear that little number you love, 'Spring Fantasy in Lavender,'" tempted Elizabeth. "Think, Jessica. You can help Larry and me to stay together–all while advertising our gorgeous gown. How can you lose?"

"Does the ensemble include a chain mail evening wrap?" Jessica doubtfully returned.

"You can handle Evan," Liz persuaded. "His bark is worse than his bite. Anyway, if he should act up, don't worry. *I'll* deck him."

Chapter Five

Saturday, May 12th

Dessert had been served, and Jessica sipped her coffee from a delicate, gold-rimmed cup. This evening was turning out all right, after all. The crystal and gold appointments of the hotel ballroom made for an elegant, antique ambiance. Better yet, the after-dinner speeches had been pleasantly shy of sleep inducing. There even was a sprinkling of celebrities presenting the awards. Rose would get a kick out of hearing that Florence Eldridge and Frederic March sat only a few tables away–at least out of the Frederic March part. The orchestra was lazing through some Guy Lombardoesque orchestrations, felicitous for pleasant dining.

The sounds of conversation surrounding their table were sprightly, excited, exuberant. And why not? THE WAR IN EUROPE HAD ENDED! GERMANY HAD SURRENDERED! Last Monday, Jessica had danced herself out, celebrating with Liz, Larry, Iris, and Lois. And the end of the war seemed to have blotted out the lovebirds' romantic troubles. That reflection hit a painful nerve, for Jessica could only wonder how long before she heard from James–if she *would* hear from James. Of course, she knew he couldn't just hop the first plane home, but she was haunted by the *Times*' enormous list of war dead, for whom the end of the European conflict had come too late.

Evan whispered in her ear, "Buck up, girl. You're not exactly selling the joys of wearing Elizabeth's creation sporting the expression of a gal who'd invested in German war bonds."

Jess glanced over at her sister, lovely in a white crepe gown and jacket, now happily preoccupied with Larry and another couple who had dropped by the table. For Liz's sake (and her own peace of mind), Jessica forced down her concerns and responded quietly, "Oh, so you're not mad at her for designing something this high end?"

"As long as she keeps her word about it only being an experiment for a limited edition and doesn't go trying to drag us into circles where we don't belong," he affably answered. "And how could I object when it adds to the loveliness of my companion?"

Jessica shot him a skeptical look over her shoulder at his blarney. Blair smiled.

But the dress *was* exquisite! The lights overhead sparkled azure and pale sapphire off the symmetric rhinestone splashes on the bodice. Complimented by Jessica's dark hair waving luxuriously down to her shoulders, Elizabeth's splendid creation of lilac chiffon over blue was a lovely concoction inspired by Jess's showing Liz a delphinium's delicate layering of the two colors.

And Jessica was excited to be helping her sister lay the groundwork for next year's nominations with this gown. Earlier, Liz had sent Jessica and Evan off on a stroll around the room to pay respects to carefully selected acquaintances at different tables. Liz's plan had worked beautifully, for people hadn't stopped asking Jessica about her dress. She'd been most happy tactfully to plug away. Much to her surprise, Evan Blair had been a good sport the whole time, and not because he was plotting some intemperate move on her, either.

A glance or two around their table, and Jess could see Larry looking delighted to have Liz to himself. Well, at least Evan and Larry had been on their best behaviors all evening. Probably they'd rather have taken their chances with General George Patton than with Liz on a rampage. So, the dress was going over well, and the gentlemen were behaving. Larry and Liz were even holding hands. Both obvious reasons for the glint in her sister's eyes. Except, to Jess, that glint seemed more one of anticipation than satisfaction. What could be up Elizabeth's elegant, white crêpe sleeve?

Jessica snapped back to reality as Evan chided, "Now, Liz, couldn't you have allowed Jessica dessert? How often since rationing came in have we been able to eat anything with this many eggs in it?"

"Not when she's wearing that dress," Liz fired back.

"And after she did so well with the marinara sauce?" Evan further insisted.

"After all that, do you think I have the nerve to watch her deal with blueberries?"

Jessica took over, "Evan, I don't think that *I* have the nerve to deal with my sister's Gorgon stare."

"Thanks, dear," Liz smiled not *quite* carbolically.

"Gorgon is a trifle harsh," Larry interjected lightly, tapping out his cigarette.

"You try trading places with me, then, Larry," Jess teased.

"I don't think that the dress would *quite* fit me."

"But it would bring out your eyes," Evan slid in deftly.

The two men smiled tightly at each other, their best behavior just slipping, and Liz's stare *did* approach Gorgon intensity. Hastily, Jessica changed the subject, "I just thank the Lord that Liz is letting me have this coffee. Except for della Mirandola's, I haven't had a brew like this since before Burns cancelled horseracing. Say, isn't it great that all the tracks are starting to open up? Jamaica in June, Narragansett and Santa Anita already. The Kentucky Derby's in June, the third."

"My sister, Damon Runyon," Liz pronounced over her coffee cup, eyes briefly telegraphing Jess a "good work" for breaking the tension.

"That's right," Evan Blair considered, leaning toward Jess's chair, "Liz mentioned you're an avid improver of the breed. So, Jessica, whom should we back in the 'Run for the Roses'?"

"Well," Jessica began, "it's hard to make a prediction, what with the racing and training schedules disrupted by the ban."

"Damned inconsiderate of Burns and Truman," Evan pronounced.

"Right, politicians need to get their priorities straight," Jess concurred, feigning indignation.

"I wonder how much the boys at the front, or your 'special friend,' would laugh with you two," Larry cut in coldly.

Jessica stiffened. Where had *that* come from?

To her surprise, Blair took her part. "Was that really called for, Sanders?"

"I think the orchestra's starting up," Liz interrupted. "Yes, yes. There's 'Begin the Beguine.' The perfect tune to show off how the gown looks for dancing. Jess, shouldn't you and Evan should take to the floor? *Now*."

While annoyance mingled with hurt from Larry's dig, Jessica heard Evan Blair concur, "Good thinking, Duchess. Jessica?"

Up and away from the table, moving out onto the floor with Evan Blair, Jess still puzzled over Larry's mean shot at her. Guided into the swirl of dancers, instinct took over, and she followed Blair into a foxtrot, but Larry's implication that she wasn't taking James's fate seriously continued to sting.

"I'm afraid that frown clashes terribly with Liz's gown, Jessica."

Evan's words had rolled out not unkindly. Again, maybe she should give him more credit–or maybe he was just a *really* smooth operator. At any rate, he was waiting for some response, and she did owe it to Liz to put on a good front.

"Do I look that sour?"

"I've seen more carefree faces shipping out for the Pacific. Ah, that's better. We don't want people to think dancing in Liz's creation is excruciating."

"They'd think I was having trouble with my dress, not my partner?" Jessica inquired a little archly.

"My talents on the dance floor go without saying," Blair answered, unruffled, and he whirled her into a sharp turn, with a smooth dip and recovery to prove his point.

"Touché, Mr. Blair," Jessica conceded.

"Not a'tall, Miss Minton. I intend to live up to my part in this show. But look at you now. I wouldn't be surprised to see Frederic March elbow me aside for the honor of swirling you around the floor."

"I think his wife, Florence Eldridge, might have something to say about that," Jessica whispered in mock conspiracy.

"So, whom *do* you like in the Kentucky Derby, Jessica?

"So we're back on horse racing, then, Evan?"

"You know I'm a gambling man, when I see a good thing. I invested in your sister, no questions asked, didn't I?"

"That sword cuts both ways."

"So it could. So it could. Well met, Mademoiselle. It is a pity that you don't trust me, Jessica."

"I've learned the hard way to dig beneath the surface. What it all comes down to is that I want what's best for my sister."

Blair glanced beyond Jess, in the direction of Liz and Larry. Then his eyes returned to her, and he considered, "I wonder if you'd believe me if I said I did, too."

If only she could tell what was in those blue-green eyes of his. Darned if he didn't genuinely seem on the square. But his reputation as a ladies' man certainly gave her pause.

That was when Blair surprised her with, "Just how happy is Liz with Sanders?"

Jessica didn't exactly exhibit the rocket's red glare, but her tone was sufficiently fiery when she retorted, "It's really not your place to ask, is it, Mr. Blair?"

"Ah ha. I've stepped too far. We're back to Mr. Blair. Well, I apologize, Miss Minton. But you should know that I am thinking about your sister."

"I'm sure you are, but it's *what* you're thinking that's got my dander up. Anyway, why are you asking all these questions? You've got plenty of fillies in that stable you call your little black book. Why set your sights on my sister?"

"Did I say that I was setting my sights on your sister?"

"*Would* you? Anyway, what makes you think she and Larry aren't happy enough?"

"Not happy 'enough'? Rather interesting that you'd qualify 'happy' that way. However, I can see by the way that you're starting to miss the steps to even a foxtrot that I've struck a nerve. Perhaps we'd best skip it."

"No, no. Let's get down to cases. Finish what you started."

"If you insist."

Jess had the distinct feeling that she'd been suckered into a trap.

"Your sister and Sanders are engaged, right?"

"Yes, of course."

"How long?"

"Maybe about a year and a half. What difference does that make?"

"It seems a long engagement for two people in love. They aren't teenagers waiting for their parents' permission."

"No, just the state of New York's. It takes a year for the decree to become final. It's a little embarrassing when you marry one fella if you're still legally married to another."

"Very true, but you just admitted that it's been beyond that requisite year. Even Liz wouldn't take that long to pick out her new china pattern."

"If you knew my sister as well as you suggest, then you'd know that she wants her business squarely on the beam before she settles down."

"Why couldn't Larry help her with that?"

Though she knew lack of money was a factor, memory of Larry's complaint in the Bryant Park Café strong-armed its way to mind: the old woman-with-a-career boogieman.

"I see that I've struck home."

Jessica fixed Evan Blair with a sharp look but didn't say anything. She couldn't. As their glide around the dance floor once more brought Liz and Larry into brief view, Jess noticed that Larry looked tense. They weren't holding hands. She coolly put to her dance partner, "Just what makes *you* such an expert on true love?"

For his answer, Evan Blair turned serious, "Reputation and all aside, I am capable of it."

Before Jessica could reply, the song ended. Evan Blair released her, and the necessity of joining the crowd in applauding the band precluded a snappy comeback. Glancing up at her partner, whose eyes were now on the orchestra, Jess wondered what she dared say. Was Blair hinting at his having more than friendly feelings for Liz or alluding to someone in his past? A pretty shrouded past at that. The strains of "I Don't Know Enough about You" came up, and Jessica mentally concluded, *I'll say!*

"Shall we?" Evan Blair took up Jessica for another dance. "I expect that your sister intends us to take at least two turns around the floor for her dress to get the proper exposure."

"Not you as well?"

"That's an odd comment."

Blair seemed a tad uneasy now, to Jess. "It's an odd evening," Jessica answered simply. "To tell the truth, though, I think you're overdoing the Garbo bit. Wanting to stay hidden. I'd think that you'd want to share credit with Liz. You did back her. Think of all the girls *that* would impress."

"I think I'm sufficiently impressive to the softer sex purely on my own merits." His tongue was 90% in cheek. Then Blair added, "Let's just say that silent partners should live up to their description. However, you never did answer my question. Why haven't Liz and Larry Sanders married?"

"It's a complicated situation," Jessica returned coldly.

"Ah, are you referring to the fact that her ex-husband abandoned her or to her fiancé being your ex-boyfriend?"

Jessica did manage not to lose her step when she bit out, "That's all really none of your business."

"Jessica, you should know that there are no secrets in an office. You're not a kid anymore."

Images of Ginger, the makeup people, the models, flashed through Jessica's brain. Was everyone whispering behind her and Liz's backs? She gave Blair a withering look and told him, "I don't want to talk about this anymore. It's nobody's business."

"Just don't let your sister make a mistake. Two in a row is murder. I know."

The quiet concern in Blair's words took Jessica by surprise. She almost couldn't be angry with him. Almost. Was he planning to make a play for Liz, himself? Did he really think she'd throw over Larry for him? Could she get more out of him if she took a softer approach? It was worth a try.

"You'll have to forgive me, Evan. It's been a long evening, a long week with the war ending in Europe. I'm almost dead on my feet. Euphoria takes it out of a girl."

"Understandable."

"You'd think that I'd been eating 'angry candy' rather than that blueberry trifle," Jessica smiled wanly.

"Jessica, I'd never accuse you of living in a 'furnished soul.' And you worry too much about your sister and everything from the doorman's aching bunions to Harry Truman's plans for the U.N. to have a 'comfortable mind,'" Blair returned easily.

Jessica cocked her head with surprise and queried, "You know e. e. cummings?"

"Not personally. But I do know a good sonnet when I read one. And I remember my pleasure in buying and reading *Tulips and Chimneys* when it came out in 1923."

"A college boy, eh?"

"Or just a man who likes to read. Erudition doesn't require a sheepskin."

"I guess not. But since you are on the same page with me about 'the Cambridge ladies who live in furnished souls,' how about we change the name of this dress to 'Sky Lavender'?"

"In honor of the last two lines: 'sky lavender and cornerless, the/ moon rattles like a fragment of angry candy,'" he quoted.

"Wonderful image, isn't it? I love *all* the imagery of that poem. A, um, friend of mine and I used to like to read it together." Jessica clammed up, realizing she was divulging more information about herself than she was pumping out of Evan Blair. Except he seemed to delight in metaphors a heck a lot more than she'd expected from a gambler with a questionable past. Maybe Blair was an English teacher on the lam?

"Indeed," Blair agreed. "It's the language of poetry that fascinates me. It's a code of a world beyond, which only its creator can truly decipher, *if* he can."

"That's right, you and your ciphers and codes," Jessica recalled. "But poetry isn't something to be only analyzed and decoded. It's something you have to feel, too."

"Feelings can get you into trouble, Jessica Minton."

Jess was about to try and mitigate Blair's cynicism when she was distracted by the sight of a vaguely familiar looking woman gliding around the tables in a sparkle of dark sequins. She craned her neck to catch the face.

"Someone you know ... ?"

Blair had turned his head to follow Jessica's attention. That head snapped back abruptly.

"Evan, what's wrong? You look as if you'd just seen a ghost."

His smile, when he spoke, was almost convincing, almost: "No, of course not."

Then Blair deftly glided Jessica into a turn, only to stop short with a painful: "Ow!"

He'd somehow twisted his ankle and stumbled–not enough to create a disturbance on the floor, though.

"You all right?" Jessica questioned, concerned, as a limping Blair guided her to the edge of the floor, the crowd now between them and where they'd been looking.

"Yes, yes. I think so. Let me just check my ankle. Not here. The lounge. Would you mind? I'll meet you back at the table. If the injury's too severe, I'm sure Liz will free up Mr. Sanders for your dance card."

"If you leave, Liz may free up your head from your shoulders." But Jessica dropped her teasing, for her companion really did look pale. "Never mind, Evan. Can you walk? Can I help?"

"No, no. Just explain to Liz. I'll join you as soon as I can. My apologies."

He was gone before Jess could say anything more. So now she had to circle the dance floor and face Liz *sans* Evan. Not a treat by a long shot.

Liz's expression at Jessica's solitary return was startled, then unsettled, as if she were afraid something had gone awry. Jess had expected annoyance, but not that.

"Jessica, where's Evan?"

"Field injury," Jess quipped in hopes of calming her sister's unease. "You know how tricky dancing and chatting can be." Sitting, she resumed, "Not to worry, though. We won't have to destroy him. He just retired to powder his nose and assess his injury."

"Well, I like that," Liz fussed.

"I doubt he did it on purpose, Liz," Jess assured her sister. "Calm down. He'll be right back."

"It would be just like him to run out on me *now* of all times," Liz fumed over the coffee cup she had raised to her lips, then impatiently lowered without drinking.

"I can't say that *I'll* miss him," Larry remarked.

Still smarting a bit over Larry's earlier implication that her feelings for James were shallow, Jessica observed pointedly, "On the whole, Evan Blair has been rather on his best behavior, Larry. I don't see that you have anything to complain about tonight."

"Don't you?" Larry replied, irritated at being corrected. However, he controlled his temper, and with a more agreeable tone apologized, "You'll just have to excuse me for wanting to have my girl to myself."

Jessica didn't feel like making nice so easily, but she wasn't about to make things worse when her sister already seemed inordinately concerned about Evan Blair's absence. Where was he, anyway? He couldn't have hurt himself *that* badly. Jess shifted in her seat, her gaze sweeping the crowded dining area, hoping to see him return. That's when she caught a flash of blonde upsweep and black sequins approaching, the same as she'd seen from the dance floor. Only now, she had a good enough look to put a name to that vaguely familiar face.

Jessica turned sharply back to her sister and questioned suspiciously, "Elizabeth, why is now such a bad time for Evan to take off?"

Jess caught Larry's puzzled expression at her question. However, she was more interested in Elizabeth's hesitating guiltily, then smoothly answering, "We're in the middle of an evening out, kid. Of course leaving you without an escort is a bit tacky."

"So's ambushing a guy," Jessica sternly returned.

"Jess, what on earth"

"Good evening, Miss Minton."

The woman's voice came from over Jessica's right shoulder. Clear tones, the beneficiary of elocution training, a timbre of velvet encasing steel.

Liz's features flashed into cordiality–not subservience, though. Jessica turned to look upon the perfect upsweep and chignon, topping the masterfully made-up features of Mrs. Wilmington Tewkesbury. Her form was womanly. As the soldiers at the Stage Door Canteen would have said, "built for comfort not speed." The dress's black sequins highlighted that form all the way up to jaggedly curling flames of ebony glinting midnight blue and emerald along the bustline to an ebony, chiffon-veiled décolletage and collarbone. The necklace of emerald and diamonds perfectly highlighted the seductive sparkle of the dress. The face came next: oval but not plump with a jaw that was more than firm—as hard as the blue eyes under the decisively long lashes. The jewelry, the glinting black dress, the blonde upsweep caught under a fall of lacquered black feathers, all spelled the powerful and relatively young wife of a well-connected, moneyed old man. Except something was not quite right. The hair was maybe a little too golden, the lips just too red, the sequins glinted a tad too demandingly. Then, there was that predatory smile.

Jess glanced at Liz. Her sister was definitely at battle stations. All charm, welcome, and warmth glowed on Liz's features. But her eyes showed that maneuvers were shifting relentlessly, albeit graciously, into place. Another glance back at Liz's visitor and Jessica fervently hoped her sister knew what she was getting into. Playing footsie with Tojo and Goering combined would bring a lot less heartache. She could see that Larry was regarding the whole situation with skeptical curiosity.

Alanna Tewkesbury slipped her finely calibrated charm into high gear: "Miss Minton, I'm so delighted you and I have been able to finally cross paths. I can't say what a fortunate coincidence it was that I decided to postpone my trip. How else could we have met tonight?"

"Mrs. Tewkesbury, what a lovely thing to say. You know I've been just as anxious as you for another chat. We have so much to talk about. Please sit down."

Larry shot Jess an ironic look. She responded with a brief, uneasy twist of her mouth.

"Thanks so much," Alanna smiled. Like a gracious barracuda.

Jessica also caught Liz's quick frown at the ready availability of a chair. If Evan Blair were where he was supposed to be, it wouldn't have been so available.

As Mrs. Tewkesbury sat down, she deigned a smile to Jessica and Larry, followed by a swift, commanding glance to a rough-featured blond man not enjoying his imprisonment in a tux. Standing inconspicuously behind and a little off to the side, he nodded before melting into the crowd. *Oh right*, Jess recalled, *the gorilla who'd accompanied our guest here into the art gallery that Sunday morning. Cute.*

"Wilmington isn't here. Poor dear wasn't feeling well this evening–but he insisted that I go out without him."

Liz offered, "I'm so sorry your husband's indisposed."

"How kind of you, Miss Minton. At any rate, I see that Wil isn't the only one missing tonight." Alanna Tewkesbury emphasized her awareness of Blair's absence with her obvious searching glance around the table.

"Oh, of course, my partner, Evan Blair. He's here."

"You know, people are starting to refer to him as the "Invisible Man.'"

"Unfortunately, he sometimes does take the term 'silent partner' too much to heart," Liz pleasantly parried, "but he will be right back."

"Speaking of the 'Invisible Man,'" Larry interjected in a cheery attempt to cut the tension, "did you know that Jessica once worked with Claude Rains?"

Liz and Alanna briefly looked at Larry as if he'd sprouted an extra noggin. With a subtle headshake, Jessica warned him against stepping between the tigresses. He blinked acknowledgement.

Mrs. Tewkesbury resumed, "Miss Minton, I really must tell you how impressed I am with how you've built up your business after all that unpleasantness with your ex-husband. Failing in your marriage is such a terrible blow for most women."

Liz didn't bat an eye. She allowed one quick glance at Jess, then another at Larry, warning both against letting their guest have it for that crack. Then, wonderfully warm but no less commanding, Liz smiled at Alanna Tewkesbury, "I'm a determined woman, Mrs. Tewkesbury. I know what I want and how to go about getting it. It takes more than a little heartbreak or someone else's treachery to knock me down for the count. But enough about me. Have you been having the fun this evening that your husband was concerned about?"

This time Alanna blinked. Then she smiled, perhaps admiring Liz's refusal to take any guff from her and proceeded, "It's quite enjoyable, thank you so much. Really rather entertaining. By the way, that's a lovely dress your sister is wearing." In a patronizing tone of voice, she ordered Jessica, "Stand up, dear. I'm afraid you aren't giving anyone a look at your sister's dress if you just sit there."

"Oh, Mrs. Tewkesbury," Liz maneuvered in before Jessica could respond to the woman's condescension with a sharp word or a blunt object, "you did notice my sister on the floor dancing with Evan Blair? Then you certainly would have seen how beautifully the dress moves."

And that Evan isn't a figment of anyone's imagination, Jessica completed in her mind.

All that the shiny blonde woman said was, "I'm afraid I was rather too busy chatting with my friends Lulu Vanderbilt and the Ronald VanRups to notice. *Now* I would so like to see how the dress moves. That's the only way a woman can truly judge, isn't it, Miss Minton?"

For a minute, both Miss Mintons were uncertain whom had been addressed, but Liz took charge. "We can solve that problem. Jess, Larry, would you mind taking a turn on the floor? I can hear a rumba coming up, and I know how you both enjoy that."

Jessica hesitated. True, leaving the table and putting some distance between herself and *La* Tewkesbury would be a blessing. That gal burned her, the way she tossed off her Four-Hundred connections to put them in their places, then dangled the possibility of her interest if everyone hopped to her orders. Jess most certainly didn't want to leave her sister alone with that sleek crocodile in sequins. Still, Liz's eyes were adamant, and, even though Larry seemed to have as many qualms as she, Jess took his hand and said, "Come on, Larry. Let's put Fred and Ginger to shame."

Larry rose and pulled back Jess's chair for her, but hesitated and asked

Liz, "Are you sure you'll be all right?"

"I'm not going to bite her," Tewkesbury smiled.

Liz gave the woman a smile of her own, which might have warned, "Try it and I'll bite back." Then she shooed Jess and Larry off, "Go. You two kids have some fun. We have some girl talk."

Larry clearly didn't like the sound of that, but Jessica drew him onto the dance floor, whispering to him, "We can have a little confab, ourselves."

He had known her long enough to catch on. "Right. Ladies, enjoy your chat."

On the floor, Larry assumed the lead, questioning Jessica as they moved into their dance, "Do you know what the deuce your sister is up to?"

Jessica didn't respond immediately, still smarting a bit over Larry's earlier comments about James and her. Nevertheless, this was her sister they were concerned about. She tamed her temper and answered, "I'm not certain, but I've got an idea–and I don't like it."

"Go on."

"Wait a minute. The boss and her evil nemesis are watching. Give them a nice big smile."

They mamboed past the table gracefully, and Jessica decided, "I don't think I like the thought of her in my dress. It's not designed for a predator."

"You're not making sense to me, Jessica. What is your sister up to?"

"You haven't guessed? Why do you think Evan Blair faked an ankle injury? It's all so clear to me now."

"I left my crystal ball at the office," Larry returned. "Nothing's clear to me."

"She's trying to reel this 'lady' in as a partner, but Evan's dead set against it," Jess explained. "He thinks she'll chew Liz up, grab the company, and run it into the ground. I wouldn't be surprised if he hadn't seen Alanna Tewkesbury come in when he was dancing with me, then faked hurting himself so he could get away before Liz dragged him into a conference with that woman."

"That's one thing on which I can agree with Blair." Larry sent Jess into a turn. When she faced him again, after her dress displayed the proper billowing effect, he continued, "But why does he hate Tewkesbury so much, or need to avoid her? He could just say no and leave–politely, of course."

"Of course," Jess concurred. "But there's more to it than that. Blair acts as if he doesn't even want to *see* her. That's my impression. I wouldn't be surprised if there had been some kind of funny business between them, years ago, the way he talks about her."

Turning Jessica into a cuddle, Larry queried, "Which is?"

"Vague, bitter." Jess let Larry turn her out and around to face him before she continued, her meaning double-edged, "Just like when someone's wounded you so much that you don't want to talk about her, but the anger won't let you stop taking digs."

"Thank you, Dr. Freud."

He didn't get the hint, so Jessica insisted, "Don't get smart, Larry. I'm right. You can see that, can't you?"

"Yes," Larry allowed. "I do know what you mean. But then why did he come at all? Fascination with the evil temptress?"

"I seriously doubt he knew she'd be here. Everyone thought she was in Virginia Beach. Liz probably has a secret connection with the woman's hairdresser and got the scoop, then masterminded this plot to sucker Blair into a meeting tonight."

Larry concluded, "So Blair will be in for a slap in the face when he comes back?"

"You really think he *is* coming back?"

Larry's brow creased as he questioned, "You think he's run out?"

"I'd be willing to bet Dusty's tuna supply."

"Mmm, you *are* confident. Tell me, Sherlock Holmes, what led you to that deduction?"

"Simple, I'm sorry, elementary, Watson." Though she hadn't completely forgiven Larry for his earlier digs, Jess couldn't resist kidding. "He came up lame right after I pointed out a familiar looking woman, when we were on the dance floor. I couldn't see her well enough to recognize her at the time, but I did when she came to our table later. He must have gotten a better look than I did, realized it was Alanna, and then faked his injury as a cover to get out of here."

Larry made one of those "guess-you're-right" frowns before going on, "I know one thing. I wouldn't want to be in Blair's shoes when Liz sees him again."

"I suspect he'll keep a low profile around the office for some time," Jessica wryly agreed.

Larry sent Jessica into a twirl, and when she came back around he admitted, "Again, Jess, I have to admit that I'm with Evan Blair on this one. I do not want to see your sister get mixed up with this woman. I don't like this Tewkesbury character; she's hard, and there's just something not right about her."

"I know what you mean. Phony isn't exactly the word. It's as if the money were sort of buying a new identity."

"Ah, so you suspect that the illustrious Mrs. Tewkesbury may have come from the wrong side of the tracks?" Larry queried.

"I don't know. I don't mean to be a snob. *I'm* not exactly a member of the Four Hundred, but there's something about that woman that says she's got a past she wouldn't want anybody to know about," Jessica pondered aloud. "Now she's hooked a guy with enough money and clout to keep people from asking embarrassing questions."

"Perhaps Evan Blair knew her when her name was Bertha Hoffenbleckel?"

"Don't get wise."

Larry wondered, "At any rate, why would a man with the family, position, and wealth of Wilmington Tewkesbury marry a Bertha Hoffenbleck?"

"Bleckel. Hoffenbleckel."

"Thank you."

"Maybe for her 38-28-38 personality."

"Was that you or Dusty speaking? Catty, Jessica, catty."

"Don't go high and mighty on me, mister. You're smiling."

"I didn't say you weren't funny." He put Jessica into the Cuban walk; and, when she faced him again, he went on, "So, you think that Wilmington Tewkesbury was a kind of Pygmalion?"

"Gee, I don't know about that. She might have, probably had, made her transformation before they met–where was it? Florida? She could have invested in the right accouterments, a little charm school, then let the hormones do the rest. Remember Betty Grable and Carole Landis in *Moon over Miami*?"

"Except that this woman has none of Betty Grable's apple-cheeked charm."

"No, but I bet it's a dead heat in the gam department."

Larry shook his head in mock disapproval, clearly amused.

The dance ended, and, as they joined everyone in applauding the orchestra, Jess suggested, "Larry, let's stay on for the next dance."

"Aren't you afraid to leave Liz alone with Madame Tewkesbury?"

"No, Liz can't do anything that's legally binding without her silent partner–and I don't expect to see Evan Blair coming back."

Larry seconded her, "No, I don't imagine so. Certainly, we can take another turn then. You *are* supposed to show off the gown, and here comes a waltz. Ah, 'The Merry Widow.'"

As they whirled around the floor, Jessica reflected that a waltz was, indeed, the perfect showcase for the floating, gracious chiffon and silk of her skirts. She also reflected a little more on Alanna Tewkesbury.

"You know, Larry, it would be interesting to dig up the straight dope on the Tewkesbury woman. If she is going to be playing ball with Elizabeth, we want Liz to be prepared."

"That makes sense–not the metaphor but what I think you mean by it."

"Liz rubs off on me more than I like," Jess conceded. "That's the second time I've mangled the language tonight."

"At any rate, Jessica, how would we go about protecting Elizabeth from Mrs. Tewkesbury?"

"We-ell, for starters, I could go back to the society pages. Those two have been married for oh, about seven or eight years, right? Then there's Ginger, in the office. She knows everything about who did what to whom in the city over the past fifteen years. Of course, I'll have to separate the wheat from the chaff there, but that should give me some leads. Oh, gee, what am I thinking about? Lois really has the skinny on Tewkesbury's set, with her cleaning service catering to the apartments and hotels of the well-to-do. And then there are her old connections to the art world. Now, if I could just get to Florida where our little gem was first discovered..."

"With travel restrictions still on?"

"I know. I know. I'm beginning to sound like a private eyelash," she laughed.

"And quite an impractical one at that." That old tinge of condescension sparked up Jess's earlier annoyance. Almost as if he were psychic, Larry surprised her with, "I know one way *I'd* like to do better, Jessica. I want to apologize for implying, earlier, you were cavalier about Crawford. I was out of line."

Jessica studied Larry. The apology hadn't been easy for him. Apologies never had been. Giving him another chance, she asked, "Larry, what on earth possessed you to take that shot at me?"

Her dance partner seemed genuinely perplexed, himself, when replying, "I don't like Blair. I don't trust him. Seeing both of you so cozy with him ... I don't know ... I guess I just couldn't keep from lashing out."

"It didn't help matters much, did it? Look, Larry, Liz is planning to marry you. She could care less about, well, that's not quite true; she does *like* Blair. But do you really think *our Liz* would fall for a guy with that many question marks in his background?"

"She let him finance her business."

"Yes, but with the cash up front–and she keeps an eye on all the books, drives all the deals. Besides, that's business. You're a matter of the heart to her."

Larry smiled a little then, at last venturing, "So, are you saying that Blair doesn't worry you? You trust him not to pull any funny business?"

Jessica wasn't quite sure if Larry meant romantic or financial funny business, so she answered, "I wouldn't go so far as saying I *trusted* him. I don't think even Liz quite does. But I do know that even if she weren't in love with you, my sister is too pragmatic to mix business with pleasure."

Should she have warned Larry about Blair's questions about Liz and Larry's fitness for each other, earlier in the evening? No, what was the use of saying something that would inflame Larry? Instead, Jess wrapped up with, "Anyway, Larry, you're the man my sister plans to marry."

"Does she?"

Jessica almost stumbled. She definitely blinked, and then, quickly got her feet back in rhythm with the music before questioning, "What's that supposed to mean, Larry?

"Nothing. Never mind, never mind," Larry shook his head. "I'm sorry. I'm just getting a little cross waiting. I know the story of her wanting to get back on her feet, chapter and verse. It's been a long night–and the Tewkesbury woman hasn't shortened it any."

"Well, then, smile, Larry. Look. She's gone. Liz is alone."

Larry's "Really?" was followed by his turning Jess so that he could view the table before he agreed, "Right. But isn't Blair back *yet*?"

"Larry, I told you: I doubt he stayed in the building more than a minute after he saw that Tewkesbury woman. I really think there's bad blood between those two."

"He *said* that?"

"Not exactly. He didn't have to. He gave me one of those sinister 'it happened to a friend' stories."

"And? What happened?"

"No details," Jess related. "Just a lot of ominous blank spaces that all boil down to her being a user, a sadistic one at that."

"Perhaps you should consider this, Jessica. Perhaps this woman is only approaching Liz so she can avenge herself on Blair."

Larry's observation was unsettling. Jessica tried to soothe her own concerns as much as his, reasoning, "No, no, not really. From talking to Blair, I think he's kept himself pretty well undercover–except, perhaps, for that incident when you clipped him. Besides, now that I think of it, Blair was acting as if he didn't want her to know he was here. No, Evan Blair would probably be a big surprise to Madame Tewkesbury."

"She didn't react to his name," Larry agreed. "So, she's either a superb actress, or..."

He scowled in a way that disconcerted Jessica into probing, "Or what, Larry?"

"She knows him by another name. Evan Blair is not his real name."

Jessica squeezed Larry's hand tensely. With all her questions about Blair, why had that possibility never occurred to her? And he came from half a continent away. How could she check *this* out?

"It's a thought that's plagued me for some time," Larry revealed. "You never considered the possibility?"

"No. It never occurred to me. I mean, he had this whole legal history out West. The lawyers never picked up on this, and they're damned good. Have you ever mentioned this to Elizabeth?"

"Yes, yes, I have."

"And?"

"She said that anyone who had a solid reputation in business for six years, albeit on a small scale..."

"Liz said 'albeit'?"

"Do you think you can allow for paraphrasing?'

"Sorry."

"Right. Where was I?"

"Small scale, solid reputation."

"Thank you. At any rate, she insisted that six years of a solid reputation proved he was a reliable business partner, especially if *her* name, not his, was on all the contracts and bank accounts."

Jessica frowned and said, "I like this less and less."

To think that Evan Blair had almost sucked her in tonight. Maybe those hints of feelings for her sister might be the first step on the road to getting both their names on the contracts, even turning bank accounts into community property. She started to share her suspicions with Larry but put the skids on it. Elizabeth was in no danger of falling for Blair, but Larry'd blow a gasket if he had any confirmation that Blair was trying to beat his time with Elizabeth. No, she'd have to be careful.

"I can call a girlfriend of mine, Arlene, on the West Coast, Los Angeles," Jessica began. "She might be able to draw on some contacts, do a little digging on Mr. Blair. After all, she plays a detective on the radio. Then there's Lois. Lots of connections on the Coast. Maybe we can hit pay dirt on Mr. Blair–at least set our minds at rest. And you, Larry, if we could get his fingerprints, could you have him checked out? You work for the government."

His features tensing, Larry answered, "You know I've been re-assigned since the scandal with your former brother-in-law. I'm not allowed those kind of contacts anymore."

Whew! That was a sore spot! Should she tell Larry that *she* might have an ace in the hole when it came to checking Evan Blair's fingerprints? That would require cashing in some awkward capital, though. Instead, Jess only apologized, "Sorry, Larry."

"Forget it. What I'd like to know is how the devil you propose even getting his fingerprints. I can't imagine that Blair would be terribly cooperative."

Hmm. How did they do it in the movies? Could she sneak into Blair's office and lift something? Could she do it Monday? Now what did he use frequently enough to print but not often enough to miss?

"If I get something of Blair's, Larry..." Here, she hesitated. What the dickens, this was her sister's future, "I could go to the F. B. I. Evan Blair's from across a state border. It must be a federal thing."

"I'd love to be there when you explain it to them. I can just picture it: 'Mr. Hoover, lay off those communists and Axis spies. I've got something important. I think a wolf is trying to con my sister.'"

"Larry, you're forgetting that I did help flush out and catch a dangerous spy. There's one F.B.I. guy who still sends me Christmas cards."

"That may be, Jess, but let's put this in perspective," Larry cautioned. "With a war on, no one has time for your little worries."

"I wouldn't think that you'd see Liz's wellbeing as a 'little worry,'" Jessica chided.

"I'm not speaking for myself, Jessica. I'm just trying to make you take a realistic look at what you're up against."

He had her there, to a certain degree. Nevertheless, she challenged, "Then let's see you come up with something practical. I'm all ears."

Larry didn't look very comfortable, conceding, "I wish I could. I wish I could. We'll just have to keep a sharp eye out to make sure neither Tewkesbury nor Blair maneuvers Elizabeth into anything foolish."

Jessica recognized she could say nothing more. How could Larry have known Liz this long without grasping that it would take more than a sharp stick, never mind a sharp look, to keep her out of trouble once she made up her mind to get into it?

Her irritation abruptly turned to uneasiness at the sight of Alanna Tewkesbury's bodyguard standing alone at the fringe of the dance floor. His sharp, cynically probing stare told her that she was playing in the big leagues. Determined as she was to protect her sister, Jessica realized she had better heed Larry's warning to take things slowly and carefully.

Jess looked her dance partner in the eye and stated calmly, "Larry, I don't intend to do anything stupid. One brush with intrigue was enough for me. However, I do intend to look out for my sister, with or without you. If you really do deserve Liz, you'll help me. Otherwise, you'll have no one to blame but yourself. No, don't say anything now. Liz is alone, so let's head back. Anyway, this will be the really tough part: listening to her rail about what she has in store for Evan Blair after tonight."

Chapter Six

Sunday, May 13

The laughing, warm voice of Jessica Minton lazed from the bedroom into the corridor. Pad, pad, pad. Dusty's trot carried her in to investigate her human's amusement. Quite a switch from last night's quiet, tense gloom. She'd had to invest a good deal of nuzzlings, braows, and catly cuddlings to take the edge off Jessica's dark mood. Of course, Dusty had ultimately succeeded, for no worthwhile human could resist her feline charm. So, what was making the human actually laugh now?

Pause at the bedroom doorway. Locate Jessica on the bed, holding the phone. A glance toward the kitchen, then back to Jessica. Now the two most important considerations: was there any liverwurst left and would her human give her some?

Pad, pad, pad–leap. The bed yielded comfortably beneath her paws.

"Oh, pet, it's you. No, nothing, Lois. It's just the cat, on the bed."

Just the cat?! Dusty pulled away from her enjoyable neck rub to knead the covers speculatively. If she weren't on the prowl for liverwurst, she'd be affronted. So, what was the human blathering about, and how could she be directed to more important matters, like a cat's feeding schedule?

"Yes, yes, Lois. I can't tell you how relieved I am we've talked. I *do* feel much better. What you're telling me puts my mind a little more at ease. I mean, I still don't trust that Tewkesbury female, or even Evan Blair, but those scoops give us some bargaining power. I wonder how much Liz already knows."

A pause. Dusty had time to blink, twice, before Jessica continued, "Yes, that bodyguard was there, too. Do you think he's a part of her past?" Jessica sat up, listening, nodding, finally positing, "Do you think that there's some monkey business going on between them?"

Silent, Jessica listened. So, Dusty settled into a demure, body-wrapped-in-her-tail crouch, feigning a doze. This might take some time. Her eyes snapped open at Jessica's louder, "Yes, I agree. She'd never take a chance on losing the money or position. But you know, I still have a feeling there was something going on between her and Evan Blair once upon a time." Silence as Jessica listened more before agreeing, "Sure, that's true, but, if he had a different name then, the one he's using now wouldn't ring a bell with her. He's made darned sure she hasn't seen him yet."

Again, more listening. Then, "No. Lois, my plan to snag his fingerprints isn't rash. He won't suspect a thing." Pause. "Yes, I have a connection who can check them. You don't know him. Well, sure a snapshot might be more straightforward, but nobody has one, and Blair won't sit still long enough to for anybody to take one. Tell me *that's* not fishy."

Jessica went silent, listening, and Dusty was beginning to think she'd been much too patient. It would soon be time for some meowing and head butting.

"Sure, getting into that contretemps with Larry the other night wasn't exactly low profile, but I think Blair might have had a snootful, and everyone believed our chum Alanna was out of town ..."

It was hard to tell if the sound of the back-door bell made Dusty or Jessica start more. Dusty was up first, padding to the doorway. She stopped and signaled Jessica to follow with a flick of her tail, before heading into the kitchen.

"Oops. Gotta go, Lois. I hear Iris at the kitchen door. You know how she likes to come up by the garden. I'll give you the lowdown on this new beau she's bringing over. And, Lois, thanks for listening. 'Bye."

Jessica swung gracefully off the bed, the long skirt of her lounge outfit shimmering green, like forest moss in sunshine. Someone was tapping at the door now, a bit impatiently. Jess smoothed out the collar of her cream blouse, randomly graced with sprigs of green. Had to look her best to meet Iris's new beau.

Reaching the kitchen, Jessica halted. The window on the door revealed, not Iris Rossetti eager to get in, but Evan Blair! He wasn't looking at her but peering anxiously back into the garden. What on earth was he doing here?

From the corner of her eye, Jessica could see Dusty studying her through the bars of a kitchen chair's legs. Softly, she proposed, "Sherlock Kitty, let's see if we can pump this sucker. Maybe even get his prints."

When Jessica turned back to the door, Evan Blair was looking right at her, gesturing to the doorknob. He wanted in.

Warily, Jess crossed room and opened the door. However, she prevented her guest's entrance with a cool, "Not so fast. Just what prompts this visit, Mr. Blair?"

He smiled more tensely than he probably realized, Jessica surmised. After a glance up the alley toward the street, he winningly inquired, "Aren't you going to ask me in?"

"You really think I should, after last night?"

Jess had no intention of driving him off, but she thought it might look suspicious if she didn't show some annoyance over his letting down Liz–even if Liz had been asking for it.

"Precisely after last night. I'd like to explain. May I ... come in?"

"This I've got to hear," Jessica warily relented, stepping aside to admit Blair.

Closing the door behind Blair, Jess noticed he was holding a medium-sized volume, wrapped in a bookseller's paper. However, she was distracted by Blair's affable, "Nice place you have here."

"Cut the small talk, Mr. Blair," Jess set him straight. "You didn't pay me a visit just to give my kitchen a once over. Let's get down to cases about that cute trick you played on my sister last night."

"That was a cute little trick your sister played, trying to spring Alanna Tewkesbury on me when she was supposed to be out of town."

He had her there. Jessica said nothing.

"May I sit down, Miss Minton?"

Jess nodded, and he pulled out a chair, placing his book on the table. *At least he's not antagonistic*, she thought. *So, what's his game?* Dusty scooted to the relative safety of the corridor, her under-the-table sanctuary invaded.

Noting the cat settle into leery watchfulness, Blair inquired, "Roommate?"

"She pays her way in rodent removal," Jessica coolly responded. "Never mind the cat, though. You said something before about explaining?"

"Yes, I believe I did." Blair looked down at his book. Lifting the volume, he proffered it, "First, a peace offering. For you."

That threw Jessica. For a minute she didn't quite know what to do.

"Please, take it. My arm's getting tired, holding it out," he wryly requested.

Jessica took the book and unwrapped it: *Tulips and Chimneys*. Flipping it open, she skimmed the volume as she spoke, "Cummings? You're giving me a copy of cummings?"

Thoughtfully gathering up the wrapping paper, folding it, and stashing it in his pocket, Evan Blair explained, "I didn't forget our conversation last night. I'm sure you remember that this is the collection with 'the Cambridge ladies who live in furnished souls.' Better to have 'angry candy' than angry Minton sisters. So, I visited a special contact who deals in old books, got him to open up his store just for me on a Sunday morning, and when I saw this volume, I said to myself, 'Now here's something to restore me to the good graces of a literate girl!' I even had him wrap it. From his hands direct to yours–no sullying by me."

Jessica carefully put the book on the table, moving aside a stack of photos of friends and family she'd been perusing earlier, then responded carefully, "This won't cut any ice with Liz."

"But you might be able to put in a good word for me. Smooth the waters."

"For a bribe?" Jessica nodded toward the book.

"I could point out that it's a rare edition, perhaps from a fine family's library."

"And which family would that be, Mr. Blair?"

"It's not polite to question gifts, Miss Minton. Maybe you've been eating a little 'angry candy,' yourself."

"Maybe I'm just looking out for my sister, so you can cut the zeugma."

"I can't fault you there. But life would be much easier all around if I were back in her good books. Though, truth be told, your sister wasn't exactly playing fair when she tried to ambush me with Alanna, especially after I've been so adamant about my objections to the whole business."

He had her on the Alanna thing. Wasn't it interesting, though, that Blair had referred to La Tewkesbury by her first name–familiarly, though far from warmly. Very interesting. Maybe if she seemed to consider helping him, she could pull a little more out of Blair.

"You'd be a lot more persuasive, Mr. Blair, if you were more definite about how you know Alanna Tewkesbury is bad news. Facts, evidence are what convince people."

"I don't know how much more definite you expect me to be," Blair insisted. "I've told you the woman is cut-throat in business. Even Liz, bless her pointy little claws, isn't in her league. Your sister's *human*."

Jessica shrugged, countering, "I saw Liz handle her just fine last night. You underestimate my sister."

Blair shook his head, frustrated, "No, no. That was nothing. Just the preliminaries. Once Alanna means business, there's no holding her back. You've never seen her in action."

"And you have?"

Blair started to scowl at Jessica's insinuation, but quickly caught himself. He smoothed his features into his trademark debonair smile and corrected her, "I never said my experience with the lady was firsthand."

Jessica leaned forward on the table and quietly insisted, "Look, Blair, you're not dealing with a four-year-old. I've been around the block." She straightened up and challenged, "Why should I trust you? I know next to nothing about you, and what I do know is pretty shady. Do you honestly expect me to just buy any old bill of goods? I intend to look out for my sister, so level with me or forget it."

Blair sat back in his chair, thinking. He surprised Jessica by, finally, facing her squarely to confess, "Whether you believe me or not, I care what happens to your sister. She's been a breath of fresh air to me, acerbic fresh air, but fresh, nonetheless. I can't remember the last time I thought I could trust anyone this much." His eyes rested momentarily on the book he had given Jessica before he determinedly stated, "I'm not one to stick my neck out, but I don't want to see your sister get tangled up with that she-wolf."

Jessica nipped her lower lip. Damned if he didn't seem on the level. She walked away, speculatively rubbing the back of her neck. Turning sharply on her unsettling guest, Jessica told him, "You don't exactly make it easy to trust you. Granted, I'm with you on the anti-Tewkesbury front, but I've got more than a few doubts about you. First of all, what exactly do you mean, you 'care' about Liz. I'll tell you right now, I wasn't too crazy about some of your hints that you'd like to break up Liz and Larry."

"Tell you what, Miss Minton, I'll leave Liz and Larry alone if you agree to help me with the Tewkesbury situation."

"Before I make any alliances, I need to know the credentials of my allies," Jessica coolly stated.

Blair didn't waver under her intimidating eye. So, Jessica upped the ante: "If you *are* genuinely concerned with Elizabeth's welfare, you'll be willing to sacrifice a little privacy, won't you?"

She knew that Evan Blair could tell her a pack of lies just now. However, it had been her experience that to be convincing, lies needed some element of truth–a good place to start digging later.

Blair smiled a little bitterly before relenting, "Well, Miss Minton, you drive a dear bargain. I think perhaps if I'm to be autobiographical, I could use a drink."

"The liquor's in the other room. What can I get you?"

"Lemonade."

Jessica blinked.

"If I'm going to make a clean breast, I want to do it with a clear mind."

Jessica was amused, but she only nodded before moving to the fridge. He didn't have to know that she had Lois and old pal, F.B.I. Agent Jeff Hooley, to help her untangle the threads of truth in whatever story he wove for her. Better yet, he didn't have to know that this nice, cool glass of lemonade would leave her with a nice, cool set of fingerprints.

"There you go, Mr. Blair. Enjoy. I made it myself."

"Not your roommate over there glaring at me?"

Jess just smiled and sat down, restraining a comment on Dusty's innate hostility to rats. No, that wasn't entirely fair. There had been sincerity in Blair's concern for Liz–but, then again, even a chisler could have a tender spot. Mmm, just look at his hand closing on the glass as he took a drink. Five beauties right there.

"So, Blair, shoot."

The telephone rang.

"I'll resist saying 'saved by the bell,'" he commented, returning his glass to the table.

"I'll be right back," Jessica promised, impatiently rising. Just her luck that the kitchen phone was on the fritz right when she wanted to keep tabs on her guest.

"I'll indulge myself in a little e. e. cummings till you return. All this talk has whetted my appetite for some 'angry candy.' It's something *you*'ll need to do when the time is right," Blair called to her back as Jessica rushed for the phone in the living room.

Boy, he sure could dwell on that poem! Jessica briefly thought as she tore down on the ringing phone. She couldn't decide if she was more irritated or relieved that it was a wrong number. At least now she could get back to Blair, if he hadn't run out on her.

No, back in the kitchen, there he was, glancing down at her stack of photos rather than the book he had brought. He didn't seem to have laid a finger on it. Dusty was still on guard, her tail flicking sharply, menacingly. Jess fought the urge to snatch the record of her personal life away from this man she didn't trust. She couldn't afford to antagonize a person she was trying to pump for information.

Blair surprised Jess by speaking first about the topmost photo, "This Chinese woman, she's beautiful. Who is she?"

A quick glance before a barely impatient, "Lois Wong. Why?"

Still perusing the Kodak, Evan Blair answered thoughtfully, "She seems very troubled here. I couldn't help wondering what would do that to such a beautiful woman."

Jessica hesitated. The snapshot had been taken not long after the family tragedy. She wasn't sure how she'd ended up with it. Not about to give away her friend's past to this stranger, Jess answered vaguely, "That picture was taken before I knew her. Things are much better for her now."

"Oh. Are they?" There was a surprising mixture of hope, happiness, even relief in his tone. "I'm glad for her. It's not easy to climb out of..."

His words trailed off and Jessica puzzled, "Climb out of what, Evan?"

The front doorbell rang.

Furiously, Jessica inhaled her impatience, looked behind her toward the sound of the bell, then turned back to Blair. She was not amused at his sardonic expression nor his, "No, I did not plan this. Scout's honor."

"Why do I have a hard time picturing you as a Boy Scout? Never mind. I will be right back." She turned and instructed Dusty, "Make sure he doesn't go anywhere. There's a peck of tuna riding on it."

Jess fairly flew across the apartment. She pulled the door open on an eager Iris Rossetti and an attractive young man, but before her friend could say a word Jess blurted, "Iris, I feel like a heel. I know this sounds insane, but, well, could you come back in twenty minutes?"

Iris blinked, laughed incredulously, then managed, "Come again, Jess?"

Jessica scrunched her mouth with embarrassment, then began again, "I, I can't explain, exactly, right now." Her voice dropped to a whisper, "There's someone here."

"Oh?" Iris queried with a knowing expression.

Jess shot the amused boyfriend observing them an awkward glance, then hissed, "No, no, you don't get it. Honestly, this is important. It's about Liz. I can't talk now, but if you give me twenty min..."

They all heard the back door slam.

"I know someone who's going to be short on tuna today," Jessica muttered.

"I take it your phantom visitor just flew the coop," Iris quipped.

Jessica raised her hands in frustration and said, "Oh, Iris, please, just come in! What a morning!"

"I've no idea what's going on," Iris's companion said, smiling, "but it sounds more mysterious than an episode of *Lights Out*. By the way, I'm Wes Castle."

"Jessica Minton," Jess smiled weakly at the handsome young man, shaking his hand, then stepping aside to allow her guests in. He was a good-looking guy, with brown hair and eyes that really twinkled. Nice dark suit, cut expensively but not ostentatiously. And, if she hadn't been caught up in pumping Evan Blair, she might even have enjoyed his humor.

Without thinking, she let slip, "I came so close."

"To what, Jess?" Iris asked.

"Close to getting the truth out of Evan Blair."

They all stopped, and Iris quizzed Jessica, "Your sister's partner? The one you don't trust any farther than you can throw?"

"On the money, Iris. I can't begin to tell you what's been going on the past few days."

The bemused expression of Iris's date slowed Jessica. Maybe spilling out the latest Minton soap opera in front of a stranger wasn't the swiftest decision just now.

"I'm sorry, Mr. Castle. I don't mean to ramble on," Jess apologized. "Circumstances have conspired against me. Someone came by whom I wasn't expecting, and he knocked me for a loop. I hope you'll forgive me. Please, both of you, come into the front room and have a seat. Would either of you like a drink?"

Iris smiled, "Just a ginger ale for now."

"I'm fine," the newcomer replied agreeably. "Is there anything I can do to help?"

"Yes, sit down and get cozy by the window or by the fireplace, whichever is more comfy."

"Actually, I'd be more comfortable if you knocked off the 'Mr. Castle' business and called me Wes."

He did have a nice way of smiling those almost chipmunk cheeks. Maybe Iris had hit the jackpot with this fella.

"Wes it is. And make sure that you call me Jessica. I'll be right back. You and Iris make yourselves at home."

"Don't worry," Iris piped in. "We will."

On that note, Jessica hustled herself back out to the kitchen for the ginger ale. She could hear their voices, their little laughs. Wouldn't it be great to glance back in, to smile with them? Instead, the realization that Evan Blair had slipped out on her took over her thoughts, hardening her mouth.

Dusty floated into sight, making a little circle before the door and hitting Jessica with a demanding meow.

"Fine. *Now* you want to go out. You're always bringing me dead mice and moles; why didn't you go after that rodent when he made a break for it?"

Dusty blinked with feline forbearance.

"I should know better than to argue," Jessica shook her head, opening the door. "Okay, kiddo, it's liberation day."

Wait a minute, what was she grousing about? She still had the glass he'd been holding. All she had to do was pick it up with a cloth, being ever so careful not to smear the prints. There were some nice clean dishtowels right here in the drawer by the sink and dish strainer ... the strainer with the sparkling clean glass in it and another towel nearby. Blair's having the clerk handle the cummings book and his gathering up the paper wrapping now revealed themselves more shrewd than "considerate."

It wouldn't be right to scream just now. Not with company in the next room. If only she had something that she could break quietly. Much as Jessica hated being outsmarted, something much worse troubled her. Evan Blair wouldn't have gone to all this trouble unless there was something pretty nasty rattling around in his closet–nasty enough to hurt Liz?

Chapter Seven

Friday, May 18

Glints of silver, gold, and icy blue sparkled in the gentle waves of dark hair brushed back off Jessica Minton's forehead. The rest of her tresses were deftly caught in a French roll. With eyes lowered, her features softened into lovely pensiveness. The tightly cinched oriental house-dress, somewhat more upscale than most of Liz's line, glinted silver and gold scrollwork over blue and lavender crêpe and taffeta. It wasn't hard to hold that pensive expression for the shot, not with everything on her mind.

"All right, fine Jessica," came photographer Blaine Lassiter's voice. "Take a break. It's about lunchtime anyway. We'll have the next set up ready when you come back."

Jessica nodded, even managing a smile, but something more important weighed on her mind than her mid-day feast of lettuce, tomatoes, and celery. Liz hadn't gotten the chance to lace into Evan Blair after last Saturday because he'd gone to ground for almost a week. Blair had called the secretary to say he'd be out of town for a while, but not for how long. No direct message to Elizabeth. Her sister had tried to hide her feelings, but Jess had seen Liz's anger morph into reflection and then into guilt over how much her "surprise" guest at the awards dinner had damaged things with Evan. That guilt had only intensified after a meeting, at the lawyers' recommendation, with a certain Mr. Lyman Gastongay. He'd spelled out in no uncertain terms how disastrous his partnering with Mrs. Tewkesbury had been. It was painful for Liz to admit she was wrong, but Jess knew her sister well enough to understand that she was more pained at the thought of alienating a friend. And, of course, there was a practical consideration: Elizabeth had some key backers who wouldn't want to keep their money in a business run by a "little lady" with no masculine guidance.

She knocked on Liz's door. No reply. If it was unlocked, Liz couldn't be far off, so it made sense to try to pop in and wait. Stepping inside, she noticed a new floor-length mirror just to her right. A note was taped there, with her name on it.

"Oh, Miss Minton, I didn't expect you."

Jessica dropped the paper she'd pulled off the mirror. Evan Blair had just entered from his office.

"Sorry to unnerve you," he went on. "I'd hoped to talk to your sister. I heard someone moving about in here, and I thought that you were she."

"I should say you'd want to talk to Liz," Jessica chided. "Do you have any idea how worried she's been about you?"

"Dear Liz," Blair shook his head. "Absence does make the heart grow fonder, but I did leave a message with Ginger. It's hardly as if I absconded with the company funds. Can you really blame me for wanting to duck her until she cooled down? Which reminds me, were you kind enough to try to conciliate her for me?"

Jessica hesitated. True, Evan should have behaved more responsibly toward Liz and the business; but, also true, Liz had created this whole mess in the first place. Finally, she responded, "The two of you can be like a couple of kids, sometimes. You're irresponsible and she's headstrong. Anyway, I told her that you both need to stop playing games and work together. By the way, she wasn't impressed with your e.e. cummings bribe. I told her the next time I was going to hold out for a pony."

Blair's mouth crooked, then he said, "I'll see what I can do about that pony, if your landlord has no complaints. However, I'd be happier if there were no next time."

He turned and left, leaving Jess pondering whether her sister and Blair *had* turned over new leaves. At least Liz didn't have to worry that she'd lost her partner. Through the open door between the offices, Jess could see Blair, frowning down at his desk, smoking, but clearly deriving none of the relaxation advertisers guaranteed. What, exactly, was eating him? The Tewkesbury woman? Unexpectedly, Blair's eyes rose to meet hers, something speculative in them. Uncomfortable that he might read her thoughts, Jess turned back toward the mirror and went searching for the note she'd dropped.

"Miss Minton?"

Jess just managed not to jump out of her skin at Evan Blair's unexpected return, but she hid her annoyance. He apologized, "Ah, terribly sorry. I didn't mean to startle you again. I just wondered, would your sister mind if I borrowed her typewriter? Some private correspondence. Not exactly for Ginger's eyes, if you know what I mean."

"Borrowing a typewriter should be the least of your worries with Liz now; but, no, I don't think it would be any big deal, as long as you put it back exactly where she had it. You know Liz is a bit of a Hun when it comes to disordering her desk. I'd leave her a note."

"You're sure? Perhaps I shouldn't do anything else to set Liz off."

Blair gave her a conspiratorial look that even Jess had to admit was rather charming. In spite of herself, she allowed, "I can't say this flak has been all your fault. Liz can be awfully headstrong."

"It's part of her charm," Blair smiled. "And I hope making myself scarce this week may have taught her not to push that type of charm too far."

The superior sentiment in his words definitely did not sit well with Jessica. Maybe Liz had pulled a boner; nevertheless, she leveled him with cold blue eyes and lowered, "Where do you get off playing games with my sister, Mr. Blair? If you ever do anything to hurt her..."

"Jessica, the last thing I ever intend to do is hurt Elizabeth."

Their eyes locked. In spite of all Larry's and her suspicions, something in Jess believed this man right now. Still, even if gut instincts were 99% right, that 1% could kill you.

Indecision silencing her, Jessica watched Blair heft the stout black Underwood and return to his office, not able to close the door behind him. Jess resumed looking for the paper on the floor–until her glance caught the reflection of Evan Blair's office in the mirror. What in Sam Hill was he doing? Tipping the typewriter on its side on his desk? Was he taping something underneath and inside the typewriter? Oh for Pete's sake, he'd turned and blocked out what he was doing!

Now, Blair moved out of the mirror's reflection; and, automatically, Jess turned for a better look. The door from his office to the reception area opened and closed, then locked. But the door adjoining *this* office was still open.

Jessica wrestled temptation and a touch of suspicion. Blair hadn't bothered to lock her out. She really had no right to sneak in and check out what he'd taped up, inside the typewriter. But it was her sister's typewriter. She was looking out for Liz's best interests.

Jess took one step closer to the open doorway, then another. If she didn't hurry, he might come back in and catch her in the act. Darn it all, Liz was rubbing off on her!

"Jessica, there you are!"

The air seemed to crackle from the slash of her skirts as she whirled to face Ginger behind her.

The secretary cocked her head curiously and queried, "Were you looking for Mr. Blair?"

"Um, sort of. He walked out without returning Liz's typewriter. I thought I'd go get it."

"Oh, you don't have time for that. There's someone here to see you. A soldier. Easy on the eyes, if I do say so!"

"A solider wants to see me?" That definitely perplexed Jessica.

"Yeah, some sergeant, named Le May."

"I don't know any Sergeant Le May. Did he say what he wants?"

"He's in kind of a hurry. Has to catch a train out, and he's limping, so I think he really can't wait. Needs the extra time to get to the station."

"Gee, that's too bad, but did he say what this is all about?"

"Not exactly. Just that he had a letter for you that he didn't think you'd want to miss. From overseas."

The implications knocked Jessica for a loop. She recovered enough to stammer hopefully, "Did he, did he say who ... whom it was from?"

"Nope. There's one way to find out, though."

Trying not to shake, Jessica urged, "Please, Ginger, send him in. Right away."

Ginger saluted, "Okey dokey. You'll have to give me the scoop, afterwards. Oh, I almost forgot, Lois Wong called and asked me to leave a message for you in Liz's office. I taped it to the mirror for you. I figured you'd notice it better there than on your sister's desk. Did you get it?"

"Note? Yes, I guess, but never mind. Just send the sergeant in, will you, Ginger? Or maybe I should follow you and..."

"You sit down. I'll send him in. Remember, I want a full report."

Jessica couldn't sit down. Was this a message from James? Did it mean he was all right? Damn! She should have asked if the sergeant looked anxious or happy or nonchalant–or *anything* that might tell her if the letter was so bad he dreaded delivering it. But if James was writing, he had to be okay, okay enough to write. But a guy could suffer a lot of damage and still be able to write. Oh for Pete's sake, why hadn't Ginger sent him in yet?

As if on cue, there was a knock on the door, and Jess had all she could do to call calmly, "Come in."

Hobbling energetically on a crutch, he did. Ginger had been right; he wasn't hard on the eyes at all. Medium height, wiry build, and a shock of dark hair swept back under his cap. His dark eyes had a bit of a glint to them, even if the lines of his handsome, hawk-like features bespoke soul-deep weariness. That glint was a good sign.

Biting back her anxiousness, Jessica gratefully welcomed the soldier, "It's so good of you to make time to see me, Sergeant. Could I have Ginger get you coffee or something?"

The "sergeant" seemed to take him by surprise; then he laughed and explained, "It's a field commission. I was a private the whole war till just last month. They pulled me out of my old squad, gave me a bunch of new recruits, and bam! I get a million-dollar wound."

"Oh, I'm so sorry. Should you be standing? Maybe you'd better sit down?" Jessica offered, trying not to hover.

He waved her off, laughing, "I've been sitting too long since I got hit. I like getting up to play mailman for a fella trying to get in touch with his girl."

"You've seen James, Sergeant Le May? Is he all right? He's alive? He's okay?"

The sergeant put a hand on Jessica's arm and said, "I think you better sit down, Miss. But, yeah, he's okay. A little banged up, but he's fine."

He got Jessica to sit on Liz's couch, and, joining her, he continued, "We were in the same hospital in England. He recognized me because my old squad had brought him in one time from the Resistance. Don't worry about him. He's going to be fine. He knew I could get this back to you sooner than the V-mail–and without the censors holding it up."

Jessica's hand was shaky once she held the letter. Le May picked up on her eagerness to read it and, with a glance at his watch, tactfully offered, "Uh oh, I've a got a train to catch out of Penn. I'm gonna have to hustle if I don't want to miss it. Sorry to deliver and run."

He'd gotten back on his feet, a little awkwardly, but with such surprising alacrity that Jess hadn't the chance to try to help. She had the distinct sense he wanted it that way.

"Isn't there any way I can thank you for this, Sergeant?" Jess raised the letter as she spoke. "Is there anything I can do?"

"Forget about it, Miss. It's good to see two people getting back together for a change." There was a world of meaning in the last three words, but then Le May grinned, "Now, I've really got to get the lead out."

Jessica moved to the door with Le May. Though her thoughts were on the letter, she had enough presence of mind to squeeze his hand gratefully. The soldier shook his head and laughed, "Just sit down and read that letter."

She could only smile, wishing him the best. As he crossed the reception area, Jess called to the secretary, who was trying to look as if she were only interested in her typing, "Ginger, I'll be in here if anyone needs me. But I really don't want to be disturbed for about fifteen minutes. Got it?"

Ginger was not happy about a delay in getting the scoop, but she nodded. Overhearing the exchange, the sergeant gave Jess a wink before he was out the door.

Slipping back into Liz's office, Jessica's hands trembled with an unnerving cocktail of emotions. She ripped open the letter and slowly sank onto the couch to read.

Jessica,

How do I start after so long? I'm all right. I'm coming back, though God knows when. But I'm on the mend. Just don't expect me to go dancing any time soon. But I will be all right. In fact, I might be out of hospital by the time you get this. I don't know where I'll be sent when I'm released, so I can't tell you where to reach me. But I had to get this letter off to you. I couldn't let you keep wondering and worrying all this time.

I can't tell you how much I miss you. Remembering New

York and San Francisco with you, that kept me sane. It pulled me through a hell of a lot. It still does. I always feel you near me, love. I'll write you through regular channels as soon as I can. Jessica, it looks like this damn war is coming to a close. First Europe, next the Pacific. Thank God. I can't come home to you soon enough. Just know that I'm safe now, and that I love you. I'm sorry to have put you through this hell of waiting to know about me. If there had been another way, but we both know we're not the only ones who've gone so long apart. Once this damned thing is really done, I'm never letting you go. And tell Dusty I've been saving a tin of premium tuna for her.

All My Love,
James

Automatically, Jessica flipped the letter over, greedy for more, though she knew there wouldn't be. One hand flicked away the tears washing off the make-up woman's careful enhancement of her features. She sat there, a little dizzy with joy, her hands now crunching the letter. The letter!

Carefully flattening out the crumpled paper on her lap, Jessica scanned it again, hungry to catch anything she'd missed. Those wonderful words: "love," "home"! And James had said memories of their time together saw him through. Through what, exactly? The question was a knife in her side. What *had* he been through? He was in the hospital? Lord, how badly injured was he?

But he would soon be out of that hospital. "On the mend," James had written. Plus, he wasn't discharged from the service yet. So it couldn't have been a million-dollar wound like with the sergeant. And that sergeant *had* said James was all right now.

God bless that soldier. Jess had such an urge to find him and hug him for bringing James this close to her. She hoped someone was waiting for him, the way she was waiting for James. Maybe Ginger would have some information on where she could at least write her thanks.

Jess got up to ask but never got beyond reaching for the doorknob. From the entrance to the dressing rooms, Liz called, "Say, where are you going in such an all-fired rush?"

Jessica whirled. Her dress swirled so beautifully that, at first, Liz paid more attention to it than her sister–until Jessica pounced on her with an ecstatic hug and pronounced, "Liz! Liz! He's all right! I've got a letter from him! James is alive!"

Liz held her sister at arm's length and demanded, "What the dickens are you talking about, and don't crush the dress."

Jessica waved the letter at Liz and crowed, "A soldier from overseas just left here. James sent a letter to me through him. I've heard from James, and he's alive!"

Liz started to say something acerbic but thought better. Instead, she took out her handkerchief and offered it to Jessica with, "Here, blow your nose, kid. Weepy doesn't go with the ensemble." Jessica gave her sister a skeptical look but complied, while Liz continued, "Look, I'm sorry, but you know your fella is not exactly my favorite person."

"It wasn't as if it was anything personal, Liz. And besides, that's all behind us now."

"Okay, okay." Liz put her arm around her sister and walked her over to the couch. "He makes you happy. That's what counts. And I'm glad this load is off your mind, Jessica. Why don't you go home and relax? We've both had a tough week. Besides, you're not exactly in premium shape to finish the shoot. That blotchy face. Take the afternoon off. Have some fun. Celebrate. You don't have to look good to do that!"

"Thanks, I think. But are you sure you don't need me? Won't Blaine Lassiter be steamed?"

"I'll take care of him. That's why it pays to be related to the boss. Go tell the cat."

"She always liked James," Jess pointed out, "even before I did."

"That's why I've always preferred dogs."

"You stinker!" Jess shot back with a grin, then caught her sister in a hug and finished, "but I love you anyway."

"I love you, too. Even if you do have lousy taste in men."

"Say, what happened to your being nicer, Liz?"

"I don't want to spoil you."

Jessica shook her head and swished her skirts toward the dressing-room, until a couple of disquieting questions unexpectedly came to mind. Should she tell Liz that Evan Blair was here today? Did Liz know? Maybe letting this temporary rift widen into a permanent chasm would be the best way to get Blair out of her sister's life. Except, Liz was really eating herself up over how things stood. Had she the right to manipulate her sister into doing what *she* wanted through a lie of omission? Still, Liz had a right to work out her own problems. Darn, Jess hated being such a Girl Scout.

"Liz, I almost forgot. Did you know Evan is back? He was in his office, but I think he stepped out, maybe only for a minute. It sounded to me as if he's ready to bury the hatchet."

"In my skull?"

"Look, Elizabeth, Lord knows I'd love to see you running this place without him, but I also know you need to square things with him. Go and ask Ginger where he is or when he'll be back."

"I thought you didn't trust him?" Liz shot back.

"I'm not saying I'm his biggest fan, just that I know what you need to do to feel right with the world."

"Sometimes, kid, I wonder which of us is the elder sister–not often, though!"

"I'll take that as a compliment," Jess returned, then added, "I just wish you could be as happy as I am right now. How lucky can I get? James is coming home, and I have a great new job. Next Monday, I get my first script and start rehearsing!"

"Well, Jess, your *job* sounds nifty," Liz remarked.

"I said it before and I'll say if again: you, sister dear, are a stinker. Just do what you think best in terms of Mr. Blair. I'll see you tomorrow night at your party."

Liz gave her kid sister a sharp salute and soon found herself alone. Alone with the prospect of what to do about Evan. Elizabeth Minton did not dine heartily on crow. Rather, oughtn't Evan have to chow down on a healthy serving after going A.W.O.L. all week? Anyway, he was back now, and she had some fences to mend. Too bad Jess and Larry couldn't give him more credit for trying to steer her away from Mrs. Tewkesbury. Well, if she wanted things back on an even keel around here, she'd better get the lowdown from Ginger on Mr. Evan Blair's whereabouts. Maybe it would be quicker to knock on his door, but a *little* stalling was mighty appealing.

That was when Elizabeth noticed the note on the floor. Okay, who was littering her immaculate office? Heads would roll!–but neatly into bins. Liz uncrumpled the paper and discovered a message from Lois, asking Jess about coming here for lunch at–five minutes from now! She'd better get out to the reception room and redirect Lois to Jess's, or at least instruct Ginger to do it.

Stepping into the main office, Liz came to an abrupt halt at the sight of Ginger leaning over her desk, gazing, flummoxed, at the main door.

"I hope you're not staring after a customer," Liz stated.

Ginger fluttered, "No, no, Liz. Lois Wong, she'd just been here a minute. She told me not to announce her, that your sister was expecting her. Then, out of the blue, she popped up, all jumpy, said something about having to go–and did!"

"Just now?"

Ginger nodded, and Liz was out the main door and into the empty corridor, trying to catch Lois. No one.

Back in the office, Liz was greeted by Ginger's, "Sorry, Elizabeth. She just jumped up right where you're standing now and said something about another appointment. "

"Don't worry, Ginger. Have Jessica give her a call to straighten things out. I'm sure it's no big deal." Liz's glance drifted across the office, to her partner's partially open door Wonder of wonders, he looked as if he was actually working!

"I see Mr. Blair is in," Liz noted, proud of how well she could disguise her nervousness.

Ginger briefly glanced in his direction before saying, "Oh, he's been here for some time. Before Miss Wong came in–and out. You must have been in the studio or dressing room when he came in."

"Fine, Ginger. Could you hold my calls until I tell you? I'll be in conference with Mr. Blair."

"Okay, Miss Minton. Do you need me to take any notes for you?"

Giving her secretary a raised brow, Liz instructed, "No thank you, Ginger. Just put some of that interest into typing up the schedule of showings that I gave you."

Liz looked back at Blair in his office, then gave herself a mental shove that propelled her across the reception area. A quick rap on Blair's door and she said, "Evan, I need to speak with you. May I come in?"

Blair regarded Liz warily before responding, "That depends, Duchess. Are you armed?"

"Only with my snappy wit," Liz returned with a weak smile.

"Then come and sit down, Elizabeth. Tell me what's on your mind." Though his words were gracious, he still watched her carefully, as if unsure of what to make of a subdued Liz Minton.

Elizabeth closed the door behind her and quickly moved to the chair before her partner's desk. Sitting there, she stared down at her hands, folded in her lap. The words wouldn't come. Damn! She'd kill for cigarette!

"Cat got your tongue?" Evan prodded.

Liz faced Evan. His expression was definitely curious, and he also seemed to be enjoying her discomfort: revenge for the dirty trick she'd tried to pull on him with Mrs. Tewkesbury.

"You're not going to make this easy on me, are you?" she grumbled.

Evan leaned back in his chair, linking his fingers in his lap before answering, "I suppose I should be grateful that you aren't planning to boil me in oil for my little disappearing act..."

"You call almost a week 'little'?" Liz flashed. At Evan's raised eyebrow, she reined in her ire and only said, "All right. Never mind."

"Fine with me, Liz. Now what do you want to talk about? No more nonsense about letting Alanna Tewkesbury into our cozy little setup, I hope."

"Not exactly," began Liz slowly. Then the dam burst: "Okay, I admit it. You had her pegged. I'm not going to push it anymore."

Blair was clearly surprised, but he probed carefully, "That's quite an about face, Duchess. What's the story behind it? Perhaps meeting her showed you just how tough a customer she can be?"

"I handled her just dandy last Saturday," Liz snapped back. "The question is, do I want to. Especially after what Lyman Gastongay told me corroborated everything you warned me about, in spades! Then Jess had me sit down with our pal Lois Wong, and she gave me the full treatment on what had happened to some of her art world friends whom La Tewkesbury got her claws into. Evan? Are you listening? What's with you?"

Evan was now sitting straight up in his chair, but he inquired with only mild interest, "The Wong girl knows about Alanna? She's met her?"

"That's not what I said, Evan," Liz replied impatiently. "But she has connections who have. You know she was just out in the reception room a short time ago. If she hadn't taken off like Barney Oldfield, *you* could have asked her. Never mind her. This conversation is about you and me. I want to make sure you know that I'm through with my plans for teaming up with Tewkesbury. Evan, are you listening to me?"

Blair was staring at the door, speculating. Liz turned, following his gaze: just a door closed on the outer office.

Blair broke into her thoughts with, "Does the Wong girl come here often?"

Turning back to him, Liz fumed, "I don't think so. I don't know. Never mind that; I'd expect you to be more interested in my coming around to your way of thinking. At the very least, I'd expect you to do some gloating over my eating crow for you."

Evan waved off Liz's annoyance with, "Now, Duchess, I would only enjoy seeing you eat pheasant. I'm just glad you avoided a train wreck, for whatever reason. So did you miss me this week?"

"I ate my heart out," Liz deadpanned. "By the way, you've got work to make up. So get cracking on the Resnick account. I need your thoughts on it by the end of the day."

"Ever the slave driver," Blair teased.

"And don't you forget it!" Liz kidded back, on her feet and relieved their little chat had been far less painful than she'd anticipated. "So, I'm glad we cleared the air. Everything's jake?"

"Of course it is, Liz," Evan answered quietly. "It always was–even if you are one of the most infuriating of women at times."

"Have to keep you on your toes," Liz cracked as she headed for her office. She stopped and turned back to Blair, to add, "By the way. I don't know if you read the papers, but yesterday there was a lovely photo of your pal Alanna at the train station under the Waldorf-Astoria, heading off for Florida with her retinue."

"Why do you think I came back today?" he smiled devilishly. "I knew you couldn't spring her on me–until she gets back in a week or so."

"Well, you don't have to worry about that anymore," Liz assured him. "Like I said, I'm through with that gal."

"Good," Blair responded, but his smile was somewhat less cheerful than Liz expected.

She regarded her partner thoughtfully, her tone now serious, and asked, "She really gets your goat. Is there something more than bad business deals between you and our uptown 'friend'?"

"Isn't that enough?" Blair laughed fairly convincingly. "Now get out of here if you really want me to study up on Resnick–or I *will* show up at the staff party you're throwing this Saturday."

"It's S.O.P. for both partners to be on hand," Liz pointed out.

"Sorry, Liz, weekends are my nights to squire lovely ladies to out-of-the-way, romantic rendezvous."

"I had to ask you. You do own the business, too," Liz shrugged. She didn't say she'd felt safe inviting Blair into the same building with Larry because she figured her partner wouldn't come. Closing the door behind her, Liz mused that crow, after all, wasn't so distasteful if seasoned with a little charm and humor. Maybe she should try this humility thing more often–Naaah! It was good to have her partner and friend back.

Chapter Eight

Saturday May 19

After James's letter, Jessica should have been having the time of her life at Liz's party. His words had melted an avalanche of care from her heart, but not all of it. Ill-at-ease, Jess kept watch from the landing above the exuberant crush of partiers in her sister's living room. One hand absently stroked the soft cream-colored crêpe of her summer dress, then yet again adjusted the dark hair gently swept off her pensive features and pulled into a bun at the nape of her neck. Standing by the apartment's front entrance, with a street-facing window to the right, she kept an eye out for the person who worried her keenly. At the moment, though, Jessica was watching the conviviality in the living room.

Bing Crosby's "Swinging on a Star" jived out of the Philco, infecting everyone with a mischievous bounce; one couple was even attempting a severely abbreviated jitterbug in the corner. Liz, Larry, and some others were embroiled in a fierce contest of charades, trying to decipher Iris Rossetti's acting out either "Coming in on a Wing and a Prayer" or an inebriated pelican choking on a mackerel. The sound of laughter, attempts to sing-along with Bing, and general conviviality inspired by the company of good friends and a near end to the war beckoned. Yet one good friend was missing, and Jessica had the sinking feeling this friend was in trouble.

Turning away from the party, Jess peered into the shadows of the street below. On this overcast night, she almost hadn't seen the figure next to that stoop, positioned so a person couldn't spot him from street-level. Only up here, with repeated checking, had Jessica discerned him–though not clearly, with his hat pulled down that way. There was even something vaguely familiar. If she could just see a little more nose, brow... no dice. He, however, seemed to have a nifty view of the comings and goings of *this* building.

"Think you might like to join the party tonight, kiddo?" Liz's query invaded her thoughts. "I was expecting you to be turning cartwheels, between your new acting job and the letter from Prince Charming."

"Something else is bothering me, Liz. It's Lois. I'm really worried. After Ginger called and told me about her dashing off yesterday, I wasn't able to reach her by phone or catch her at her apartment. I haven't heard from Lois at all!"

"So that's why you're on the lookout here."

Jessica nodded tightly, explaining, "I feel so guilty."

"Guilty? For the love of Mike, why?"

"If I hadn't gone home to 'celebrate' hearing from James, I'd have seen her at the office. Maybe I could have found out what was wrong before she bolted. But I wasn't there, and I haven't been able to track her down."

"Well, now, don't beat yourself up. Ginger didn't say Lois was all upset when she came in. Only that something seemed to strike her, and then she took off. Anyway, let's quit wasting time worrying over spilled Milk of Magnesia. Have you tried her mother in Massachusetts?"

"There's the rub, Liz. Her mother's English isn't great, and since my Chinese consists of being able to say "Hi," "I'm full," and "I have a gray cat," I don't think we'd have an awfully fruitful conversation."

"I see what you mean. You might even get her all nerved up."

"Exactly. So, I thought I'd keep an eye out for Lois here. She was supposed to come."

"I see. But you do understand, Jess, that your standing here won't affect whether Lois shows."

"I know."

"Well, to put it bluntly, you're making *me* a wreck. Come down and at least pretend to have a good time," Liz urged.

As Jessica started to protest, Bing Crosby's vocals chimed in, "Or would you rather be a mule?"

The sisters cracked up, and Liz started to guide her kid sister from the window. But Jessica stopped them with, "Liz, wait. There's something else. Take a look out that window–across the street, by the steps. What do you see?"

"Why?"

"Never mind 'why,' just take a gander," Jessica insisted, nudging her sister to the window.

"Okay. Where? I don't see anything."

From around Liz's shoulder, Jessica directed, "No, not there–*there*, to the left of the stairs and down. Look down. See?"

Thank God, there he was! Liz couldn't accuse her of an over-active imagination tonight.

"So? It's a guy with his collar turned up. It's cold tonight, for spring."

"Don't you think it's a little odd, a man standing out there, all this time, in the cold rain?"

"He's waiting for somebody."

"Waiting in the shadows? He's up to no good, I tell you. He's definitely hiding."

"From whom?"

"I don't know. That's what bugs me. He's on the lookout for someone but doesn't want that someone to know."

"Big deal. That's nothing to do with us."

"You don't know that, Liz."

Elizabeth shook her head and, gesturing out to the convivial party, tried to be reassuring. "Jessica, please. Do you see anyone here on the lam from the law *or* the 'criminal element'?"

"Not here, but what about Lois? She's missing, and he's on the lookout. What if ... ?"

"What if? What if? Don't be daffy. You're coming down with a king-size case of the heebie-jeebies. I know you. I know how that imagination of yours works. That's one thing I could agree with Mr. James Crawford about. Besides, Lois, of all people, being stalked by a gunsel..."

"Be fair, Elizabeth. I never said he was a gunsel."

"Fine. But think about it: a steady girl like Lois involved in a mystery? Really?"

Jessica's concerns were not soothed, though. She pressed, "So why did Lois take off abruptly yesterday? Why no word from her since? And isn't it an odd coincidence that now some joker should be watching your building?"

Liz was decidedly unconvinced: "Jess, there's more than one apartment in this building. There's more than one building on this side of the street. My place isn't the only one he can get an eyeful of."

Jessica didn't have a good rejoinder for that. There was one, she was sure, but it danced somewhere beyond her grasp.

Liz continued, "Look, kiddo, Lois is fine. You're just making a mountain out of a Mohawk. Anyway, if you have to blame someone, blame me. *I* sent you off on your merry way yesterday. So if anything's wrong–and nothing is–blame me and go down there and have a good time."

Jessica regarded her sister doubtfully before beginning, "Liz, I really do appreciate your trying to make me feel better, but..." Three brisk raps on the door cut her off. Jessica ventured, "Shall we have the Porter answer it, Lady Macbeth?"

"Porter, nothing. It's probably Lois, you big goose! Let's answer it and take a load off your mind!"

Relieved, Jessica couldn't help sharing her sister's grin. Liz reached forward and opened the door. Evan Blair!? Jess exchanged a double take with her sister before they both anxiously surveyed the crowded apartment. Thank God, no Larry in sight!

"May I come in–or would you prefer we chat in the corridor?" Blair's query brought them back to him.

"Don't be silly, Evan," Liz recovered herself. "Please come in. Were all the romantic hideaways booked for the evening? Misplace your little black book?"

Blair gave Liz the slightest of smiles at the reference to his earlier excuse. However, on entering, he became serious: "I wouldn't have come, but I've been doing some serious thinking, Liz, and I need to discuss something with you tonight. Is there any place where we can talk, alone, briefly?"

Jess could tell by Liz's quick glance toward the kitchen that the room was Larry-free. Her sister answered, "Yes, Evan, follow me. Sure you can't stay, though? It's quite a lively gathering."

Jess wanted to warn Liz not to overplay the gracious hostess role, but she had bigger concerns. For Blair not to wait until Monday but to show up unexpectedly here, he had to have something pretty big up his sleeve–or in that briefcase she noticed him carrying. What was in there?

Jessica carefully inquired, "Something wrong, Mr. Blair?"

"Not at all, Miss Minton. Just a few business questions I thought needed attention while they're still fresh in my mind. You know how hard it is for a playboy like me to keep my nose to the grindstone. At any rate, if Liz can turn over a new leaf and not push so hard, perhaps I can turn one over and start doing my fair share, right, Liz?"

"Why not?" she pleasantly concurred "Just follow me." Then Liz added, "Jessica, please see to the guests. Keep things running smoothly out here; you know what I mean. I know I can count on you."

With that code for "keep Larry occupied when he comes back from wherever he is while I worm Evan's story out of him and sneak him down the back fire escape," Liz swept her charge off to the kitchen.

Inwardly, Jess griped, *Darn you, Liz, do you really think I've nothing better to do than ride shot gun on your personal life?* Jessica loved her sister, she really did, but she certainly didn't want to deceive Larry; there'd been too much of that in the past. Still, the prospect of a volcano erupting in the midst of all this shiny, bright conviviality was not particularly appealing. A quick, thorough scan of the room revealed no Larry. Fine, her moral dilemma was temporarily postponed, but the questions of exactly where Larry had gone and if he'd return while Evan Blair was here still threatened.

Iris Rossetti caught Jess's eye, smiled broadly, then sailed across the room in a swirl of shiny green and silver rayon, greeting her, "Hey, Jess, you gloomy Gus! What are you doing all by yourself? This is a party! Let your hair down!"

"After I spent so much time fixing this nifty coiffure?" Jessica kidded.

"Never mind that, Jessica Minton. What's with the sour puss?"

"Just something on my mind, Iris."

"What? You have that great new radio gig and all those juicy roles where you get to go crazy and kill people! You should be dancing around on the furniture with a lampshade on your head."

"Gee, Iris, I don't think Liz has any lampshades that go with this dress. What do you think?" Jess couldn't help smiling at her pal's zaniness.

Arms akimbo, Iris decided, "*You* need a drink to loosen you up."

"Iris, I'd say that you're loose enough for both of us right now. What have you been imbibing?"

Iris's smile was devilish as she answered, "Stingers–and I *know* how to mix them. C'mon over to the bar. You could use one, Jess, old girl."

Jessica hesitated. What with worrying about Lois and wondering whether Larry would waltz in and spark off a powder keg, Iris couldn't find enough liquor to mellow her out tonight. Still, she acquiesced, "Okay, Iris, hit me. But just one. Dusty sometimes checks my breath."

"Not to worry," Iris brightened, guiding her friend to the bar. "Liz has plenty of mints."

Jess leaned on the bar and, hoping to sound casual, inquired, "Say, Iris, have you seen Larry around? I had something to ask him."

"Uh, well, he's somewhere. Could be getting a whiff of air on the fire escape outside the kitchen. What's with that look? No, wait a minute, I think he stepped out to buy some smokes. Never mind him, wait till you've had one of my Stingers! More of a kick than those Singapore Slings you like."

Jessica made a mock grimace. They both knew the story of Jess's having a few too many Singapore Slings, with the next thing she recalled was waking up in bed wearing only a sequined beanie and a string of pearls. It had been her own bed and she had been alone, but Iris never let her forget it–mischievously embroidering on exploits Jessica could never remember. Still, the following morning Jessica had found herself the possessor of a trophy as the Felicitous Feline Club's jitterbug champ.

"So, Jess, how's the radio gig going? Nervous about your debut next week?" As she queried, Iris was busy digging up her ingredients behind the bar with all the relish of Boris Karloff creating life in a test tube.

"I always get the jitters at first, but I'm really thrilled, Iris. Our first script is 'A Rose for Emily.' It sounds like a real spine tingler."

"'Rose for Emily'?" Iris paused in her mixology. "Isn't she a crazy, whacked out eccentric?"

"She sure is, but she's a starring crazy, whacked out eccentric, and the part sounds juicy. That's what counts."

Iris pushed the glass forward with a big grin and, "There's your poison! Bottoms up!"

Iris's heels almost got out from under her then, and Jessica dryly advised, "Just the glass, not you."

"That's the ticket. Laugh it up. Say, have you heard anything more about your friend James..."

Iris's words trailed off at the sound of raised voices emanating with increasing volume and ire from the kitchen. The rest of the guests were no less attentive.

"Well, at least we know where Larry is," Iris muttered uneasily.

"And how," Jessica tensely agreed. "Iris, I have to go in and break it up. Could you distract the people out here? Put a record on the hi-fi and teach them a new version of the, uh, merengué?"

"I don't think I know an old version, Jess."

They both winced as a dish smashed–and the guests began the low-level buzz characteristic of people shifting into eavesdropping mode.

"Okay, okay, Jess, I'll improvise. You go see if you can break up Schmeling and Louis."

Iris was off to the hi-fi, chattering brightly about a new dance called the Lemon Merengé Conga. Carmen Miranda had taught it to Betty Grable in *Moon over Cleveland*, or something. She had the music up to fight-camouflaging level before Jessica even got to the kitchen. Ironically, at that point, Liz and Larry had reached a lull.

Entering the small kitchen, Jessica found Larry glaring down at Evan Blair, who sat with irritating calm at the table, legal papers spread between him and Liz. Her nibs must have just jumped up, for her chair was shoved back from the table, and she was icily staring down Larry. There was enough electricity in the air to illuminate Manhattan several times over. But it was too late to make a break for it now: Liz had already raised an eyebrow at her.

"Well, at least I won't have to ask you kids to retire to your corners," Jess observed coolly.

"And a lovelier referee could not be requested," Evan Blair smiled.

"You can stow the *faux* charm, Blair. Jessica is wise to you," Larry derided him.

"And I suppose I'm some kind of a sap?" Liz zinged.

"Did I say come out fighting?" Jessica warned. "Your guests thought that they were sitting in on a broadcast of *The Bickersons*."

Liz's face contorted in horror: social humiliation! Nevertheless, she was sharp enough to swiftly shift blame, narrowing her eyes, and firing off, "If you'd been running interference, Jessica, none of this would have happened. Evan and I would have had our chat..."

"And I've have been none the wiser? Unfortunately for you, you couldn't see me on the fire escape getting a breath of air," Larry finished, righteous, but quieter. He clearly had in mind the public circumstances of this contretemps.

"You don't have to worry, Larry. This is business, pure and simple," Liz corrected him, still annoyed but no longer antagonistic.

"I imagine you were holding his hand 'purely' and 'simply'? Really, Elizabeth, what do you take me for?"

"Don't answer that, Elizabeth," Jessica took over. To her surprise, Liz listened, gathering her thoughts before addressing Larry with surprising tact and earnestness, "I was just saying good-bye, wishing him well, letting him know I appreciated his friendship. It's not every day your silent partner turns over his end of the business to you–and assets to help you carry on."

"What?" Jessica blurted out.

Everyone ignored her. Larry spoke next, sarcastically addressing Evan Blair, "No strings attached?"

"None," Blair replied simply.

Larry shook his head and said to Elizabeth, "You can't believe this man. You Minton girls are far too trusting. How much of a fool could someone be?"

Elizabeth fumed, and, truth be told, Jessica started scanning the room for her sister's rolling pin.

Evan Blair rose and spoke, reasonably and forcefully, "Look here, Sanders, I may not have the trustworthy face of Gary Cooper, that's fine. You may not like me, fine again. But I don't ever want to hear you talk to Elizabeth so disparagingly. You're right about one thing: I'm not a prize catch. Elizabeth is too good for a fellow like me. That's why I'm leaving. I can see that sooner or later I may cause her grief. She can make it on her own now, without me. Just in case, I've given her some capital to tide her over. But I'll tell you something else, as shady a customer as I may seem to you, I know a first-rate woman when I see one. In any case, I'm a gambler, and the gambling is over in this business. And I don't want to cause any more friction between you and Elizabeth. Frankly, though, Sanders, I think she's too damned good for *you*. Whether I'm in the picture or not, I sure as the devil hope she calls it quits with you."

Jess and Liz practically had to jump on Larry to keep him from letting Blair have it. Larry, however, was too civilized to let fury–or two women–control him. He glared at Evan but shook down his anger, himself. The sisters stepped back, and Larry gave Elizabeth one last penetrating look before saying coldly, "I need some air."

Liz, for once, didn't know what to say. Only after the kitchen door had slammed behind Larry did she exhale a flummoxed, "Oh."

"Are you all right, Liz?" Jessica asked, steadying her sister.

"I'm sorry, Elizabeth."

It was Evan Blair. Jessica gave him a furious look, but Liz almost floored her by admitting, "This whole mess is my fault. I handled everything badly, so badly. Poor Larry."

"I think there's plenty of blame to go around," Jessica corrected, eyes leveling on Blair. He looked away.

"Well, there's nothing more for me to do but go out, find Larry, and bring him back," Elizabeth concluded, exhausted emotionally.

"Oh, Liz, I don't know," Jessica warned. "Larry's pretty steamed right now. Don't you think he needs time to cool off? I know you two. The state you and he are in, I'm really afraid you'll both say something you'll regret."

Blair tendered agreement, "Your sister is right. I also think that since he ran out, Larry should be the one to come back."

"Funny, advice coming from one of the reasons he left," Liz pointed out. Turning to Jessica, she continued, "What if he's too angry to come back? What if he thinks I don't care enough? And maybe he's right. Maybe I should have thought more about him and his needs."

Blair held back a moment, then spoke his mind: "Then it's his loss. 'Tender yourself more dear' or some such thing Polonius said."

"I seem to recall my sister once saying that Polonius was a dope."

Jessica carefully explained, "Far be it from me to agree with Mr. Blair, but I do think Larry needs to cool down. Besides, Liz, you've got an apartment full of guests. If you and Larry both disappear after a blow out, what will people think?"

Jess didn't really worry about what people thought, but she knew that if she played that card with Liz she might prevent her from making a major mistake.

"That's true, Jess. Perhaps if I go out there and turn on the charm they won't notice that Larry's nowhere to be seen." Liz turned to Evan, "But you had better go."

Blair nodded and agreed, "Yes, of course, but, if you don't mind, I'd like to speak to your sister for a moment, alone."

As puzzled as Jessica by the request, Liz raised a brow, then pointed out, "You know I'll just worm it out of her later."

"I thought as much," Evan smiled.

"It's *so* nice that you two have such faith in me," Jessica commented sarcastically, knowing that Liz hadn't wormed everything out of her about James Crawford.

Liz didn't respond to her sister, but faced Evan Blair seriously with, "Make sure we talk before you leave the city–and thank you, Evan, for the business."

Blair nodded, with nary a quip nor a sardonic twist to his smile now.

As soon as Liz left, Jessica leaned forward on the table and demanded, "Okay, just exactly what *is* going on here?"

Blair smiled dryly and observed, "Why, Jessica, I thought that you'd be happy to see me out of your sister's life."

"I'll be happy if you're on the level," Jessica replied straightening.

While she spoke, Blair had been collecting the legal papers, tapping them together against the tabletop. He answered her, "That's what these papers are; that's what we were up to here in the kitchen. We'd finished when Sir Launcelot charged in and started making noises like an outraged fiancé. I've signed the company over to your sister, lock, stock, and seamstresses."

"*Can* she afford to run it on her own? I mean, she needed the capital of a silent partner in the first place."

"We're in the black, and, as I promised, I've left your sister with sufficient liquid assets to cover any emergencies."

"Isn't that just oh so generous. What's in it for you?"

"The satisfaction of getting a fine businesswoman off to a roaring start on her dream? No, I didn't think you'd buy that, Jessica Minton. To be honest, I've made a pretty tidy profit, and now it's time to take my profit and stake it on a more exciting gamble somewhere else. Take a look at the paperwork. You'll see that I've set up your sister nicely."

Jess took up the documents. Sitting down to read, she found, to her surprise, that it all seemed on the square. He'd even protected Liz's interests by having Bushey, Baggot, and Greene put their imprimatur on his plan. Finally, she looked up and said, "Okay, this looks good. But I'm sorry; I still don't trust you. Exactly how far are you heading out of my sister's life?"

Blair leaned back and informed Jessica, "Far enough that she'll never see me again. None of you will ever see me. That's one of the reasons I want to talk to you, alone."

"Go on." The suspicion in Jessica's voice was clear.

"Still skeptical? Well, I can't blame you. No one wants a man of mystery endangering her sister."

"Liz is in danger?"

"No. No. Especially with me gone. I admit, I don't possess a sterling character, but I haven't done anything to hurt Elizabeth. And if I leave now, things will stay that way. If my past catches up with me, I want to be too far away for it to touch Elizabeth."

"So, there is a troubled past? Exactly how bad is it? This money that you put into her business ... ?"

"It's clean. I won it fair and square. But that's not what I want to talk to you about. Even with me gone, I can see someone else bringing her grief. You need to talk her into breaking it off with Sanders."

"Break up Liz and Larry? That's crazy!" Jess paused before going on, "Even if I thought you were right, she'd never listen to me about something like this. In case you hadn't noticed, Liz has a mind of her own. Anyway, where do you get off criticizing Larry? He's a hardworking, loyal, decent guy. And you seem to be forgetting that he was there to help Liz pull herself together after what happened with her husband."

"I won't argue that Larry is far more respectable than I am. But I think you see as clearly as I do that those two are not getting along. I don't want your sister to get into another bad marriage..."

"Take my word for it; Larry definitely doesn't have the same problems that Peter did."

"Be that as it may, Larry can still create problems all his own. You see that, too."

Jessica was silent before taking a different tack: "There's something else,

Blair. I'm sure with office chatter what it is, you know that I have a 'history' with Larry, myself. If I say something, it will just look like sour grapes."

"Jessica, what's more important: how you look or your sister's happiness?"

That hit home, and how. Resentfully, Jessica retorted, "And I suppose all this concern is because you're so madly in love with Liz, yourself?"

Blair didn't answer right away. Then he smiled ironically to admit, "I've been 'madly in love' once. I haven't had that in me for years. I learned my lesson. I can't afford to indulge in those kind of emotions, but I can afford to try to do my best for Liz. Don't let my 'noble gesture' go for nothing."

Jessica tightened her lips, but Evan Blair, flip as he was, had revealed enough earnestness to shake her. Carefully, Jessica allowed, "I think you really do care about my sister, in your own off-beat way."

"You're not going to go all starry-eyed on me, are you, Jessica?"

"Don't get cute. You better believe it'll be a cold day in Agua Caliente before I start tossing orange blossoms at you." Jessica paused, then, "Are you really so sure about Larry?"

"You saw him tonight, Jessica, jumping to conclusions, not trusting Liz. And I've seen you watching them together, waiting for the bomb to explode and wondering how you're going to pick up the pieces afterwards. You don't think he's the right man for Liz any more than I do."

"Maybe after you leave..."

"Am I their only bone of contention? Isn't he competing with more than another man, in his own mind anyway?"

Jessica sighed, remembering too well her own problems with Larry, remembering that conversation with him in the Bryant Hotel Café recently. Frustrated, she admitted, "I just don't know what to do. I don't want to stab Larry in the back, but I don't want Liz getting into another bad marriage. Maybe she is still on the rebound from Peter, and this thing with Larry feels safe–when they're not fighting. But they could also work through their problems. Sometimes, when I talk to Larry, I think he's trying to change, but other times .... If I'm wrong and break them up, Liz will never forgive me. *I'll* never forgive me. I don't want to ruin their lives."

"You'll have to make up your mind, Jessica. I can't stay. Things are closing in. I still have time to get out of here before anyone starts to see me as a familiar face."

"Familiar face," Jessica repeated slowly, something uneasily clicking into place. "Evan, when you said 'closing in,' did you mean someone not something?"

"What do you mean by that?" He was genuinely disturbed by her words.

"Well, like someone is spying on you, following you."

"What makes you say that?"

"This sounds odd. I couldn't figure it out. Liz said it had nothing to do with us."

"What?"

"Outside, tonight, I saw a man watching the building from across the street. Really difficult to see unless you were looking from an upper storey. I connected him with Lois..."

"Did he look like a pro?"

"Well, he *did* look as if he knew what he was doing. He commanded a good view of the street, both ways."

The more she spoke, the paler Evan Blair became, like a man waiting for the verdict in his murder trial. Staring Jessica down so intensely her shoulder twitched, he pressed, "This man, you recognized him?"

"No, not exactly. He looked vaguely familiar. But from where ... ?" she spread her hands as her words trailed off.

"Kind of a mug?"

"Yes, yes. But that covers half the population of the city. Now that I think of it, he had a kind of long, straight face, what I could see of it. Why that funny smile? You know him, don't you? He wasn't watching for Lois; he was waiting for *you*."

The mention of Lois seemed to rattle Blair even more. Why?

"What gives here?" Jessica demanded. "Is he after Lois or you? Both of you? What exactly is going on? Are you in on something concerning my friend?"

"Just take it easy, Jessica. I can 100% assure you that our friend outside has no interest in Lois Wong. But I don't like him hanging around Liz's place. It's high time I left–for good. Just one thing, does this kitchen door lead back to the main street? Or can I get out on the back street or an alley without our friend seeing me?"

"It opens onto an alley with some off-shooting alleys onto the next block. He's not going to see you unless he has X-Ray vision. But, Evan, who is he?"

"Someone you never need to know now that I'm leaving."

Blair was on his feet, glancing toward the door that led to the living room. As Jessica's eyes questioned his hesitation, he considered aloud, "I promised Liz I'd say goodbye, but there's no time. Jessica, you explain it to her. She'll understand."

"No she won't. You know that."

"Then tell her I'll write her and explain when it's safe."

"Will you?"

"You'll just have to trust me."

"Oh, *that's* reassuring."

"It's the best I can do. Take care of her."

With those words, Evan Blair took all his charm, wit, and mystery out the door.

Jess longed for one of Iris's Stingers but settled for a glass of water. What had Blair done? Who was after him? The underworld? If he'd been tracked here, seen here last, would some torpedo lean on her sister to find out to where Evan had disappeared? That guy outside, maybe she'd better take another look to see if he was still there or even if she could place him. If she was going to look out for her sister, she'd better have the goods on the opposition.

Returning to the living room, Jess was almost relieved that Larry hadn't returned. Fortunately, the food, liquor, and music had been plentiful enough to send the party rolling away from Liz's tempestuous love life.

But now here was Iris, powering across the room to question *sotto voce*, "So, chum, what's the story? Only Liz emerged. Did she plant both her rivals six feet under?"

"Nothing so dramatic. No, they both took a powder out the back, but not together."

"No fisticuffs for your sister's honor?" Iris queried.

"You're enjoying this entirely too much, Iris. Stop drooling. This is Liz's life not *John's Other Wife*. Speaking of Liz, where is she?"

"Powder room. Putting everything back in order. She swept through, showed off her charm, got everybody chattering about Truman and the U.N., then slipped off to do some damage control on the makeup."

"Okay," Jessica sighed, then beckoned, "Follow me. I want to double check something out this window."

As Jess led her friend to the landing, Iris queried, "On the street? D'you think Larry and Blair went outside to settle things 'man to man'?"

"Gosh, I hope not," Jessica replied, dismayed at yet another possibility of how wrong things could go. "No. Here, take a look. Do you see ... ? Oh, he's not there now. Where did he go?"

"Who? Where did who go?"

Jessica didn't like this at all. Why had her dark angel suddenly flown right after Blair left? Had he gotten tired of waiting or was he hot on Evan's trail? At least that trail led away from her sister. Still, in spite of herself, she felt a twinge of concern for Blair.

A rap on the door brought Jessica back to Earth. Now what?

Iris provided the answer to that question, flinging open the door and bursting out, "So there you are! It's about time! Jessica was having kittens over you!"

The voice that answered was more than welcome to Jessica's ears, "Sorry, my train was late from Boston..."

"See, Jess, what did I tell you," Iris grinned, pulling Lois Wong into the apartment.

"Lois, I was so worried after I missed you Friday. Especially after Ginger told me you left abruptly–and then I couldn't get in touch with you," Jessica poured out to her surprised friend.

"It's a little embarrassing," Lois quickly explained. "I was checking my portfolio, waiting for you, when I came across a memo for a meeting scheduled in twenty minutes. That meeting was a beaut! When I finally got away, I had to rush 'cross town to catch a train out of Grand Central to go see my mother. I ended up forgetting all about our lunch. What can I say? I'm really sorry, Jessica."

"Well, that's one load off my mind," Jess allowed a little grimly.

Lois's brow creased and she queried, "*One* load? Why? What else is wrong?"

Iris explained, "We had some fireworks here, and you missed it, kiddo. Larry hit the roof because of something between Evan Blair and Liz in the kitchen."

Lois shot Jessica a piercing look, demanding, "Your sister is in the kitchen with Evan Blair? Now? There's something more between them than business?"

"No, not at all. I mean they were in the kitchen, and Larry came in and got the wrong impression. But it's only business, and I don't mean monkey business, Iris," Jessica finished by fixing her blonde friend with a warning look.

Iris protested, "I didn't say that, exactly. But, gee, I wonder which one Liz would choose if she weren't already spoken for? They're both so handsome and charming. Larry has that British accent, and Evan Blair has that gentlemanly charm. He kind of reminds me of someone."

"Brian Aherne," Lois interjected a little impatiently.

"Huh?" from Iris.

Lois's uncharacteristic asperity with Iris left Jess curious.

"Brian Aherne, the actor," Lois elaborated, her tone smoother now. "He looks something like the actor. Anyway, Jessica, don't worry. Liz is too sharp to be taken in by that kind of phony charm. You can trust her to stick with a swell guy like Larry."

Jess smiled, a little weakly. If someone as level-headed as Lois liked Larry, maybe she was wrong to doubt him. So, she should be happy: Lois was safe, and James was safe, and she could delight in her acting assignments. Almost as nifty, Evan Blair was finally out of the picture. It was just too bad that the picture of Liz and Larry haunting the periphery of her thoughts was as jagged as a Picasso.

Chapter Nine

Sunday May 20, 1945

In red, orange, gold, and black splashes, an enormous water-color tiger brooded fiercely over the couch in Liz's apartment. Much more in the mood of Dusty than the Bengal denizen above her, Jessica Minton gracefully curved into the corner of the gold-striped couch, her lemon-ice gown falling in soft folds on her torso. She regarded her three companions thoughtfully.

This had been the darnedest "celebratory" evening out. She and Iris seemed to be the only ones having a good time–and her spirits were beginning to wear out after an evening of Liz's and Lois's separate preoccupations. You'd almost have thought they'd gone to see *King Lear* instead of a play about a giant, invisible rabbit. Jess understood Liz's state after last night's scene. However, Lois was a question mark. She had said she'd been tied up Friday and Saturday settling a Mah Jong dispute between her mother and aunt–her "radio silence" no big mystery, after all. So what was on her mind tonight?

Lois was speaking now, one hand playing with the red frog clasps on her white-satin, mandarin evening jacket, "Now that Liz is making coffee in the other room, tell us, Jess, has she heard anything from Larry?"

"No, she hasn't," came Liz's voice as she sailed into the room, elegant in black silk that draped down to the floor from folds gathered flatteringly at the waist. "As far as I'm concerned, *he* strolled out on me, so *he* can stroll back in on his own. He blew *his* stack; unfairly, I might add. Now let him take his medicine. I'm not running after *him*."

Liz settled on the love seat next to Lois. She reached up and smoothed her coif, hair coiled atop of her head and clipped into place with pins that sparkled. But that hand froze as Jessica corrected, "What I think you mean is that Larry can call back after you spent all day unsuccessfully trying to reach him. The operator won't speak to her anymore."

"I think it's romantic!" Iris declared. "Don't listen to her, Liz. Think how much fun making up will be!"

"You have to be able to *find* someone to make up with him," Jessica dryly observed.

"You're just not romantic enough, Jessica," Iris disapproved. "I hardly ever see you pining over your fella. I only got it out of you by chance that you just heard from him. You don't appreciate the excitement of romance."

Jessica briefly mused, *Oh, Iris, if you only knew!* However, she zipped her lips and maintained national security.

Lois made Jessica smile with, "Maybe after playing all those murdered *femme fatales*, Jess *de*preciates excitement."

"I'm glad to see you're back to your 'gay' self again," Liz noted.

"As perky as Fred Allen," Lois replied with about as much animation as Mr. Allen usually failed to muster.

"Hey," Iris began, "speaking of radio, why don't you put on yours, Liz? There's a good mellow music program about now."

Liz got up, but before she reached the radio the telephone rang. Betraying her earlier *sang-froid*, she dashed to the bar where the phone had remained since her last batch of calls.

Iris excitedly proposed, "Maybe it's Larry, wanting to kiss and make up!"

"Let's retire to the kitchen and give them some privacy," Lois suggested, observing Liz turn rather quickly away from them as soon as she recognized her caller.

"Then we can't hear anything," Iris protested.

"Brilliant extrapolation!" Jess teased, getting up.

However, all three women came to a surprised stop when Liz let slip the words "Evan" and "office."

"That's not Larry," Irish-whispered Iris.

"C'mon town crier," Jess ordered, with a nod enlisting Lois to usher Iris beyond earshot. Not for one instant, though, did Jessica stop trying to figure out what Evan Blair was up to.

Barely into the kitchen, Jess had to scramble to the stove to prevent the coffee boiling over. Meanwhile, Lois tried to keep Iris from out-boiling the coffee. And now Liz was stood on the threshold of the kitchen hesitating. *Liz*, hesitating?

"Elizabeth, you look worried. Everything okay?" Jessica questioned. "Is there something we can do?"

Liz gnawed her lower lip, actually marring her Max Factor. But she took control of her turmoil and calmly directed, "Nothing for anybody to do but have some coffee, relax, enjoy. There's cheesecake in the fridge. Bring it out, will you, Jessica? I have to step out for a bit."

"Out? It's after midnight! Where?" Jessica questioned, even though, from what she'd heard Liz let slip over the phone, she had a pretty good idea.

Lois interrupted, "Okay, Iris, let's get going. It's late and..."

"Lo-*is*, they have cheesecake!" Iris protested. "When was the last time you saw a cheesecake? Who has the dairy coupons?"

"Iris." Lois's glare at her friend was as cold as her voice.

"No, no," Liz assured them. "It's okay. I insist that you stay and start the coffee and dessert. I'll be back in a jiffy. Remember Blair turned the business over to me last night? Unfortunately, the big goof forgot about an important paper. He's got to make a late train, so I have to dash over and sign it."

"Why can't he bring it over here?" Jessica questioned skeptically.

"It's out of his way getting to the station," Liz answered with almost convincing nonchalance. "If he misses his train, he'll never make his next connection. He explained it all. Makes perfect sense to me."

"But..." Jess started.

"No, you girls enjoy your coffee and dessert."

"Then I'm going with you, Liz," Jessica decided.

"Don't be ridiculous. Who will entertain my guests? Not that you're exactly Sophie Tucker," Liz returned smoothly, and immovably.

"Liz," Lois began, "Iris and I really had better be going. I do have to get up for work, so..."

"But the cheesecake," Iris lamented.

"Oh for heaven's sake," Jessica blurted out, "take the damned cheesecake with you."

"Not the whole thing," Liz gasped. Then, more graciously, "I mean it's so rich. You'll make yourself sick."

"Don't worry," Lois took over. "Here's the compromise. We'll leave now, without the cheesecake. Tomorrow night, we can come back to splurge on calories. How does that sound?"

"Sounds fine," Jessica agreed, helping Lois usher a grudgingly acquiescent Iris out of the kitchen, then the apartment. Returning to continue the argument with Liz, Jess found her sister waiting in the living room, white fox stole already over her shoulders, black bag in gloved hands.

"That was quick," Jessica noted, as she went over to Elizabeth.

"Look, Jessica, don't let's quarrel. To be honest, I would like your company tonight, but I can't bring you."

"Why on earth not?" Jess asked, concerned.

"Evan has to see me alone," Liz quietly revealed.

"For Pete's sake, Liz, doesn't this sound more than a little fishy to you?"

"No, you don't understand. He wants to explain to me why he has to leave. Jess, I think I can help him, maybe set him straight."

"You're not the Salvation Army, Elizabeth."

"No, I'm not, and I've no intention of playing reformer or therapist. But you seem to forget, Jessica, that Evan set me up in business, supported me, kept me going when no one else could or would. Now he's given me the whole operation. Jessica, I owe the man, and I pay my debts. I have to give him the chance to stop running. Is that so risky? You've taken some pretty big risks yourself to help someone you believed in. How can you, of all people, hold me back?"

Jessica wanted to protest that Evan Blair was not in the same league with James, but she knew Liz wouldn't believe her. She'd have to play her cards skillfully.

"All right, Liz, how about this? We both go. If he's not on the level, he'll have a harder time pulling the wool over both our eyes, all our eyes. You know what I mean."

That had been a crashing success.

Liz shook her head, "No, no. I need someone to field Larry if he calls. I don't want to miss his call completely."

"Then don't go."

"I have to. What I need is for you to stay here and cover for me."

"'Cover' for you? I think you mean *lie*. I'm telling you: watch your step with Evan Blair. He acts as if he's doing a swan song, but I'm beginning to wonder if he isn't trying to hoodwink you into a duet."

"What's that supposed to mean?" Liz demanded, her tone revealing she had an inkling she didn't want to acknowledge.

Jess hadn't wanted to make the possible more real by saying it, but maybe it was time to take a long, hard look at the situation. Besides, Blair's trying to turn her against Larry still rankled.

"What if Blair is trying to make a play for you, pique your interest by seeming to leave with a wounded air of mystery?"

"Oh for the love of Mike, I'm not about to give up a good guy like Larry for a Romeo like him. I'm just being a friend. Case closed."

"Liz, don't get all riled up. I'm concerned about you. But, hey, why not call Blair back and have him meet you here? I could hide out in the bedroom, just in case you need me."

"And what if Larry should come back? How would it look to have Blair here *again*?"

"Not any better than if Larry calls and I have to tell him you went to meet Blair *alone*."

"I don't want you to tell him *that*, for heaven's sake."

"I'm not going to lie, Elizabeth."

"Don't lie. Just don't tell everything. Say I can't come to the phone at that minute, but that I'll call him right back. Then you can phone me at the office, and I'll call him pronto. It's not really untrue. If he should show up, say I had to drive the girls home, but you're sleeping over."

"I bet there'll be dozens of Nazis clamoring for you to defend them when those war crimes trials get rolling." Jessica's humor was not light-hearted.

"I'm sorry, Jess, but this is how it has to be."

After leaving, Liz decided she was glad not to have told Jessica Evan's injunction to make sure no one followed her. Jessica was already too concerned. For her part, Jessica watched her sister from the window overlooking the street and searched for any sign of that ugly mug in the shadows. No one. She still wasn't relieved. If she hadn't promised to deal with Larry, she'd be tailing Elizabeth right now! She could just kill Evan Blair for putting them through all this.

Elizabeth Minton's flashlight sliced down the corridor, hitting the office door diagonally. Of course no one lurked in the shadows, not even the night watchman. Maybe, for once, he was off locking *all* the side doors. She'd just been complaining to Larry, Jess, and Lois about his laxness securing the building, and the old guy's bouts of amnesia did not mix well with Evan's warning that she make darned sure she hadn't been followed. Maybe it was nice that her tenant's elevator key had allowed her to skip the stairs in these shoes, but, with all her dark thoughts, Liz wouldn't have minded some company from the daytime operator.

Walking down the corridor to her offices, Liz couldn't help noticing the deep quiet surrounding her. Like a tomb. Really unfortunate metaphor.

So why *was* Evan concerned about someone following her? Worried what Larry might think? Or Larry, himself?

Liz hesitated before her door, then quickly checked both ends of the corridor with her flash. No one. She was being silly, downright silly. Still, it was awfully eerie.

Fishing the keys out of her purse, Liz once more wondered what Evan had to say that was so important, so requiring of secrecy. Over the phone, he'd told her there was one last thing he had to do, something only she could help him with. Liz would not let him down. She also couldn't resist a mysterious secret. That was beside the point. Maybe, she could even straighten out Evan Blair. It was worth a shot. He wasn't any angel, but he wasn't as bad as the others thought. If he had a chance, he might pull himself together, and she was just the gal to help him.

Liz was barely inside the reception area, before Evan opened the door to his office and fastened a surprisingly genuine smile on her, saying, "Thanks for coming, Liz. You don't know how much I appreciate it." His features clouded before he questioned, "You're sure no one saw you come here? You weren't followed?"

"Not unless Daniel Boone's on my trail."

"Good. We can enjoy the safe ... privacy of my office."

The tone was perfectly urbane, but Liz saw something flit through Evan Blair's eyes that made her wait until he had shut his office door on the outside world before she went to town on him.

Tossing her bag on his desk, Liz fired off, "Okay, Evan, exactly what gives here? I don't go for this cloak and dagger business at all. I'm only here because I feel I owe you something."

"Sure you won't have a drink first, Elizabeth?"

Liz's eyes narrowed and she considered, "No 'Liz'? No 'Duchess'? This must be serious. Quit stalling. Exactly what's going on here? Over the phone, you sounded as if you were in deep trouble, maybe even danger."

Evan's lips tightened, then he answered, "Not yet. That's why I'm getting out now, before I drag you and the business down."

Liz managed to keep her outer composure, but she couldn't deny an inner chill as she probed, "Which means?"

"Which means, if I get out now, no one gets curious, no one asks you any embarrassing questions, no one expects you to be involved–and I escape the biggest mistake of my life."

"You're in trouble with the law? And our business ... ?"

"Don't look so stricken, Liz. We're completely legitimate. You need to know that, in case anyone tries to put questions into your head on that account. I wouldn't do anything to let anyone take the business from you. But there's something you have to know that's not so pretty."

"Maybe I'd better sit down."

"Maybe you had better. I'm afraid I've quite a yarn to spin for you before the night is through. And then I really am going out of your life."

From her seat next to his desk, Elizabeth questioned, "That bad?"

"That bad. I wouldn't even be telling you, except I need you to set some of it right. I know you're pretty damned shrewd, Liz. If you know your enemies' hands, you'll be better able to bluff them. I don't want any unintended false steps by you to make my sins any heavier a burden than they already are."

"Just exactly what are you trying to protect me from?"

Blair turned away, wouldn't meet her eyes. Part of her was as relieved as the rest of her was curious.

"Sure you won't have a drink, Liz? It's a long story." He faced her again.

Now Liz couldn't quite meet his eyes when she answered, "No, but I will have a cigarette."

Blair nodded sympathetically, procuring one from his silver case and lighting her up.

After her first exhale, Liz directly questioned, "Exactly from whom are you running, police or crooks?"

"Both." Blair tried to smile wryly, when Liz's cigarette trembled in her hand.

She recovered herself to note dryly, "Popular boy, aren't you?"

Evan smiled at her delivery, but they both knew she was getting the kind of jitters that nicotine did *not* soothe. She almost wished she could vamoose from the office now, except she did owe Evan, and she'd never get to the bottom of his secret if she didn't stay.

Evan had been musing, too. He lit a cigarette of his own and took a bracing drag before exhaling and continuing, "Sure, quite the popular chap. I broke a lot of promises, Liz. Now people are dying to collect."

"Just as long as *they* do the dying, not us."

"That's why I'm getting out tonight, Duchess."

"You must have gored a pretty big sacred cow to have both sides of the law on your back and down your throat."

Blair furrowed his brow as he translated Liz's conglomeration of clichés. A man with a talent for decoding, he succeeded and continued, "I guess you could say that. It's a long story, one that requires some background. Have the patience?"

"I'm all ears."

"And what lovely ears they are."

"Deep six the soft soap. I'm not one of the models, remember?"

"No, you're something else, all right."

Liz looked away, tapping ashes from her cigarette into an ashtray, not wanting to lock eyes with Evan Blair. She wasn't afraid of a wolf. Heck, she'd had enough practice with that type to merit a hunting license. No, what she'd seen in Evan Blair's eyes was not at all lupine. That's what scared her; and, worse, she wasn't 100 % sure why.

However, he got back on track: "Did you know that I was born in Philadelphia? Last of an old Main Line family. Grew up in an elegant mansion, well, it doesn't really matter. My aunts raised me."

"This *is* a long story."

"But germane. I'll skip the short-pants years. Let's just say that a not-too-distinguished career at the University of Pennsylvania got me exiled from the old homestead, so I worked in the jewel trade. I learned to custom design for the kind of people I used to belong with. Let's say that experience rekindled some tastes a little too rich for my income. To make a long story short, I ended up in Chicago a little over ten years ago, after a mutual agreement with my employers that I shouldn't confuse my tastes with other people's possessions."

"So you're afraid someone here will recognize and prosecute you?"

Evan laughed, not hard, but with deep irony, "Ah, Liz, you ought to have much more imagination than that. I'm afraid that my crimes are far more Byronic."

"Knock off the Byron jazz, Evan. My sister's the literary nut, not me."

"So, she is. I hope she enjoys that volume of cummings I gave her. Maybe one day she'll 'decode' some of the writing for you. I hope she never has to," Evan decided with a bitter smile, seeming to consider a private but not very happy joke.

"Sure, like I really need a personalized English lesson," Liz snapped. "Are you stalling or are you planning to get on with the story?"

Evan resumed, "Well, Chicago in the '30s was a toddling town."

"So the history books and Tin Pan Alley say," Liz remarked, impatient that Evan still wasn't coming to the point.

"And my experience in the jewelry trade, to the shrewder criminal mind, proved a godsend."

"I see. You waltzed into town, introduced yourself as a disgraced jeweler, and Al Capone and Dutch Schultz beat a path to your door. All that charm lured them in."

"Not quite. I'm afraid that I and a tender little mob led by a Mr. Paul Weisenthal mutually bamboozled each other."

"That must have been a scream."

"Poetic justice, at least. Weisenthal had a darling little wife, Betty–red hair, piquant crooked nose, and the lushest of female attributes. She was the bait used for running wealthy sports into debt at his gambling establishment. I looked like a prime mark: a well-dressed chap talking up elite Philadelphia connections, but not my fall from grace. You know how I love to gamble. I think you can guess the rest."

"And charming little Betty must have been quite an incentive to you."

"Unfortunately, the joke was on the Weisenthal gang. I kept losing, and the wealthy relatives back East who still cared that I'd fabricated to impress Betty turned out to be..."

"Fabricated."

"Precisely."

"So, what kept you from being custom fitted with a pair of concrete overshoes and swimming with the sturgeon?"

Resolutely, Blair proceeded past Liz's malformed clichés, "Betty was a shrewd one. She decided that the gang could work a whole new con with a man who knew jewels, how to appraise and reset them. In fact, she was so taken with one piece I did–diamonds and emeralds in a silver lily–that she persuaded Paul to let her keep it."

"So not everyone had to rely on the WPA during the Depression? Continue."

"Betty could talk a good game, flatter the sports, young or old. She charmed her way into their homes when the wives or parents or servants were out. Get the lay of where the jewels were."

"Among other things."

"Exactly. We'd send our boy in to knock the place over. I'd re-cut or rework the booty. Then, even if the saps put two and two together about Betty, who would squawk over an insurance-covered theft if the alternative were admitting to adultery or something equally embarrassing? After all, no one collects an insurance check for a divorce or disinheritance."

"Cute. And you were part of it, Evan."

He frowned. "Yes. I was. I could tell you that was then–but you won't understand why you should believe I've changed until I finish."

"Oh, by all means." Liz let an exhalation of smoke gently waft away. "Do go on."

Was she projecting a control? Did he know that she was shaking inside? What had she gotten herself into, being in business, even friends, with this man?

"Things were going fine for a time. Then Betty got wind the police were setting a trap."

"How?"

"I told you she was a clever girl, Betty. She always had some connection with the local gendarmes, wherever we worked. She enjoyed seducing people."

"Mr. Weisenthal must have been quite the understanding husband, between the police and the marks."

"He knew which side his bread was buttered on."

The words were bitter. Liz wondered about the younger Blair's feelings for Betty. After all, she had worked her magic to lure Evan into her ring in the first place. But now wasn't the time to ask. Later.

"After Chicago?"

"A grand eastern tour: New York, Albany–Philadelphia was out of the question with my background–Providence. Then Boston. That's when it all fell apart: Boston, 1935."

Why had he watched her so carefully for those last words? Should she know? Something did nag at the back of her brain, but ... he was starting again.

"Betty made her contact. Some cop, a young guy. Ultimately, he got burned along with the rest of us. I don't know where he is now. But that's not what made me turn them in..."

"*You* turned *them* in?"

That was not where Liz had thought the story was going!

"I had to. I gave up, turned state's evidence when I realized how she destroyed that kid and his family."

"Yes. Go on," Liz prodded carefully, uncomfortable possibilities falling into place.

"He couldn't take the shame for himself and his family. He committed suicide. That was it for me. I wasn't going to let them get away with any of this anymore."

"But you still didn't want to take the rap. So you cut a deal and went state's evidence," Liz coolly concluded. Her suspicions moved closer to an infuriating conclusion at Evan's last words.

"That's about it. I never said I was an angel, Liz–and let's face it, the only stripes I look good in are pin stripes. But I've paid for it ever since."

"Living on the run? Afraid of your colleagues catching up to you some day?"

"Yes and no. I probably would have done all right for myself in the witness protection program, but I got itchy, jumped my keepers."

"Not very bright of you."

Blair shrugged, then admitted, "No, but out West I had too much time to think, about what I'd done to that family. So, when I met you and you offered me this opportunity, I tried to run away again, from myself, this time to New York. I was sure enough time had passed, that if I kept a fairly low profile, I was still sufficiently distant from the scenes of my crimes to be safe. Funny, isn't it; that brought me smack up against the guilt I was trying to escape. That's why I need your help." Liz could see from Blair's strained features what this admission was costing him. If her suspicions were right, though, it damn well ought to. Finally he confessed, "I can still help what's left of his family. A Chinese family, Liz. Name of Wong."

Ah, that's why Lois had taken off like a bat out of hell the other day! Liz realized. *She must have gotten an eyeful of Evan in his office.* Perhaps Elizabeth would have felt more than passing curiosity over Lois's not revealing Evan's identity if she weren't so furious now. On her feet, glaring and trembling, Elizabeth sputtered, "You! You're the low-down, dirty skunk who ruined Lois's family. Never mind your playmates, I'd like to kill you myself, Evan Blair. My God! To think I've been working with you all this time, treating you like a friend." Suddenly struck by a horrifying possibility, Liz demanded, "The money you invested to start the business, did *that* come from..."

"No." Blair was emphatic. "That was gambling money not blood money."

"How can I believe you?" That wounded him, but Elizabeth didn't care. She railed at him, "I knew you were no angel, but this, this is horrible. I never dreamed that *you* could have been responsible for the hell my friend and her family went through!"

Now Blair was on his feet, but far from angry. He almost pleaded, "Listen to me, Elizabeth. It had never come to this before. The others, Betty's victims, were just a bunch of fatuous lechers. They were rich; they could spare the loss–and they were just as crooked as we were, collecting on the insurance. It was almost like Robin Hood–we worked harder for the jewels than they did. Until Boston, the Wong kid, that was where I drew the line."

"You drew it a little too late, Evan."

Blair hung his head, nodding, "I know, I know. I wasn't crazy about the set up to begin with, but that crew, they had me. Get this straight: there's no weaseling out on Paul Weisenthal. I had qualms but not enough to risk a one-way ticket to the morgue."

"Too bad Lois's brother didn't have a better travel agent."

"I deserved that."

"Don't you know it!" But there was something in his weary, tortured tone that weakened Liz's fury, just a little.

"Well then, Liz, perhaps after you hear what I have to propose, you'll feel a trifle less harsh."

"That will take some doing."

"This will be some doing."

Liz dropped her eyes at Blair's intensity. He'd be damned before she let him see he was getting to her, no matter how sincere he seemed.

"I'm going to try to make amends," he calmly promised.

"The kid's name wasn't Lazarus," Liz retorted harshly.

"No, I can't bring him back, but I can do something to help your friend, Lois."

Liz forced disapproval into her voice to mask her hope and curiosity, "This I've got to hear."

"The police thought Weisenthal had the jade. It was my word against his. His main gunsel was killed at the arrest, and Betty blew town–her contact tipped her off."

"But Weisenthal didn't have the jade. You did."

Blair managed not to wither under Liz's accusation, but just barely. He soldiered on, "Yes. I hid them as insurance against the future. But in these past months, the time I've spent working with .... The time I've spent here, I've changed. I want to do *something* that's right. Look, Elizabeth, I'm not asking for forgiveness, only the chance to do what I can before it's entirely too late. I'll cut to the chase. I stashed the jade squares where I could get at them when I needed them. Funny, I never realized I'd need them for someone else. Once I leave town, I'll send your lawyers an anonymous letter telling them where and how to collect the stones. From your scrupulous vetting, I can see they're trustworthy. They're in no one's back pocket. So, I'll make a clean breast of everything the man I used to be had done and clear the Wongs. I know that if I require Bushey, Baggott, and Greene to act discreetly, no one need suspect that your lawyers being involved has anything to do with you."

"You don't have to tell me this story for your plan to work." Liz was genuinely at sea. "Why Evan?"

"Elizabeth, I had to come clean completely before I left. It matters to me that you know the whole truth, the good and the bad. I know how good a friend you've been, and I didn't want you brooding over what you'd done wrong or how you should have helped me."

Liz was overwhelmed. How *did* she feel about Blair now? He'd told her something dreadful about himself, yet he'd also revealed his determination to make things right. Maybe the best way to repay her debt for his past support would be to convince Evan to stop running and completely square himself with the law.

"Evan, wouldn't it be best to go to the police? You might even get them to arrest Betty. That would save you from her."

Blair shook his head, "Too dangerous. She probably has connections with the law even here. That was part of her old m. o., and she's a gal who got around. Besides, I held out on the jade when I made my original deal. The law isn't going to look kindly on me for that. I have to leave town while there's still time to get some place I can't be traced..."

"By the police."

"They're the least of my problems."

"Paul Weisenthal and his lovely wife Betty?"

"You're half right. Paul died in prison, and his crew bought it in a shootout with the police. Betty's the only one left, and she hates me for putting away her husband, making her go on the run, and, worst, keeping the jade. My handlers told me that there was talk on the street that she wanted nothing better than to kill me herself–and get her hands on the jade. Just my luck, I landed right in her home territory, and now she knows I'm here. She put on an act as if she didn't see me, but she did. Why do you think I was lying low all week? She and her hired hands are out of town now, so I'd better take advantage of my grace period to make tracks. The only thing that keeps me from naming her in the letter is that an accusation without a flesh and blood corroborating witness or some other irrefutable evidence wouldn't hold up well against the lawyers of a woman with her clout. It would just make her madder."

Liz straightened, too much clicking horrifyingly into place. Locking eyes with Evan, she added, "She's not called Betty anymore, is she?"

"No. She's come a long way, beyond the new name, the nose job, and the peroxide..."

The telephone's shrilling from Liz's office sliced through the dark, empty building.

Evan shot her a look so hunted it nearly broke Elizabeth's heart. No, she couldn't let herself go soft on him. Liz raised a quick hand to calm Evan, then dashed to her office, not sure how she'd unlocked the door, scrambled through the darkness, and flicked on her desk lamp to find the phone.

The voice crackling through the receiver was anxious: "Liz, Liz, it's Jessica. Is everything okay?"

"Yes, yes, fine," Liz lied. "Except you scared us half to death. Did Larry call?"

"Just a minute ago."

"Thank God he didn't drop by. He's all right?"

"He's not planning to jump off a bridge or push anyone else off, if that's what you mean."

"How sensitive you are, dear. Were you able to stall him?"

"I hope so. I said that you'd stepped out to Casey's All-Night Market to pick up some sugar. Darn, I hope that doesn't contradict the rationing schedule for the time of the month. Do you think he'll check?"

"He's probably got more important matters on his mind now, Jessica. Can you call him back?"

"Not exactly."

"What's the catch?" Liz demanded sourly.

"Larry was calling from a phone at Sam and Al's All-Night Diner. Apparently there's something wrong with his phone. He wants you to meet him there and talk to him alone. I went with your cover story. He probably believed he woke me up, so he didn't want to come here and throw me out on the street in my jammies."

"That means I'll have to leave now," Liz surmised, not pleased at an interruption.

"You sound upset. Hasn't Blair finished giving you the low down? Just what has he told you? He's not thinking of staying, is he?"

Liz sighed, then answered, "No, not at all."

"Well that's a relief."

"I wish it were."

"What's that supposed to mean?"

"It's too complicated to spill over the phone, Jess. You'll have to wait until I see you."

"I don't like this, Elizabeth. Has he got something shady up his sleeve?

"It's all right. I know what I'm doing. You've done your duty tonight, kid. Go home now. I'll explain everything to you tomorrow morning."

"That's it? I have to wait till tomorrow to get the lowdown on Blair, on you and Larry? I don't think so, Sis."

"Please, Jessica, trust me. I can't tell you anything more tonight. I don't want you waiting up."

"As if I'd get any sleep at home. Anyway, I want to make sure that you're all right."

"I'm fine. Just do as I say, will you, please? I can't handle worrying about you, too. I'll see you in the morning."

"All right. This time. But you be careful. Don't buy any bill of goods from Blair and take it easy with Larry."

"How did he sound when you talked to him?" Liz asked nervously.

"Tired. Not angry, not contrite. Mostly weary. I didn't want to press him."

"Okay, thanks, kid. Go home and get some shuteye. My apologies to Dusty. And don't worry."

"Oh, *that* reassures me. Don't do anything rash, Liz. Promise?"

"For Pete's sake, Jess, don't have kittens on me. I can take care of myself. You just get a good night's ... morning's sleep. Really, kiddo, I'm fine."

"All right, Liz. Good night."

Hanging up the phone, Liz reflected that she could have sliced the concern in Jess's voice with a machete. But she had to fly solo to get things done right.

Now to take on Mr. Evan Blair. Liz marched back across her office, steaming at the predicament he'd put her in, not so much with Larry, but with his convoluted offer of reparation to Lois. Shoving open the door to his office, Liz had planned to give him an earful. She couldn't. Blair's head in his hands, then, the naked pain in his eyes when he looked up and faced her, were all too much for her. This man was staring straight into the black hell of his past, not letting himself off the hook for a minute. Had she ever seen any man do that? Could she?

Blair gathered himself and questioned, "The phone call?"

"My sister. Larry called and wants me to meet him."

"Now?"

"Pretty much."

Blair sighed, then said, "All right then. What do you say, Elizabeth, will you help me?"

Liz slowly approached Blair, circling his desk, "You really put me on the spot, Evan. Of course I want to set things right, as right as they can be for Lois. But I'm not going to do anything that's not on the up and up."

"You probably don't feel you have much reason to believe this, but I wouldn't ask you if I thought I'd be putting you in a tight spot. I want this done so that you're out of the line of suspicion. As I said, your lawyers can keep their involvement on the q.t. and return the jade to, I guess, the owner or some insurance company. I have no idea after all this time. That it was *your* lawyers doing this never need come out. One thing I do not intend to do is hurt you."

Liz couldn't face him after those words. They moved her, and she believed him, even after all her first husband had taught her about how deceptive a man's words could be. Damned if she'd let him see that!

"Yeah, fine!" she tossed off skeptically. "All I care about is helping Lois. So all I have to do is act surprised when Lois tells me that she and her family are cleared? You won't forget to mail that letter will you?"

Evan actually looked wounded, but gave Liz an ironic smile when he said, "I guess I deserve that, probably much more. Don't worry. I've set up some insurance just in case the letter gets lost in the mail."

"Getting lost is not what I'm afraid of."

"Liz, if I weren't going to mail the letter, I could have left without a word, retrieved the jade myself as soon as I was certain no one was on my trail, and completely disappeared. There's no reason to tell you this incriminating story if I'm not going to follow through on my promise."

Liz didn't have an answer for that. She even felt a bit small for accusing Evan. Abruptly, she asked, "So, I can go now, and meet Larry?"

"If that's what you want."

"Of course that's what I want. What are you getting at, Evan?"

"Nothing much, but, just, take care of yourself, Liz. Don't jump into anything too hastily. You're quite a gal. Don't sell yourself short."

"I don't think that I do. I think Larry's quite a fella. Most girls would."

Did Evan pick up on her defensiveness? Liz didn't like the feeling, herself. All he said was, "You're not 'most girls,' Duchess. Anyway, you better get going. I've got a few things to wrap up here first, and you have somebody waiting for you."

That was when it really hit Liz that she would never see her partner again. And whatever he had done in the past, he had been her staunch ally. Those thoughts must have shown in her face, because a strange kind of lightness briefly came to Blair's features. Standing in front of her, very near, he stiffly squared himself before saying, "You've got to go your way, Liz. I've got to go mine. Someone's waiting for you."

He turned away, crossed to his own window. Time for her to go, for Liz was too afraid of what could happen if she stayed. So afraid that she was halfway to Sam and Al's Diner before she realized that she'd never gotten Evan to confirm her suspicion of Betty Weisenthal's new identity: Mrs. Wilmington Tewkesbury.

Chapter Ten

Monday, May 21, 1945

Ascending in the office-building elevator, Liz Minton smiled and nodded at many a familiar face, but her mind was elsewhere. The encounter with her sister earlier this morning had gone better than she'd expected, which was still not to say it had been anywhere near smooth. Liz was hardly at ease concerning Jessica's cold skepticism with Evan Blair, his plan to square things for Lois, or Liz's announcement that she was dead sure Betty Weisenthal was none other than Alanna Tewkesbury. After some reasoning, Jess had come around on that last point, but she wasn't happy, even if Evan was supposed to have blown town.

Well, Liz would just think happier thoughts. She and Larry seemed to be back on track, even though their planned rendezvous hadn't started well. When she'd gotten to the diner, there'd been no Larry. All steamed up, she'd huffed off home, but Larry had called and explained he hadn't been thinking straight and gone to Shaftner's by mistake. The big lug had sounded beside himself, over mixing up the two late-night places she and Jess frequented. By the time he'd figured out his mistake and hot footed over to Sam and Al's, he'd missed her. But Larry had been so sweet when he called, apologizing that he'd been wrong to misjudge her and that an all-night diner was no place to make up, anyway. Better yet, after today's business trip, he was going to take her out to some place special, really make it up to her. Boy, she'd made out on the deal!

Liz came off the elevator and marched down the corridor with more authority and alacrity than her dark-brown suede, sling-back sandals and a night with a minimum of sleep should have permitted. But Liz was always the mistress of her shoes, and it was hard not to move forcefully in a pin-striped suit with lapels this wide. Still, even the impetus of her wardrobe deserted Liz at the door to her offices. What gave with her? Maybe realizing that having the business all her own now meant she had to prove she'd been the brains and heart of this outfit all along?

Liz pushed the door open, tipped her hat, and pronounced, "Here I am, Ginger, even after a wild night on the town with the girls."

Looking up from the paperwork on her desk, Ginger grinned back, "And looking fresher than Betty Grable."

Liz nodded her agreement, and Ginger cocked her head toward Evan's old office, "I guess you weren't the only one on an all-nighter, though I'd never have expected him to pull one at *work*!"

"Come again, Ginger?"

"Mr. Blair, he must have been in his office all night. Take a look, but quiet-like. The poor guy. He's out like a light in there. With his door ajar, I could see him when I came in."

Liz's eyes flew to Evan's office door. It was shut. Vaguely, she heard Ginger say something about tip-toeing over and closing it some time ago. Could Ginger see her shaking, or was that only happening inside her? Why hadn't Evan gone? Why was she relieved? Did this mean he was going to face the music, take a stand, and all sorts of other clichés? Liz was a little proud of him right then.

"Don't worry, Ginger. You get the coffee started, and I'll rouse him with a little sunshine and cheer."

"Sure thing, boss lady! I could go for some Joe myself."

Liz's sling-backs carried her across the room as if they were sling-shots. One push of the door, and there she found Evan, his head cradled away from her in the crook of his arm, out for good and all on the desk. With an authoritative hand on her hip, Liz mischievously prepared to growl a command to make her partner jump to attention faster than a private at the finish of basic training. Then she'd let him know how glad she was that he hadn't run out on her and himself.

The sun was deliciously warm on a feline's fur. On the hassock by the window seat, Dusty was basking in the leisurely pleasure of being a cat at home with her human. Usually she dozed, but, occasionally, her eyes focused on Jessica, sitting on the nearby couch, studying a collection of bound papers intently. Ah yes, the "radio" script.

That's when the speaking device startled Dusty fully awake with its irritating jangle.

"Hello..." Jessica had been interrupted by her caller. Something was definitely up.

"He–what? Where? There? How did it happen? Are you absolutely sure ... ? Well how many *have* you seen?"

Dusty swiveled one ear. This sounded interesting.

"No. Stay there. The police will want to quest ... Liz, it will look bad."

Oh, it was Liz! No wonder something was wrong!

"No, but you really should stay put for the police. But ... but..." A huge sigh, then, "All right. Shall I come and get you? Okay. All right, I'll meet you at the apartment. Yes, I still have the key. And, Liz, I'm really sorry."

Jessica hung up the phone, staring ahead, troubled, not even seeing Dusty.

Dusty stretched and offered a concerned, "Raow?"

Good, Jessica came back to herself and focused on her.

"Gee, Dusty," Jess shook her head in disbelief. "He was causing us all a lot of heartache, but this ... He's gone all right, Dusty. Dead gone. Someone roughed him up first and shot him. Damn, Liz and I may have been responsible for setting up the poor guy. If it weren't for us, Evan Blair might still be alive."

Jessica stood by the couch, surveying the tea she'd set out and thinking that she and Elizabeth could use something stronger than Darjeeling right now. However, with the police scheduled to arrive any minute, tea was clearly the better choice. The first thing Liz had done when she saw Jessica was pronounce Alanna Tewkesbury the murderer. Jess had warned her sister in no uncertain terms to tread carefully on that topic with the police. Mrs. Tewkesbury was big game with even bigger influence. It wouldn't pay to run off half-cocked about her. Tewkesbury's striking back through high-powered attorneys or that low-class Kubek was not something to be provoked without solid grounds for their accusations. Funny thing, though, thinking about Kubek, Jess had the darndest feeling she'd seen him in some strange, off-kilter context.

At the moment, Liz was lying down in her room, recovering from the shock–and a night of probably only fifteen out of the prescribed forty winks. To Jess's way of thinking, it would have looked much better to the police if her sister had stayed at the office. Not that Liz had anything to hide, but perhaps to the cops ... Too many unpleasant memories of dealing with Inspector Winston two years ago left her silently praying, *Give me a break, Lord. Don't let this be his precinct.*

Suddenly, Elizabeth sailed into the room, hair upswept into a chignon and clothes changed into navy slacks and box jacket with a linen-colored blouse.

"That was a quick nap!" Jess remarked in disbelief. "And for someone recovering from shock, you look awfully well turned out, Elizabeth."

Liz scoffed, "I never said I was shocked out of my good taste. Oh, you made me a sandwich. I don't know. All this shock."

CHIIIING!!!

The doorbell made them both jump.

"Okay, I'll get it. But, Elizabeth, I told you: don't let your anger control you. Be careful what you say. You don't have to hide what you know about Mrs. Tewkesbury but be prudent in how you say it. All right?"

"Of course, Jessica," Liz dismissed her sister. "I'm not a babe in the woods."

Crossing to the room, Jessica made it to the door before the third chime, thinking, *No, you're no babe. You're a hound baying for your prey–except you're hunting a wolf not a bunny. I'm going to have my hands full today.*

Jess opened the door on two plainclothes men.

"Elizabeth Minton?" queried the taller of the two. He *was* tall, too, over six feet. Under his dark fedora, his hair was black, somewhere between curly and wavy. His face was a little too long, his nose a little too straight, his mouth a little too far down for him to be handsome, except for his eyes: brown, intelligent and wry, even though they were clearly tired. The voice was light and easy.

The voice of his partner, who repeated the query, was not: "Miss Minton?"

The second detective was much shorter, maybe no taller than Jessica. Sandy hair, set jaw, dark eyes, and an expression almost as hard as his tone, he snapped Jessica back to attention.

"Jessica Minton. Elizabeth is my sister," she informed them. "She reported the, um, discovery of Mr. Blair. You are the police, right?"

The shorter one cracked irritably, "We ain't the Good Humor men."

The tall one took over, disarming Jessica's scowl at the other's sarcasm, as he revealed his detective's shield, "I'm Detective McLaughlan. This is my partner Detective Boyd. We'd like talk to your sister about Evan Blair."

"Please, come in. Join us down here," called Liz, standing next to the love seat.

"Gentlemen," Jess said, standing back and gesturing the way.

Boyd gave her a suspicious look on the "gentlemen." McLaughlan seemed to have better things to think about, his attention on Liz as she apologized, "I'm sorry to drag you both out here, but I just couldn't stay in the offices. I couldn't."

"That happens," McLaughlan agreed, but Jessica wouldn't swear it was sympathetically.

"We were business partners," Liz offered.

Jess noted that Boyd definitely wasn't sympathetic. In fact, he seemed to be doing a mental estimate of the apartment's cash worth before he laconically inquired, "Successful partners?"

"Well, yes," Liz answered slowly, not sure of whether to read anything unsavory from his tone. Jessica's instincts left her less unsure, and not pleased. McLaughlan quietly let it all unfold.

But Liz merely gestured for them to sit. When they had, she resumed, "As I said, I'm sorry you had to come all the way over here to interview me. I was so beside myself after, after finding Evan. I promise, though, that I'll make your trip worthwhile. I know who killed Evan Blair."

Jess sat still only because she knew it would look too odd if she dope-slapped her sister.

Processing Liz's announcement took the detectives a second. Boyd demanded sharply, "You were there?"

Liz clarified impatiently, "Not at the actual event, but..."

Decidedly annoyed that his time might be wasted, Boyd snapped, "Then just how do you know that, lady? You got the low down from someone who was there?"

"That's it. Kind of it. I saw Evan last night," Liz excitedly answered.

"*You* saw him last?" Boyd calmly interrupted, but not calmly enough for Jessica to miss the hard flicker of interest in his eyes. "Around what time?"

Ice shot up Jessica's spine as she realized where Boyd's questions were leading, but how could she warn Liz without making it look as if she had something to hide?

"Listen to me and I'll make it perfectly clear," Liz impatiently instructed. "Evan told me that he was terrified because someone from his past had recognized him and wanted him dead–out of revenge. That's why he was taking off and leaving me the business."

"And when did you leave him, Miss Minton?" McLaughlan asked. He had been taking notes all along.

"Around 1:00 a. m.," Liz answered.

The detectives couldn't help looking at each other at that admission. Liz finally caught on and tried to set them straight. "No, no. You've got it all wrong. I was here with my sister and some friends after going to a show when he called and asked me to come to the office."

"That's a new name for it," Boyd observed dryly. "Was he in the habit of buzzing you at all hours?"

McLaughlan gave him a sharp look but not before Liz snapped, "Do you want to hear the facts and solve this crime or just sit around making snide cracks?"

"Go ahead, Miss Minton," McLaughlan urged respectfully.

Jess liked him for that and offered her explanation directly to him: "We were all here, Detective McLaughlan, after twelve o'clock. We'd just gotten back from seeing *Harvey*. We *all*, including Liz, thought it was odd for Evan Blair to call so late." She made sure to briefly toss Boyd a look that clearly said, "So there!"

Unfazed, Boyd queried, "So they didn't make a habit of after-midnight overtime?"

"Certainly not," Liz bristled. "We were friends and business partners. That was it. If you were as smart as you seem to think you are, you'd have found that out from the people at the office. Anybody with a brain knows that there aren't any secrets from office gossip mills. Besides, I'm already engaged."

"We know that," McLaughlan concurred neutrally. "Suppose you get to the part about knowing who killed him. You said you didn't actually see him shot."

"Of course not," Liz declared, frustrated. "I'd have called you in then and there. Do you think for one minute that I'd ever let that woman get away with killing my friend?"

"What woman? Lady, you're taking us all around the mulberry bush here," Aaron Boyd jumped in. "Suppose you just tell us what you actually know."

"I know," Liz began with biting patience, "that I left Evan Blair alive in the office around 1:00 A. M. I went there because he called to tell me he had one last business paper for me to sign, and we had to meet at the office, or he'd miss his train. We talked for a half hour or so. I left Blair alive, and when I came in to work this morning, my friend was dead in his office. I swear we'll all be damned if I let Alanna Tewkesbury get away with this!"

This time the detectives really were flummoxed. Boyd finally puzzled, "Alanna Tewkesbury, who's..."

"A big society type." McLaughlan cut in. "Silver-plated Rolls Royce, hot and cold running ermine stoles (so to speak), married to Wilmington Tewkesbury. Not the kind of uptowner you want to mess with. That's a pretty stiff charge to level at someone with her clout, Miss Minton. You're telling me that you and Blair knew her."

"I was slightly acquainted with her because she was interested in investing in our business," Elizabeth explained. "I couldn't understand why Evan kept avoiding meeting her, until last night, when he told me that he'd known her years ago, both of them under different names. He'd ended up in Chicago after being kicked out of a wealthy Main Line family in Philly. All of them gone now. He got hooked up with this jewel-robbing gang of Paul Weisenthal's in Chicago. She was part of the gang, married to Weisenthal. She went by Betty back then. Evan helped put her husband away by going state's evidence for a case in Boston and broke up their gang. He had an attack of conscience over what happened to their victim. She managed to get away, but she hated him for betraying them and sending her husband to prison, where he died. Evan was sure she'd recognized him at this awards dinner last week and was planning to even old scores. He was hot to get out of town before she could get to him."

Jess didn't like the looks Boyd and McLaughlan exchanged. Boyd spoke first: "Lady, that's got to be the most cockamamie story I've ever heard. And I've heard some lulus in the near ten years I've been on the force here."

Liz's back stiffened as she challenged indignantly, "What?! You think I'd make something like this up?!"

Cooler than his partner, McLaughlan observed, "Usually these kinds of things happen between people who know each other. More a matter of passion than an intricate plot."

"Evan might have been a bit of a flirt, but no one would say any of the ladies in his little black book wanted to kill him," Jessica interjected decisively.

She didn't add that if Lois Wong knew Blair's real identity, *she* might have wanted him dead. Jess believed she knew her friend well enough to realize that for Lois "wanting" wasn't the same as "doing." Still, only now, with thoughts of Lois and the jade dancing in her head, did she remember Blair's letter. Was Liz going to bring it up? How might that affect Lois?

"Your boyfriend couldn't have been too happy about Blair calling you for an after-hours conference," Boyd observed a little too knowingly.

McLaughlan shot his partner an annoyed glance for pushing Liz too far, which her reaction confirmed.

"Just where do you get off talking about us like that?! Not everybody's mind is in the gutter, Mr. Boyd."

Jessica had to restrain herself from clamping a hand over Liz's mouth before she antagonized their interrogators further. Happily, Liz hadn't mentioned Larry's not being in the diner when she got there.

McLaughlan told Liz, "Look, Miss Minton, no need for anyone to get hot under the collar. We want the truth, like you. Unfortunately, my partner isn't as smooth as Nick Charles when it comes to getting it. The only reason we're bringing up Sanders is that there's been talk about some bad blood between him and Blair, particularly an incident at the Skylight Club, as well as at your Saturday night party. Could you clear that up?"

Despite McLaughlan's calm tone, Jessica's heart sank. She could smell this good cop/bad cop routine a mile away: Boyd would needle, while McLaughlan played it Bing-Crosby mellow.

Liz also seemed to have tumbled to the cops' routine. Far more calmly, she answered, "I don't know who you were talking to. Some blabbermouth who likes to exaggerate. There was a mix up, at the nightclub, when *Evan* had had a few too many. Larry felt bad about that. That's old history, though. *More* recently, we all had a wonderful time at the Designers Awards Ball. It's a pity your Hedda Hopper neglected to inform you about that. As for the party, well, I just told you that Larry and I kissed and made up."

"That's right," Jessica chimed in. "You can't convict a guy on that. Anyway, why would Larry kill out of jealousy if Evan Blair was out of the picture? Once you talk to Larry, you'll see he's not the type to kill anyone."

"We're going to do just that," Boyd smiled.

"You go right ahead," Liz returned sweetly. "Now, do you want to hear the whole story about Mrs. Tewkesbury, or are you going to let her off the hook?"

"Look lady," Boyd informed her. "A society dame going after a small-time dressmaker doesn't wash with me. Sounds like you're trying to throw up some kind of a smoke screen, a whacky smoke screen, but a smoke screen just the same."

McLaughlan signaled his partner to pipe down, then told Liz noncommittally, "Go ahead, Miss Minton, give us the rest of Blair's story about his past."

"All right. Here's the God's honest truth," Liz began earnestly. "As I said, Evan Blair called me last night and asked me to meet him at the office–but to come alone and make sure I wasn't followed."

"Afraid your boyfriend might be tailing you," Boyd skeptically glossed.

Liz's cool was defrosting under Boyd's heat, so Jessica eased in, "No. Blair had been jittery for weeks. Ask anyone in the office. And not over Larry. It began earlier, when Liz took an interest starting a business affiliation with Mrs. Tewkesbury. The lengths he went to duck her would have almost been comical, if it hadn't ended so tragically."

"If I'd only let it rest then, he'd still be alive," Elizabeth punished herself. Jessica touched her arm in sympathy.

"You wanted to go into business with Alanna Tewkesbury and he wouldn't let you?" McLaughlan clarified.

Seeing where the question was leading, Jessica tried not to tense.

"Initially," Liz began, "but, after I did talk to people who had firsthand experience with her business practices, I realized Evan was right. I told him so and assured him that I wasn't interested in having anything to do with her." Jessica was a little surprised to see McLaughlan taken aback by her sister's grief and the self-accusation when she finished, "If I'd never had that crazy idea, Evan would be alive. If I'd just listened to him in the first place, Alanna Tewkesbury might never have run across him again and killed him."

"If this isn't just some kind of yarn," Boyd scoffed.

McLaughlan frowned at his partner, leading Jessica to decide that if he were putting on an act, it was a good one.

Meanwhile, Liz icily turned on Boyd: "Listen, rube, get this and get this straight. I'm telling you the truth. I don't know about your partner over there, but maybe *you* don't want to hear it because you'll have to ruffle some important feathers to make your pinch. I guess it would be a lot easier to hang a frame on an innocent civil servant who doesn't have any connections or platinum-plated law firms to look out for him."

"Say, what're you gettin' at?"

McLaughlan cooled his partner with a sharp look–and a sharper rebuke aimed at both him and Liz: "The two of you can both settle down. We're not getting anywhere as long as you both toss wisecracks back and forth like hand grenades."

Boyd settled grimly back, apparently knowing better than to push his partner too far. McLaughlan gave his attention to Liz, informing her briskly, "Miss Minton, you'd better understand that you can't make accusations without giving us anything solid to back them up. We're not going after anyone, member of the Four Hundred *or* working stiff, without real evidence. So, let's get to the bottom of this mess. Do you have any hard evidence to support your charges against Alanna Tewkesbury?"

Jessica cooled Liz with a very firm hand on her shoulder and offered, "I can give you something, Detective McLaughlan. The night of Liz's party, Saturday, I saw a man hiding in the shadows outside Liz's apartment, watching who went in or out. He looked vaguely familiar. I told Evan Blair about it. He got all shook up and decided to leave by the back way. I didn't see the guy after Evan left. It took me a little while to place the guy's face, but I realized that I'd seen him trailing Alanna Tewkesbury, like a bodyguard. I think his name's Eddie Kubek."

The two detectives seemed to recognize the name, but Boyd only said skeptically, "You just remembered this minute?"

Ignoring his partner, McLaughlan allowed, "It's a link, worth looking into. Can you definitely swear it's the same guy? Did anyone else see him, to identify him?"

Jessica's heart sank, and she had to admit reluctantly, "I was the only one, and, um, it was dark. He was in the shadows, but it looked like him."

"I can attest that she told me there was someone out there!" Liz insisted.

"But did you *see* him, Eddie Kubek? Could you positively identify *him*?" Boyd challenged skeptically.

At Liz's deflated admission that she couldn't, Boyd opened his mouth for a sarcastic comment, but McLaughlan forestalled him with a reasonable, "I'm afraid that weakens your sister's claim, Miss Minton." Then he added, "And I still have to ask, why would Blair come back so close to Boston, again, if this threat were hanging over him?"

Liz explained impatiently, "Evan told me last night that he came back East because he thought enough time had passed for the coast to be clear, so investing in my dress business would be a good gamble. I actually met him in California, through mutual friends. He told me that the witness protection guys placed him somewhere else in the West, but he got antsy and jumped the program."

McLaughlan sent Boyd a warning glance before his partner could comment on exactly what Blair had been gambling on and repeated, "I still don't see a definite Tewkesbury connection."

"Then try this on for size: Blair identified Mrs. Tewkesbury as a member of the Paul Weisenthal gang: the leader's wife, Betty, whom they used as a decoy to lure in the men they wanted to rob," Liz asserted.

"Wait a minute," Boyd interrogated skeptically, "You're telling me that your pal Evan Blair unequivocally accused *Alanna Tewkesbury* of being a gun moll? He specifically named her to you."

Jessica bit her lip in disappointment as her sister's forcefulness seeped away in having to admit, "Not exactly directly."

"How, exactly, if not 'directly'?" McLaughlan questioned, a little skeptical himself.

Elizabeth insisted, "Evan said he'd seen her, that she'd gotten a peroxide treatment and a nose job, but he recognized her still–almost right after he ducked her at the awards. People in the office knew he was always trying to avoid her. Evan said he was trying to get away before she *got back from out of town*, and Mrs. Tewkesbury had just left for Florida."

"So she had an alibi?" Boyd undercut Liz. "Listen, lady, if we bought your crazy story, we'd have to suspect three-quarters of the dames in New York. Your pal isn't the only one to color her hair and take a trip."

"But those 'dames' don't have a big ape who works for them trailing Evan Blair," Jessica argued. "If he did her dirty work, that alibi wouldn't count for much, would it?"

McLaughlan surprised the sisters, maybe even his partner by asking Boyd, "You ever heard anything about this Weisenthal gang, Aaron?"

"Yeah, well. He was before your time. Operated mainly out of Chicago. But it sounds like a mighty convenient story to me. The guy and the rest of his gang are dead, either in a shootout or in prison. You can believe her load of hooey, but remember, nobody's exactly around to deny it."

"Nobody except Alanna Tewkesbury, now that Evan is gone," Liz countered, shrewdly.

"And your friend just waltzes right back into her backyard?" Boyd doubtfully observed.

"I'm sure he didn't expect to find her here, since the case that broke up the gang took place in another town all those years ago," Liz parried.

Jessica kept her best poker face at that reference to the scandal in Lois's family. She really hoped Liz wouldn't bring up the letter Evan supposedly sent. It didn't unmask Alanna, and it would just drag Lois into this mess–maybe even make her a suspect if someone could show she had figured out that Blair was involved in ruining her family.

Boyd shook his head, cautioning his partner, "Think about it, Leo. Even if he had identified Mrs. Tewkesbury as the Weisenthal dame, he's dead. He can't be cross-examined. A good defense lawyer, which I'm sure that family has plenty of, would make mincemeat of the testimony."

"You don't believe me," Liz accused, "Are you even going to check out the Tewkesbury woman?"

McLaughlan calmly assured Liz over his partner's scowl. "Sometimes my partner likes to think out loud. I can promise you, we'll look into every possibility." McLaughlan stood up, with his partner following. "I think we've gotten all we can here for now."

Liz shot Jess a quick glance before she got up first. There was an awkward moment, but Liz earnestly asked McLaughlan, "Do you believe me?"

It was his turn to be a little surprised, but he answered, "It's early in the investigation, Miss Minton. We're going to look into all avenues. The ones you want, and some of the ones that maybe you don't. We have to look everywhere if we want to find the truth. That's what you want, too, isn't it? Evan Blair *was* your friend."

Liz looked McLaughlan in the eye to say, "Fair enough. You see, I have faith that the truth will lead you smack dab to Mrs. Tewkesbury."

"Yeah, lady," cut in Boyd, "if the truth is out there, we'll find it. Trust me."

"We'll want to speak to Larry Sanders," McLaughlan took over. "Where can we find him?"

"Today, you'll find him in Connecticut. He's on a business trip for his office. He works for the civil service. But he'll be back tomorrow. You can check with his office in the Browning Building. I can tell you how to get in touch with his supervisor."

"Well, thank you for your cooperation," McLaughlan smiled.

"Think nothing of it, Detective; Larry Sanders has nothing to hide. The sooner you talk to him and clear that up, the sooner you can go after the real criminal, silver fox and all."

As McLaughlan wrote down Liz's information, Aaron Boyd watched sourly. Jess wondered, could she trust either of them? Was this just a good cop bad cop act or the real deal? And why was Liz so forthcoming when she knew that Larry didn't have a great alibi? In fact, he didn't have any. And why *hadn't* these two cops asked if Larry had one? This felt bad all around.

McLaughlan closed his book, smiled slightly at Liz and Jessica, then finished, "Okay. That about wraps it up for now. Thank you both for your help. You ready, Aar?"

"I been ready since before the Lieutenant sent us over here," his partner grumped. "Let's get the lead out. I'm dreaming about a nice bucket of hot water and Epsom salts to soak my aching bunions."

Elizabeth stopped them, "Just one more thing. I don't think Evan has anybody left, at least anybody who'll acknowledge him. I'd like to claim his remains. I'll take care of the funeral."

McLaughlan shot Aaron Boyd a look that nixed an oncoming snide observation and told Liz, "I'll look into it, Miss Minton. Of course, that will have to wait until after the autopsy."

Liz visibly repressed a shudder at the thought of that intrusion on what was left of her friend, but she just nodded, and started her callers on their way out. Still, she didn't fail to ask again, "You will talk to Alanna Tewkesbury?"

"Sure thing, lady," Aaron Boyd cracked as they all stopped at the door, "right after we grill Mrs. Astor and her pet horse."

McLaughlan quietly warned his partner, "Okay, Aaron, cut it out."

Regally, Elizabeth responded, "Thank you, Detective."

"Don't mention it. Oh, by the way, where was Larry Sanders last night from midnight to 3:00 a.m.?"

That question caught Elizabeth with her Panzers down. It wasn't often Jessica saw Liz stammer, but then she, too, hadn't expected McLaughlan's out-of-the-blue query.

"At home, I would imagine," Liz replied, marshalling her dignity.

"And you know because... ?" Boyd prodded.

"Your mind must get awfully slimy wallowing down in that gutter," Jessica couldn't help commenting.

"Okay, ladies, settle down," McLaughlan told them with a calming spread of his hands, "Aaron's a little out of line, but he has a point. Your friend ought to have a decent alibi if he wants to get himself off the suspect list. Maybe this is sticking our noses into your business, but, if you can alibi him, you better not worry about whether we think you're a nice girl, Miss Minton."

Jessica could see Elizabeth realizing that even if sacrificing her reputation might save Larry for the moment, the detectives were too sharp not to discover the truth sooner or later.

"No, Detective McLaughlan," Jess cut in. "My sister wasn't with him. She went home after her meeting with Evan Blair."

"This true, Miss Minton?" McLaughlan's features were relaxed, but his eyes were sharp on her sister.

"Yeah, my kid sister speaks the truth," Elizabeth admitted. "But that still doesn't mean Larry is guilty. He can't be the only one with a weak alibi–and as I've been trying to tell you, there's someone out there whom Evan was genuinely afraid of."

"I'm listening. But we have to cover all the bases."

Jessica added her own two cents, "Detective, I would never in a million years believe Larry capable of murder. I know him. He would never wantonly take a life. I also know that Evan Blair has been afraid of running into Alanna Tewkesbury for some time. He even faked spraining his ankle on the dance floor so he wouldn't have to meet her at an awards dinner. And this is God's own truth, my sister may be the biggest wise guy in spectator pumps, but she would not cover for a murderer, least of all one of her friend."

"Thanks, kid," Liz said.

"Yeah, yeah, but she sure has some crazy imagination," commented Boyd, not as a compliment.

McLaughlan suggested to his partner, "Aaron, why don't you get the car warmed up while I finish here, huh?"

Boyd started to say something, then changed his mind and agreed, "Yeah, fine. Just don't let either of these two sell you on anything even nuttier."

To keep from throwing something, Liz just grimaced and said, "If you'll excuse me, I need to lie down," before sailing off to her bedroom. Jess stayed to manage some damage control.

McLaughlan spoke first: "I guess my partner forgot to read his Emily Post today." Seeing the corner of Jess's mouth turn up, he continued, "Look, Miss Minton, we've got to go where the case leads. Your sister tells an interesting story. There could be something to it. I'll be looking for mug shots of Betty Weisenthal, tracking down fingerprints. But I'm not about to go bothering someone as prominent as Alanna Tewkesbury without a darned good reason. As I said, I'll need something better to go on to make the charges your sister is pushing for."

"Once you see what Betty looks like, even if she's changed her hair and her nose, it should be clear that she is Alanna," Jessica persisted hopefully.

"Or it could just as easily prove you're wrong. Like I said, I have to follow where the evidence leads me. But I'll guarantee you, I won't let politics interfere."

Jess nodded, almost smiling, before saying. "Okay, Detective, fair enough. You know where to find us if you need us."

"That I do. Oh, and a word to the wise, don't let your sister go shooting off her mouth to anybody else with this story. It could make things tough for me to get at the truth, but it could go a lot worse for you two. If your sister's right about the Tewkesbury woman's past and her involvement in Blair's murder, that lady's not going to go easy on you two for trying to expose something she killed to keep secret. I don't think her husband would cut you any slack for embarrassing him, either."

Jess's eyes widened as McLaughlan's warning struck home. She assured him, "Don't worry. I can play it quiet."

"I'm not sure that you're the one I really have to worry about," the detective surmised, his gaze moving to the bedroom door Liz had closed on them.

Jessica promised, "I'll do my best to keep a lid on her. Please keep us up on what you find."

McLaughlan nodded, replying, before he left, "Will do, as long as it's according to regulations. And thanks for your help. It's been ... interesting."

Alone now, Jess returned to the couch and flopped down, both hands clutching her aching forehead. Gosh, she missed the good old days when all she had to worry about were Nazi fifth columnists!

Chapter Eleven

Wednesday, May 23, 1945

Six o'clock, a delicious May dusk for Jessica Minton. Especially so at this garden table of della Mirandola's, waiting in the hum and chatter of voices, amongst the clatter of silver ravenously applied to china. What a treat for this tender evening breeze to play with the black hair curling past her shoulders or to sigh into the flowing sleeves of her blouse, a startling white against the black of her skirt. No, on an eve like this, Jess didn't even mind being alone. Not too much, with that letter from James tucked in her bag.

James could afford this place under his cover. After long explorations of the crooked streets and fantasies of old architecture in the city, she and James would come here and stuff themselves with pasta against the cold New York winter. Here, Jess had learned about the grimness of the northern industrial town where James had grown up, relieved only by the love in his family and the exceptional generosity of the woman who'd run Thornton Mill and helped him find an education. Or maybe they'd talk about the books they read, the movies they watched together, or the music they'd to which they dreamed. Anything and everything to keep at bay the war that they knew would inevitably part them when James was needed again across the waters.

Her eyes sought out the sliver of moon in the darkening sky, then returned to the glass of red wine, scarcely touched, in front of her. A sweet, tangy indulgence. A cup of celebration? The excitement of yesterday's rehearsal still tingled. To be back acting, with a grand ensemble of fellow players! Jessica was all revved up for going live tomorrow night. Wouldn't James be proud of her? Would that he could be at the broadcast, when she and the rest of the cast led their audiences in the studio and across the airwaves into the realm of mystery. Bittersweet was the memory of James's hand closing over hers, his dark eyes melting into hers, ironic in some dry observation but decidedly pleased that her heart was open to his.

Some diner loudly thanking God that there would be no delicatessen strike, after all, ludicrously yanked Jessica back to reality. To think that not so long ago, people were praying they wouldn't be blasted by air strikes! Another man was grousing to his wife about Truman's making sure some kid in the service got a birthday cake because his mother wrote to say she couldn't afford to buy him one. The diner's wife was a little confused, asking why a service mother would want to buy Truman a birthday cake.

Amused, Jessica pulled James's letter from her evening bag and spread it on the table to reread for the millionth time. There was comfort in having at least this much of him with her. All her thoughts weren't comforting, though. She and Liz still didn't know if Evan had been able to mail his letter. Even if he had, how would they know? Their lawyers were supposed to keep Evan's message under wraps. Probably the only clue would be Lois Wong's starting a one-woman ticker-tape parade down 5th Avenue. But neither she nor Liz knew how hard the jade would be to retrieve or what lengthy complications would be involved in straightening everything out.

Lois, herself, gave Jessica further cause for uneasiness. It was probably just her imagination, but their friend had been surprisingly incommunicado since Evan's death. Knowing Evan's true connection to the Wongs, neither Jess nor Liz had felt comfortable talking to Lois about his death. Uncharacteristically, Lois had never bothered to offer Liz comfort or condolence. Peculiar.

That wasn't the only reason thoughts of Lois troubled Jessica. She and Liz hadn't been forthcoming with McLaughlan about Lois's connection to Blair, even if their intentions were for the best. Elizabeth had confirmed Jess's guess that she'd kept mum to save their friend undeserved trouble and to avoid diverting attention from the real murderer. Liz's justification had been convincing at the time. Yet every day since, Jessica's belief strengthened that as the police dug deeper into Evan's background, his involvement with the Wongs would come out. Wouldn't that Boyd just love such a confirmation of his suspicions about her and her sister! More than that, though, Jessica didn't like the thought of not leveling with McLaughlan. She sensed that Liz shared her feeling.

"Those must be some pretty dark cogitations."

Speak of the devil, or rather of Detective McLaughlan!

Jess swiftly folded up her letter, stuffing it away, and McLaughlan apologized, "Sorry, Miss Minton, I didn't mean to startle you."

At least he didn't say "Guilty conscience?" Jess folded her hands in front of her and queried, she hoped, casually, "What brings you here, Detective McLaughlan? My guess is this isn't a chance meeting."

"Not at all, Miss Minton. I stopped by your sister's office on my way off-shift. The secretary told me she was meeting you here for dinner at six." He glanced at his watch and wryly noted, "She's running late, I see."

Jess checked her watch and explained, "No, I'd have to give her another twenty minutes before I'd say she was late, running on Liz-time."

"Hmph, I guess I'd hate to wait for your sister in a fire."

Jessica asked mischievously, "Would you really wait for *anyone* in a fire?"

"No, wouldn't be my first choice. Would you mind if I sat down and waited with you?"

Jess shook her head, but she saw that he'd noticed her tense. Rats! Just when she thought she'd disarmed him.

As he sat down, McLaughlan surprised her with, "Take it easy, Miss Minton. I've been working on some of the leads you and your sister came up with. But I could use some help from the two of you."

"Us? I think we told you everything, Detective," Jess responded pleasantly, hating not being completely forthcoming.

"As a matter of fact, I've been doing a little digging on your friend Mrs. Tewkesbury. That's where you and your sister come in."

Jess cocked her head, interested, "How so?"

He settled back in his chair and explained, "You know as well as I do what kind of clout her husband pulls. I can only dig so deep without red flagging what I'm up to, and, right now, I can't go any deeper than to make myself curious."

"What exactly *did* you come up with?"

"Let's just wait until your sister shows," he returned.

Jess started to protest, but McLaughlan's calm determination convinced her otherwise. She took a different tack, "It must kill your partner that you found something. He doesn't seem to think Larry merits special treatment, like a trial by jury or any of that reasonable-doubt malarkey."

"Boyd's okay–and don't think that I'm letting your pal Sanders entirely off the hook, either."

"But you're still pursuing other leads. You haven't dismissed what Liz said."

"Let's just say I like to keep an open mind, and what I have found out so far about both Betty Weisenthal and Alanna Tewkesbury gives me an itch," he explained.

"Come on, give over, Detective. You *did* find something on her? "

"Something, but not enough to stick my neck out over, yet. I need more proof that Mrs. Tewkesbury was ever mixed up with Evan Blair, or whatever his real name is. But let's wait for your sister, so I don't waste time repeating myself."

Jessica sat back and sighed, "You don't know Liz. The war could be over six years before she gets here."

"Relax. This isn't your first brush with murder, anyway, is it?"

Taken by surprise, Jessica sharply demanded, "What's that supposed to mean?"

"Jim Winston had a few things to say about the Bromfield case."

"Did he?" Jessica queried neutrally, mastering her disquiet. Detective Winston had investigated the murder of a spy who'd tried to kill her. But Winston hadn't known about the espionage angle, only that the Feds had made her look like an innocent caught in the crossfire. She added, "I understand the case was taken out of his hands by the Feds. Did they ever get who was behind the murder?"

"You were closer to the case than I was," McLaughlan shrugged. "Funny thing, their taking over the case."

"Maybe there were connections to racketeers or something," Jess suggested.

"You Minton girls travel in interesting circles."

"I was in a play with the victim, that's all. As for Evan Blair, we were hardly in the same circle. I barely knew him."

McLaughlan threw Jessica a bit of a curve with, "Winston's case, that was around the time your brother-in-law left."

Not liking this drift into top-secret territory, Jessica offered a noncommittal, "Yes, I guess it was. But Peter didn't even know Bromfield..."

"That wasn't where I was going. I was just thinking that it must have been pretty tough on your sister."

"Well, yes, yes of course it was. How could it not be, your marriage breaking up after ten years? I mean, they weren't always the smiling couple. In some ways, though, I think it was better for her. Let's just say Peter had something of a mean streak."

"And she found someone else," McLaughlan observed neutrally.

Jess looked him right in the eye and answered, "Yes, she did. They had always been good *friends*. Larry was there for her *after* the marriage broke up. He's a good guy. That's why neither of us can believe he'd kill Evan Blair."

The detective studied her, and Jessica wondered if he were thinking, "If he's so swell, why did *you* let him go?" He seemed to have tumbled to everything else in their lives.

Abruptly, Alfonso della Mirandola descended on them, urged dinner on McLaughlan, and finally succeeded in getting him to accede to a cup of coffee. Mission accomplished, he bustled off to another table of regulars.

"The old fellow's persuasive, isn't he?" McLaughlan noted, mildly amused.

"He just wants everybody stuffed and happy. You're off-duty, aren't you? Why didn't you go for something with a little more octane?" Jess returned, softened by della Mirandola's aura of good spirits.

"I think I'll try keeping my wits sharp, dealing with the two of you."

McLaughlan's eyes took the edge off that remark, and Jessica considered that maybe memories of her brother-in-law's betrayal, not McLaughlan, had made her so prickly.

Her mouth relaxed into a little smile as she explained, "We're not exactly Mata Hari and Axis Sally. Don't trust us, do you?"

"Don't know you, Miss Minton."

The coffee arrived, and McLaughlan flashed the waiter a smile of thanks before taking a sip. His face brightened, and the usually laid-back detective enthused, "Hey, that's some java. Quite a switch from what we get down at the station."

"Bad?"

"Let's just say that you don't have to be a saint to walk across it."

Jessica lightly laughed, "That sounds exactly like something my sister would say, except it actually made sense."

"In a brain-dead, world-weary kind of way."

"Exactly."

"Well, well, Detective McLaughlan, you just can't keep away from us Minton gals."

Jess and McLaughlan looked up to the landing across the patio to see Liz, resplendent in a wine suit, fitted and peplummed. Upsweep held in place by a dark veil with silver stars gleaming over her hair, Liz looked downright regal. Now they could get to the bottom of McLaughlan's news.

Jessica good-humoredly admonished, "Well, Elizabeth, it's about time."

Reaching their table, Liz said to McLaughlan as he started to rise, "Take a load off your feet, Detective. Haven't been grilling my sister too severely, have you?"

"Look, no rubber-hose marks," Jessica joked.

"Actually," McLaughlan corrected dryly, "rubber hoses don't leave marks. That's the idea."

"Learn something every day," Liz returned sardonically. Then she cut to the chase: "I did *not* expect to see you so soon, Detective. Did you find out anything on Alanna Tewkesbury?"

"It's more what I didn't find out."

"So..." began Jessica.

"What..." Elizabeth continued.

"Gives..." Jess finished.

McLaughlan couldn't figure where one sister began and the other left off, but Jessica caught him smiling faintly as she and Liz exchanged irritated glances for stepping on each other's lines.

"First, I made some calls to Chicago and came up with some interesting dope on Betty Weisenthal. My connection told me he knew about the gang, though the department didn't have much of a line on *her*. Apparently, she'd been too slick to ever get arrested. And since none of her marks was willing to press charges, no one even had a sketch artist do her portrait. The insurance companies that paid off on the stolen jewels would love to track her down, but they never saw her. There was talk that she had a connection with a guy on the force, but apparently he blew town long ago under a cloud. Dave's pretty sure he's dead."

"So, why don't you just show a picture of Alanna Tewkesbury to someone in Chicago?" Liz insisted.

"To whom? The cops who never saw Betty Weisenthal, the marks who all developed amnesia, or the dirty cop who made like Yahoodi?"

"I see your point," Liz admitted, disappointed.

"Then I made some calls to Boston."

He waited, giving them both a penetrating stare. Jess knew the jig was up, and before McLaughlan could call them on leaving him in the dark about Lois, she spoke up, "You found out about Lois's connection to Evan: her brother's suicide and the family being ruined because of that gang Evan was a part of. I guess we didn't say much because we were afraid to make her live through that hell when it didn't seem necessary."

"Maybe you should let me decide what's necessary. Try to remember, *I'm* the detective," McLaughlan sternly advised Jessica. She looked down, ashamed, but was happy to feel Elizabeth's comforting hand on her arm.

Her sister spoke intently to McLaughlan, "Don't blame the kid; blame me. It's my fault. We both made a mistake Monday, not telling you everything. But since then Jess has been trying to convince me to make a clean breast of everything. It just seemed too cruel to drag Lois through another criminal investigation. Besides, Evan was trying to make restitution. That last night he promised to send a letter to our lawyers, anonymously, so Alanna wouldn't make any connection to me. In it, he cleared Lois's brother and instructed the lawyers how to recover the missing jade. Doesn't that remove any reason like revenge for considering her a suspect?"

"Miss Minton, according to your story, if Blair sent the letter, it would never have reached the lawyers before he was killed," McLaughlan pointed out, not harshly though. Then he continued, "As it is, I talked to Miss Wong after I found out her story, and you'll be relieved to know she has an alibi. It seems she stayed over that night with your other friend, Iris Rossetti."

"I'm surprised you didn't read either of us the riot act the minute you saw us tonight," Jessica ventured, still feeling bad.

McLaughlan took a sip of his coffee, leaving her time to think things over some more, before answering, "I figured I wouldn't have to. I could see when I came in tonight that you were beating yourself up better than I could." To Liz he said, "And I appreciate that you didn't let your sister take the rap for you. I can also see that you care about getting the right thing done. So, I'm giving you two a pass *this* time. You don't want to get in trouble for obstructing an investigation."

The sisters both nodded, with Liz actually looking contrite. Still, as much as Jessica appreciated the "get out of the doghouse free card," part of her wondered if McLaughlan was playing a neat game of good cop on them again.

"Okay, now that I know we're all on the level, I have something you might want to hear," he commenced. "Don't get your hopes up too much, but I did find some interesting dope on Alanna Tewkesbury that makes me wonder about her –– a lot."

"Well?" Liz excitedly questioned, casting aside contrition.

"I didn't want to arouse anyone's notice by trying to check out her background up here. So, I decided to make some calls and do some digging in Florida. The record of her marriage license down there seems to be conveniently damaged, so you can't decipher her date and place of birth. Even funnier, the trail on her background hit a dead end when I tried to find out anything before she showed up in Palm Beach eight years ago..."

"Ah ha!" Liz burst out.

"'Ah ha' nothing," McLaughlan returned flatly. "I'm telling you I didn't find any information before that point, not that I found hard facts confirming what you said Blair claimed. It's not the same thing."

"But why obliterate her past if she doesn't have something to hide?" Liz persisted.

"Because she could be hiding a lot of things that have nothing to do with Evan Blair."

"And the marriage record?" Liz argued. "What about that?"

"Records do get damaged or lost, Miss Minton, without there being some big cover up going on. She might not have wanted anyone to know how long in the tooth she really was, or her bridegroom might not have wanted his social set to see that the younger woman he was marrying wasn't from the ritzier part of town. Still, I'll give you that the facts indicate she's hiding *something*, and the year she married Tewkesbury jives nicely with the time frame you gave me from Blair.

"And there's something else. I didn't want to tell you until we cleared the air about you two leveling with me. My friend Dave in Chicago told me that even though no one had any images of Betty Weisenthal, the F.B.I. had gotten her prints from some of her belongings when they raided the gang's hideout. Unfortunately, they didn't find her wedding picture with Weisenthal."

"So now, all you have to do is get Alanna's prints and match them with Betty's!" Liz almost squealed.

"Hold your horses, Miss Minton. I can't exactly command someone with a husband like hers to trot down to the station and ink up her little digits. This Tewkesbury gal is a big fish. If you expect me to fry her, I need more. I can't afford to get her so steamed she makes a call Downtown. I don't want to be told to lay off before I even get started."

Jess could see the smoke roiling in Liz's eyes, so before any could pour out her ears, she stepped in, "Exactly what *do* you need from us to tie her into the case?"

"To start with, I need as much solid evidence as I can get that Tewkesbury is this Betty Weisenthal. I need anything and everything Blair told you about the gang, especially Betty. I want to know about the cities they operated in, too. Whatever he told you about the victims."

"First of all, what your pal in Chicago said matches Evan's story," Liz agreed. "But let me go back to the beginning."

"Just not back to when 'dinosaurs roamed the earth,'" Jessica interjected, knowing her sister's propensity to verbally meander.

"If it helps the case, she can tell me about Blair's pet stegosaurus," McLaughlan returned. "We came up deuces searching his apartment, so I need everything he told you. No matter how inconsequential it may seem."

Elizabeth filled in McLaughlan on every iota of information she could muster about Evan, even down to his love of ciphers and e.e. cummings. She voiced her conclusion that he had not been using his true name, given his fear of retribution. That point led her to emphasize how afraid she believed Evan was of Alanna/Betty, citing that fear as his reason for not unmasking the woman in his letter to the law firm.

At the conclusion, Liz questioned hopefully, "So, Detective McLaughlan, did I give you enough to go on?"

"It's a start," he allowed.

"We still need to crack her alibi, though," Jessica reluctantly pointed out. She felt Elizabeth's eyes bore into her for raising that objection.

"She may call Eddie Kubek a bodyguard, but with a guy like him on the payroll she wouldn't need to pull the trigger herself," McLaughlan noted.

Elizabeth shook her head, and disagreed, "No, Evan said he was convinced she wanted that pleasure all to herself."

"You know you're torpedoing your own case," McLaughlan informed her dryly.

"Not if we can crack her alibi!" Liz shot back.

"*We*? Don't think so. Leave the detecting to us, Miss Minton." Then he reflected and added, "Of course, this could all be moot. I still have to put in a call to the F.B.I.'s Fingerprint Bureau in D.C. to share those prints before I can compare them. Right now, though, the Feds have their hands full chasing down fifth columnists."

Liz queried carefully, "If Jess and I had some pull with them, would that help you?"

McLaughlan perked up, but Jessica, not liking where Liz was heading, questioned carefully, "What pull?"

"Your pull, you dope."

Jessica managed a taut, "Me? I don't get you, Elizabeth."

Was her sister nuts? Was she going to uncover the whole spy plot in front of McLaughlan?

"You did answer questions about Frederick Bromfield's murder when the F.B.I. took over the case, Jessica," Liz pointed out, tactfully.

"For a couple of interviews. I hardly think J. Edgar Hoover is sitting by the phone waiting to find out what he can do to thank me, Elizabeth."

"*Hoover* might not be waiting, but *Hooley* is, I'll bet."

Jess couldn't hide her blush. Killing her sister in front of a cop was probably a bad idea. Unfortunate. She heard McLaughlan's puzzled, "Hooley? Who's Hooley?"

"Agent Jeffrey Hooley. F.B.I. He was one of the G-men who questioned Jessica. He really took a shine to her, right, Jess? You said he'd been assigned to Washington, and he even gave you a special number for contacting him if you ever needed help. Don't you think nailing a killer qualifies?"

"It's a big F.B.I., Liz, and he's only one little agent."

"Hardly little. I'd say about six feet of agent. Anyway, I'm not asking you to marry him, just ask him for a favor."

McLaughlan cut in, "This is all very interesting, ladies, but, unless you can actually do anything, we're wasting time."

"Jess," Liz pressed, "Larry needs our help. You could just ask Hooley to grease a few doors, open a few wheels. Wouldn't he want to help an innocent man? As I seem to remember, Hooley was pretty much in the corner of the underdog, and..."

Jess cut her sister off, "All right, all right." She still felt bad about earlier considering going to Hooley, if she'd gotten Blair's fingerprints. She didn't like the thought of using him. Still, this would help Larry. She told Liz, "I could give Detective McLaughlan Hooley's number." Turning to the policeman, she finished, "If you tell Hooley I referred you, that might help speed things up. I can't promise you that he has any pull with the Fingerprint Bureau, though."

"All right, then, thank you, ladies," McLaughlan said, polishing off his coffee. He was on his feet, finishing, "Well, I'm on my merry way."

"To do some digging?" Liz queried hopefully.

"Home. I've been off-shift for some time now. Even a cop needs to catch his forty winks."

McLaughlan reached into his jacket pocket for his wallet, taking out some cash and saying, "This should cover the coffee."

"We could spring for it," Jessica wryly suggested, "or are you afraid somebody might interpret that as a bribe?"

"I'm not that easy," McLaughlan kidded back, leaving enough to cover his tab.

Jessica turned her smile to Liz, only to find her sister staring tensely at her wine glass. Abruptly, Liz levelly told the detective, "Thanks for not giving us the brush off over Alanna Tewkesbury. I don't want Larry railroaded or Evan's murderer to get off."

McLaughlan sobered when he answered, "I'm with you on both counts, but don't get me wrong. The chips will have to fall where they may, wherever the evidence leads. Can you take it?"

He wasn't antagonistic, but Jessica didn't expect her sister to be any too pleased with him. Liz surprised her by calmly telling McLaughlan, "You dish it out, we can take it, Detective, as long as you play square with us. You're forgetting, though, we *know* Larry. Just get to the bottom of things."

Once McLaughlan was gone, the two sisters faced each other. Jessica questioned, "Well, what do you think?"

Liz studied her wine, then shrugged, "He's not completely against us, probably."

"Probably?" Jessica sat back, surprised. "He *is* pursuing the Tewkesbury lead."

"He *says* he is."

"What's that supposed to mean? You think he's got some kind of an angle?"

"He could be lulling us into a sense of false security," Liz reasoned. "He could be setting us up, so we'll let something slip about Larry."

Jessica shifted uneasily before asking, "Do you really think he's so devious?"

"I don't know," Liz sighed. "I just have a funny feeling–and you know that my feelings are always on the money."

"Except about being married to a Nazi."

"Not amusing, little sister."

"Okay, okay. Sorry. Maybe that was out of line." As much as Jess wished she had James here to bounce conjectures off, she was almost glad for him that he was presently incommunicado. It was certainly better than being stuck in a morass that was enough to make Charlie Chan and sons numbered one through twelve turn tail and run.

Chapter Twelve

Thursday, May 24, 1945

Two floors of the Baxter Building housed the offices and studios of the station broadcasting Jessica's program. The fifteenth floor was the beehive of creativity, blood, sweat, and pure anxiety: two studios, one with a theatre for live audiences, broadcasting booths overlooking each one; several rooms designated for the writers, rehearsals, a lounge, and storage. The sixteenth floor was the world of suits: business offices devoted to accounting, advertising, the general manger and his minions, and two sponsors who had invested in this station, rather than in just specific programs.

"A Rose for Emily" had gone off like a dream for cast and crew; and, from the looks on some of the audience's faces, Jessica figured some of them might be having nightmares tonight! Voices bubbled off adrenaline and champagne in the lounge. Her hair in a French roll under a black pillbox hat matching her light, wool-crêpe suit, Jess smiled to see her friend Vic run a hand through his rush of light brown hair, intent on planning next week's script with Scott Zimkewicz. Vic had already told her that they were adapting the role of one of the male professors in "The Dunwich Horror" for her. She grinned, thinking about how she'd get to save the world from Yog-Sothoth. Then again, a week devoting her life to Lovecraft would mean the audience wouldn't be the only ones having nightmares.

Maura Robinson, sitting next to Jessica on the couch, nodded her titian upsweep and black lacquer cap toward Vic and noted, "Our young man's so excited about switching into writing, I hope he doesn't pop before the night's over. We still have twenty-five weeks to go."

Maura's husband, Guy, classically handsome with wavy black hair and a twinkle in his dark eyes, kidded, "Hey, Maura, give the guy a break. He boiled Faulkner down to forty-five minutes, in sync with commercial breaks–and still avoided writing stage directions like 'the villain creeps noiselessly.'"

"I think Vic would know better, having been an assistant sound man," Maura smiled.

Jessica confessed, "I'm just so happy I didn't rattle my pages or mix them up!"

"Jessica, you did just fine," Maura assured her. "You've got a natural talent. Some of the Broadway and Hollywood actors just can't cut it. They don't know how to color the words or when to tone down the voltage–and some just can't act."

"Thanks!" Jess appreciatively replied. "You don't know how excited I am for this new start. It's great that Mr. Wellstone and Scott wanted to bring in new people like me and Vic and Gerry Davis over there." Jess nodded at a tall, round-faced, handsome young blond man sipping a drink. He leaned slightly off-kilter, thanks to an artificial leg replacing the one shot up in Italy. Gerry was talking to a writer, Nataska Turtletaub, and their announcer Claude Coleman. Claude stood all of 4'11" but his voice sounded 6'4"–all that mattered in radio.

It *was* a good night. Par for broadcast practice, a transcription had been made of the performance for later transmission in California; after all, 10:00 P. M. live from New York would only be 7:00 on the West Coast. *Hmm, would any kind of transcription make its way to England and James?* Jess had wanted to call Liz and ask her how she'd liked the show, but the excitement of performing and the good times she was now sharing with her comrades had nixed that plan.

A tap on her shoulder brought Jess out of her reverie as Gerry Davis told her, "Jessica, there's a call for you, on the line at the receptionist's desk, just outside the door. I think they said it was your sister."

"My sister? Oh, maybe she called to congratulate me for the show. Thanks, Gerry."

Jessica excused herself and made her way into the corridor leading to the reception area. At the desk, the day girl had been replaced by a night watchman. He handed the phone receiver to Jessica with, "Say, would you mind holding down the fort so's I can get myself some cake and coffee? I'll be right back."

Jessica nodded, refraining from asking him to leave her his gun and the one bullet he kept in his pocket should her sister make her too crazy.

She queried the phone, "So, Liz, what gives?"

"I just got home and found a letter from Evan."

Jessica sat down, hard, in one of the visitors' chairs.

"Jessica? Are you there? Hello?"

"I'm here, Liz. I just ... did I hear you right? You got a letter from Evan Blair. Did he send *the letter* to you rather than the lawyers by accident?"

"No, Jess, this letter is something entirely different! But it's definitely from him."

"Just how does a dead guy send you a letter?" Jessica puzzled.

"When I brought in the mail, after I got home just now, there was a letter with a note from the post office saying some mix-up picking up the mail in our office building Monday morning delayed delivery. So, Evan must have dropped it down the mail chute Sunday, as insurance. Wait till you hear what he has to say."

"Well?" Jess demanded, grateful there was no witness to her excitement.

"Okay. Here's the screwy part: he writes about you."

"Me? I don't get it."

"To be honest, neither do I. But here goes:

Liz,

When you receive this, I'll be long gone–but, with luck, still on this mortal coil. I'm hoping this letter is unnecessary, that we'll have had our meeting already and I'll have explained why and how I will make restitution to Lois Wong for the stolen jade. I also know that I may not live to clear my plans with you and get that other letter out–or that someone might interfere with it. So, this is my insurance. I wish I could just write, "Here's the booty, turn it over." But there's too much chance that this letter, too, might fall into the wrong hands–the hands of whom I won't name here for fear she'll come after you if she knows you know her secret.

Let me just say your sister holds the "key" to this mystery in her memory–I made sure of that when she was in a kind of Oriental dream last week. That key opens a door in a little town yo<u>u'll know well</u>–from your past.

Liz interjected, "That's underlined, the '*ll know well.*'"

Check your offices to me, and we'll be done, in part. Sometimes a few steps lead to reward. Ask your sister not to turn down 1 to 2 mad Hershey bars back home in town. Zeugma's the key to felicity for Cambridge ladies, so that one near twin leads to his match.

Good Luck,

Evan

Okay Jess, for the love of Mike, what does *that* mean?"

"Elizabeth, I get the reference to e. e. cummings, but, beyond that, I'm lost," Jessica confessed.

"But he says to ask you. He seems sure that you'll know. Think, kiddo, it must mean *something* to you."

"You did just spring this on me, Liz. Give me time..."

"Okay! Then I'll be right over to get you."

"Hey, hold your horses. We're all celebrating our first broadcast here. Did you listen?"

"Yes, yes, but, Jess, this is bigger."

"I guess," Jessica grumbled. "He'd have made it a lot easier by simply telling you where the jade was, as well as adding, 'By the way, don't tell Alanna Tewkesbury because she's really Betty Weisenthal.' Oh, did you call Detective McLaughlan? What did he say?"

"At this hour? I don't think he's on duty. We can call tomorrow, which means you and I can take all night to figure this thing out. Maybe if we put our heads together we can come up with something other than a headache."

"It's too late for that, Liz."

"Then take two aspirins, and I'll pick you up in fifteen minutes."

"Liz, I'm exhausted," Jessica protested.

"Jessica Minton, this letter can help us make restitution to Lois's family, maybe clear Larry. Don't be selfish."

Jessica started to argue, but with the champagne, the hour, and the head-spinning language of Evan Blair's letter, pinning down the holes in her sister's argument seemed a lost cause.

"Okay, okay, you win," Jess gave in. "I'll make my excuses and meet you in front of the Baxter Building. You know the address. But I warn you, my brains are turning to mush."

"Fine. I'll take you to Sam and Al's Diner. It's closer to your building than either of our apartments. The coffee there should turn on a few lights in your head. We're going to nail this one, Jessica! You wait and see!"

The receiver clicked off.

Jessica sighed, hanging up the phone as the security guard returned with two pieces of chocolate cake and a coffee. Hmm, should she ask him to load his single bullet and put her out of her misery then and there?

Wearing a beige, felt boater and black pinstriped suit, Elizabeth Minton pulled her Buick up in front of the Baxter Building. She'd been so keyed up over this new turn of events that she'd almost thought she'd been followed! Anyway, a few quick turns, and Liz had convinced herself no one was on her high-fashion tail.

Jessica was standing under the awning, chatting away with the doorman as if the fate of Evan Blair's killers and Larry Sanders weren't in their hands. At least she didn't have to honk the horn before Jess saluted her companion goodbye and made a beeline for the car.

Opening the door, Jessica riveted her sister with, "I think I've figured out part of Blair's letter, Liz."

"Well, praise the Lord and pass the ammunition. Hop in, kiddo, and give."

Sliding into the front seat, then slamming the door, Jessica settled back and told her sister decidedly, "Lowell."

"Lowell?"

"Lowell. Where Aunt Grace lives. That's the place from your past the letter refers to. Now, let's roll. Caffeine helps me think!"

"But why Lowell of all the places in my past? Why not Europe or Salem or Boston or even our hometown? Why Lowell, for the love of Mike?"

"Simple. Vaudeville."

"Vaudeville? How much of that champagne did you imbibe tonight, kiddo?" Liz queried suspiciously.

"Never mind that. Just drive. I'll explain."

Liz gave her sister an impatient snort but engaged the gears and zipped them both into the flow of traffic, a little too sharply for Jess's comfort.

"Do you mind, Liz? Another maneuver like that and we can ask Evan Blair ourselves."

"Don't get wise. I'll get you there in one piece. How many accidents have I had in the past fifteen years, forgetting the nun? And not to repeat myself, *vaudeville*?"

"It's like this, Liz," Jess began. "When I went back to say goodbye, Maura was talking about hearing John Carradine say one of the toughest places to play was at the Royale in Lowell."

"And?"

"So, I remembered the letter, when you read it–do you still have it? Maybe I can show you..."

"It's in my inside pocket," Liz replied, managing to pull out the letter, while driving. Only part of Jess's life flashed before her eyes.

Jessica unfolded the missive and switched on the dome light to read, explaining as she did, "Let's see. Okay, here, right here: 'you'll know well.' Slur it together, into l-no-well. Get it? Lowell?"

"Are you serious?"

Jessica challenged, "I'd sure as the devil like to see you do better."

Liz relented a little, "Look, you could be on to something, but that's a big 'could.' Even if you're right, Lowell's too large a burg for us to go knocking door-to-door."

"That's the other thing, where e.e. cummings comes in!" Jessica eagerly revealed.

"So, spill with your brilliant deduction, Miss Marple," Liz urged doubtfully.

"The mad Hershey bars–they're 'angry candy,' from a cummings poem Blair and I talked about enjoying." Jessica's excitement increased as she elaborated. "Then, get this, when he was trying to make nice with me, he made a point of telling me he'd picked out a volume of *cummings* to give me because it included the poem with that line..."

"Huh," Liz concluded.

"Huh what?" Jessica questioned, irritated at the interruption.

"Huh, Evan once told me that coming up with something keyed to your recipient was essential for creating a successful code. Something that would click with the way that person thought or with his interests yet would go over the head of most everyone else. Thank God I didn't nod off until *after* that part of his exposition. Oh, oh, and the last night, he brought up giving that particular book to you. And omigosh, Jessica, he talked about 'decoding' the poetry and hoping you'd never have to do it! I thought it odd at the time, but it makes sense now." Then Liz's crest fell as she concluded, "Big deal: 'angry candy'? What does *that* mean?"

"I'll tell you, sister o'mine," Jess answered. "I've looked over the book more than once since then and noticed he'd underlined 'Cambridge' and 'angry candy.' You've been to Lowell often enough to know that right near the train station there's a Cambridge Street with all those seedy rooming houses. Just the place to lie low, with a quick and easy exit on the B & M line. And here," she stabbed the letter with her tapered nail, the words 'one to two.' That's likely the street number: 122!"

"Okay, let's say that you got it right about the address. What then? What's at the address? A scrapbook with photos of Alanna aka Betty cavorting with him and her husband? Her diary confessing her criminal past? How do we even get *in* for that matter?" Liz demanded, pulling up and parking. After setting the parking brake, she turned to her sister to finish, "And what's all this nutty jazz about an 'oriental dream'? "

"That, Elizabeth, is why we need to get into the diner and charge our brains up with some hot coffee," Jessica directed. "And while we're at it, I want some cherry pie. Everyone at the party got a piece of chocolate cake but *me*!"

The waitress had finished pouring their coffees and taking their orders. The Andrews Sisters were skulking in harmony through "One Meatball." Jessica carefully spread the note on the table before her and said, "Okay. Let's get down to business."

The script was hasty, almost scrawled, nothing like the graceful flair Jess had seen a time or two before. The rest of the message still taunted Jessica, and she told her sister, "I just don't get how I'm supposed to figure out this 'oriental dream' business. I can't think of anything Oriental or dreamy about the few times I talked to him one-on-one. I was trying to trip him up, well, figure him out."

"What *did* you talk about?" Elizabeth tried to prod helpfully.

The truth was embarrassing to admit.

"Umm, ah, you–and Alanna or Larry."

"Planning my future?" Liz queried, more than a little resentful.

Jessica allowed, "To be honest, Liz, I have to give him credit. He was worried about you."

"So, he's not quite the cad you thought him, after all?"

"Liz, just because Al Capone isn't Hitler doesn't mean he's Shirley Temple." Jess shook her head. She was beginning to sound *far* too much like her sister.

Liz ignored her, grousing, "We're getting nowhere. Let me see the letter again. Hmm, this 'oriental dream' seems important. Something to do with Lois?"

"But what, Elizabeth? Blair never mentioned her to me. Besides, he says that *I'm* in the orient not Lois. And it was last week. I know I never talked with him about Lois then."

"Last week, you're right. Last ... Damn, Jessica! How could I be so dense! It's right in front of me, just a little to the left."

"Huh?"

"Last week, Evan and I discussed it, one of the numbers you modeled. I wondered why he made such a big deal about that one. He thought it was 'really you'! He even said so a few times. Of course!"

"Of course what, Liz? Mind letting me in on your little epiphany?"

"Last week you modeled a number called Persian Fantasy, a hostess gown, remember?"

"Ye-es. Yes! You're right. So that's it! That's ... nothing! What about the dress? Some clue! A fancy, too-tight-in-the-waist dress and an address in an old Massachusetts mill town. Unless you think he hid the jewels in the dress?"

Elizabeth shook her head, "I was hoping you'd say that he'd told you something significant when you were wearing the dress..."

Jessica shook her head; and, before they could struggle any further, the waitress arrived with her pie. After the woman left, Jess now found herself too concerned with this enigma to dig in. Like Liz frowning into her coffee cup, she wondered, what was the significance of Evan's other clues?

Finally, Liz probed, "Jessica, you're sure Evan didn't say or do anything significant while you were wearing that number?"

Frustrated, Jessica answered, "No, we hardly talked, that I recall. Although now that I think of it, I hardly remember *anything* from *that* day. It was when I heard from James. In fact, I almost forgot that note you posted on the mirror, because of the letter ... No, wait, that's not right. Something happened before that, something screwy, something to do with Evan."

"What? What? What?!"

Impatiently raising her hand, Jessica silenced her sister and questioned, "Where's your typewriter?"

"My what?"

"Your typewriter, your office typewriter."

"In my office, where else?"

"You're sure?"

"I can't say that I've checked its timecard lately, but what's my typewriter got to do with the price of tea in China?"

"Just this, Elizabeth. I'd dropped something by your mirror, and, in his own office, Evan actually looked toward where I was. Get this; he *acted* as if he hadn't seen me. He must have, though, from that angle. *That* was his plan, for me to see him. But why pretend?"

"Pretend? See him? See him what? For Heaven's sake, Jess, what are you getting at?"

"Liz, keep your bloomers on and listen!" Jessica ordered. "Blair must have wanted me to remember his borrowing the typewriter. I was wearing that 'Oriental' get-up at the time, and he made a big deal about asking me if he could borrow your typewriter and then letting me see him pretend to furtively tape something underneath it."

"And you just thought of all this *now*?"

"Good Grief, Liz, it wasn't an issue until just now. And I did have more important things on my mind, like finding out that James was alive."

"Okay, fine. Let's go!" Elizabeth decided.

"Go? Where?"

"The office and get the typewriter, you dope!"

"What about my pie?" Jessica protested; her hunger returned.

"What about the clues?

"Wait a minute," Jess cautioned. "Shouldn't we call Detective McLaughlan about this?"

"At this hour?" Liz countered. "Like I said before, he must be off shift. Besides, you remember how those two detectives treated us when we brought in Alanna Tewkesbury's name. If we bring them this crazy letter and its clues don't pan out, they'll really think we're a couple of dizzy dames. They'll never believe anything we say about the murder, and there goes Mrs. Tewkesbury scot-free! Look, all we'll do is check to see if there *is* a clue. We won't mess up any evidence. Okay?"

"I have a bad feeling about this," Jessica demurred.

"Have all the feelings you want," Elizabeth countered. "But I'm going. Now, you can come along to make sure no evidence gets meddled with, or you can sit here feeling righteous. It's up to you–plus, you'll have to find your own ride home."

Jessica narrowed her eyes and informed her sister, "You really know how to make a girl wish she were an only child."

The corridor of offices stretched long, forbidding, and murky under Elizabeth's flashlight. As with her last nocturnal visit, Liz had used her key to the elevator. Even if Elizabeth had a right to be in her own building, it just didn't seem prudent to advertise their mission, so she whispered, "Jessica, do you think we were followed?"

"What put it into you head, Liz. *Did* you see anything fishy?"

"No, no. Not really," Elizabeth answered. "I thought there might have been something, a car, when I left my apartment, but I'm sure I was wrong. I didn't see anything on the drive here. I just have one of my feelings..."

"Feelings? Oh no you don't, Elizabeth Minton!" admonished Jessica. "I have enough of the creeps already without you getting one of your 'feelings.'"

"But aren't my feelings usually right? What about that break-in at your apartment two years ago? Or the Japanese sneak attack?"

"You predicted the Japanese would attack Alaska in '43, Liz. Just quit monkeying around, and let's get into your office," Jessica ordered.

At her suite of offices, Liz found her keys while Jessica held the flashlight, tensely. Then the door swung open, and, of course, it creaked.

"Where do you rent from, Liz, *The Inner Sanctum*?"

"Yeah, Raymond is going to be our new receptionist," Elizabeth returned. "He's the only one I could find who puns worse than I do."

As Liz reached for the light switch, Jessica stopped her and prudently suggested, "Just the flash. We don't want anyone wondering what we're doing here now."

"I don't know. All these shadows give me the creeps."

Their whispers rustled disquietingly in the dark silence.

"Liz, we might have some living, breathing creeps in here if any light escapes the office door or the windows."

"So you *do* think we were followed."

"I think we'd better not take any chances," Jessica returned. Satisfied, somewhat, by Liz's grimly acquiescent expression, Jess closed and locked the main door, then nodded to her sister, "Onward, MacDuff."

"Couldn't you quote a nicer play?"

"Okay, how about if I call you Touchstone?"

"What's he from?" whispered Liz as they cat-footed by beam of the flash.

"*As You Like It*. He's the clown."

"He-e-e-y," Liz hissed.

They reached Liz's office, and she unlocked the door, pushed it open, then softly announced, "Okay, all menacing thugs come out with your hands up. Give yourself up within the next three minutes, and we give you a free set of dishes. Nope, no one? Okay, Jess, safe to go in."

Liz switched on her desk lamp and stared at her empty desk, empty of her typewriter. She turned to the little table to her left: no typewriter there, either.

"Liz," Jessica began, trying to suppress the nasty little chill creeping up her spine, "where is your typewriter? Please tell me that nobody lifted it."

Liz was awfully silent. Not a good sign. Uncertainty in this dark silence left Jess feeling vulnerably alone. Then Liz rolled her eyes, embarrassed as she remembered, "I'm such a dope. I forgot that Ginger's machine was broken, and I lent her mine. I feel so silly."

"You mean we could have had our hands on the typewriter already?" Jessica lowered.

"Exciting, wasn't it?"

"Elizabeth Minton, you'd better hope that Alanna Tewkesbury gets her claws into you before I do," Jessica growled, but quietly.

Back by Ginger's desk, Liz breathed, "Thank God!" when her flashlight revealed the typewriter.

The two women circled Ginger's workstation from opposite sides. Flashlight resting on the desk, Liz was illuminated with her curved hands and red nails poised over the machine. Jessica tensely jogged her string of pearls.

Liz ordered, "I'll lift it, you feel underneath. See if he hid something on the bottom or inside. Okay?"

Jess nodded. Up went the typewriter and out went Jessica's hand.

"Oh, My Gosh!"

"Found it?" Liz's eyes fired anxiously as Jessica pulled back her hand.

"No. Cracked a nail. Darn that hurts!"

"Oh, for the love of Mike! "You hold the flashlight and we'll both look," Liz griped, turning over the machine. "I don't know why we both didn't just..."

"Look, Liz!" Jessica cut in.

"Where?" Liz peered, her neck craning like a heron's.

"Up in there. To the right..."

"Oh, sure, yeah, I see it!" Liz announced. "Good grief! You'd really have to know what and where to look to see this baby!" Reaching under and up, Liz pulled out, "A key, Jess! It's either a house or a room key! I'll bet you dollars to donuts it's to 122 Cambridge Street."

"Omigosh, Liz!" Jessica gasped horrified. "We've just tampered with evidence! You promised we wouldn't! Maybe whatever Evan was trying to point us to in 122 Cambridge Street will be inadmissible because our grubby little paws contaminated the key. What are we going to say to Detective McLaughlan? We promised we'd play square with him!"

Elizabeth's hand closed on the key, as she awkwardly admitted, "Oh, I guess you've got something there. Boyd I could not care less about, but McLaughlan deserves better from us..."

"Shhh!" Jessica silenced her sister. Liz was only a moment behind in hearing a heavy tread in the corridor, moving closer: the tread of someone much bigger than the watchman, of a man unafraid to let you know he was coming.

Liz killed her flashlight, and Jessica found herself shoved away from the desk, towards her sister's office. They might have made it, too, but Jess, unlike Dusty, could not see in the dark–both women went down in a flailing of high heels and shoulder bags.

The only sound louder than their crash was the crack of wood as the front lock was splintered from the door by a savage kick.

Jess and Liz managed to untangle themselves and face the intruder. He snapped on Ginger's desk lamp, revealing himself in its dim light: Eddie Kubek. With the smile of a sadistic goon who overrates his wit, he cracked, "All this nice furniture and you two ladies have to sit on the floor? Real shame, a real shame."

"That's why we went with the wall-to-wall carpeting. So much more comfy," Liz coolly returned.

Kubek continued to flaunt that smug, dangerous grin, while Liz carefully helped her sister up, both glad that their "gentleman" caller wasn't about to do the honors. He did get curious when he caught Jessica looking down and trying to inconspicuously sight something on the floor.

"Looking for something, sister?"

"No, no," Jess answered a little too quickly, hoping he wouldn't perceive her anxiety or see that her eyes had frozen on a particular object on the floor. But she couldn't catch a break.

"Oh this?"

Kubek scooped something off the floor, and Jessica gulped. Back by the desk, he glanced at his hand with that same mug's smile, then queried, "Couldn't wait to see me, girls? Knocked each other down running to unlock the door and let me in? But you didn't have to hurry. I'm a guy who can take care of little matters like locked doors."

"We're comforted," Liz acidly smiled.

"Yeah? I bet you wouldn't be, comforted or in a big hurry, if you knew why I followed you here or the message I have for you."

He was still smiling, but the steel in his eyes hardened his features and tone.

"Suppose you enlighten us, Mr. Kubek," Liz directed, putting more than a little steel into *her* delivery.

"Oh, you know my name? Ain't that swell. Well, I guess I can get right down to cases. You knowing who I am has a lot to do with that–say, your sister is looking kinda antsy there. Something bothering her?"

"Aside from your breaking down my door and talking tough to us?" Liz queried, but her last words slowed as she noticed that Jessica seemed to be trying awfully hard not to look at the clenched hand Kubek rhythmically bounced. What was he holding? And why was it giving her sister the heebie-jeebies?

"Yeah, I guess your sister has tender nerves. Sorry, honey. Don't worry. This won't take long."

"How considerate of you," Liz returned.

"Yeah, ain't I just, though? My friend thinks that you girls could use a little advice. See, I like your sister, there, nice and quiet. I'd like you both to stay nice and quiet. You don't want to make no trouble for nobody, do you?"

"Like Alanna Tewkesbury?"

Kubek's eyes hardened even more, and Liz wished she hadn't pushed him quite so far. Jessica's hand on her back was an unnecessary warning.

"We don't need to go naming names, here, but, if we do, I might name Larry Sanders. If the cops go nosing around my boss, maybe she has a way to make them more interested in him."

"Mrs. Tewkesbury has nothing to fear, if she's innocent," Liz replied with velvet charm. "Besides, what makes you think I have any control over whom the police investigate?"

"Don't get cute with me, sister," his tone still not *overtly* threatening. "Your gums have been flapping, and there's people who are feeling persecuted–and when people feel persecuted, they can make *you* feel uncomfortable."

"Are you threatening us?" Jessica finally intervened, carefully but not fearfully.

An expression of wounded innocence: "Who me? Threaten? Do something illegal?" Kubek's hands opened both to express his "innocence" and to reveal what had made Jessica so antsy: Evan Blair's key. "Perish the thought, girls. I just want to see justice done."

Jessica could see that Liz had all she could do not to flip at the sight of that key in Eddie Kubek's big mitt. Clasping her sister's elbow, Jess steadied Liz from giving away the show. Luckily, their visitor seemed to believe them crushed by his chutzpah.

"My friend wants to see justice done–an' maybe that includes giving the cops a little evidence that don't look so hot for your pal Larry Sanders–like his gun."

Jess and Liz felt like a couple defenseless ten pins when that revelation bowled into them.

Liz found her voice first: "Gun? What gun? What are you talking about? Larry Sanders doesn't have a gun."

"Not now he don't. But ask him if he's missing a sweet little .38."

"You're just whistling in the dark," Jessica cut in. "Even if Larry had a gun, he's still not the killer. *You* have to prove he is: that he was here, that *his* gun killed Evan Blair. Maybe the caliber is the same, but ballistics and fingerprint tests will show that Larry is no murderer."

"You sure about that?"

Eddie Kubek was not rattled. Jessica even more unhappily noted that he had started to bounce the key à la George Raft. He smiled at her and stopped, saying, "This bothering you, honey? I'll fix that."

He dropped the key in his pocket. It was all Jess could do not to scream. Liz was even with her, but, again, Kubek seemed to misread their horror as caused by his threats against Larry–not that either sister was bearing up awfully well under that strain.

Kubek smiled, then continued, "So, girls, do we have a deal, or does your pal take the rap for Evan Blair's unfortunate demise?"

Liz snapped, "This is a frame, pure and simple. You're covering for Alanna Tewkesbury, but her putting up this frame job is like admitting she's guilty."

Kubek shrugged, "You can try and tell the cops that when they haul away your boyfriend, but I wouldn't count on them buying some half-baked yarn when they have a nice tidy solution handed to them, gun and all. Now, play ball with us and my friend will be happy, your boyfriend will be happy. Everybody wins."

"Except Evan Blair," Liz countered tightly.

Eddie Kubek shrugged again and pointed out, "He wasn't no saint, honey. He messed with the big leagues, and he got his. *You* don't want to make the same mistake. Think about it. You play ball; we'll play ball. Evidence don't go bad, not this kind, anyway."

But even through all her fear, Jessica's brain had been working overtime. She screwed up her courage to enable her to calmly, forcefully challenge Eddie Kubek, "Sorry, but you don't hold quite as strong a hand as you think. Unless you have proof positive that the gun is Larry's, you've got nothing. Once you take it out of his house, you snap the link chaining that gun to him. You just outsmarted yourself, chum."

Eddie Kubek grinned, and returned, "Think so, girlie? How about you chew on this. If we could get the gun out of Sanders' house without anybody knowing it, we can get it back in the same way–and make a helpful little anonymous tip to the cops telling them where to find it–all before you can do anything about it. It's not like you're about to call in the cops to keep an eye on his place. An' you two can squawk all you want about tonight's little chat, but I got a boatload of poker buddies who'll place me at a game all night long. But, somehow, I don't think you're going to be wanting to call too much attention to this chat."

Jessica barely managed a deflated, "Oh."

Kubek smiled and turned to leave, putting his hands in his pockets.

"Oh, here girls." He turned back. "You might need this for the new lock."

The key clattered onto Ginger's desk. Jessica and Liz found themselves alone in the office.

Finally, Jessica squeaked, "So, so what happens now?"

Elizabeth didn't answer right away. Instead, she walked carefully to the door, leaning out to peer into the corridor.

"Is he gone, Liz?"

Liz pulled back in with a glum, "He's gone." She fixed Jess with a steady eye and continued, "There's only one thing to do, you know."

"Move to the South Seas?"

"I guess I would rather face those sons of Nippon than Eddie Kubek," Liz remarked, circling the desk determinedly to take up the phone.

"Who're you calling?"

"Who do you think?" Liz barely glanced up.

Jess concluded, *Ah, the police!* Funny how the thought simultaneously comforted and alarmed her. But if Liz thought calling Alanna's bluff was the right thing to do, maybe she had something. They had nothing to fear as far as Larry was concerned. Jessica just hadn't expected her sister to take the normal approach, turn everything over to the authorities, especially when one of them was that Aaron Boyd. So why was it taking so long for the cops to answer? Long line at the donut wagon? Liz was looking mighty impatient.

The name Liz's crisp voice sent across the telephone wire startled Jessica: "Larry? We'll be right over. You've got a little explaining to do, my lad. Yes, I know how late it is–I just wonder if *you* do. Melodramatic? You ain't heard nothing yet! No, I can't explain over the phone. It's complicated. No, *I'm* not in trouble, but we have to talk and get all the stories straight. We'll be right over. Yes, Jess and I. Goodbye."

"Liz, why aren't you calling in the police? They can handle a big ape like Kubek much better than we can. And we owe it to McLaughlan," Jessica argued indignantly.

Liz allowed, "I know what you're saying about that detective. He did give us a break. Believe me; it kills at me, not leveling a solid guy like him. But I don't have a choice. That Tewkesbury dame has Larry on the mat. We're talking about his life here. Even if we report our interview with little Eddie Sunshine, it's only our word against his–and his poker buddies. Don't forget, we can't say anything without implicating Larry."

"Elizabeth, if you'd listened to me in the first place and gone to McLaughlan about the letter, Eddie couldn't have threatened us here, and the police would have these clues," Jessica chastised her sister.

"We don't even know if those clues lead to anything legit, even credible. But, Jessica," Liz reasoned, not happy, herself, where she was going, "Mrs. Tewkesbury has a damned convincing frame all nailed together to hang on Larry. I will tell you one thing more. No matter how bad I feel about not being on the level with someone like McLaughlan, I will not let Larry hang because

I got him into this mess. I took on Evan as a partner; I pursued the Tewkesbury woman. I owe it to Larry to put him first now."

Jessica clenched her hands in frustration, knowing that Liz was right: playing according to Hoyle would play right into La Tewkesbury's hands. And like her sister, Jess also felt she owed Larry for the troubles she'd brought him in the past. In the end, Jess asked, "So what do you want to do now, Elizabeth? What *can* we do?"

All business, Liz decided, "We've got to warn Larry, on the double. Let him try to clear this up–or at least give us a clue how we can. In fact, maybe if we can come up with a good cover story for Larry, we can call their bluff."

"Cover story, Liz? What about the truth? I never even heard of Larry having a gun before this. Neither did you, right? I don't like the sound of 'cover story.'"

"How hard do you think it would be for someone like Mrs. Tewkesbury to coerce or pay off some chump to testify that Larry bought the murder weapon?" Liz argued back.

Jess didn't have an answer. Grudgingly, she conceded, "We-ell, we do need to at least talk to him. Still, Liz, I don't like playing fast and loose with the police. It's bound to jump up and bite us sooner or later." To herself, she brooded, *Where is any of this going but down a dark, treacherous path?*

Chapter Thirteen

Thursday/Friday, May 24/25, 1945

Larry Sander's study was softly lit. Jessica couldn't help thinking about how once before she'd tried to clear Larry of suspicion in this room. Larry had been innocent then. Shouldn't the past repeat itself?

At Liz's revelation of Eddie Kubek's ambush, Larry's annoyed half-asleep look had vanished into deep concern, "He didn't hurt either of you, did he?"

"No. We're fine, Larry," Jessica calmed him from next to her sister on the couch, "but what about Kubek's accusation?"

"That I shot Blair and left the murder weapon around for Eddie Kubek? A bit absurd, don't you think? I'm much more methodical than that."

He absently patted the front of his dressing gown for his cigarette case, and Liz advised, "The end table, top drawer. You usually keep some in there. In fact, I could use one myself."

Jessica almost protested her sister's request. But with far more vital concerns at hand, she asked Larry, "We can just ignore him, then, and keep pushing the police to connect Alanna Tewkesbury to the murder?"

Larry stopped abruptly and ordered, "I don't want either of you to antagonize that band of hooligans. I won't have a minute's peace unless you promise to stay out of this mess. This isn't a play, Jessica. It's not just a gaggle of recalcitrant buyers, Elizabeth. You're antagonizing powerful people, whether or not they're murderers. Let the authorities handle this."

"The police, some of them, anyway, seem to be handling this all in your direction, Larry," Elizabeth warned. "Boyd wants to pin this on you. Didn't you tell me that they pulled you in for questioning a second time, and he gave you quite a grilling?"

"I can take it, Liz," Larry tried to assuage her. Putting a hand on her shoulder, he pointed out, "I'm still free, aren't I?"

"Leo McLaughlan seems to have more of an open mind," Jessica added hopefully.

"True," Liz agreed. "He seems a much nicer man..."

"Should I be jealous?" Larry laughed, a little nervously, it seemed to Jessica. He had his cigarettes now and lit up quickly, apparently forgetting Liz's earlier request.

Jessica got up, explaining she needed to stretch her legs; she actually wanted to move where she could better watch Larry and Liz interact.

"So, Elizabeth, and you, too, Jessica," Larry was admonishing them again. "I expect both of you to swear you won't do anything to provoke Mrs. Tewkesbury or her henchman."

"Larry, I can't let them get away with Evan's murder," Elizabeth disagreed hotly, "even if they can't pin it on you."

Jessica watched Larry scowl before he asserted, "They *won't* pin it on me, Liz, and I wish you'd stop worrying about Evan Blair. He was quite the scoundrel, himself! You seem to forget that he destroyed Lois's family. That kind of man..."

"Doesn't deserve to be murdered in cold blood, Larry, especially since he was trying to make amends. And let that crew get off Scott free? That's the right thing to do? Who knows what else that Tewkesbury female might do to us–or anyone–if she walks away from another crime," Elizabeth countered, for once not so much angry as trying to reason.

"I'll grant you that the Tewkesbury woman may be no angel, may even have blood on her hands, but proving that is not up to you, Elizabeth," Larry tried to convince her. "Let the police do their job and stay out of this imbroglio."

"Larry," Jessica slowly shook her head, "you don't understand. I've already set things in motion that will unavoidably lead to Mrs. Tewkesbury and Co."

He actually looked ashen, and Jessica sank inside, even as Larry tried to wave her off with, "Don't be absurd, Jessica. What could you have done?"

"I'm afraid I gave Detective McLaughlan the number of Jeff Hooley from the F.B.I. He may be able to help the local gendarmes get Betty Weisenthal, aka Alanna Tewkesbury. I can't undo that, Larry. I'm sorry."

"Damn!" escaped Larry.

Jessica slowly came forward, continuing, "What can I say, Larry? I had no way of knowing that attempt might further antagonize Mrs. Tewkesbury against you. How could I? But thinking over some of the things James had said to me two years ago, about the basis for his suspicions about you, things I'd never have expected, maybe I should have expected the unexpected to be true when it came out of Eddie Kubek's mouth."

On her feet, Liz demanded, "Jessica, what the devil are you talking about?"

"Larry, you did have a gun, didn't you?" Jessica questioned levelly.

"You do own a gun?" Liz blurted to Larry. "You're the last person in the world I'd expect to have a gun."

Larry stiffened, thought hard, then confessed, in a tone somewhere between bleakness and black humor, "*Had* a gun, my darling Elizabeth, *had* a gun."

"*Had*?" the sisters echoed.

Hand to her forehead, Liz shook her head and muttered, "I don't like the sound of this, not at all." She looked up hopefully, "I don't suppose you could have sold it to a little old lady from Manitoba a year before the murder took place? There isn't a lovely corroborating sales slip hanging around, is there?"

"Unfortunately, no, Elizabeth. I'm afraid it's as bad as it can get." Another long drag on his cigarette, a longer pause to struggle with something, then an exhalation of smoke. Larry went on, "I got the gun two years ago, around the time Jessica's 'friend' had me under surveillance. I knew something was up, and I wanted protection, but I didn't want to arouse anyone's suspicion. So I didn't get it through proper channels. It was, obviously, never registered. After Peter's trial, when things had quieted down, I put the gun away and forgot it." More thinking, then: "I forgot about the gun until after the second chat with the detectives, where it came out Blair was killed with a .38. I thought I'd just take a look at the thing, but it wasn't where I believed I'd stored it. I've been telling myself that I must have just misremembered, but after your bulletin from that Kubek thug..."

"You didn't notice that your house had been broken into?" Jessica questioned.

Before Larry could respond, Liz interposed, "Come on, Jess. Kubek and his crowd are pros. If anyone could break into a house without you knowing, they'd be the ones."

"Sounds logical," Larry agreed. "So now, ladies, I am caught between the proverbial rock and hard place. I can't prove the gun was stolen from me. Even admitting that the gun was mine in the first place puts me in the stew. Any possibility, Jessica, that you could call off that F.B.I. chap?"

Jess shook her head miserably.

Going to Larry, Elizabeth argued, "Why does this have to hang you? We don't know that they can prove your gun *is* the murder weapon, just because it's the same caliber. Ballistics could clear you."

"Unless Alanna had the gun stolen in order to commit the murder," Jessica suggested. "They could have planned this whole frame up from the start. I wouldn't put it past her."

"Thank you for that uplifting analysis," Liz snipped.

Jessica shrugged, walking toward her companions, saying, "I can't change the facts. I wish I could."

She faced Larry with genuine sympathy.

He shook his head. Weakly smiling, he crushed out his cigarette and said to Liz, "It's not Jessica's fault, Dear. I'm afraid we all have to face some painful, difficult facts. There's nothing more to be done. Nothing more. I might as well make a clean breast of it all."

"No!" Liz thundered. "I've got it! I've got it! They wouldn't dare release anything incriminating on you if we had something on them."

"That sounds like an extraordinary 'if,'" Larry countered bleakly. "I won't have you two doing anything to endanger yourselves for me."

"But we have something," Liz excitedly explained. "A letter from Evan Blair with a clue to finding the jade for Lois."

"That helps Lois," Jessica countered. "What good does it do Larry?"

"Remember, we figured out some kind of address. If we search there, I bet we find some connection to Alanna Tewkesbury. If we do, we've got leverage over her."

"Again, Elizabeth," warned Larry, "that's another big 'if.'"

"It's better than nothing, Larry. Have a little faith. Evan wouldn't have given me these clues if he didn't think we could follow them somewhere, and I aim to make that somewhere lead us straight to the goods on Mrs. Fancy-Pants, which of course we'll turn over to the police. But if we don't do this, she stands a good chance of getting away with all her dastardly little crimes, maybe even having something to hold over all our heads forever. So," turning to her sister, "Jessica, let's make tracks to your place. You have all the family dope on Lowell, so we can make our plans there."

Jess mightily resisted telling Liz that *she* was the family dope, giving Larry the chance to argue, "Wait, wait. Exactly what are you proposing, Elizabeth? I can't have you girls sticking your necks out for me. I won't allow it."

Liz waved her hand, disagreeing, "What danger, Larry? We're just going to see if we can find an address in Lowell."

"That's all?" Larry smiled skeptically. "I think not, Elizabeth. I rather think that Miss Marple and Nora Charles believe they can trot off to dig for clues, regardless of the threat of Mrs. Tewkesbury and her crew. And suppose that you do find evidence against her, what next? Do you really believe that you could just drop in on her for a little tea and counter-extortion, with no repercussions?"

An index finger punctuating her words, Liz shot back, "First, Larry, I better be Nora Charles in your little analogy..."

"Thanks a lot," Jessica interjected.

Ignoring her, Liz continued, "Second, we can hold our evidence in reserve until we know they're going to act." Reading Jessica's doubtful expression, she explained, "That's why we have to hold out on the police with this, so we have leverage over Alanna Tewkesbury. She was nervous enough about her social standing that she sicced Eddie Kubek on Jess and me after I merely raised a few questions about her. I imagine she'd change her tune if we let her know any more nonsense from her and we'd let her in for a full-blown scandal. The point is, we need insurance against Mrs. Tewkesbury, and we can't get any if we don't go to Lowell."

"I'd feel a blessed sight better if I could go with both of you," Larry temporized.

"But the detectives wouldn't like your leaving town," Jessica warned.

Larry added, "They also wouldn't like you rummaging around that apartment. If there is any evidence, isn't it better for the authorities to find it there? Doesn't that make it more reliable than for you two discover it?"

"He's got something," Jess reluctantly agreed.

Liz shook her head and countered them both, "I understand, but if we tell McLaughlan we'll have to wait for him either to get to Lowell or to try and get the Lowell police to do the search. Who knows how long that will take?! Kubek's showing up tonight to threaten us tells me his boss lady has a huge stake in this, and she's impatient. Larry, since she was so chummy with Evan in the past, there's a good chance she *knows* about this apartment. Jess and I have to go out there pronto and do some investigating before Mrs. Tewkesbury can grab or even destroy whatever clues Evan wanted us to find. It may even be too late now, but we've got to risk it. Otherwise, we're all sunk. Heck, I might even argue that Evan's letter gives me his permission to go to his apartment. And, say, what if I promise we won't remove anything unless it would be a useful clue no matter who found it or how it came to light?"

Larry didn't argue, but his strained expression showed he was not happy, let alone completely swayed.

"Anyway, Larry," Liz pushed her point, "we have to go, but not just for your sake. There's Lois to think about. We've got to get the jade back for her. Right now, though, we can't have the police in on this, until we know what we've got. So, we've got to do this on our own. You must see that you can't put a monkey wrench in this chance to bring Alanna Tewkesbury to justice for all her crimes. If she gets away with this, there'll be no catching her and making her pay for what she did to Lois's family."

Liz's words gave Larry quite a bit to chew on. Finally, he relented, "All right, all right. I don't feel right about this, but, since you put it that way, that it's for Lois and all the others, I understand what you have to do. I just wish there was some way I could protect you."

"Don't worry," Liz smiled, coming forward to give the lapels of Larry's smoking jacket a little tug. "No one will have any idea that Jess and I are heading to Lowell. Leave it to me."

Jessica could see that Liz's charm was working on Larry. He didn't look thrilled to agree, but he seemed willing to believe Liz wouldn't be getting herself and Jess into hot water. Jess wished *she* could be so sure. Sure it was vital to beat Alanna Tewkesbury to whatever Evan wanted them to uncover in the apartment. Nonetheless, Jess not only dreaded a possible encounter with the woman and her minions, but she wasn't at all comfortable about leaving McLaughlan out of this deal.

The good-bye kiss between Larry and Liz prompted Jess uncomfortably to peruse her black pumps. Now why was she so antsy over a little romance? Because she missed James or because she still wasn't sure Larry was the right guy for her sister?

Friday, May 25, 1945

Leo McLaughlan tossed a pile of reports on his already crowded desk, stared at the entire mess, then dropped into one of the most uncomfortable chairs in the precinct. He knew he really was bugged because he found himself irritatingly aware of the stale smoke and salt sweat of cops and outsiders. The horse snort that escaped him as he flipped through his list of messages and didn't find what he wanted betrayed how much he'd been banking on it.

Aaron Boyd, at the desk across from him, cocked an eyebrow but didn't comment, yet.

McLaughlan turned for a rough kind of solace to the ceramic mug of coffee on his desk, and wasn't so much disgusted by its tepidness, or even the ribbon of congealed milk on the surface, as by the soggy, floating cigarette butt. His long jaw twisted into a scowl, and he muttered without even looking up, "Say, Aaron, you take a call for me from an Agent Hooley?"

"Agent Hooley?"

"Yeah, Agent Hooley. Agent Jeff Hooley. With the F.B.I."

As he spoke, McLaughlan stared his dissatisfaction into the Evan Blair folder, knowing he'd find nothing new in it but giving it the once over anyway.

"Getting pretty palsy with the Feds, aren't we? What gives?"

"You know what gives." He shot a quick glance across to Aaron, then lit a cigarette and added, "The Blair case."

"The Blair case," Boyd snorted. "What do we need the Feds for on that one? It's open and shut–it's the boyfriend."

"Not clear enough without some hard evidence, Aar," McLaughlan clipped out. "You know better."

"I know we got a motive." Boyd ticked off the points on his fingers, "And the guy's got a flimsy alibi. It's just a matter of time before we pull everything together. If you'd of just let me sweat him a little more the other day."

"We don't have a murder weapon, and we came up deuces on the paraffin test."

"Maybe the guy owns a pair of gloves. Like I said. If you'd just let me work on him a little more–my way gets results."

"Yeah, but not the truth. Work a guy over enough and you'll get anything you want to hear. He'll make up stuff, so you'll lay off."

Boyd shrugged, countering, "Hey, gotta bust a few eggs to get an omelet."

"Or just some broken yolks."

Boyd gave his partner an odd look, and McLaughlan briefly wondered whether he'd been talking to that Elizabeth Minton too much. She kind of grew on you. Seeming to read his thoughts, Boyd questioned, "You aren't buying any of that baloney about the Tewkesbury dame?"

"Aaron, there's more going on here than a jealous boyfriend. What we have on any of them right now isn't strong enough to take to the D.A. Let me tell you, I talked to Sanders' lawyer, and he's no hack. If we jump the gun, this case is going south, no matter who's guilty. Besides, I want to know the straight dope on this thing."

"Yeah, well, I'll give you the low down, Leo. Oldest story in the book. This Minton broad's feeling guilty about getting one guy killed by driving the other nuts with jealousy. Now she's trying to turn Tewkesbury into the Wicked Witch of the West to let herself off the hook."

"Guilt transference, huh?" McLaughlan crooked his mouth.

"You're the college boy, not me. I don't need those fancy words. Let's just say I know dames."

"Your wife must think you're a real prize, Aaron."

"Not any worse than I think of her. Anyway, if you do buy Minton's story, why haven't we been up to have tea and crumpets with Mrs. Tewkesbury?"

"Told you." McLaughlan leaned back in his torturous excuse for a chair. "I'm not going to see that gal until I'm armed for bear, and this Hooley fella is the one with the ammo."

"Yeah, well, just don't go sticking those two big flat feet in your mouth or Tewkesbury may use her clout to get you reclassified as nonessential personnel, and you'll find yourself playing dodgems with Jap bullets."

McLaughlan tapped his head and said, "Strategy, pardner. I'll use what I know when it will do me some good."

"Hunh, well five'll get you ten; Tewkesbury'll tell you to take a vacation somewhere hotter than Florida. And when she does, just remember she's married to some heavy-duty juice."

"Don't worry, son, I'm building a nice pension. I intend to collect it."

"Yeah, well how about the fact that Boston never came through with anything on this Blair being in protective custody?"

"Might be a Federal case, out of their jurisdiction," Leo countered unperturbed. "But you're forgetting that my pal's low down on the Weisenthal gang jibes with Blair's story. And Madame Tewkesbury's past is pretty cloudy before she married her sugar daddy."

"Big deal. Maybe she was a showgirl or a stripper or just from the wrong side of the silver spoon. There are plenty of dames out there with a shady past who didn't run with a jewel-heisting gang. Besides, witnesses put her in Florida when Blair was murdered."

"Aar, you know as well as I do that she didn't have to pull the trigger herself, not with Eddie Kubek as her bodyguard."

"Maybe, Leo, but until I can make the same kind of link to Blair as I can with this Sanders, my money's on him. Hell, if you want to put the finger on a dame, there's that Lois Wong. You know how those Orientals are about family honor and all that stuff. Hari kari."

"She's Chinese; that's Japanese, and it's a form of suicide not murder. Besides, she's got an alibi."

"Iris Rossetti? I bet I could shake a different story out of her."

"You don't want to bruise those tender mitts of yours, Aaron, working over too many suspects."

"Don't be a wise guy. Aw, hell, this ain't the only case we got, anyway. Instead of waiting for your Junior G-Man to call, let's take a bite out of some of these other cases, huh, Leo?"

"Sounds jake to me," Leo agreed. Yet he still wondered what it was about this case that seemed much hinkier than so many others he'd handled.

Chapter Fourteen

Still Friday, May 25, 1945

Two o'clock in the afternoon. Through the grimy window of the drugstore, Liz Minton had a perfect view of their objective across the way. One in a row of identical tenements, number 122 stood on the corner of Cambridge and a narrow, dark side street. She nervously patted her pompadour, shifted her hat, adjusted the collar of her beige-and-yellow-checked blazer, and looked at her watch. Again. Jessica was long overdue. She and Jess had traveled separately to divert suspicion, with Liz leaving word at the office that she had a business trip in the opposite direction of her true destination. But could Tewkesbury and her goon squad have waylaid her sister? No, they wouldn't have any idea how much she and Jessica knew–would they?

Still, Elizabeth's stomach churned like a cement mixer at the possibility she might have gotten her kid sister into some horrible fix. What had the two of them been thinking? She looked down and started rummaging in her shoulder bag for a cigarette. Yes, she'd promised Jess she'd lay off, but this was an emergency! Then Liz halted, spotting outside a blonde in a summer dress of raspberry swirls on creamy silk.

Snapping shut her bag, Liz moved to the street to intercept the blonde with, "What took you so darned long?"

Jessica quickly glanced around before quietly cautioning, "It's all good, Liz. Don't jinx us by attracting attention."

"Fine," Liz agreed, trying oh-so-hard to hide her nerves. "But what happened to you?"

"A melodrama of errors," Jess answered. "First, I almost forgot that I had to wait for this week's script to be delivered. Then, I thought I was followed, so I did some extra hiking to lose the guy. Don't go green on me. I said I lost him."

"Do they know you're in disguise?" Liz questioned tensely.

"No, I changed in a department store ladies' lounge. I could see the joker still watching for a brunette when I waltzed out as a blonde in a different outfit. I kept my eyes peeled, though, to make sure no one else followed me. What about you? Pick up any unwanted baggage?"

"No."

"You're absolutely sure?"

"Yes," Liz snapped a little too loudly, piquing the notice of a passerby.

"Take it easy, Liz," Jessica calmed her sister before directing her toward the building across the street. "No sense hanging around. The street looks clear to me, so let's get this over with."

Across the street, at the foot of the worn, rust-brown steps leading to the entranceway, Liz suddenly blurted, "Uh, oh."

"Uh oh what?" Jessica queried uneasily.

"Uh oh this is a rooming house. How do we know what room? There must be twelve names by the door. How do we know which one is the right one? What if he didn't use 'Evan Blair'? We don't know what his real name is, if he even used it."

Jessica started to answer, but she had nothing–at first: "No, wait. He wouldn't have sent us the key, along with these clues if he didn't think we could figure it out. Let's look at the names and see if any of them connect with his letter."

"All twelve of them?"

"It's not like plowing through *Forever Amber*."

"Actually, I thought *Amber* was pretty exciting."

"Argh!" Jessica growled at her sister then bounded up the stairs to look at the names.

Elizabeth followed cautiously, with piercing glances up and down the street. That twelve-year-old on the roller skates had lingered just a little too long as he sped down the sidewalk.

Liz no sooner joined Jessica, than her sister crowed, "Ha! Well, what do you know!"

"What? What?"

"Get a load of 001, Liz."

"'William Blue Buffalo'? An Indian? What do Indians have to do with Evan? Are you nuts, Jessica?"

"Nuts like a fox. That name pulls together words from a cummings poem: 'Buffalo Bill's /defunct' and 'how do you like your blueeyed boy/ Mister Death.' Get it?"

"You know that's just looney enough to be right. Okay, Sherlock, lead on."

"I only hope the rest of this caper is as easy for us," Jessica told her sister, not too confidently, as they went inside.

"Lovely," Liz sniffed in the gloom. "Mildew, must, liquor, burnt potatoes, and cabbage. I'm too much of a lady to comment on the rest."

Jessica was no more enchanted by their surroundings, but she was too busy getting her bearings to comment. To the left, stairs lead up. At the first landing, a telephone hung from the wall under a grimy light. On their floor, to the right, doors flanked them with numbers in varied states of mutilation. The word "Superintendent" was barely discernible on one. Maybe the Super wanted the tenants' memory of him to fade with the paint. The number under the title was "1." That gave Jessica pause.

She paced down the corridor, anxiously reading off the numbers to herself before returning to Elizabeth with, "This isn't good."

"What isn't good? We have the number and the key. All we have to do is go to the room and..."

"Therein lies the rub. This is the first floor and there's no 001, only 1 through 4. So where in blue blazes is the door that fits Blair's key?"

"Do I look like an architect for run-down firetraps?" Liz snapped. "What now?"

Gnawing her lipstick seemed to inspire Jessica. She decided, "We ask the Super."

Looking back at his door, Liz proposed, "You knock. You have better resistance to infections."

Jessica hesitated before rapping, wishing her gloves were asbestos mitts. No answer. She gave it another try. Nothing.

The building's outer door opened, admitting a gnarled old man. He eyed them suspiciously before demanding, "Whatcher want? Whatcher doin' here?"

"Um," was as eloquent as Liz could manage.

Jessica answered for them both, "We want to see the Super about a room."

The old man eyed them with disbelief and asked, "You two wanna room here?"

Finessing the truth, Jess explained: "Not us. A friend of ours was here on a bender and left something behind. But there's this woman in the neighborhood, and if she sees him, she'll make a terrible stink. We're his secretaries. If we don't find the room and get his things, we're out of jobs."

"Aah, why didn't ya say so in the first place? I'll get him up for you. He likes ta take a nip and nod off this time o'day."

The man went to the door and slammed it a battering tattoo with his palm, yelling, "Macrodotus, get up an' earn yer pay! Get out here! Ya don't have to fix anythin'!"

Liz remarked out the side of her mouth, "He has quite a set of pipes for a little guy."

Jessica nodded, grateful, nonetheless.

A guttural gripe emerged from within "1": "Knock it off, Shanahan! I'm comin! Keep your shirt on!"

The old man winked at the sisters and shuffled up the stairs before the Super opened the door. Jess and Liz made sure to offer him a grateful, "Thanks, Mr. Shanahan."

When the door opened, it was hardly Cary Grant who greeted them. Jessica managed not to cough openly at the waft of stale cigarette smoke accompanying the long, dough-jawed face of a fiftyish sort. His eyes were bleary, just slightly more from sleeping than drinking.

"What do you two want? I'm a hard-workin' guy. I need my rest."

"We're looking for a room," Jess explained.

"I'm full up. Go away."

He almost closed the door on them, but Jessica caught it, insisting, "We want to see 001."

The Super stopped, looked at her suspiciously, and said slowly, as if testing her, "It's taken."

"That's right, and the renter gave us the key," Jessica returned, pleasant but determined. "We just can't find it."

The Super's nosiness outweighed his laziness and suspicion. He threw them another question, "Yeah, how come he didn't tell you where?"

Jessica shrugged, "I don't know. Maybe he assumed we could find it. You know him: doesn't say much, only wants results."

The man ran a hand through his mess of greasy, probably brown, hair and said, "He never did say much. Kind of a wise guy when he did, but nothing you could pin him down on. Sometimes quoted poetry, for cripes sakes. Some character."

Liz took over: "That character wants us to pick up something in the room. Can you show us there?"

"I could." Not he *would*. He speculatively raised his chin and questioned, "You say you got the key?"

Liz smiled and fished the key out of her shoulder bag. Holding it up, she announced, "Right here."

The Super reached toward that key, but Jessica calmly pushed her sister's hand back and asserted, "We've got it, and as long as he's paying the rent, he decides who keeps it. He gave it to us for today."

Macrodotus rubbed the black and gray stubble on his chin, then gave his cheek a determined scratch before saying, "I only see him every so many months. How do I know what he's up to? Maybe it's no good?"

"Oh, we can assure you he's not doing anything he shouldn't right now," Jessica replied innocently. "But if you show us where the room is, we might fill you in as we go."

He narrowed his eyes, thinking, before he suggested, "I'd like you to fill me in on a president. Andy Jackson, yeah, Andy Jackson, written up with a picture and all in nice green ink."

"How about Alexander Hamilton?" Jessica bargained.

"Hamilton was never a president," Liz corrected.

Jessica gently whapped her sister with the back of her hand, then calmly took a ten-dollar bill from her wallet (Liz breathed an "Oh" of comprehension), and sweetly continued, "Another Alex Hamilton shows up *after* you take us to the room."

With that, Macrodotus sauntered out into the hall, in all the resplendence of faded dark pants and an aged undershirt, ingloriously topped by a vest that had also seen better days.

"Okay, follow me. It's no wonder you couldn't find 001. It's in the cellar."

"The cellar? I can't believe Evan lived in a cellar!" Liz let slip as they trotted after their lumbering guide.

"'Evan'? That his name?" the Super nonchalantly queried with a glance at Liz. "I coulda swore it was something different. I'll have to go back an' look at his mailbox. Not that he ever gets any mail."

Jess gave her sister a "nice going" look and ad libbed, "It's a nick name."

"Aah, to each his own. He paid up in advance. I heard he had this place years before I got here. I don't like to dig too much into tenants' business."

"You respect their privacy," Liz approved as they stopped at the cellar door.

"Yeah, well, I figure if the tenants forget I'm here, they won't always be botherin' me to fix stuff. Works pretty well. Old Shanahan, there, is pretty much the only one who knows me by name."

"Macrodotus, right?"

"Shhh, lady. Don't be spreadin' that around."

"Maybe *you* should be giving *us* pictures of presidents to keep us quiet," Liz archly observed.

"You know, it's pretty dark in that basement. Maybe you don't want to get so cute until you get what you want."

"Maybe we all had better think nice thoughts about Alexander Hamilton and shut up," Jess suggested. "The sooner we get to the room, the sooner you can go back to your apartment and rest, Mr. Macrodotus."

"You got a point, sister. He was a smart guy to hire you." He unlocked the door and pushed it open into darkness, turning back to remark, as he switched on an anemic overhead bulb, "I don't know what he was thinking when he hired the other one."

As he turned away, Jessica prevented Liz from pouncing. They followed Macrodotus down the shaky wooden stairs, as confident as if they were crossing a minefield. The bulb didn't much supplement the light eeking through the barred, grimy cellar windows. Jessica vaguely noticed the furnace to the right of the stairs, with archaic heating and plumbing hulking overhead. Macrodotus lumbered ahead of them across the dirt and cement floor, provoking a phantom scurry or two in the gloom by rodent tenants. With only an occasional battered box or suitcase littering the floor, at least there didn't seem to be any place for someone sinister to hide. At the far end, on the left, three steps led up to a door in a wall that cut off nearly half the cellar.

What made Jessica pause was the bulkhead entrance, near this other door, its lock swinging on a broken chain. Liz shot her a look that pierced the dimness with shared concern.

"Say, Macrodotus," Jessica questioned, "How safe is our boss's place? Anyone could get in through there." She tipped her head toward the bulkhead.

The Super brushed off Jessica's concerns, "Who'd want to break into this rat trap? You see anything down here worth stealing? Besides, the cellar and this apartment are locked up."

Jessica's and Liz's eyes exchanged the uneasy thought: what a snap for Mrs. Tewkesbury to have the room's lock picked. But they had no time to pursue that fear; they'd reached 001.

"After you, ladies," Macrodotus offered with a slight forward tilt of his shoulders, the closest he'd ever come to offering a bow.

Liz told their guide, "We have the key. We can take it from here."

"Not so fast, lady. You owe me something."

"Thanks a lot?"

"You can thank me with that saw buck you promised–after you let me in for a looksee."

"We'll pay you off, buddy," Jess coolly informed him, "but our boss pays the rent. That makes the room his, not your, private palace."

"And I'm bigger than both of you put together, so if I want to throw you out on your ... ears, it wouldn't be much trouble."

Before Liz's temper could reach critical mass, Jessica took charge, "Fine, fine. Take a look, but don't get in our way. Fair enough?"

"Okay by me," Macrodotus shrugged.

Jessica pushed Liz up the steps. Her sister fumbled a little, but finally got the door unlocked to admit them to Evan Blair's subterranean hideout. All three blinked. These ground-level windows above them were much cleaner than those in the rest of the cellar, letting in a surprising amount of light through their barred glass panes.

"Say, this ain't half bad," decided Macrodotus, surveying a good-sized studio, dusty but fairly bright, the books and furniture ordered as if someone had straightened up before stepping out–but never came back.

Liz pulled off her jacket, slipped it over her shoulder, and pronounced, "What I couldn't do with a Hoover in here."

"Herbert Hoover? What bill's he on? "

"You've got a real one-track mind, haven't you, Macrodotus?" Jess cracked, giving him a quick glance before speculatively surveying the apartment. In *her* mind, all that existed were drawers and nooks to be emptied, cushions to be turned over, and books to be shaken.

"Doesn't smell very appealing," Liz commented, wrinkling her nose and starting halfway down the three steps into the body of the apartment.

"I don't smell nothing,'" their low-brow Virgil shrugged.

Jess resisted the obvious cheap shot and observed, "The place doesn't seem to get much of an airing."

"Like I said, a few times over the past years or so I seen him sneak in an' out–who knows how often before I got here. You two know when's he comin' back?"

"I wouldn't expect him any time soon," Liz returned coolly, going to the couch in the room's center, continuing to look speculatively about.

"But he does want us to make sure his rent's up to date. He can get forgetful. That's why he has two secretaries," Jess smiled. "So how long is he paid up for?"

"Rest of the year. Like clockwork, Western Union wires the money in for the year. Don't you know that? You're his secretaries, aren't cha?"

"We're new," Liz smiled, turning gracefully to him. "We have to straighten out the mess his old one left. Now, don't we owe you something; something you can take back upstairs with you?"

"Huh? Oh, yeah. Which one of you has the rest of the dough?"

"My partner," Liz smiled.

"Thanks," Jess grumbled with narrowed eyes. "Here's the other ten, Mr. Macrodotus. Live it up."

"Sure you girls don't need no help down here? For a little extra somethin' I could do any dirty work you might come acrost. Youse girls are dressed awful nice for all this dust."

"No problem, Mr. Macrodotus," Liz assured him. "We packed some aprons. Be prepared is the secretary's motto."

"Yeah? I thought it was the Boy Scouts'."

"It was. We borrowed it 'cause we didn't want to get caught flat-footed when those Boy Scouts grew up and started chasing us around the desk," Liz returned.

"Yeah, makes sense," Macrodotus nodded. Jessica shook her head.

Macrodotus started through the door, saying, "If you need anything else..."

"We know, just call," Jessica finished, trying not to be too obvious about pushing him out the door.

He shook his head, "Nah, I was gonna say, 'Don't bother me.' You got your twenty bucks worth. I'm going back to ... rest."

With that, Jessica shut the door on the world outside Evan Blair's old hideaway. She faced her sister, who tossed her the key and said, "Lock it up. We don't want Mr. Macordotus sneaking in on us."

Jess nodded and complied. That done, she descended into the room and joined Liz, querying, "So, where do we begin?"

The sounds of kids and traffic clearly filtered in; no conversation outside the windows would be any secret from the Minton sisters. The reverse prospect prompted them to keep their voices down.

"Not a bad little hideout, is it?" Jessica considered. "Closet space over there in the far left corner, a Murphy bed, a table, a hot plate, a refrigerator, even a little sink. Think he left anything in the fridge?"

"If he had, we'd have gotten wind of it when we opened the door, kid."

"Yeah, sure," Jess nodded. "All right, let's get cracking, then! I'll take the desk and bookcase over there, to the left, and work my way around. You start from directly behind me and go around the room in the opposite direction. We can meet in the middle and then work inward."

Accompanied by some initial grousing about dust, dirt, splinters, and unnecessary wear and tear on their nylons, the Minton sisters went doggedly to work tapping, scraping, peering, and prying. Then Jessica stopped before a little rickety, sparsely populated bookcase and shook her head, "I'm not sure we'll find anything that will clear Larry. I mean, if we get a lead on the jade, that could help Lois, but Larry would still be in trouble over the gun."

"We don't have to find the jade itself, Jess," Liz contended. "All we need is evidence that Alanna *is* Betty to get leverage on her. I think Evan sent us here because he stashed some kind of insurance against that dame."

But Jessica had something more than Liz's conjectures on her mind as she took a closer look at the bookcase and announced, "Say, this looks interesting."

"What'd you find?" demanded Elizabeth. She rushed over to her sister, but what she saw only left her snorting, "Big deal. You got me keyed up over six measly books?"

"Six books, five of which are on gems or gem cutting, but number six," Jess shook the volume before her sister, "is by e. e. cummings."

"Him again," Liz observed curiously. "Does the book have any clues?"

"Keep your bobby pins in and give me a chance to look," Jessica remarked, flipping open the cover. She looked at the opening pages and thought: *Darn! No inscription.* Running her finger and eyes over the paper to detect an anomaly that might indicate something had been inserted, she commented, "I'm willing to bet if our chum or her playmates *were* here, a book of poetry would be the last thing they'd give a second look."

Perusing the table of contents, Jessica continued, "It's different from the book he left me, although some of the poems are the same. Say, take a gander at these funny pencil marks on some of the poems. Oh boy, here's 'Cambridge ladies' marked off in the index."

Jess eagerly flipped to the poem, then paused to ask, "Liz, what do you make of this? There's a date written in here: September 1935, the same year they arrested Evan and the Weisenthal gang, right? Say, a couple of pages are stuck together."

"The only ones?"

"Actually, yes. And if you look carefully, you can tell these pages aren't just uncut; they're actually re-glued!"

"You think he hid something in there, Jessica?"

Jess made a little *moue* before replying, "Well, not the jade. You could feel it. But it may be another clue. Quick, do you have a letter opener or something sharp I can use to slit the pages?"

Liz swiftly grabbed her bag and dug out her manicure kit, presenting it to Jessica with, "Try the cuticle snipper. The blades are sharp but tiny, so you won't cut whatever's inside."

Thanking her sister, Jessica drew on all her discipline to ignore Liz's hovering as she managed a tiny puncture at the ends of the pages by the binding. Carefully, Jess sliced her way forward, then down the front of the pages. Cautiously, she reached in with her long, manicured nails and extracted....

"Pictures," Liz breathed.

Two 4 ½" by 3 ½" photos from a Brownie. The resolution wasn't great, but the figures and faces were definitely recognizable. On one, the clothes and hair of the Asian man and a Caucasian woman in the picture said the 1930s; and, though the man's face was vaguely familiar, the woman's definitely was: Alanna Tewkesbury. The nose wasn't as delicate, and the hair hadn't yet enjoyed an expensive peroxide rinse, but you could clearly identify their nemesis.

"Bingo," Liz triumphed.

"More like 'bing,'" Jess corrected, flipping the photo over in search of any identifying writing. Nothing.

"What do you mean, Jessica? We have a ten-year-old photo of Alanna Tewkesbury with George Wong that we found in Evan Blair's apartment–an apartment Evan's letter gave us permission to enter." At Jessica's skeptical expression, Liz corrected, "Okay, roundabout permission. Still, here's an inarguable link between her and both guys! This proves Evan's story. And the best thing is it doesn't matter who found it. It's still a picture of the two of them, whether we're against Tewkesbury or not."

Jess put down the picture and pointed out, "Actually, Liz, this only proves Evan has a picture with Alanna in it back then. We don't know how Evan got it or for certain that her knowing George Wong definitively links her to theft of the jade. It's a base hit but not the whole ball game."

"Whose side are you on, anyway?" Liz groused, knowing her sister was right.

Jessica flipped the photo over once more. No, she hadn't missed anything. A disgusted sigh escaped her.

"What about this picture?" Liz insisted, tapping the other photograph: Evan Blair in someone's kitchen, with a tall serious man, the badge on his suit vest giving him away as a plainclothes detective.

"That's interesting," Jessica decided thoughtfully. "If we can find this guy..." Her words trailed off while she turned over the picture. As she started reading the name on the back, almost getting to an address, the voice of Eddie Kubek drifted through the windows from the obscure side street outside.

"You're sure this is the place, Mrs. Tewkesbury?"

Through a street-level window across the room, they saw two pairs of feet, one shiny black ankle-strapped, the other shod in men's shoes, equally shiny.

Jessica was grateful she and Liz had been shocked speechless. Perhaps they hadn't given themselves away! She was not grateful, however, for her sister's claw grip on her shoulder.

Carefully removing the hand, Jess glared at Elizabeth. Gratuitously, Liz put a finger to her lips, then cupped a hand to her ear. Jessica nodded but quietly pulled her sister into a crouch so that the desk shielded them from any eyes that might spy them through the windows.

"Okay Mrs. Tewkesbury, let me try and talk you out of goin' in there one last time. You don't want to risk someone seeing you here. We got a good thing going with you married up and all."

"How many times do I have to tell you that jade is worth the risk? We could lose everything if my friend left anything in there incriminating me. Anyway, no one's going to see us in this side street," she snapped, her voice and vocabulary far from the cultured lady she pretended to be. "Who'd see us going in through that bulkhead? A dump like this, they probably don't even have it locked up. Even if they did, you can get us in and out without anyone knowing."

"Yeah, maybe," Kubek grudgingly allowed, "but you searched the place seven years ago and didn't find anything."

"Don't be such a sap, Kubek. My friend's been back on the East Coast since our last visit. I'm betting that when he saw we'd tossed the place once and hadn't found anything, he thought we'd write it off. For all we know, he might even have stashed the jade here when he came back. Now quit wasting my time. Your job's to protect me from trouble–and you've fouled up royally today."

"Sorry, Mrs. Tewkesbury, but you're over-exaggerating. So Mickey and I got a little lost in Connecticut. So we got here a little late..."

"A little late? I have to be back for a big 'do' at eight o'clock! That doesn't leave much time to scour this dump. Inside. Now." Her tone was controlled but biting as January frost.

Jess and Liz exchanged terrified looks of "How the hell do we get out of here?!"

As the two sets of ominous footsteps moved to the back of the building, Liz looked at the narrow cellar windows.

"No dice, Liz," Jessica discouraged her. "Unless we can each drop about forty pounds in the next two minutes, we're not getting out that way."

Liz flared, "I'm not going to let them get me! Wait, the cellar! Maybe we can make it to behind the furnace or up the stairs..."

But they heard the bulkhead opening.

"No time, Liz," Jessica hissed, grabbing her purse and tossing Liz her shoulder bag.

"The closet," Liz softly declared, grabbing Jess's arm and dragging her across the room, all the while forcing them both into a crouch. "We might even overhear where they hid Larry's gun!"

"Don't you think they're going to open the closet when they search the apartment? And why are we crouching, Liz?"

"(b) so no one can see us if another of her mugs happens by and (a) we can hold on to the door together, so they think it's stuck."

"For crying out loud, Liz, the two of us can't hold off Eddie Kubek."

"You have a better idea?"

With nothing to offer, Jess let Liz shove her toward the closet. They were almost home when Jessica tore free, hissing, "The pictures! I forgot the pictures!"

She sprinted to snatch the two pictures from the desk–and the book, too! Oh, God Alanna and Kubek were just outside the door! Soon they'd be working the lock. With Liz frantically gesturing her home, Jessica made a mad dash for safety–and took a flyer!

The book seemed to sail in slow motion toward Liz, while the pictures fluttered gracefully to the floor

Outside the apartment, a voice questioned, "Did you hear something?"

Jessica found herself on the receiving end of a bum's rush into the closet, but not before she'd managed to snatch up the cummings book. Liz pulled the door shut, and the apartment door opened.

Through a crack in their door, Jessica spied Eddie Kubek enter first, tense against the wall, his body a shield for his boss. He was armed, and Jess's knees almost melted.

Kubek put away his gun and nodded an "all clear" over his shoulder. The grand lady paused only long enough to give the room her own once over. Jess gave their adversary a thorough once-over of her own: a black pill-box hat sitting elegantly atop blond hair that was pulled off her face and deftly styled into a sleek French roll. Over a black jersey, her suit was burnt orange, fitted to show off her figure: luscious and commanding. Those cold eyes. Jess found herself recalling a *National Geographic* story about rattlesnakes. No! She wouldn't give in to the willies! Focus on something else. That broach! That enormous swirl of diamonds and emeralds in a silver lily, every gem as hard as those eyes.

"Where do you want me to start?" Kubek grumbled.

Jess considered that Eddie didn't seem to relish tearing apart anything that couldn't scream or bleed.

She heard Mrs. Tewkesbury observe with superior irony. "My dear partner was never a fastidious housekeeper. He'd had maids to do that sort of business when he was growing up. Not like us, Eddie. Where's he now, with all that fancy upbringing?"

Hmm, were those words bitter or triumphant? How close partners had

Evan and this rattler in Lily Dashé been? Had Mr. Weisenthal had any clue?

Eddie was giving Alanna Tewkesbury one of those c'mon-don't-go-all-philosophical-on-me looks–except "philosophical" probably wasn't in his vocabulary. Finally, he answered her rhetorical question, obviously not clear on that concept, "He's dead, and we're in this stinking, damp cellar. Didn't you say we didn't have much time?"

"We'd have had more time if you and Mickey hadn't gotten lost."

"You wanted to take the back ways; you didn't want to use the chauffer–alls so no one would know about us coming up here."

"You know as well as I do keeping a low profile concerning my late, former 'partner' has been smart." Then she growled, almost to herself, "Although if I hadn't had to keep up appearances about being in Florida, we could have tossed this joint before today."

Jess felt Liz's hand tighten on her shoulder, both relishing the implications of Alanna's admission of knowing Evan Blair–but they both were equally frustrated that no one else was around to corroborate what they'd heard.

"Yeah, well, alls I know is if you were in such a hurry," he jerked a picture off the wall, flipped it over, then finished, "you'da had Mickey come in and help."

Kubek took out a knife, shot his boss a questioning look, and, at her approving nod, began carefully to slice the picture out of the frame, pick apart that frame, and probe for anything on the back of the picture. It was a nasty, sharp knife, and Jessica winced empathetically for the disemboweled picture and frame.

Examining the odds and ends on the desk, Tewkesbury seemed to be thinking out loud, "Mickey's checking up on the sisters. One went out of town. I don't like that."

Pausing in his skilled gutting of a cushion, Eddie assured her, "Look, Mrs. Tewkesbury, the older one went on a business trip. I checked up, and our guy tailed her to a southbound train out of Penn. We got someone else watching the actress's house."

"We haven't heard from him since we got on the road," Alanna snapped, pulling open a drawer and checking its contents. "I want to know exactly where those two are at all times. They can make trouble for me with their insinuations. It might not have turned out exactly as I planned, but I worked hard for all the perks that go along with being Mrs. Wilmington Tewkesbury. I'm never going back to being Betty Weisenthal. She's dead and so's anyone who wants to bring her back!"

She viciously shoved the drawer closed. Even Eddie started.

"Hey, Mrs. Tewkesbury, calm down. Those two are scared little rabbits. They won't do nothing as long as you got the murder gun. And that'll never change. You were really using your noggin, stashing it with Roarke at the Ballard. Nobody even knows that you rent that apartment with his name on the lease."

"Will you shut up, you damned fool! Don't even talk about it!"

The blow Alanna struck him resounded around the grimy little hell-hole, even jolting Jess and Liz. Kubek's eyes blazed for a moment, and his hand moved almost imperceptibly toward his pocketed knife. But Alanna Tewkesbury's expression caught and imprisoned him. The wolf's eyes sank under the gaze of the Medusa.

She smiled, a terrible little smile, before advising, "These are high stakes, Eddie. You'll be in hot water if the cops figure out we had a reason to kill 'Evan Blair.' Now, check the closet."

Those words swept Jessica like ice; she had no doubt of the like effect on her sister. Eddie Kubek moved toward the door. In that second, Liz's hand reached around Jess, gripping the doorknob. It wouldn't work. Jess knew it. Still, she added her strength to her sister's. Maybe they wouldn't be killed. After all, it was the middle of the day. People would hear guns or screams, right? If they suddenly turned up dead or missing, wouldn't that look suspicious for Mrs. Tewkesbury? Unless missing was read as taking a powder out of guilt. Oh God, why couldn't she see James just one more time?

"Say, what's this on the floor?"

The voice was Eddie's; that's all Jess could tell from this angle.

"Never mind trash. No wait, Eddie..."

"It's a picture, Mrs. Tewkesbury. Huh, darned lucky you said 'wait.' It's a shot of you with some Chinaman."

"What?"

"Some Chinese kid. Nice picture of you. You look good with the different hair, even in those outdated duds."

"Give me that!"

A pause, then Jess could hear the woman ruminating, "Hmmph. I'd forgotten that face, but I remember him. There were lots of faces like his."

"Chinamen?"

"No, sap, saps! I'd never played one like this, though. He believed me. Can you buy that? Usually, they thought they were conning me. It was quite a kick working over this one. Those Orientals aren't as inscrutable as everyone says."

Only fear of death kept Jess from kicking down the door and having at that fourteen-karat creep in high heels. Sensing Liz tense, Jess knew she was just as furious at the racial insult.

"Eddie, that haul was the biggest ever. I really pulled the wool over his eyes. Paul said it was my best job. Then the kid kills himself, so 'Mr. Main Line' has to grow himself a conscience and turn state's evidence on us."

"Good thing your inside man tipped you off," Kubek said as he continued to search. "He didn't get caught either, did he?"

"No, but he didn't get off completely. Too much suspicion to let him stay on the force, not enough to prosecute. He blew town, too, and got himself a new identity."

"Ain't you afraid you might run into your snitch, and he'll put the finger on you?"

"Oh, Eddie, I know exactly where he is–and believe me, he's in no position to take me down unless he wants to go down with me. Besides, the Chinaman wasn't the only one really stuck on me."

"I guess those Kodak guys are right, Mrs. Tewkesbury; pictures do bring back memories."

The tender moment was interrupted by a new voice: "Mrs. Tewkesbury, we got a problem."

"And what is that, Mickey?" Tewkesbury questioned, in a tone that made Jess glad she couldn't see the woman's face.

"Actually, it's more like three problems. Maybe not three problems. Maybe a problem and two glitches."

"Cut to the chase, Mickey!" his boss lady ordered.

"Which do you want first, the problem or the glitches? Okay, don't look at me like that. I'll work my way up. Our tail lost the Liz lady in Philly. Big station there. He checked into her appointment, but the secretary wouldn't say exactly where she was supposed to be."

"And the other sister?"

"She went into a ladies lounge in Bergdorf's, but he lost her coming out."

"Those are *glitches*?" Alanna snarled, before turning on Eddie, "What are *you* standing around for? Rip apart that damned closet! Snap to it..."

Jessica was too terrified to realize right away that the angry woman had abruptly gone silent. They all were silent, as if waiting. And in their silence, Jess could vaguely hear other voices, muffled by this door and the closed window. One of them sounded like, yes, it was: Macrodotus. He was arguing with someone. Had she heard the word "officer"?

There was scuffling in the room, and then the apartment door slammed hurriedly. Were she and Liz alone at last?

The sisters waited in the darkness a few moments before Jessica whispered, "Is it safe to get out?"

"Wait a minute, to be sure," Elizabeth softly warned.

That minute stretched out an eternity. No sound of Tewkesbury and company. Only the faint argument outside the window between Macrodotus and ... whom?

Liz swung open the door and practically had to shove her sister out. Jess's first impulse was to run screaming from the room. Bad idea. Not only undignified, but what if Alanna and her two minions hadn't left the cellar yet?

Thank God the apartment door was closed. There was a lull in Macrodotus's argument outside. Liz whispered in Jessica's ear, "Think they're gone? How 'bout we make like Jesse Owens and get the hell out of here?"

Macrodotus's voice suddenly boomed through the glass, "You cops got no respect for us taxpayers!"

Her eyes flying to the window, Jess noted one pair of pants up there was uniform blues! Macrodotus *had* called the police. Momentarily, she felt safe, even relieved, but then she softly gasped, "Shoot, Liz! Macrodotus heard Alanna and her goons tearing this place to shreds and called the cops. If he brings that officer down here, it will look as if we did this and..."

"The last thing we want is to explain what we're doing here to the *police*, especially after that cock and bull story we gave Macrodotus," Liz finished in tones equally muted, equally anxious.

"Fine, Sullivan! I'll handle it myself! Who needs you cops, anyway? Go ahead, take a hike," came through the window.

To their relief, the women saw Macrodotus walking off towards the front of the building, while the cop went the other way.

Liz breathed, "He's not coming in!"

"Maybe not the cop, but our lovable super probably is. I've got the book and the pictures. Let's scram," Jessica urged, already starting for the door.

"Not the pictures," Liz contradicted, grabbing Jess by the arm. "You dropped them when you fell. Eddie Kubek nabbed that snapshot of Alanna in her Betty days with George Wong! The best evidence to date and you lost it!" Now using her grip on Jess's arm to propel her forward, Elizabeth ordered shakily, "C'mon, let's get out of here before Macrodutus catches us and does God knows what to us for this mess!"

"No, wait, Liz. There were *two* pictures." Jessica yanked herself free to search where she'd last seen the photos float to earth. "Kubek didn't say anything about the other one. It must still be here. Yes, there!"

Jessica fairly pounced on the Kodak, grinning as she held it up and claimed, "This is still useful evidence."

"Better than a shot of the Black Widow with a robbery victim?" Liz questioned as they hurried back across the apartment.

"Well, I think the picture of Evan and the man had a name and address on the back. I only saw it for a second, but it just may lead us to someone who knew the case," Jessica enthused as she raced her sister up the steps, wishing she had time to confirm her hopes with a peek.

Jess reached for the doorknob, hoping to take a quick look outside to ensure Alanna and company weren't around, but that plan and the doorknob were taken entirely out of her hands.

The door swung open. Jessica and Liz jumped back, and Macrodotus gave them both a skeptical look before inquiring, "Find what you were looking for girls?"

Chapter Fifteen

Momentarily, the sisters stood flummoxed, but Liz recovered first and nonchalantly replied amidst the carnage, "Why yes we did find it! How kind of you to ask. So, we'll just be on our way." Starting forward, almost dragging Jessica, she finished, "Have a lovely nap–and do remember to buy bonds."

"Hold it right there," he ordered. "You two did quite a job here!"

Nervously, carefully, Jess and Liz backed down the steps, arms defensively linked. Hoping to break the tension, Liz offered, "I suppose you'd like us to tidy up?"

Macrodotus shocked them both by bursting into a belly laugh.

The women exchanged bewildered glances, but Macrodotus grabbed their attention with, "I know you didn't do this. It was that big blonde and her goons. I'm just havin' some fun here."

Jess and Liz laughed nervously, with Liz commenting, "Good one. Well, we'll see you!"

With one step, Macrodotus blocked her and smiled, not exactly warmly, "Not so fast. Let's chat. Lucky for you, I, ah, shall we say 'lingered inconspicuously' the other side of the furnace–just in case you girls needed me."

Jess sarcastically decided, *How thoughtful.*

"So when's that crew blew in through the bulkhead, I laid low, just to see what would shake down. You didn't call for help, but I couldn't hear you when I was listening to them talkin', so I figured you was hidin'. I didn't like what I did hear, so I took off to grab the beat cop, my pal Sullivan, before that crew found you. An' I made sure him and me had a loud argument, so's they could hear and get the idea blowin' would be in their best interest. Then I got rid of Sullivan as soon as I figured they had time enough to hightail it. But I'll tell you right now, I don't want no beef with them. So if anyone asks, I couldn't identify them if I tried."

"Very thoughtful of you," Liz observed suspiciously.

"Yeah, I thought you'd be appreciative." He smiled and held out his palm.

"Looks like Alexander Hamilton is lonely for more friends," Liz shot out the side of her mouth to Jessica.

Jess nodded, but before Liz could put her on the hook for another palm greasing, she told Macrodotus, "Talk to my sister. She's the one with the expense account."

Jessica had collapsed, exhausted onto her couch: eyes shut, blonde wig on her lap. Two such brutal days in a row was more than General Patton could take! Crouched on the hassock, Dusty was watching her–no, watched the wig, probably thinking that some kind of crazy, jumped-up Persian had invaded her territory. At least she wasn't growling at it anymore.

In the study, Liz was fixing highballs for both of them. Getting the drinks should have been Jessica's job. It was her apartment. But Liz had insisted that her baby sister looked bushed and needed to be pampered. The baby sister figured Liz's thoughtfulness was really an attempt to soften her enough, so she'd agree not to let the police in on what they knew just yet.

The joke was on Liz. True, Jessica wanted to level with McLaughlan and wash her hands of the business, but then what would happen? They had heard Alanna Tewkesbury admit she was Betty Weisenthal. Hearsay evidence at best, and even less credible coming from two people vocal about their antipathy to her. And how hard would it be for the woman to come up with an alibi undercutting their claim? Macrodotus had pointedly insisted he'd never stick his neck out to back them up.

Still, they had discovered where the gun was hidden. With some guy named Roarke at the Ballard–mostly likely the Ballard Arms on 56th Street. Yet telling the police where to nab a gun that belonged to Larry would not exactly clear Mr. Sanders and put the blame on Mrs. Tewkesbury.

And wasn't it just too cruel of fate to tell them where they could find the weapon Tewkesbury was holding against them but not how they could manage to get at it!? Irritably, Jessica flipped the wig off her lap and onto the couch. Dusty gave a startled hiss and threateningly arched her back. Then, realizing the hairy monster no actual threat, her arch morphed into a nonchalant stretch and back to a crouch, enacting the sentiment, "*I* wasn't scared. I was going to move anyway."

"I know how you feel, pal," Jessica wearily concurred, leaning forward to retrieve from the coffee table the picture they'd salvaged. Re-examining it for the thousandth time, she concluded, *Nope, nothing different*. Still only the name "John" and a number 75, part of what was likely an address. The rest was one great big, beautiful smudge from Eddie Kubek's shoes. Big help that!

But there had been a picture of Betty/Alanna with George Wong, a picture Eddie Kubek had waltzed off with. On the train back, Liz had revealed that loss was doubly devastating. She'd spotted on Betty Weisenthal's coat the same elaborate pin they'd seen on Alanna while they hid in the closet. For the thousandth time, Jess wanted to kick herself for losing that picture.

The ringing phone interrupted those frustrated cogitations.

Liz approached with the drinks, grumbling, "Swell. Who could that be? Oh my gosh! I hope it's not Larry. We haven't figured out what to tell him!"

Jessica was startled speechless by the caller's identity: "It's Lois! I must see you right away! Is Elizabeth there? I need to talk to her, too!"

"Yes, Lois, Liz is here. What's wrong? You sound so upset," Jessica worried over the line. They hadn't seen her all week and now this anxious desire to tell them something?

Lois was speaking again, "I'll be right there. I can't keep this in any longer. It's been eating me alive all week, about Evan Blair. I'll be right over!"

"Lois..." Too late. The line clicked dead on Jessica's confusion.

"What did she say?!" demanded Liz, startling Dusty into jumping down and scurrying under the couch.

"Liz, she wants to come over and talk to us. About *Evan*." Growing hopeful, Jess suggested, "Do you think the lawyers contacted her? Would they have been able to retrieve the jade this soon?"

"I don't know, kid," Liz admitted, pensively tapping a finger on her upper lip. "Did she sound happy? Excited?"

Jessica sat back, not pleased, and decided, "Excited but not really happy. She said something had been 'eating her.' That doesn't sound like a girl whose family honor had just been resuscitated."

"No," Liz conjectured. "More like someone who's feeling guilty. But why would Lois feel guilty, especially concerning Evan. *He* did *her* wrong."

Jessica had no answer. So the two sisters sweated it out until an anxiously ringing doorbell announced that answers to their fraught questions were at hand. The Lois Wong on whom Jessica opened the door was a far cry from the supremely capable, dry-witted woman she knew. Instead, they saw a strained, pale face, ghostly in contrast to black hair and trench coat. Lois's haunted eyes gave Jess pause before she finally urged, "Oh, Lois, please come in."

"Goodness, you look terrible," Liz less than tactfully compassionated.

The usually mordant Lois, oblivious to Liz's tactlessness, only said, "Thank God you're both here."

Taking her friend's arm, after grimacing disapprovingly at Liz, Jess guided Lois, saying, "Let's go to the living room, where you can sit down and get yourself together, Lois."

"All right," Lois agreed, leaning on Jessica. "I'm sorry for keeping this from you, but I must tell you what I know about Evan Blair and his connection to my brother and the jade."

"Ah!" Liz crowed, relieved, even delighted. "So the letter did go out! The lawyers were able to act on it already! This is great!"

Lois stopped dead in her tracks and stared at Liz before finally quizzing her, "Letter? What letter? What lawyers? What are you talking about, Liz? What's this got to do with my brother and Blair?"

Jessica gave her sister a look of "Now, you've really put your foot in it!" Still, Lois was demanding answers: answers that she deserved. Which raised the unsettling question: if Lois didn't know about Evan's letter attempting restitution, exactly what did she want to tell them about Evan and George Wong?

"I'm waiting, Elizabeth," Lois demanded, for the moment more her old take-charge self.

Elizabeth plunged forward, "Okay. Maybe you'd better sit down. Maybe we'd all better sit down. I don't know which one of us has the story that's doozier..."

Jessica made an impatient reeling motion with her finger, and Liz cut to the chase, "Lois, last Sunday when I met Evan in our offices, he came clean with me about his past with the Weisenthal gang and how your brother's case was one of the last jobs they pulled. But at that point, you already knew who he was, didn't you? You saw him in his office Friday, and that's why you took off. I just don't understand why you didn't tell us. Jess and I would have been there for you to lean on."

"I couldn't say anything at first. I was in shock, and I wasn't completely sure it was the same man. After all, it was ten years ago," Lois explained, taking the chair next to the couch, "Then, I was so angry, remembering..."

"Lois, I wish I could have told you this earlier," Elizabeth tried to comfort her friend. "Evan told me that last night that he was going to send an anonymous letter to our lawyers clearing your family name and telling them how to retrieve the jade..."

Jessica would have sworn that Lois couldn't have gone any paler than when she'd come in, but her friend's reaction to Liz proved her wrong. Then Lois burst out, "Oh, no! No! Then he wasn't lying! After all those dreadful things I said to him, he *was* truly trying to square things–and I left him there to die!"

Now it was the Minton sisters' turn to go pale and speechless. Jess stopped nervously bouncing the wig on her lap.

Jessica spoke first, "Lois, you saw Evan Blair that last night? But you told the police that you were with Iris! You both lied?"

Lois shook her head, "Not Iris. I'd insisted on taking the couch to make slipping out easier. After Liz announced she was going to see Blair, I'd already made up my mind to take a chance he'd still be in his office. I hoped that I could find a way to sneak in–bobby pin-pick the lock, maybe. I don't know. I was desperate. I *had* to know for sure that he was the same man who'd ruined my family. And, Liz, I had to know who he really was to warn you. I was afraid he was up to no good, even if he seemed to be leaving you the business. Fortunately, Iris snores like a bulldog with sinus trouble, so she never heard me leave."

"Wait a minute!" Liz demanded, shocked. "You're telling us that you saw Evan Blair the night he was murdered? After I was there?" A pause as multiple conjectures roiled in her brain. "Lois, what happened between you two?"

Jessica held her breath, awaiting Lois Wong's answer. Exactly why had she needed to give the police a fake alibi? Why had Lois been afraid to face her and Liz since that fateful meeting? How maddened with anger and resentment had Lois been in confronting Evan Blair? A truly dreadful possibility assailed her.

"It wasn't pretty," their friend admitted. "As I told you, I had to know for certain if this was the same man. I'd only seen him a few times in court. I won't even give you the name I knew him under. I doubt it was his real one. But, damn it all, it was the same man, and it seemed that every iota of my fury ten years ago took possession of me!"

Jess and Liz sucked in their breaths. Dusty, who had finally ventured out from under the couch, ducked right back.

Lois continued, "I confronted him about 1:30, apparently sometime after you had gone. He was speechless when he saw me. I let him have it right off the bat."

Lois's words were hard and cold, moving Jess to glance at her sister as Liz repeated nervously, "Let him *have* it? How?"

Remorseful, Lois explained, "There was a gun on his desk, near me. I grabbed it and pointed it at him. Then I told him what I thought about him. I called him every name in the book; 'murderer' was the nicest one. I let him know that I wanted to destroy him. Take away everything he cherished, the way he'd done to my family."

"And then ... ?" Liz gulped, her heart sinking that clearing Larry would not lead to Alanna Tewkesbury but straight to her friend.

"He didn't beg; he didn't plead. He said I wasn't the first person that night who'd wanted to plug him, but I was probably the one who least deserved the consequences. He *seemed* to really mean it. That floored me. I put the gun down. I still hated him. He did start to tell me something about being on the level, trying to square old accounts. That's when I really let him have it."

"With the gun?" Liz breathed.

Lois scowled at Liz, then set her straight, "No, of course not. I couldn't commit murder. But I could let him know what he had done–all the lives he'd wasted. He couldn't give me back the ones I loved. But he was right; he wasn't worth destroying my mother or my humanity for. I left."

"So, he *was* still alive when you left?" Jessica pressed.

"Yes, yes he was–and I wasn't the only one to see him that night. I got to your main office, Liz, and managed to pick the lock with a hairpin. I slipped in and was startled to hear voices in Evan Blair's office, arguing behind the closed door. Someone moved to open the door and look into the outer office, so I ducked behind Ginger's desk. Even though they couldn't see me, I could see Mrs. Tewkesbury and Eddie Kubek in there making some ugly threats against Blair. I was frightened but not frightened out of wanting to confront that man for what he'd done to my family."

"What?" Jess and Liz burst out in unison. Liz added, "Lois, you don't know what a wonderful gift you've given us. Alanna is actually Betty Weisenthal, one of the gang that stole the jade. She's the woman who played your brother! I know from Evan, and he also said that she had recognized him and was aching to kill him. You just blew her Florida alibi sky high! This is your chance to right the score for your family and bring a murderer to justice!"

"Except for one little messy detail," Jessica quietly pointed out, referring to the gun.

"We can work that out," Liz countered testily. "We'll find a way. What matters is that Lois has just given us proof positive that Alanna was at the scene of the crime!"

"But Alanna wasn't around when Lois confronted Evan afterwards," Jessica corrected, not happy to be right. "That makes Lois the last person to see him alive. Lois, that's why you kept this to yourself, isn't it? Self-incrimination?"

Lois answered reluctantly, "That's part of the reason, Jessica. There's more to the story. Those two did leave before I confronted Evan Blair, and you're not going to like the reason why. Someone else came into the main office, while I was still hidden, and made a noise, bumping into something in the dark. I could hear those two hurry out through Liz's office. Probably they kept going through the dressing rooms and out of the offices altogether from there, though I never actually saw them leave the building. I stayed hidden; the one who came in, he didn't know I was there."

"He?" Liz repeated shakily, not having difficulty guessing that "he" was....

"Larry," Lois sadly revealed. "I saw Larry Sanders go in. It wasn't for long, but they exchanged angry words, and it sounded as if he exited the same way as Tewkesbury and her gunsel. So, I figured it was my turn at bat, and I was damned determined to take it before anyone else jumped the line." The "humor" in Lois's words was cold and biting. Then, remembering to whom she was speaking, she sadly offered Liz, "I didn't see any more of Larry at the office. I can't imagine that he would hang around, but I'm sorry that I can't testify that I actually saw him leave the building."

"That certainly takes the ever-lovin' cake," Jessica exhaled, flipping her wig onto Liz's lap in disgust.

Liz barely noticed the hairpiece, chafing in anger and disbelief, "He lied to me. Larry never told me he was there. He must have followed me there! Or been waiting for me, checking up on me!"

"Technically, Larry just didn't tell you. When you do the same thing, you claim it's not exactly lying," Jessica corrected her sister. "However, I'll grant you that he ought to have been more straightforward."

"And not checking up on me!" Liz steamed.

"Well, maybe he was just worried about you," Jessica offered, not entirely convinced, herself.

"We're getting off the track," Lois warned. "The point is that I can't swear he wasn't still somewhere in the building when I left. Innocent as I'm sure he is, Larry has an alibi as shaky as mine. "

"Shakier," Jessica surmised.

Lois gave her a "How so?" look, and Jessica explained, "Alanna Tewkesbury has a gun, stolen from Larry, that she claims is the murder weapon, and she's holding it over our heads to keep us quiet. It may even be the one you saw in Evan's office. If we aren't good little girls, she's going to give the police an early Christmas present: suspect and murder weapon all tied up nice and neat. Of course, your handling the gun probably put some prints on it, so now you're in jeopardy, too. Swell, isn't it? The only person who could place Alanna at the scene of the crime would have to incriminate herself and Larry to do so."

"This is awful," Lois groaned.

"It gets better," Jessica continued. "Thanks to a coded letter that Evan did manage to mail, we went to an apartment in Lowell where we found a picture of Alanna with your brother, and she was wearing a pin in the picture just like the one she had on in the apartment! Unfortunately, I dropped it when we rushed to hide because (Surprise! Surprise!) Alanna and her ape, who knew about the apartment, had to pick the same day as us to search it. The final jewel in our crown of thorns was when they came across the picture and took it."

"They didn't find you, did they?" Lois questioned, alarmed.

"We're still here, aren't we?" Jessica answered.

"But it's not *all* bad," Liz insisted, "First of all, you said you didn't actually see Alanna leave the building any more than you did Larry. Maybe she and Kubek hid out in the dressing rooms or my office and came back to finish off Evan once you'd left. And there's more. We still know the apartment where the gun is hidden, and we did find this snapshot of Evan with some cop. We can't make out much of the information on the back, but maybe you can recognize him, Lois, from the trial."

Lois took the picture, hopefully, but shook her head, "No. I don't remember seeing this guy. I think your best bet is to get that gun. Anything you dredge up on the past will only inflame that Tewkesbury woman, unless you have something ironclad to hold against her. If you know where the gun is hidden..."

"Knowing and getting are two different issues," Jessica corrected.

"A maid could get in. Every hotel has maids to clean rooms," Lois posited. "And if the apartment building is serviced by my company..."

"The Ballard Arms?" Elizabeth queried hopefully.

Lois smiled, "Looks like we're in business, ladies. I'll just have to check which day we're supposed to clean in there. We don't want to arouse any suspicion by jumping the schedule."

"But we can't send someone else to do our dirty work, so to speak," Jessica protested. "It could be dangerous."

"We wouldn't have to send in one of Lois's girls if one of us were disguised as a maid," Elizabeth suggested.

"Which one of us?" demanded Jessica suspiciously.

Liz shrugged, but began to twirl the blond wig on her finger, before looking straight at Jessica.

Jess was on her feet, stalking away, "No, no way! No dice! Uh, uh!" Then she stopped and pointed out, "The best person I know for both cleaning detail, and snooping, is *you*, Liz."

Sweetly smiling, Elizabeth countered, "I'm much too imperious for the part–and parts do require great actresses–a woman who can transform herself."

Jessica pointed at the wig and suggested sourly, "How about if we plop Mrs. Merkin there on Larry's head, pad him up in the right places, and stick a uniform on him? It's his after-hours chat with Evan that got us into this fix in the first place."

"Larry can't know anything about this plan until after we've pulled it off. He'd go to the chair before he'd let us go through with it. I won't have that," Liz insisted.

Jessica scowled. The whole plan was daffy. But this wasn't just a case of Tewkesbury literally getting away with murder, even of setting things right for Lois. Larry *could* get the death sentence. And even if they did play ball with Alanna Tewkesbury now, what would prevent that dame with an iceberg for a heart from pulling a fast one on them later?

"Larry's not going to have to take the fall," Jessica relented. "But you can get yourself another girl to play Nancy Drew for you. I'm not about to poke my nose into that nest of rattlers. There is absolutely no way I'm going into that apartment. Hell will freeze over first!"

Chapter Sixteen

Wednesday, May 30

The numbers on the elevator panel above the door flashed: basement, one, two, three, four–racing up to nine. Jessica Minton turned her eyes to the room-cleaning cart in front of her, thinking, *Sonja Heine must be doing figure eights in hell about now.*

Service elevators didn't merit an operator at the Ballard Arms. Her only spark of sunshine was having the car to herself. An extremely dim spark. The shiny panel reflected back the image of a plain girl in a black maid's uniform: no makeup, hair imprisoned in a bun, and the grumpiest of expressions. The last detail wasn't acting.

The elevator stopped. Jessica said a quick prayer, took a metaphorical whip and chair to the demons raging in her stomach, then hit the "Door Open" button and pushed her cart into the corridor.

The Ballard Arms was nice. Certainly not as exclusive as the Tewkesbury digs at the Waldorf Towers, but maybe that was the point. Who would expect Alanna to hide herself or anything valuable here? Pushing the cart down the corridor, looking for 912, Jessica shaped her expression into that of a little maid who scooted in and out, too mousey to attract notice.

She did slip out of character long enough to check her watch: 10:32. Keeping track of time was vital for a dead serious reason: Jack Roarke. He seldom went out, good little watchdog that he was, but he liked to take off every Wednesday from 10:30 to 12:00. Lois had tipped them off, pointing out that only she and her contact in hotel management knew about this predilection. Roarke had paid a handy sum to keep his "employer" in the dark. No one knew why or cared because this was the only margin of time they could send in a maid without her having to hotfoot it out of his clutches. Thank God for Roarke's overactive libido and Alanna Tewkesbury's having the same trouble getting good help as everyone else during the war.

So, here was 912. Jess knocked and squeaked out, "Maid service," relieved that this should just be a formality before she whipped out her passkey and let herself in. What she wouldn't have given to have James here for support–as if he would have encouraged her to get herself into this mess! A dog yapped within, and Jess prayed it wasn't a Dachshund. It'd snap onto her ankle, and she'd never get free!

No answer, aside from the yapping pup. Quick glances up and down the corridor, then Jess had the key in the lock. Before she could even turn it, though, the door opened, confronting her with a tall, dark-haired, expensively suited man who would have been handsome, except that his eyes were mean. Don Ameche as a Nazi.

"Come in. Hurry up, girlie. You're not going to do much cleaning standing out there."

This could only be Jack Roarke. What in blue blazes was he doing here? Feeling like a fly blundering into the spider's web and having no idea of what to do other than wing it, Jessica turned around and pulled her cart into the room. Instinctively, she glanced over her shoulder to confirm her suspicion that Mr. Roarke was sizing up her caboose in ways that would normally have elicited a sharp crack from her–verbal or physical. But Larry's freedom and her safety depended on her staying in character. Jess ducked her head down, vaguely aware of the dog now impatiently barking rather than yapping behind one of the doors in the apartment. Roarke closed the door. Alone together. Lovely.

A woman's voice from another room startled Jessica. Could it be Alanna, herself? What had she walked into?! The little dog kept barking.

"Lucky for you my company's leaving, doll," Roarke fired off, preoccupied with one of the rooms down the corridor to their left.

Just before ducking her head down into the side of her cart, Jess caught a glimpse of a blonde coiffure, high cheekbones, striking black hat, and matching satins that clung in places most pleasing to the likes of Mr. Roarke.

"I really have to leave now, Jack. Too many appointments, darling. Oh, what's this?"

Jessica straightened. Being referred to as "this" was not exactly her cup of tea, but she was relieved that the voice did not belong to her arch nemesis. Nevertheless, Jess had to draw deeply on reservoirs of self-restraint not to sling a few disparaging pronouns of her own.

"Nothing to worry about, honey. Sorry, I couldn't meet you like usual, but I have to stick around. Expecting an important call."

Jessica surreptitiously studied the two on either side of her, noting Roarke had been careful not to let slip that the apartment wasn't his. She was willing to bet that the call had been to ensure he was faithfully baby-sitting the darling little .38. Even so, he wasn't letting it interfere with his love life. Fine with Jess. This nine-foot-tall blonde (give or take a yard or two with that hat) was just the distraction she needed. Who would look at a plain-Jane when he had Miss High-Pockets to play footsie with?

"Something funny, mouse?"

Roarke's tone wasn't suspicious, but it wasn't nice.

"No, no, sir," Jess lowered her eyes, kicking herself for having slipped out of character.

"Then wipe the smile off your face and do what you came here for."

"Yes, sir."

Playing meek, Jess silently had the last laugh of: *Son, I'm only too glad to reclaim Larry's gun and put you in the worst kind of Mulligan Stew with your boss!*

Jess maneuvered the cart to head down the corridor to the bedrooms, but Roarke halted her with, "Not the bedrooms. Do the kitchen first–and watch out for the dog."

As if on cue, the barking recommenced.

Pushing her cart toward the kitchen, Jess could hear Roarke sweet-talking his doll: "Baby, you got appointments to keep, remember? Let me give you a sendoff that'll keep you in the pink till the next time. We made some beautiful music together, didn't we?"

Her back to the couple, Jess mimed a gag. She also concluded that Tewkesbury really knew how to set up her flunkies. It was one heck of an apartment: bright, with a white-walled living room that stretched around her. Sliders led to a balcony across from the front door, showcasing a beautiful cityscape–and an even more beautiful steak and egg breakfast set out on the balcony. A wolf like Roarke needed his protein.

Unexpectedly, the kitchen door burst open and out charged a fierce, black Scottie. Jess found herself standing on a chair, with the Scottie dancing and yapping around her like the Sioux circling Custer.

"You're not going to do a hell of a lot of cleaning up there."

"Does he bite?" Jessica gulped.

Maybe this Scottie was a dead ringer for the President's Fala, but he was behaving more like a passel of Nazis. The dog was small, but Jess knew from the Daxies her sister had once owned that canine fierceness was often inversely proportionate to size.

Roarke glanced at his watch, scowled, then strode forward, ordering, "Hey you, mutt, Jamie, you mutt! Get back there!"

Seeing Roarke was ready to land a kick, Jess forgot the dangers of miniscule canines and jumped down, coming between him and Jamie–taking a blow meant for the dog, even though Roarke caught himself and pulled back before connecting with her shin.

"Jeez!" she cursed, limping over to rest on the couch. Jamie, appreciating her protection, now bounced worriedly and tried to lick Jess's face or hand as she checked her shin.

"Now, what'd you want to get in my way like that for?" Roarke groused, then checked his watch again.

"What do you want to kick your own, well anyone's, dog for?" Jessica couldn't help retorting. Maybe it was out of character, but, for Pete's sake, kicking a dog?! Jamie nuzzled against her arm, and she paused from rubbing her injury long enough to give him a reassuring pat.

"What, that mutt? Mine? If I had a dog, it wouldn't be a runt like that..."

Jamie growled.

"Yeah, I mean you. A friend got tired of having him around and dumped him on me. Wouldn't drop him in the river 'cause he's an 'investment.' Can you believe a squirt like that is worth five-hundred dollars? Blue-blood Scotch Terrier they say. Even has a human name, James Stewart. Beats me, though, why anyone names a Scottish dog after an American actor."

"Especially such a tall one," Jessica agreed, the soul of innocence. A "mouse" wouldn't have been able to explain that the dog was probably James *Stuart* VI, named after a Scottish monarch rather than an American MGM star.

"Yeah, well, I don't have time for jawboning. I have an appointment coming."

"Another one?"

That slipped out. It was damned hard to stay in meek character with such a louse.

"Are you getting wise with me, mouse?" He took one menacing step forward, and Jamie growled protectively.

Jessica put a hand on Jamie's furry black back. Roarke, in spite of his earlier scorn, thought better of getting in the range of the canine's canines.

"Just get to work. Never mind the kitchen. I need my bedroom done, pronto. It's the first door on the left, back down the passage there. Then I want you out of here."

"Yes, sir."

Jessica was on her feet, shaking out her limp as she scurried past Roarke.

He called after her, "I'm going to finish my breakfast, so don't bother me."

Jess only thought, *Brother, you'll need that steak with your schedule.*

If he was in this much of a hurry to get rid of her, she didn't have much time. And what if the next "guest" was her nemesis? That froze Jess as she hit the juncture of the living room and the passage. The Scottie had followed and now eyed her quizzically. Where should she look first?

"One more thing, mouse," Roarke's voice preceded him as he approached.

Jessica turned and offered a timid, "Yes, sir?"

"Stay out of the master bedroom."

"But my boss wants me to be thorough. I could lose my job..."

"No one's using it. Its john's on the fritz. You do what I tell you. Go only where I tell you. Stay out of that room at the end of the hall. Now hop to it."

He returned to his steak and eggs before Jess could finish nodding.

Silently, Jess thanked Jack Roarke for his unintentional tip-off. She'd give 2-1 odds that he wasn't only worried about tidying up for the next cutie on his dance card when he told her to concentrate solely on his room. If he didn't want her in the master bedroom, that was exactly where she was going! The Scottie trotted merrily after her.

One glance behind her as she pushed the cart down the corridor. Out on the balcony, Roarke couldn't see a bit of what Jess was up to, and he'd closed the slider doors. Great. But to give herself some cover, Jessica pushed her cart into the room Roarke had pointed out as his. Sheets, pillows, bedspread–sheesh, it had been a blitz in here! He probably needed two steaks, no, the whole bull!

Jessica glanced over her shoulder. How much time did she have? Much as the thought gave her the creeps, she probably ought to at least change the sheets in case Roarke checked up on her.

With a snort and a jingle of his dog tags, Jamie was up in the middle of the bed. After a quick root through the whirled and twisted sheets, he playfully "whoofed" at her.

"C'mon, Jamie, get out of there before your distemper shot gives out."

Jamie's tail waggled. Jessica smiled and turned back to the cart to grab a pair of rubber cleaning gloves. A quick glance around confirmed they were still alone, and she whispered conspiratorially to the Scottie, "No sense in leaving any prints."

Moving past the cart, Jess thought better and turned back, deciding she'd better do a quick, cursory cleanup to make herself look legit. Now she made a swift reconnoiter of the corridor. Yup, Roarke was still preoccupied with rebuilding his strength for his next hand-to-hand (amongst other things) encounter. Thank God the carpet muffled her nervous footfalls. The doors of the master bedroom loomed close. What if they were locked?

The doorknob was under her hand and with a determined push, open sesame! All right! Alanna must have thought that a twenty-four-hour guard would be enough to keep her dirty little bargaining chip safe. But she hadn't reckoned on the "in" that Lois's business gave them or on Roarke's libido double-crossing her. Slipping inside, Jessica started to close the doors behind her, only to see Jamie eyeing her quizzically from the other bedroom. With a silencing finger to her lips, Jess closed the door on the little Scottie.

Now she turned to face the boudoir stretching around her. Gorgeous! Pale mauve walls, white furniture, enormous king-sized bed with surging, sculptured scallop-shell headboard almost directly in front of her. To the bed's right, a frosted-glass door led to the bath. The room bathed her in mauve ambience of walls, spread, and light filtering through curtains draping floor to ceiling windows on the left.

A tentative step brought Jessica close to the vanity, along the right wall, about half-way down the room. That was when she heard the door slowly creak open behind her.

Jess whirled, backing into the vanity, to face–no one?

"Woof!"

Having squeezed through the doorway, Jamie dropped a rubber toy before him and wagged his tail expectantly. He nuzzled the ball toward Jessica, then expelled a hopeful, "Woof."

Relieved, Jess sank onto the vanity's chair and put a finger to her lips, before sighing, "Jamie, you're going to be the death of me yet."

The pup nuzzled his toy toward her again and started to bark; but, before he could, Jessica got up and silenced him by tossing the toy toward the window. Jamie was soon gnawing on his prize, all around pleased at last to be back in the company of someone who didn't consider him a general annoyance. That left Jessica to make her next move: actually looking for the gun. But not for long.

"Rfff! Ark!"

Jamie wanted more than tolerance. Up for a playmate, he was again being far too vocal about it!

After a swift glance at the door, and relief that no one was coming, Jess pounced (Dusty would have been so proud!). With a hand firmly, but not cruelly, silencing the barks, Jess scooped up her canine pal and his toy, stashing both under the bed's muffling comforter. The bedding bubbled up over the Scottie's playfulness, then settled into a neat lump as Jamie decided to focus on the business of gnawing his toy.

Neatly dusting her hands with that business completed, Jess was ready to check the bathroom.

"Hey! What the hell are you doing in here?! Didn't I tell you to stay out?"

Whirling to confront a glaring Jack Roarke, Jessica was too unnerved to summon a defense as he stepped forward and lowered, "You think you can get away with this, don't you?"

"With, with what?" she fumbled, finally grabbing a desperate excuse. "My shin. Where you kicked my shin. I bumped it again, so I came in here to get a towel to make a compress. It's closer than the kitchen, and you don't have a bathroom off your room. You told me not to waste any time. Honest, Mister, that's the only reason I'm in here."

It killed Jess to reveal her genuine alarm but putting up a tough front now would hang her.

Roarke stopped. He clearly enjoyed seeing a weaker person squirm more than he was concerned at catching her in off-limits territory. She'd use that.

"Please don't get me in trouble with my boss. I'm new. I can't afford to lose my job."

"And that's why you came in here?" He was thinking it over, but Jess wasn't sure she was completely out of the woods.

"That's the God's honest truth, Mister. So help me."

"Arurf!"

Jamie poked his upper torso out from under the comforter at the end of the bed to confirm her story in caninese.

"And what's going on here?" Roarke demanded, as if moving in for the kill.

One hand placed demurely over the other, Jessica cocked her head to the side and commented, "He just gets into everything, doesn't he?"

Roarke grabbed Jess by one arm. She had all she could do not to kick him to free herself, as he accused, "Tell you what, honey. I think you didn't want the dog to bark at you when you were up to no good."

"No," she struggled against Roarke, without getting too far out of character, "I just wanted a compress–for where you kicked me."

"Or maybe you figured there'd be some jewels or loose money around in here."

"I'm on the level. Honest."

She couldn't play timid with this wolf much longer. Her hands were itching to grab something off the vanity and conk Roarke on the noggin. But before she had a chance to lose that inner battle, he suddenly pinned both her arms and snarled into her face, "Hey, don't worry, mouse. I just got a call. My next appointment is off, and I'm feeling awfully disappointed. Maybe if you're nice to me, I'll let you off the hook. You may be plain as a mud fence, but I can see some real moxie in your eyes."

Jess wasn't sure if it was fear or the fact he'd called her plain, but she snapped, "Yeah, pal? Well, how's this for moxie!" even as she scored a well-aimed assault to *his* shin. She'd learned that move from Joan Bennett in *The Man I Married*, and if it worked on Nazis, it ought to do the trick with this creep.

Roarke let out a yell and grabbed his leg. Released, Jess lunged for the door, only to feel herself yanked back by an arm around her waist. Roarke's snarl, "I'll fix you," mixed with her own, "Not if I fix you first." A move James had taught her for protection back in San Francisco instinctively came to mind, but, before she could use it, a different James came to her rescue.

James Stuart VI snarled and leaped at Roarke, sinking his fangs deep into the man's leg and clamping down until Jessica's attacker howled and jumped away. The man staggered off, trying unsuccessfully to free himself from the dog. Horrified, Jess saw Roarke snatch up a lamp to crush her defender, who hung tenaciously onto him. Instinctively, Jessica stuck out one of her shapely gams and tripped the distracted Roarke, who crashed down, cracking his head on a table leg. The man lay very still.

In the terrible silence, Jamie snarled once more at his enemy, then trotted to Jessica and nuzzled her leg. She wanted to reach down and pet him, but all she could think was: is Roarke dead? Could she actually have killed someone while trying to clear Larry of a murder frame?! Hot and cold washed over her at once, and her stomach heaved a little. Only Jamie's repeated nuzzles brought Jessica back.

"I'm okay, boy," Jess finally breathed, hoping Roarke was only knocked out. She'd have to check–and shuddered at the prospect. But she had to know. If he *were* still alive, she'd have to move fast. How long before he came to?

Carefully, slowly, cautiously, Jessica approached the limp form and crouched down, ready to kick or stomp and spring away should the need arise. Gingerly, her hand reached for Roarke's neck. She hesitated. Jamie snorted and nearly sent her out of her skin! Licking her lips, Jess tried again, touching his jugular. Nothing. Her horror flared, then collapsed into stupid relief. She'd forgotten to take off her cleaning gloves.

Off came the glove and Jess's fingers, tentative with loathing, checked Roarke's jugular. A pulse. A definite pulse!

Jess quickly stood up, her mind calculating. *You have no idea how long he'll be out, so snap to it!*

Roarke's earlier offhand comment about this boudoir's bathroom problem had raised a red flag that had never lowered in her mind. Marching into that room, Jessica went straight to the toilet. Putting her rubberized glove back on, Jess lifted the top of the lilac porcelain tank and smiled. Reaching in, she pulled out a water-tight container, a container for Larry's gun. Probably Roarke hadn't even known exactly what he was guarding. Alanna Tewkesbury wasn't the kind to share, and chumps like Roarke weren't given to asking too many questions if the price was right.

Turning, Jessica nearly fell over Jamie. He woofed his disapproval.

"Watch it, kid. You're supposed to be on my side."

Jess gave the Scottie a quick pat, before dashing with her container into the bedroom. Roarke was starting to groan. She sprinted out of the room, while Jamie trotted after her, toy in mouth. Turning on a dime outside the bedroom, Jess closed the door and dragged over a chair to brace it shut. Roarke was groaning louder now.

Jessica dashed into Roarke's room to pull out her cart and block the corridor. Movement and muttering grew in the bedroom. Now Jess was galloping for the door, the container with the gun tucked under one arm. Jamie met her there with his leash in his mouth and a pitiful look in his eyes.

"Kiddo, I don't exactly have time to walk you right now," she apologized, starting to bypass the Scottie to open the door.

That's when a roar escaped the master bedroom, "God damned bastard mutt. I'll throw him off the balcony!"

Jamie cocked his head at Jess, and she knew that there was no chance she'd leave him victim to Roarke's temper.

Jess scooped up the dog with her free hand, muttering, "Okay, pardner, let's beat it!"

She deliberately left the door ajar, hoping it would look as if Jamie had wandered off in all the commotion rather than that she'd liberated him. Too bad .38s couldn't be said to do the same.

Dashing down the hall for the service elevator, Jess cautioned her pal, "Just don't think you can stay with me. I've got a roommate who would not appreciate you, *at all*!"

The dark car sat waiting in the alley by the service entrance, pointed outward for a fast getaway, its engine humming. Elizabeth Minton tensed behind the wheel, dark fedora low over her face. Suddenly the passenger door jerked open. Liz prepared to battle off an attacker–but it was Jess–and a dog?

Before Liz could utter a word, Jess leaped in, dropped something in the back, and commanded, "Let's get out of here, and don't spare the horses!"

"But the gun. Is that it in ... ?"

"You heard me, Liz, step on it!"

They roared up the alley and plowed into traffic. After the last half hour, Jess didn't even bat an eye at her sister's driving. Still clutching the Scottie, she turned to peer anxiously behind them.

Liz repeated, "So, you're okay? You got it?"

Heaving a terrible sigh, Jessica turned forward and sank back into her seat to answer, "Yes. Yes, I got it all right."

"Well, where is it? In the dog?"

"No, it's in that container I threw in the back."

"You threw a gun onto my back seat?!"

"I was in a bit of a hurry, Elizabeth."

"Then who's this? An accomplice? A hostage?"

For the first time in what seemed like a lifetime, Jessica smiled, then answered, "No, an ally." Her features went serious when she added, "Roarke *was* there after all."

Liz nearly rear-ended the car in front of them.

"Jessica, are you all right? Did that son of a, well you know, did he hurt you? I should never have let you go in there alone."

"I'm all right, Liz. It's over. He tried some rough stuff. Keep your eyes on the road! I'm okay. My pal here gave him quite a savaging, and Roarke ended up out cold, but I'll tell you one thing, Elizabeth, I will *never, ever* do anything like this again. Got it?"

"You're darned tootin' you won't! Jess, believe me, if I'd have thought for one minute he was there, I'd have had Lois find another time, somehow. Please forgive me. And God bless that Scottie! Thank heavens you're safe and we have the gun."

"But they'll figure out who has the gun now, even if no one sees through my terrific disguise. Who else would take it? And they'll come looking for it."

"They may look, but neither you, nor I, nor Larry will have it."

"Huh? Who will?"

"I talked this over with Lois. She wants to take the gun. Now wait a minute. She insists that she's already involved, what with her brother's death and being a witness who can't come forward. Lois told me it's something she can do to help prevent the crooks who ruined her family from ruining another life–and they don't know who she is."

"Hmmm."

"'Hmm'? Just exactly what's that supposed to mean, sister dear?"

"It means that there's more at stake than the threat of Alanna and her pals. That's one of the reasons I resisted this crazy scheme from the get go. This gun is evidence, Liz, whether or not that evidence points to the real guilty party. Any time we don't turn it over to the cops we're obstructing justice. Did you think of that? Did Lois?"

Liz shot Jess a sharp look, returned her attention to the traffic, then finally said, "As a matter of fact, we did discuss it, and Lois wants the gun, anyway. She said she was already in it up to her neck, being around the office at the time of the murder, seeing Larry there, and keeping it all under her hat. I know we're not playing square with McLaughlan. He seems like a right guy, and we did promise to level with him. It bothers me, too, Jess. But giving the police this gun means we're risking Larry's being railroaded. If you turn in the gun, you might as well sign his death warrant and hand that evil woman a get-out-of-jail-free card for *all* she's done!"

Jessica didn't know what to say. What would you say when you were too much of a girl scout to want to stonewall the cops, but you knew playing square would only hurt the wrong people? Reluctantly, she muttered, "My sister and her own Boston Tea Party. What if we all end up in the drink over this?"

"Look, Jessica, are you with me or are you going to throw Larry to the wolves?"

"One wolf almost got me, but good," Jessica observed coldly, turning away from her sister to look out the window. The Scottie licked her face sympathetically. She relented enough to say, "Well, let's just see. Maybe the cops don't need to know, if we can get the goods on Tewkesbury quickly enough. Then the gun will be a moot point. I just hope Hooley comes through in time. But you know Alanna will never sit crying on her tuffet when she finds we've outmaneuvered her. "

Liz deftly careened them around a corner, causing the Scottie to woof anxiously. Jess stroked him comfortingly.

"Listen, Jessica, if they come after us now, make any false moves, they only prove we were right all along. McLaughlan would be down on them like that!" A snap of her fingers. "No, Madame Tewkesbury's not that stupid. For the moment, anyway, we've pulled Larry's bacon out of the fire and put it on his plate, nice and crispy–meantime, we have these monkeys over a barrel and in the soup!"

Jessica couldn't help furrowing her brow at the conglomeration of images her sister's tortured metaphors conjured up, but, before she could comment, Liz continued, "Anyhooo, we'll drop the 'evidence' with Lois, and then I'll take you home so that you can shower and rest."

"Okay, Liz, deal. But there's one catch. What about Fala's twin, here? If Dusty welcomed him with open paws, the claws would be out."

"That is a prob ... Say! What about Iris? She loves dogs. We could say he was a stray," Liz suggested.

Jess nodded and, looking down at Jamie, said, "No way that I'd have left you with that big creep, especially after you came to my rescue."

"Much better than that other James's rescuing efforts," Liz couldn't resist saying.

Jessica was too tired to argue. What she wouldn't give to have James Crawford here right now–maybe not sitting in her lap but definitely snuggled up close. How many times had he longed for her across the ocean, but she couldn't be there for him? That was when it sank in that even without James, she'd entered the wolf's den and conked him out! She'd won! Not that she was eager for a return match. She was just never, *ever* going to get herself into this kind of a jam again. You could take that to the bank.

"You did what?!"

Larry slowly sat back into Jessica's living room couch. The evening was the soonest they had been able to get him there, since he'd been conscientiously putting in overtime. He was shaking his head, "I never expected things to go this far, Liz. Do you have any idea where all this will lead? I wanted to protect you, to keep you out of this!"

Back on his feet, Larry gripped Liz's arms with deep concern and persisted, "It wasn't just for my sake. I wanted to protect *you*. Now you, Jessica, even Lois are all involved–not only with Tewkesbury and her crowd but the police. This is breaking and entering, theft."

"Actually, no. Roarke voluntarily let Jessica in; she didn't break into anything. And *they* stole *your* gun in the first place. Can't a friend retrieve and return property stolen from her friend?" Ignoring Jessica's cringe at that sketchy legal reasoning, Liz finished, "Besides, the last thing Alanna and Roarke are going to want to do is call in the police and claim ownership of a murder weapon. To my way of thinking, we're in the clear."

Larry argued, "Darling, I can't let this go on. I'm going to the police and tell them the truth. It's not pretty."

Liz overrode Larry's concern, "Now you look here, mister! No one's about to railroad the man I care about. But it's also more than you! This is our one opportunity to nail that Alanna Betty Weisenthal Tewkesbury dame. Do you want to be responsible for letting her trot merrily on her way, for ruining Lois's family's last chance to set their suffering to rights?"

Larry hesitated, torn and confused. Liz didn't let up: "There's more than just your gun at stake, anyway. That's not the only link between you and Evan's death. Lois saw you go into the office building the night Evan was murdered, and she never actually saw you leave."

Larry blanched. Jess moved to ease the shaken man back to the couch, but he abruptly pushed her away, demanding, "Lois? What did she say? Why didn't she say anything before?"

"Partly because she didn't want the police to know that she was there. Partly because she didn't want to unjustly incriminate you, which is all horribly frustrating because she also saw the Tewkesbury woman and Eddie Kubek there after you went in. She can't place them at the scene of the murder without making herself, or you, look bad. And if the cops grill her, that will be the living end. She might break and both of you could be charged, then think what will happen to her mother. No, for everyone's sake we've got to make sure that Alanna Tewkesbury takes the rap for her crimes."

"That is a dilemma," Larry contemplated. "I'd hate to see Lois get into any kind of a jam, and her mother's been through far too much over her children already. So Tewkesbury can, definitely, be placed there that night?"

"That's what I'm telling you. We just have to find a way to link her to the crime without putting the finger on you or Lois. But you know, Larry, you never did tell me what went on between you and Evan. I think I'm entitled to know," Liz pointed out.

Jessica waited for Larry's answer as intently as her sister. That thought had nagged her since talking to Lois, and she'd bet her bottom dollar the only reason Elizabeth had held off questioning Larry this long was that she hadn't wanted to chance his getting wind of their little plot to "recover" his gun. Larry was taking his time, likely thinking about how best to phrase something that was sure to upset Elizabeth?

Finally, he spoke, "A chap might find this a bit difficult to admit. The minute I confronted Evan Blair, I realized that I was so angry that I was bound to make a fool of myself. I got hold of myself, but I think I still warned him that if he didn't make good on his promise to leave, I'd hire someone to investigate him so you, Liz, would see him for what he really was. He almost laughed, and I became so furious again that, I must have gotten flustered, and stormed out through Liz's office and blundered out through the dressing rooms. That's probably why Lois didn't see me leave. Liz, do you really leave all those doors unsecured?"

Jess answered, "She doesn't, but apparently Alanna Tewkesbury and her favorite strong arm paved the way for you. Inconsiderate of them not to lock up after themselves."

"Unless they planned to come back," Liz knowingly surmised. She added, disappointed, "So are you saying that you didn't see the Tewkesbury woman or her big ape there?"

"And if I had, Liz? The authorities would hardly consider my asseveration reliable. Wouldn't they be suspicious about what *I* was doing there?" Larry responded with bitter irony.

"I guess you're right," Liz agreed, downcast. She tried to perk herself up by adding, "At least we got the gun away from them."

"The less said about that the better," Larry grimly noted, continuing, "I want both of you to promise me that you won't go off on any more crackbrained 'adventures.' I won't have you endangering yourselves for my sake. I couldn't live with myself if I brought you to grief when I could have prevented it."

"Well..." Liz waffled.

"Swear," Jessica intoned, *à la* the ghost of Hamlet's father. She was not really in a laughing mood, though. Larry was right, and he didn't know half of what she'd horrified Liz with about her adventures with Roarke. On top of that, his concern that they'd skated on the shady side of the law sat in her stomach like a lead mitten.

Elizabeth finally nodded. "All right. All right. Fair enough." She squeezed Larry's hand then said, "Now, you sit down, and I'll make us all some tea. We can go from there. At least that crew shouldn't have the same power over us they had before."

After Liz left them, Larry ran a hand through his hair, then skeptically eyed Jessica and Dusty before observing, "This is the sort of insane scheme I'd have expected from you, not your sister."

Coolly, commandingly, Jessica replied, "Larry, you ought to be grateful rather than critical. I went through a hell of a lot for you today. And there wouldn't even have been a 'cracked-brain scheme' if you hadn't been crack brained enough to buy a gun in a shady manner then *lose* it, for cryin' out loud."

"Sorry, Jess," Larry apologized. "You're 100% right. Since this terrible mess has exploded into our lives ... I just don't know what to do, how to act. You see me as rational, cool as a cucumber; but once I get beyond the pale, I'm completely out of my element. You've got to believe me that if I'd known things could have gone this far, I'd have squared off against all questions with the police. Now, all three of you are in too deep. If I could just go back in time..."

"So you'd never have met the Fabulous Minton Sisters?"

"Never that."

Larry's eyes held hers, and, for a moment, Jessica remembered why she'd once thought she'd been in love with him. But that was water long under the bridge. Then Larry really made her think she was hearing things, for he admitted, "I never thought I'd say this, but we could use a spot of your sly James Crawford about now."

Chapter Seventeen

Saturday, June 2

Sunlight streamed into the reading room of the New York Public Library, where Rose Nyquist perched on one of the tables, hands folded in the lap of her aqua-green surplice dress. A smidge past noon, and the girls had just cleared out. As Rose cocked her head thoughtfully, light brown hair waving down to her shoulders, she might have been considering that she and Jessica deserved pats on their backs for keeping the kiddos interested in such a gorgeous weather. She might even have been musing on what a perfect day it was to have lunch outdoors before her train ride back to Connecticut.

Instead, Rose watched her chum in black sequin-laced cap, with matching suit and white surplice blouse, make some guilty farewells to the cat she'd snuck into the library in a disguised cat caddy. Always forthright but never rude, Rose cut to the chase, "Jess, you're sure you only want me to take the cat because of the exterminator?"

Jessica smiled, "That's all there is to it. He has to put poison around the house to get all the rats. I can't take a chance on Dusty getting into it."

"It's just that Dusty *is* a cat. She should be able to kayo a few rodents."

"We're talking about rats the size of Sidney Greenstreet," explained Jess.

"If they're built like Sydney Greenstreet, shouldn't they be easier to catch?" Rose posited.

"They're *built* like Sydney Greenstreet, but they *think* like Peter Lorre."

"Peter Lorre in *The Maltese Fal*con or Peter Lorre in *All Through the Night*?"

"More like *All Through the Night*–you know, where he bumps off nice German immigrants, people who don't want to be spies, and Judith Anderson," Jess explained matter-of-factly.

"Gee, Dusty's as least as spry as Judith Anderson," Rose decided. Then, as if something had just occurred to her, she added, "Or would those rats be pals of your Mrs. Tewkesbury?"

Jess forced herself to laugh, "Oh, c'mon, Rose. Maybe I shouldn't have told you about Liz's silly suspicions..."

"Maybe you shouldn't let that daffy sister of yours sucker you into her nutcase schemes. Listen, Jessica, I know how loyal you are, and I know how persuasive Liz is, especially when she lays on the guilt, maybe about you trading in Larry for James Crawford..."

"I didn't treat Larry like an old Packard, Rose. I *know* that..."

"Consciously, sure, but, Jessica, you are such a softie. Besides, you can't handle this whole magilla by yourself, or with Liz–let's face it, being with Liz can be worse than being on your own."

"Look, Rose," Jess began, "It all comes down to the fact that the police don't want to hear about investigating Alanna Tewkesbury–well, maybe one of them is open, kind of. Anyway, she's got enough clout to make nudging suspicion toward her a delicate task, to say the least."

"You've made up your mind, haven't you?" Rose resignedly shook her head.

"'Fraid so, kiddo. Now relax. I know what I'm doing," Jess tried to be reassuring.

"Said Dr. Jekyll before he took that first swig of the Hyde cocktail."

It was time for Jess to make her goodbyes to Dusty. The nuzzle, lick of a pink tongue, and guilt-inducing amber-green eyes left Jessica biting her lip, her back to Rose. A quick hug for Rose, and Jessica beat a hasty retreat, calling over her shoulder, "I'll be out to pick up Dusty in about two weeks. The vermin should be gone by then."

Heels clicking down the marble floors, Jessica couldn't help thinking it was tough to be parted from her furry pal, but Tewkesbury would have to be pretty darn dense not to figure out who had lifted the gun. Jessica in no way put it past that woman not to be vicious enough to seek revenge at the expense of a helpless feline. And then, there were other formidable worries assailing her: not being on the square with the law, as well as wondering what the dickens had happened with Jeff Hooley! He was their main chance of getting Betty Weisenthal's prints, and no one had heard a peep from him! Coming to the grand double doors opening onto the terrace and broad steps leading to the street, Jessica carefully wiped her eyes and gave her nose one last blow on her handkerchief before stepping out to look for a cab.

"Hey, Miss Minton, you seem in kind of a hurry."

Eddie Kubek stepped from behind one of the portico's stone pillars and had her elbow in his grip. His tone was amiable, and yet not.

Promptly extricating herself from Kubek's paw, Jessica retorted, "I'm in a hurry, and I've nothing to say to you." She hoped he couldn't tell that inside she felt about as stalwart as a jellyfish.

"Then I'll just walk down the steps with you, if you don't mind."

"I do mind," Jess asserted, leaving him behind.

"Now, that's not friendly, is it?" he queried, catching up. "We have so much in common."

Searching for an available cab, Jess warily kept Tewkesbury's torpedo in the corner of her eye. At least there were too many people around for him to try any funny business.

"Aw, you're looking for a hack. Let me help you."

They were almost down the broad stone steps, level with the lions, and Jessica realized if she wanted to keep the upper hand, she'd have to square off with Kubek. Otherwise, no matter how tartly she spoke, she was just running away.

"All right, buster. I know you're not here because you ran out of old ladies to help across the street. What are you selling?"

The direct approach seemed momentarily to flummox him. Unexpectedly, Kubek burst into a grin, more wolfish than endearing, "Like I said, we've got a lot in common."

"Like we both know that peroxide viper you work for killed Evan Blair? Or maybe *you* pulled the trigger for her."

The wolfish grin widened. For a second, Jessica thought he might swallow her, but she refused to be quailed. Then Kubek pushed back, "It's your pal Larry Sanders' gun that did it."

Ah, the opening she'd been waiting for. Jess challenged Kubek, "Go ahead. Turn it over to the cops. Of course you've had it so long, you're now a bunch of accessories after the fact. No, more like 'during,' since one of you is the killer."

"We don't have the gun, but I think you know that, don't you, honey?"

He had blue eyes. They were like blue steel, the stuff of razor blades.

"You know, we can make things nasty for you and that cat of yours, if we don't get that gun back."

Something snapped inside. Jessica grabbed Kubek's tie and jerked his head down so forcefully he couldn't breathe. She snarled, "You even *look* threateningly at my cat, and I'll fix it so that you can audition as the Andrews Sisters' new soprano. Get me?"

Jessica shoved the startled thug back so hard he almost hit the steps, rump first. Before he could regain his respiration or his wits, she stormed out to the street, hailed a miraculously available cab, and popped in.

"Take me to..."

"Not so fast, girlie," came Eddie Kubek's low growl as he leaned into the cab window.

"Ignore him," Jessica commanded the driver.

"Not if you know what's good for you, bud," Kubek threatened before turning on Jess with, "Look, sister, don't play games with me. You ain't gonna pin nothing on my boss."

"*You* aren't going to pin anything on Larry Sanders, Buster Brown," Jessica shot back fiercely. "At least he has the advantage of being innocent."

"Honey, we got the advantage of money and muscle, and that's all that matters in this doggie dog world."

"That's 'dog *eat* dog,' Einstein."

"I oughta..."

"You ought to what?" The voice was Leo McLaughlan's. "Let the lady have her cab?"

"McLaughlan, you're a little off your beat, ain't you?" replied Kubek still dialing back in front of the law.

Jessica watched silently. Interestingly, Kubek didn't seem in much of a hurry to rat out Larry. She relaxed just a notch.

"Even cops go to the library. Didn't you think I could read, Kubek?"

McLaughlan's style was easy, but an underlying edge checked Tewkesbury's strong-arm.

"I was just helping Miss Minton, here, get her cab, and giving her a friendly greeting from a mutual friend."

"Uh, huh, would that 'friend' be Mrs. Wilmington Tewkesbury?" Leo McLaughlan's query was casual but had its intended effect. Eddie Kubek took a step back.

Good, Jess concluded to herself, *Alanna's not immune to suspicion if she doesn't have something to hold over Larry.*

"I got places to be." Kubek's tone was short, a play at saving face. Jess could see he wanted to give her a parting shot–hopefully not the .45 caliber kind–but he couldn't risk validating her and Liz's claims about Alanna by threatening her in front of the cop. So he left, tossing the detective a crack, "Enjoy your reading."

Turning to Jess, McLaughlan inquired, "Do you think he really means that?"

Jessica almost smiled, but the incisive glint in McLaughlan's eyes gave her pause. Still, he'd just saved her bacon. She owed it to him and the law not to leave him completely in the dark. So, Jess began to formulate a plan to tell him something about what she and Liz had discovered–and still not end up in the soup.

"You look as if you had something on your mind. Something you want to tell me?"

Jessica looked him in the eye and said, "As a matter of fact, yes, but we need Elizabeth. Hop in. We're going to my sister's office. We both need to tell you something important. What are you waiting for? Get in!"

He'd clearly been thrown off by her direct response, but only for a moment. Sliding in, McLaughlan commented skeptically, "You're being awfully mysterious. You're not Nancy Drew, you know. I saw you playing tag on the steps with that big baboon. I'm not always going to be around to save your skin."

"You may not have to be," Jess informed him. Then she gave the cabbie her sister's office address, adding, "and make it snappy."

She *loved* saying that.

On the short ride over, McLaughlan didn't say much, but Jess distinctly felt that he had something he wasn't telling her. Since she was doing some major holding out, herself, she couldn't exactly resent it, but Jess wasn't sure how much she could afford to tell him.

When they entered the main office, Ginger gave McLaughlan a quick once over, before greeting them, "Hiya, Jess. Here to see Liz? She's showing some designs to a manufacturer."

"We've got to see her, now," Jessica called over her shoulder, traversing the office like the Big Red One across Europe.

"No, wait! She'll kill me if you interrupt her!" Ginger cried.

"Then it's a good thing she brought the law," McLaughlan affably quipped.

Jessica rapped on her sister's door, barely waiting for the "Come in," before marching through.

Towering over her seated business associate, Liz was holding up a design sketch from the winter collection. Her expression at the intrusion frostily matched that season, until she saw McLaughlan. Liz's eyes went from alarm to hopeful puzzlement as she connected Jess's bright expression with the detective's presence.

Liz exuded irresistible charm as she explained, "Mr. Maxfield, I'm sorry for this interruption. You have to excuse us for a moment." She hustled the surprised man to the door with such alacrity that Jess was sure her sister had blown a business deal. Then she saw Maxfield's expression when Liz said, "Tell Ginger I said to fix you some of the real coffee with actual cream and sugar. Nothing but the best for *my* associates!"

The door closed, and Liz faced them, giving a little tug to the green-and-rust-striped tunic jacket she wore over her black skirt. "Okay, this had better be good, for me to have hustled a few grand out of the office."

"Your sister seems to think you have something to tell me that will help clear up the case in your friend Sanders' favor," McLaughlan started the ball rolling.

At first, Liz stiffened; Jess knew her sibling was thinking about the gun. But Liz was too sharp to give much away.

Jessica piped up, "I ran into Detective McLaughlan outside the NYPL today."

"Looking for a good book, Detective?" Liz dryly inquired.

"Something without pictures, too."

Jessica looked from one to the other. There was definitely a different dynamic here from the similar exchange with Eddie Kubek. Were these two enjoying themselves?

"Ahem," Jess cut in, "as I was saying, I ran into him at the library, when Eddie Kubek tried to threaten me about our implicating Mrs. T. He thinks he's such a big gun, but he doesn't have it, what it takes, I mean."

Liz got it. Her glance at the detective was almost imperceptible, but he still knew something was going on. Just not what. McLaughlan took the bull by the horns, informing Liz, "Your sister says you both have something for me. I'd advise you to spill it, forget the double talk."

Liz smiled coolly, walked over to her desk, reached for her cigarette case, thought better of it, then turned back to the detective with, "Sit down, McLaughlan. My sister and I have a little story to tell you about Evan Blair's hideaway in Lowell."

"What?" McLaughlan was not pleased.

Jessica came to stand near her sister and explained, "We couldn't say much before because we didn't figure this out until just two days ago. We'd have come clean before today, but we weren't sure if what we found was solid enough. The long and short of it is that we found evidence linking Mrs. Tewkesbury to the Weisenthal gang in that apartment."

McLaughlan frowned at them, "And you sat on it?"

The sisters exchanged glances, then Liz proceeded, "Not exactly. As Jess just explained, we weren't sure about bringing it to you."

"And the difference is ... ?"

"Well, it's this way," Jess began, not exactly answering McLaughlan's question. "We *saw* Alanna Tewkesbury in the apartment. She and a couple of her trained apes were talking about Evan Blair deserving what he got. "

"That's just your word against theirs," McLaughlan pointed out, doubtfully. "Anyone else see them there?"

"The landlord?" Liz offered.

McLaughlan looked interested now, but Jessica shook her head, "Liz, you mean the guy who told us he went out of his way not to get an actual look at them? The guy who was so darned adamant he wouldn't identify them even if he could?"

"Let's back up here a minute. How did *you* manage to see them there? How did you know about this apartment, period? How did you even get in?" Leo McLaughlan was *not* happy.

Jessica gave Liz a helpless look, thinking that Evan's Byzantine puzzle of a letter would lose McLaughlan before they could even get started on the rest of his questions.

"I'll take this," Liz decided. "Here's the abbreviated version: we received a coded letter from Evan Blair telling us to go to the apartment and where to find a key to get in."

"A letter from a dead man?"

"We're willing to make a leap here and assume he mailed it before Alanna and her pals offed him," Liz retorted.

"Big of you–although it would have been bigger and smarter if you'd brought the letter to me right off the bat. I guess you're not guilty of breaking and entering if he sent you the key and told you to go there, but I warned you about playing fast and loose with information relevant to the case..."

Liz argued, "We're giving you the lowdown, and the letter, now. Besides, we had to make sure it was legit."

"Didn't think we flat foots were up to figuring that out for ourselves?"

"You haven't been up to giving the Tewkesbury woman a good grilling," Liz returned.

"Mmm, well, I'm up to pointing out that by waltzing in the apartment before me you've contaminated the chain of evidence. Evidence looks a lot more legit when the police find it, not a sister act that doesn't like the woman it incriminates. Do you two gals follow me?"

"You mean that what we've found, what we heard, is no good?" Jessica blurted, crestfallen.

McLaughlan studied them both a moment before answering, "I didn't say that. I don't know what you found out, or how incriminating it is. But I do know that you two should stop playing detective and let the pros do the work–and withholding evidence is a criminal offense."

Liz's chin came up, and she challenged, "So, you're going after us for trying to help you?"

Still there was a trace of a quiver in her voice, which McLaughlan must have noticed. His comeback was not nearly as threatening as Jess had expected, "Lady, you haven't helped me one bit in the last ten minutes. Why don't you tell me what you do know, and maybe I can chalk it up to overzealous good citizenship."

Jessica jumped for that life preserver, "We found a picture of Alanna Tewkesbury from ten years ago with Lois Wong's brother. You remember, he was the guy they pulled a fast one on so they could steal the jade from the jeweler he worked for. Her hair and her nose were a little different, but you could clearly see it's the same woman."

"There's another thing about that Kodak," Liz eagerly added. "When I saw Mrs. Tewkesbury, she wore this unique pin. It perfectly matched one that Betty was wearing in the picture, which was one Evan described making for her."

"That's right," Jessica affirmed. She went on, "There's another picture, of Evan Blair with a man, a policeman, from about the same time I'd say. Maybe after they arrested him. But the two, they don't seem adversarial. There's a first name on the back–and a smudged address–but you can't read it."

"So, you had all this, and you didn't bring it to me right away?"

Jessica knew McLaughlan had every right to be suspicious, and if they hadn't been blackmailed by that deadly woman, they would have given him everything in a flash. But under the prevailing circumstances, neither she nor Liz could entirely come clean with him. Yet, giving McLaughlan as much of the truth as was safe might win them some credibility, as well as salve their consciences just a little. Jessica only prayed that Liz would trust her enough to play along.

"Detective McLaughlan," Jess continued, "Mrs. Tewkesbury had a hold over us. When we were in hiding in the closet..."

"Wait, you two were what?"

"Hiding in the closet," Liz snapped. "You thought she'd have invited us for tea and crumpets while her big ape tossed the place? We got there first, heard through the window that they were coming in, and hid in the closet because we didn't have time to get out. May my sister continue?"

"Oh sure," McLaughlan shook his head in disbelief. "This, I've got to hear."

"*Anyway*," Jess resumed, "we heard Alanna saying she'd frame Larry if Liz and I didn't lay off."

"Yes, yes," Liz chimed in excitedly. "I was there. I heard it all, too."

"So you still only came to me just now? What changed?"

Here came the half-truth, just true enough for Jess to get it out, "You took the measure of Eddie Kubek for me today. I saw that crew would back down if someone got tough back at them. That's when I really knew we could depend on you not to be swayed. And I guess I felt I owed you something for going to bat for me. So, can you do anything with what we've given you?"

McLaughlan studied Jessica. Guilt gnawed at her. Could he tell that she still wasn't entirely on the square? She hated having to play it that way with him, even for Larry's sake.

Finally, he said, "Let me see the pictures and the letter from Blair."

Jessica and Elizabeth looked at each other before Liz answered, "We've got some good news and some bad news on that account, Detective."

"Why am I not surprised?"

"It's not that bad, entirely," Liz amended. "We have the letter, although Jess may have to translate–we'll need a copy of e. e. cummings. You'll get what I mean when you see the letter."

"Okay, okay, now let me have the good news."

"Um," Liz hesitated, "that is part of the good news."

"Swell."

"The other part is that we do have the picture of Evan with a plainclothes cop, er, officer," Liz announced.

Skeptically, McLaughlan told her, "Go on. Let me have it; what's the bad news?"

"The juiciest piece of evidence..." Liz began.

"The picture of Alanna and George..." Jessica clarified.

"We, I mean my sister..." corrected Elizabeth.

"Thanks a load, Liz."

"Yes, my klutzy sister, here, dropped the pictures when we scrambled to hide. Mrs. Tewkesbury got it and took it away. Is it all over?"

McLaughlan settled back, then smiled, "Only if she walked off with the negative."

"What do you mean?" both sisters demanded.

"If she doesn't have the full skinny on the negative, she doesn't know if there are more copies floating around or if more could still be printed. Interesting."

"Then what we gave you," Jessica questioned hopefully, "it's worth something?"

"What you heard her say, without corroboration, is hearsay, Miss Minton. I could try having a chat with your landlord friend, but I don't see my lieutenant being too cheerful about sending me out of town when I've got so many other cases to work. But the pictures, they might be worth something, even if you dug them up on your own. Since Blair sent you to his place in Lowell, you didn't exactly get them illegally. And it's what's in them that makes them evidence not who found them."

Liz gave Jess an "I-told-you-so" look, silently referencing the point she'd raised to her and Larry earlier.

McLaughlan resumed, starting sternly, "Just remember, you're just barely on this side of the law. Don't press your luck any further. Still, I might be able to shake something loose from her with what you've given me, maybe enough to justify getting her prints. Then we can see if there's a match."

Jess perked up, but Liz spoke first: "Match? Match with what?"

"With the prints for Betty Weisenthal. Your friend, Hooley, from the F.B.I. is supposed to deliver them to me Monday. Now I have some leverage on her."

"Jeff? Jeff Hooley will be in town?" Jess repeated, feeling a touch uneasy.

"Sure. He might even be here already, somewhere. He had an assignment to deal with in town, but he's making time to see me Monday. He seemed pretty interested in our case. Funny thing, he asked quite a few questions about you when I took the call, but that's neither here nor there. I do need to see this evidence of yours right away. Then I can decide whether to make a move on Alanna Tewkesbury today, before she gets any more cute ideas." McLaughlan stood up, putting on his hat, and said, "All right, ladies, pony up what you have for me."

"It's at my house. In my safe," Jessica explained. "We'll have to go there."

At Jessica's apartment, McLaughlan gave their evidence a healthy once over. Despite Elizabeth's questioning, his reaction to the book and photo was laconic. Still, the sisters' hopes began to spark. However, that spark was somewhat dampened when McLaughlan checked the time. He immediately called in at the precinct about another case and ended up bolting to interview a witness *tout de suite*, with no time to check in their evidence in at the station. McLaughlan instructed Jessica to secure the materials in her safe, promising to return for it as soon as he finished his assignment.

He didn't tell the sisters that the picture had prompted him to plan his interview with Mrs. Tewkesbury right after he got through with his other one. Too bad Aaron hadn't been at his desk. Leo could have had him swing by to pick up everything. Then again, knowing how little the Minton sisters trusted his partner, coupled with Aaron's attitude toward them, Leo wouldn't have been surprised if the combination to the Jessica Minton's safe had inexplicably refused to work until he, himself, showed up. Never mind, Leo could prepare Aaron for their afternoon interview without actually showing him the evidence.

For her part, Jessica was not 100% sure that McLaughlan had bought their explanation for not giving him their finds from Lowell earlier. One other question did trouble her: if Jeff Hooley was in town, did she want to see him?

Chapter Eighteen

Saturday, June 2

Leo McLaughlan sourly lit up another cigarette across from the Waldorf Towers on 50th. Where the hell was Aaron? Hadn't he gotten the message to meet him here?

The interview had wasted a big chunk of Leo's afternoon. So he couldn't get back to retrieve Jessica Minton's evidence before *this* little interview. Not his first choice. At least he'd had enough time with the stuff to know how to use it, though. Still, he didn't particularly want to pay Mrs. Tewkesbury a visit without his partner to corroborate what he uncovered, even if Aar was more interested in Larry Sanders. Not that Leo could entirely blame him. Motive and a weak alibi didn't exactly clear the guy. Nevertheless, Sanders had a Sunday-school-teacher record, and no murder weapon or witnesses tied him directly to the crime.

Alanna Tewkesbury, now there was a gal with a spotty record–no record, in fact, before Florida. This "suspect" did, however, have a whale of an alibi: train tickets and witnesses who placed her in Florida before and after the murder. Curiously, no one had definitely seen her the night of the murder. But he didn't know of any train that could go from Florida to New York and back again fast enough to crack her alibi. He'd also been unable to uncover any record of airline tickets under her or her husband's name. Still, Leo had no doubt that Tewkesbury understood the concept of incognito. He just had no proof she'd put that understanding to work.

Yet Evan Blair had fingered her as his "colleague" in jewel heists, well according to Elizabeth Minton. Keeping that kind of a past under wraps was arguably an even stronger motive for murder than jealousy. Then there was the alleged photograph of her with Wong and that brooch. Not the proverbial smoking gun, but a chat with the lady did seem to be in order.

Leo would have felt better, though, if he had that photo in hand or if that screwy letter of Blair's had named Tewkesbury outright. He wasn't entirely dismissive of Aaron's cynicism concerning the Minton/Sanders camp, but his gut feeling said Elizabeth Minton was onto something–even with her bias in favor of Sanders. He had to admit that he got a kick out of watching those sisters in action, especially that firecracker Elizabeth: as if Noel Coward had been writing for the Three Stooges.

Another gut feeling, though, said that the sisters were holding out on him, even after he'd warned them. Edward G. Robinson had his little man, his indigestion, in *Double Indemnity*, and he had ... what? Itchy feet? Leo just knew something wasn't quite right.

Where in Sam Hill *was* his partner, anyway? Another look at his watch, and Leo knew that he was going in alone. After ducking traffic, he hesitated only a moment at the portals of the Waldorf-Astoria. A little research told Leo that Mrs. Tewkesbury would stonewall him if he tried to take her in for questioning and intimidate her. However, if she thought she was doing *him* a favor, as well as had the home court advantage, she'd be more likely to get cocky and slip up. She'd just love to think that the local gendarmes scrabbling to keep those pesky Minton dames out of her hair.

Fifteen floors and one door chime later, Leo was facing the butler: a young, good-looking guy. She knew how to pick 'em for aesthetic value. Jeeves wasn't impressed by the badge or the title, insisting, "Do you have an appointment, sir?"

"Don't worry, son. Once Mrs. Tewkesbury knows I'm here to discuss real estate with her, a little apartment in Massachusetts at 122 Cambridge Street, she'll want to see me."

Before the puzzled butler could put him off, Leo slipped casually but insistently into a foyer that opened on the right into a corridor crossing the length of the apartment.

In spite of the daunting stretch of regal estate, Leo reiterated calmly, "That's 122 Cambridge Street, Massachusetts."

"Massachusetts," the butler repeated skeptically.

"That's right, Junior. They'll be promoting you to concierge in no time."

"You can wait..."

"Right through here," Leo easily took over, leading the butler out of the foyer where he'd tried to relegate the detective. Let Mrs. Tewkesbury think she had the upper hand, but no sense overdoing it.

The corridor was bright from the ceiling-high window with a magnificent view of the city ahead. On the right of the cream-tinted corridor, an enormous living room could be accessed by descending a flight of stairs. The furniture was modern, tasteful, and dripping with expense. An enormous fireplace loomed against the right wall. Little Betty Weisenthal had done all right for herself. But this was too much of a showroom for Leo's purposes.

"I'll just wait in the library, son. That way if Mrs. Tewkesbury has to mull over my message, I'll have some books to keep me company. But don't let her mull too long. She wouldn't want me to get antsy. Remember, 122 Cambridge Street, Massachusetts."

"That's all, sir?"

The butler had wanted to be supercilious, but Leo nipped that in the bud with an edge in his affable, "That's it."

They proceeded along the hall before the butler opened a door to their left. A spiral flight of stairs led down into the reading area of the library. The books lived in floor-to-ceiling, built-in shelves. Leo McLaughlan's kind of room.

Taking in the books with barely a glance at the butler, McLaughlan queried, "Mrs. Tewkesbury much of a reader?"

"Mr. Tewkesbury," the butler corrected.

"Ah," Leo concurred, then a casual, "Mr. Tewkesbury home today?" He knew that Tewkesbury was in Chicago on business. He'd planned on it.

"No, sir. Did you need to talk to him as well?"

"Not at all. Just give my message to the lady of the house."

The door closed behind the butler, and Leo McLaughlan was alone with a room the Tewkesburies lived in, not a stage for performances. No props, just the story of their lives.

Leo didn't let the smells of leather book covers or acidic paper distract him, much as he savored them. Moving almost casually about the room, his eyes evaluated everything: the leather chairs, the teak tables, the pipe rack and crystal ashtrays, the prints of Hudson River Valley artists (no, these would be the real McCoy), the copy of *Leave Her to Heaven*, face down to save the reader's place. *The Strange Woman*, yet uncut, waited on the same table. Did Alanna pick up tips in *femme fatality* from Ben Ames Williams's "heroines"? Not the best guide, since they mostly ended up deader than doornails.

On the mantle of a dark-wood fireplace, several framed photos resided in state. All of them starred Mrs. Wilmington Tewkesbury. Alanna with a racehorse in the winner's circle; Alanna boarding a private plane at a small field outside of town; Alanna in her private railroad car, the one that must have pulled out of the Waldorf's siding and carried her away to her Florida alibi; Alanna with a string of good-looking polo ponies and even better looking players; Alanna on their yacht; Alanna....

Well, that was enough reviewing Wilmington Tewkesbury's trophies–all of which orbited the biggest trophy of them all, Alanna. Or were they really her trophies, even Tewkesbury himself? Leo compressed his lips in speculation, then quickly took out his notebook and began to write, his gaze rapidly shifting back and forth from the photo parade to his pad.

"Do you see something you like, Detective McLaughlan?"

The tones were firmly modulated, not exactly those of a dame who'd found the joys of elocution, just a little too controlled, too perfect.

To see his hostess, McLaughlan had to look up to the landing. Where they stood relative to each other put his gaze square on a honey of an ankle bracelet, around a honey of an ankle. Slowly putting away his notebook, Leo suddenly felt like Fred McMurray being reeled in by Barbara Stanwyk in *Double Indemnity*. But he wanted to see opponent's face.

The trouble was, to get to her face he had to go past the rest of her. Those graceful gams seemed pretty darned long for a not very tall woman; the lemon-ice silk dress curved with her hips and waist, past the bare midriff to the full curves of ... Then there was her face, enjoying every minute of this. The mouth smiling, knowing, and not giving anything away. Offsetting the dress and eyes were those brows curving below the soft curl of blond bangs and a gently waving school-girl page boy. He'd better watch his step today.

"I was admiring that filly you owned. The one that beat the colts. She paid for some smart nights out for me."

"Oh," starting down the stairs. "Should the police be betting? Is that legal?"

"As long as I do it at the two-dollar window."

"I don't know much about gambling, or horse racing for that matter." She'd reached the bottom step, smiled, and continued, "Do you?"

"I know it takes a good filly to beat the colts. One with a lot of grit. Doesn't happen very often, though."

"But when it does, the filly would have to be exceptional, wouldn't you say, Detective ... ?"

"McLaughlan. No argument here. I'm willing to bet on it. In fact, I did. But that's not the way things usually work–on the track."

Only a few feet away now, she smiled up at him and agreed, "On the track, yes." Then, she smoothly changed the subject: "Do sit down, Detective. Can, may I get you anything? A drink, perhaps?"

"I'm on duty, Mrs. Tewkesbury, but thanks for asking."

He had to look down at her. Leo made sure he didn't look any lower than her face–not that it was easy–but then wasn't that the game she was playing–the one she'd play if she was Betty?

Leo waited till Alanna Tewkesbury settled languidly onto the couch before taking a chair. She seemed to cross those long legs casually before smiling, "Now, Detective McLaughlan, what can I do for you? Milton told me your message, and I'm afraid I haven't the slightest idea what to make of it."

"That's why you're seeing me," Leo summed up reasonably, "because the address means nothing to you?"

"Well, of course, if I can help the police in any way, I'll be more than happy to do so."

"Of course. I know you're that kind of woman."

"Does this have anything to do with, oh what is that name, oh, the Evan Blair murder?" She was all helpful concern.

"Would you mind if I smoked, Mrs. Tewkesbury?" he queried, absently looking for a cigarette. Let her get a little unsettled, wondering.

Alanna graciously shook her head when Leo politely said, "May I offer you one ... ?"

She cut him off, "No, I have my own–but this Blair business, that's your case. I know that you've been asking questions. I've heard some of the rumors those odd Minton sisters started. Why else would you be here?"

Nice and logical answer. What would she do with a little push, though?

"That was my first reason. Gotta cover all the bases, no matter how offbeat. But now there's something else, too. A brooch was found at that address I gave you, by one of the boys investigating another case. One of the lady clerks at the precinct identified it as one she'd seen you wearing in pictures on the society pages a few times. Thought I'd kill two birds with one stone and check it out. Diamonds and emeralds, in a silver lily pattern. Sound familiar?"

McLaughlan caught her hand unconsciously move to her chest, just about where that broach he'd described would have been fastened. She stopped, though, so naturally one might almost have believed she hadn't made the move at all. But she had, and her words weren't so effective, "Certainly, Detective McLaughlan, I'd know if I'd lost a valuable piece of jewelry."

"Makes sense, but I just noticed in some of those photos on the mantle, you're wearing a pin just like that. Sure you don't want to check? I'd hate to see you lose a beaut like that," Leo offered with convincing sincerity.

"I don't have to, Detective," Mrs. Tewkesbury insisted confidently. "You're both certainly mistaken. I doubt either of you have as much expertise in recognizing a fine piece as I have. Besides, I don't think that I've ever even been to Lowell, let alone Cambridge Street."

She finished, smiling warmly, almost laughing. Leo smiled, too, just as warmly, and filed away her slip. He'd gone out of his way *not* to say in what Massachusetts city his Cambridge Street was.

She continued, much put upon, "I think I know what this is all about. Those dreadful Minton sisters. You don't know how I've suffered with their beastly insinuations that I'm not only a murderess but have a disreputable past as some kind of gun moll! They are so lucky that I haven't sued them for slander. I don't know why I haven't."

"Darned forbearing of you, Mrs. Tewkesbury, considering what you say they're putting you through," McLaughlan sympathized. "You must have a heart of gold."

"Well, Detective, I don't know about that," she almost purred, then waving a hand expansively, she continued, "but it would just create more scandal, and my husband's a mature gentleman, his health, you know..."

"Of course," Leo concurred, letting her enjoy believing she'd soft-soaped him.

"I imagine I should feel sorry for them. Perhaps I do. That's why I can't bring myself to add to their grief. After all, the older sister's fiancé is the main suspect, isn't he?"

"We have our eye on him," Leo assured her. "Among others."

"Others?" She seemed surprised. "Who else could it be?"

"I'm really not at liberty to say, Mrs. Tewkesbury. I'm sorry." Still pleasant and firm, trying not to sound too dumb–just patsy enough so she'd feel confident enough to overplay her hand.

"No, of course not," she agreed warmly. She got up, walked to the desk, maybe swayed would have been more accurate, and removed a cigarette from a teak box. Leo was on his feet with a light as soon as she had the cigarette in its silver holder.

Alanna smiled at him invitingly. Nothing tacky, but it would certainly have drawn a lot of men in. Would this be the way Betty Weisenthal worked her inside men?

"You know Detective McLaughlan, as much as I pity for those women, I can't help thinking they are an odd pair. First one, then the other, involved with the same man. Then the older one, Elizabeth, divorced. And her relationship with Blair? How did she come to know him? Those stories about him running around with jewel thieves. I honestly don't want to be the one to cast stones, but really..."

"As I said, Mrs. Tewkesbury, we have an eye on the whole bunch of them." He smiled.

She sighed, smiling her relief back, as if they were old pals, and resumed, "You don't know what a load off my mind that is. I have a certain, well, standing to maintain. And above that, how do I know those three are, well, stable? They could be a threat to me."

"So that's why I ran into Eddie Kubek chatting with Jessica Minton this morning."

Alanna Tewkesbury studied him a minute. They weren't such pals now. She was calculating whether irony lurked beneath his innocent-sounding words. But she didn't get all indignant, as a woman with nothing to hide would. It looked to Leo that, instead, Alanna wanted to figure out the best way to keep working him. Finally, she played it safe with, "Mr. Kubek may have just been advising the girl not to threaten me. I certainly hope she didn't twist things."

"Shouldn't talking to her be a lawyer's job, or even mine?"

"I don't want a fuss," Alanna explained, showcasing her generosity. "I don't want to get the poor, deluded girl into trouble with the law. Is she claiming that I've had her threatened? Has she lied to you?"

"Eddie Kubek isn't known for his delicate touch, Mrs. Tewkesbury. I don't want you to get yourself in trouble by being mixed up with a shady customer," McLaughlan pointed out, sounding concerned.

"Has he been arrested, charged with anything since becoming my bodyguard, Detective McLaughlan?" All perfectly reasonable.

"No, you've got me there, Mrs. Tewkesbury. But where you just emphasized the importance of your standing, I thought I'd warn you that associating with a mug like Eddie Kubek doesn't make anyone look good. I know you wouldn't want anything to upset your husband."

"My husband approved of Mr. Kubek," the woman stated reasonably. "He believes in helping people turn over a new leaf, especially if they do it by keeping me safe from the riff-raff after a wealthy woman. But no harm done, Detective McLaughlan. I see you're only interested in my well-being. Now, let's just sit down, shall we? You must tell me more about this 122 Cambridge Street. This pin, is that the connection you made to me? When was I supposed to have been there? Who on earth told you this pipe dream, or need I guess? I can't imagine why any sane person would think I'd leave my jewelry behind anywhere, much less in such an out of the way place."

"That's why I thought it didn't make much sense. The place belonged to Evan Blair."

His tone had been perfectly sympathetic. Alanna Tewkesbury paused and flicked her cigarette ash into a crystal ashtray before she spoke dismissively, "I suppose those two sisters are trying to tie me in to that place in Lowell. How preposterous! I should think you'd be more discerning, Detective. Were they there, leaving behind phony clues?"

That slight edge to her voice would have been imperceptible if you hadn't been really listening for it. Again, why wasn't she acting indignant, rather than trying to figure out how the Mintons had gotten into the apartment? Before or after her? Which was worse?

Leo let Alanna go on with, "I didn't even know this Evan Blair."

"That makes sense. Actually, his real name was Gabriel Stuyvesant," Leo added helpfully.

"Sorry, Detective, doesn't ring a bell, either. But I can't help thinking it says something about that Minton woman; she'd consorted with a man running around under an alias."

Inwardly, Leo smiled at the cool maneuver. Still, something in her eye told him he'd struck pay dirt. There was also something warning him to be careful how deep he dug right now, or Madame Tewkesbury would bury him under his own questions.

"Detective, I'm fascinated by how you find all these different clues, sort out the bad ones, and make enough sense to pull them all together," Alanna flattered him in a honey-mellow tone, but her fingers gripped the cigarette holder viselike. "For instance, how did you find out about that apartment, may I ask?"

"Sure. Your friends the Minton sisters told me. They received a letter from Blair, Stuyvesant, conveniently posthumous." He grinned, implying an alliance against the Mintons. He was pleased that her response was tenser than she'd have wanted him to discern.

"The Minton sisters? They were in the apartment? When?"

There she went again, still harping on the Mintons in those secret Lowell digs–and how did she know 122 was an apartment building? He hadn't said. Not a big enough slip on its own; it could just be a good guess. Then again, the little slips were adding up, just not to quite enough to make a move, yet.

"I never said they were there," Leo nonchalantly corrected.

"Then they were never at the apartment?" She looked *so* serene as she took another drag on the cigarette in its elegant holder.

Leo casually eluded her question, "They gave me the letter sent to Elizabeth Minton. The letter gave me the address."

"And you've been there already?"

"I have the brooch," he misdirected.

Leo could see her move to pin him down on that one, but she thought better of it, perhaps not wanting to appear too concerned whether the police spotted her there. He was a little surprised, but not nonplussed, when she took a different tack.

"Ah, so it *was* those Mintons who came up with the pin."

Maybe he was going to get even more out of her than he'd planned. She shouldn't be this het-up about the two Mintons being in the apartment if she weren't afraid they'd found something she'd missed or overheard something incriminating.

"Why would you want to say that?" he queried, leaning casually to the side, interested not threatening.

"Why? Because those two have been trying to hang, blame, me for this murder all along. I wouldn't put it past them to go there and plant incriminating evidence or remove something that would incriminate their friend Sanders. I've tried to be kind, since she must be in such desperate straits losing her partner, but her craziness has gone far enough."

This gal was good, Leo had to admit, turning his story to her advantage, not that he was buying all that she was selling.

She pressed on, "Have you actually seen their so-called letter, Detective? Perhaps if I took a look at it, I could verify it for you."

"You'd recognize Stuyvesant's handwriting?"

"Well, I, no, of course not. I just thought I might be able to pick out some sign of a frame, isn't that the word?"

"That's the word, all right, Mrs. Tewkesbury. But you can trust us to smell out a phony letter."

"Of course."

She smiled, but Leo knew she wasn't happy. She really did want to get her claws, fiery-red lacquered, on that letter.

He rose and smiled, "Well, I guess that will be about all for now."

"For now? You still have doubts, Detective?" The innocent surprise was a nice touch, Leo inwardly acknowledged.

"Just a manner of speech. Since the pin isn't yours, and if nothing else surfaces to connect you to the case, which I'm sure it won't, you can write all this off as just a bad memory. And it's not as if anything's going to happen to the Mintons to confirm their claims against you. Sorry to take up your time, but I had to come here and cover all the bases, though I'm sure everything'll be fine."

"That's reassuring, Detective. I do wish I could be more help, but I'm afraid I know nothing useful."

They were walking toward the stairs leading up and out of the library.

"I just want to make sure that the pin isn't yours. It does look mighty similar to the one in those pictures..."

"Honestly, Detective, I really do know my own jewelry. Perhaps someone had a similar piece, or a knock-off. Did you have it appraised?"

"I haven't gotten an answer on that yet." Not really a lie. You couldn't get an answer to a question you hadn't asked.

"Then I'm sure you'll find that I'm right. I certainly hope those Minton women didn't plant it just to harass me. I don't know why I'm so patient with them."

"*Noblesse oblige.*"

"Mmm." She smiled, a tad at loss. Apparently her makeover hadn't quite gone as far as bringing her up to speed on clichés in French.

They had reached the top of the stairs, and Leo McLaughlan said, "Mrs. Tewkesbury. I just wanted to thank you for your cooperation. You've been more than accommodating on a case that must seem like a thorn in your side. I'm sure we'll be on the right track now. If you should think of something pertinent, make sure to give me a call. It's Leo McLaughlan. Here's my card."

"I can't imagine that I would, Detective, but certainly." She hesitated, then added, "And I'm so glad that you're sharp enough not to take those Minton women at their word."

"A guy can't afford to jump to conclusions in my job." That was open-ended enough.

"Of course. Milton will show you out."

"Swell, Mrs. Tewkesbury."

Yeah, it was swell. Alanna Tewkesbury knew damned well about the apartment in Lowell. She was pretty nervous about whether the Mintons knew about it, or if he connected her to the place. There was no reason for a woman with no connection to Gabriel Stuyvesant or Evan Blair to be jumpy, but there was plenty of reason for Betty Weisenthal to be.

He might have tried to shake her more by letting slip the contents of Blair's letter, but that would be too much, too soon. No, this was a barracuda who needed careful playing. Besides, rattling her too much might also send her south of the border to a country not keen enough on the good neighbor policy to send her back. And he still had to discredit her alibi. True, the trophy shelf in the library had given him a healthy shove in the right direction, but he needed to do more legwork for anything that would stick. Boy, Aaron would be real sore when he blew his pet case against Sanders out of the water. That was all right. Aaron'd come around when Leo came up with a good collar for both of them.

Yeah, Alanna Tewkesbury was smart, but not smart enough to get around a cop who knew when to play just a little dumb.

In the squad room, the sun glared through open windows that weren't much of an antidote to the stale air. Guys were at their desks, filling out reports, taking calls, and putting collars and complainants through the grill, but the one guy Leo wanted was like the bear–nowhere. Where the hell was Aaron Boyd? Here Leo had a lead he was chomping at the bit to follow through on with his partner, and he was on his own.

Reaching his desk, Leo scanned the room again, his eyes resting on the guy across the aisle.

"Scottie, did Aar get my message? You know where he is? It's important."

Shooting Leo an annoyed look, Scottie Doyle groused, "I dunno about any message, and never mind where Aaron's got to. Lieutenant Bandonie's been looking for you."

Leo paused in lighting up, dropping the flaring match into a heaped ashtray.

"You're pulling my leg, right?"

Scottie sank back in his chair, answering, "I ain't his confidant, Leo. But I wouldn't be surprised if it had to do with the Blair homicide. Word to the wise: get in there before he comes looking for you again."

"How long ago was he looking for me?"

"Fifteen minutes, give or take. Didn't write the time down, bud."

Leo's mouth twisted. Recent enough for Alanna Tewkesbury to drop a nickel on him. Maybe he hadn't played dumb and accommodating enough.

"Tell me something, Scottie, was Aaron here, when Bandonie came out?"

Doyle tipped his chair back, thinking, then shook his head. "Nah. A lot earlier, he got a call, went in to see the Lieutenant. They come out and looked around for you, then the Lieutenant sent him out, pronto. But that wasn't the last time he came looking for you. Like I said, go see him before he makes another trip, if you're smart."

"Yeah, sure, thanks, Scottie."

"Don't mention it."

Leo nodded curtly. This wasn't looking good. At least Aaron was out of it, though. So why *had* Bandonie sent Aaron off? The Blair case? Damn, he should have swung by Jessica Minton's apartment first to secure the evidence. Looked like he was going to be busy for a while.

Leo rapped on the opaque, rough glass on the Lieutenant's door. From the other side came a gruff, "Come in."

McLaughlan moved in easily, but not too nonchalantly. You never took Bandonie for granted. You could depend on him in a crunch, but he wasn't your pal.

The man behind the cluttered desk didn't look up. He just growled, "Close the door behind you. Be right with you."

No invitation or command to sit down. Hmm. Leo turned away just long enough to close the door, deciding that he'd better take the initiative before he found himself heading out to the woodshed.

"I've been looking for Aaron. Scottie says you sent him out. Something I should be in on?"

The beetled black brows of Lou Bandonie thrust forward on his wrinkled forehead as he tossed off, "You tell me. Maybe I don't have this detective-partner whos is down right. I've only been on the force twenty-three years, but I thought the idea was that you guys were supposed to work together."

"C'mon, Lieutenant, don't give me the runaround. Aaron was supposed to meet me for a questioning on the Blair case, but he never did."

"Yeah? If you ask me, Boyd showed good sense missing that boat. While you were knee-deep in tea and crumpets with Alanna Tewkesbury, Boyd was here to run down a lead from a call that came in on your case."

"Lead? What kind of a lead?"

"A lead about the murder weapon. Seems like someone thinks one of those Minton dames was covering for the boyfriend. Supposed to have his gun, the murder weapon, hidden in her apartment. Aaron's with one of the teams at the apartments now. We were able to get a warrant quick this time, and I sent him and a few Blues to do a search."

Knocked for a loop, Leo McLaughlan uttered in disbelief, "What? Are you pulling my leg?"

With elaborate patience, Bandonie replied, "Son, if I was going to pull someone's leg, it would be Betty Grable's, not yours. Sit down."

None of this jibed with what he'd gotten in his chat with Alanna Tewkesbury or his instincts on the case. But Leo had a good idea how a warrant to search the Mintons had been so easy to get.

Leo sat, but he seized the initiative, "Look, Lieutenant, there's something hinky about that call. I just got back from a little chat with Alanna Tewkesbury..."

"That's half, hell, two-thirds of why you're in here now, McLaughlan,"

Bandonie said. "What did I tell you about mixing it up with the wife of a bigwig like Wilmington Tewkesbury?"

"To lay off unless I had something solid to go on–and I have."

"Yeah?" Bandonie was interested, skeptical, but interested.

"Yeah. I've got some links between her and Evan Blair, when he was Gabriel Stuyvesant in that jewelry heisting ring."

"How solid?"

Leo hesitated, and Bandonie scowled.

"No, wait, listen," Leo persisted levelly. He related the details about the apartment in Lowell, the photo, the pin, and Alanna's slip about knowing the apartment *was* in Lowell. Bandonie listened impassively. You never knew what he'd decided until he told you. But before Leo got to his clincher, "the old man" cut him off.

"And it was the Mintons who tipped you off in the first place?"

"They told me about the apartment, about Blair's putting the finger on Tewkesbury, but I..."

"You got nothing, nothing but trouble from where I'm sitting. Your partner was the lucky one–lucky I sent him out before he could meet you at Tewkesbury's and flush his career down the toilet. You know how I knew you went to see Tewkesbury?"

"Aaron must have told you."

"Nah. Aaron was covering your butt. Didn't say where you were, just you had gone out to run some leads and he couldn't get ahold of you."

"Then who?" As if Leo didn't know.

"Who else? A mouthpiece of the grande dame herself–and she was not a happy woman, Leo."

That was bad. Bandonie's tone had not only reverted to elaborate reasonableness, but he was on a first-name basis.

"I treated that woman with kid gloves," Leo asserted. "She's not happy because she has so much to hide."

But Leo was kicking himself for not realizing Tewkesbury was just as capable as him of putting on a sunny face while she was already lowering the boom.

"Be that as it may, Leo, she and her husband have a lot of juice. Probably why we got the warrant so fast. Enough to send you, me, and Aaron cleaning out horse stalls on 42nd Street, the environs of which do not allow us to enjoy the lovely air of the nearby Hudson River."

"So, you're going to let this broad walk for murder, just to keep your cushy seat?"

"The only cushy chairs would be in the Commissioner's office, not this rat trap. You listen to me, Leo. If I have to muck out stalls with you and Aaron, it'll be for something that's gonna stick. Leads from those Minton dames are tainted unless they put you onto something definite. That slip about the apartment in Lowell, it's your word against hers. Who you think the D.A. will back when her hubby starts flexing his political muscle?"

"Look, Jeffrey Hooley from the F.B.I. is getting me Betty Weisenthal's prints on Monday. If I can match those to Alanna Tewkesbury..."

"Leo, after that call from Tewkesbury's lawyer, you can bet she won't be volunteering to take off her pretty white gloves and dirty up her digits with ink any time soon. And you're kidding yourself if you think you can get away with hauling a Tewkesbury in here against her will."

"So that's it. We just let her skate? Hell, I know this Blair or Stuyvesant was no saint, but murder's murder. Money doesn't give her the right..."

"Money gives her power, and no one gets around power by just mouthin' off. In fact, mouthin' off gets you knee-deep in horse shit. You plan to go any deeper, don't drag me or your partner down with you. You're officially off this case."

Leo stared.

"Boyd can continue on it with Martinelli. I've already made the reassignment," Bandonie finished.

"You can't do that."

"Sure I can, McLaughlan. I'm the lieutenant and you're the sergeant."

"Boyd's already made up his mind," Leo argued. "He's going to railroad this Sanders if he can. He must be going to town with this tip on the gun."

"If Sanders is innocent, there won't be any gun, and Boyd will have to come up with someone else. Anyway, it's done. Work on the Hornette swindle of those orphans and old ladies."

"You're just going to let the money talk, Bandonie?"

When the lieutenant spoke, his tone was more measured than a chemistry project, "Look, McLaughlan, unless you have something more than conjecture, let it die. You don't have proof of motive, you don't have a weapon or witnesses, and your suspect has an alibi."

"What if I can shake that alibi?"

"You can shake a thousand-mile alibi, right now?"

"I have to run down..."

Bandonie raised his hands to shut up Leo, warning, "Unless you have something real, unshakeable, more powerful than a guy who the Commissioner squirms to get a golf date with, I don't want to hear it. In fact, you go blabbing anymore and I'm going to have to make Mrs. Tewkesbury, her lawyer, and the Commissioner pink with delight by suspending you, *capice*?"

Leo was almost stunned. Then he noted something funny in Bandonie's eyes. Testing, Leo began, "So, what you're saying..."

"I'm saying get the hell out of my office, go do your job–and don't be getting the rest of us into the soup with ideas that are still half-baked. That's all I want to know. You're a college boy, you dope out what you gotta do."

And that was it. Leo was on his feet, thinking. If the Lieutenant didn't know everything, then Leo was out on a limb, alone. At least he could stop worrying about taking Aaron down with him. So if he worked on the q.t., he could pursue a lead that could blow Mrs. Wilmington Tewkesbury's alibi right out of the water. Wouldn't that just be a fourteen-karat pleasure?

Back in the squad room, Leo spotted Aaron chalking out. His back to Leo hid any hint of what he'd come up with at Elizabeth Minton's.

"Find what you were looking for, Aar?" Leo hadn't spoken until he was almost on his friend.

Aaron Boyd turned sharply. His face was tired.

His own expression couldn't have been too welcoming because Aaron's reply was a short, "You got a beef with me, Leo?"

Leo took the time to snap a match aflame on the corner of his desk, light up, and take a drag and exhale before answering: "Nope. But I'd say from the look on your pan that you ought to have one with the screwball who sent you on that wild goose chase after Elizabeth Minton. Maybe if you'd stuck with your partner, you wouldn't have blown an afternoon."

"Yeah, like you made out so well. What did I tell you about nosing around those Tewkesburies? If you'd minded your ps and qs, then I'd still have my partner. Instead, I'm stuck with Martinelli. That guy never clams up. Gimme a smoke, will you?"

Leo shook out the cigarettes, waiting while his partner took one. You got more out of Boyd if you let him do things on his own terms. An occasional needle helped, too, but it had to be timed just right.

Just before Aaron took his first drag, Leo blew out some smoke and observed, "So that's why you never showed to back me with Tewksbury, the 'hot tip' on Elizabeth Minton?"

Boyd snorted, "It came in right about the time I found your message. What else was I gonna do? It wasn't like I could give you a buzz at the Waldorf. I had to go right to the Lieutenant, and he sent me out with Martinelli. Let me tell you, Bandonie wasn't exactly tap-dancing with joy when he finally wormed it out of me why you'd gone missing. Anyway, the Lieutenant calls all the shots, and I can't say I disagree with him on this one."

"Except your tip didn't pan out."

Boyd scowled and took a long drag on his cigarette before he snorted, "They could've moved it. We got the warrant to check both sisters' places. Hell, those broads were madder than a couple of wet hens. They won't want to see us around any time soon."

"*Us*? You were the guy playing D-Day in their apartments, not me," Leo corrected dryly.

But he was thinking, *It didn't sound as if they'd gotten the evidence Jessica Minton had showed him–or would that only appear to be evidence if Minton put it in the right perspective?* Leo doubted either sister would have volunteered evidence that they feared might be dismissed or, worse, "lost" by Aaron.

Boyd was enjoying this smoke after a useless, miserable afternoon. He continued, "Brother, it makes no never mind. We're just a couple of flat-foots to them. Interchangeable parts. What'd you come up with, anyway?"

Leo was taken off-guard. He'd been wondering why Elizabeth Minton's lumping him in with Aaron should sit funny. He started to give Aaron the straight dope, but caught himself and said, "Not enough to impress Bandonie. You know I'm off the case now."

"Yeah, but you said you had something on the Tewkesbury dame."

Leo only commented, "Aar, I thought you didn't want go near the Tewkesburys."

A phone was ringing somewhere in the vicinity of Leo's desk, but he was more concerned with keeping Aaron clear of his trouble.

"Yeah, well, if you really have something, Leo..."

"Like I said, not enough to impress the Lieutenant. I got a strong feeling from some of the great lady's answers that she had something to hide about both Gabriel Stuyvesant and Evan Blair."

"Not enough to perk up the D.A.'s ears?"

"Nah." Well, that much was true–and it was worth bending the truth to save Aaron's hide.

Boyd started to say something more, but Scottie interrupted, "Hey, McLaughlan, I ain't your secretary. There's a lady on your line and she don't sound happy."

Boyd smiled, "Tewkesbury or Minton, you're in for it, brother! Have a ball!"

"Yeah, thanks a load," Leo shot back as his partner slouched off.

Leo turned to take the phone, when Boyd called back, "Say, if you do get anything on her majesty Tewkesbury, let me know."

"I knew you were a right guy, Aar."

"Nah, it just beats having to go up against those two Minton dames again with only Martinelli for back up."

Leo snorted his amusement, stubbing out his cigarette as he took the phone. Now for the unknown dragon lady on the other end of the line.

"Detective McLaughlan here."

"What's the matter, McLaughlan, afraid to face me?" Liz Minton's voice sizzled over the wire. "Have to send your pal to do your dirty work? What on God's green earth is going on? Are you playing my sister and me for saps? We give you some pay dirt on Alanna Tewkesbury, you make nice, and then you send some storm troopers in to massacre our apartments."

Rather than snap back at her, Leo held the receiver away from his ear and let Elizabeth rave. It saved his hearing and ought to exhaust her soon enough. At least it would most people. Maybe the army could save on ordnance by dropping Elizabeth Minton on Japan. That gal was something else.

Leo glanced at his watch. He was supposed to be going off duty soon. At last, a lull from the receiver. La Minton finally needed to come up for air.

"Got it out of your system, Miss Minton?" Calm but not infuriatingly so, Leo McLaughlan knew how to work a potential riot.

"You think this is funny?"

"No. I think it's dead serious. And you need to know some facts. You're an intelligent woman–an angry, intelligent woman."

"Your darned tootin' I'm angry!" But his assessment seemed to mollify her somewhat before she continued, "I deserve to know what's going on. I gave you some important information. We were planning on giving you evidence! What gives here?"

"What gives is exactly what I warned you about," Leo answered calmly, keeping his own resentment under control. "Tewkesbury flexed some political muscle and, presto, they pulled me off the case. I had nothing to do with the search. The whole thing went down while I was questioning the great lady. She probably had it all in the works even before I sat down."

A stunned silence on the other end of the line. Finally, Liz asked, concerned, "You didn't lose your job for helping us, did you?"

"No, Mrs. McLaughlan's little boy is still collecting his check from the city, but not for working on the Evan Blair murder."

"Does this mean that storm trooper Boyd is going to come after us tooth and tongs..."

Leo would have pondered the mangled amalgamation of clichés but, not having the time, stopped Liz with, "I can't talk here. Look, I'm going off shift. Meet me in a half hour at that Italian restaurant where I interviewed you and your sister?"

"Della Mirandola's?"

"That's the one."

"I'll be there before you can say Lake Chargoggagoggmanchauggagoggchaubunagungamaugg."

"That takes a long time to say."

"I have to change my outfit."

"Just make it snappy. I have something interesting to tell you."

"What?"

"See you there."

Leo hung up. If he'd read Liz Minton right, curiosity would outweigh tardiness. And he could use a nice big plate of fettuccine about now. It had been a long day, and the night wasn't going to make it any shorter.

Chapter Nineteen

Saturday, June 2

Sitting back in the bustle of della Mirandola's, Leo McLaughlan asked himself why he was giving away so much to a civilian during an ongoing investigation. But then he wasn't investigating, officially, anymore, was he? Besides, his instinct told him that Elizabeth Minton was holding back a chunk of the puzzle. He knew she wouldn't share it unless he secured her confidence with the straight dope on Mrs. Tewkesbury. Maybe he also figured he owed her a little something after the raw deal she'd gotten this afternoon.

Now, if that Fed, Hooley, would only come through with those prints. Then there was his own plan for a little "private investigating" tonight. And as long as Alanna Tewkesbury had her hooks into the official investigation, it was better if the evidence Jessica Minton was holding stayed off the record. Leo McLaughlan wasn't thrilled not to be playing by the book, but, since Mrs. Tewkesbury had smacked him in the kisser with that book, he was willing to be flexible for now.

McLaughlan glanced down at the remains of the fettucine on his plate, wondering about Elizabeth Minton. If she'd been in such a rush to give him a piece of her mind and find out what he had to say, she should have been here before the entrée. Even now, the waiter was clearing the table and promising to bring a cannoli and coffee.

Dessert eventually appearing, Leo dug in, silently cautioning himself, *just enough to keep up your strength, son, not too much to dull the senses. You'll need them sharp when that Minton gal shows*.

"Don't you look full and satisfied."

She was right before him. Those damned high heels really gave the gal altitude–and the almost stove-pipe crown of her blue-and-black striped hat, matching the chevron stripes of her suit, put her even further into the stratosphere.

"A guy needs to keep up his strength," Leo replied, getting up like the gentleman he was.

Liz waved him back into his seat, continuing, "You must be exhausted, what with harassing civic-minded citizens who've been trying to help you."

As the waiter seated her, McLaughlan remarked, "Aren't you going to order? You must have had quite a day. Eaten yet?"

Liz dismissed the waiter as she answered, "Eat? Who could eat? I barely touched a bite. Only two or three bananas, a peanut butter and jelly sandwich, the Hershey bar I was saving for V-J Day..."

"I get it. But you know I had nothing to do with the search. A call came in when I was talking to Alanna Tewkesbury, an anonymous call."

"Gosh, I wonder who *that* could have been?" Liz's query dripped irony.

Leo started to speak, but Alfonso della Mirandola had swooped down to greet Liz. So, while seeming intent on his cannoli, Leo worked on calibrating exactly how much he could afford to tell Elizabeth Minton and how much *she* knew but wasn't telling him.

With della Mirandola gone after persuading Liz to take some dessert, Leo said, "I've got to hand it to you, Miss Minton, you're not half as steamed as I expected."

At first, Liz's dark eyes were icy. Then, she actually smiled, though it could have been warmer, before responding, "You said you had something that points at Mrs. Tewkesbury. And my sister thinks that, in the long run, since your search came up empty, the whole thing actually worked in our favor. That clears us of having any evidence to hide"

"It proves you don't have the gun now," McLaughlan allowed neutrally.

Liz Minton's eyes narrowed, but she bit back what she wanted to say. Instead, what came out was almost disarming in its frustration, "What do you people want? What do I have to do to clear Larry and get you to focus on that woman?"

"I'm already on her track, Miss Minton. That's why I wanted to see you."

Her expression hopeful, Elizabeth leaned forward, her hand just stopping short of touching McLaughlan's wrist. "Yes? She let something slip? Something you can nail her on?"

Leo McLaughlan shook his head, then elaborated, "Wish I could tell you I had this wrapped up in pretty pink ribbons, but not yet."

"Yet?"

"Yet. What do you know about Alanna Tewkesbury's private plane?"

"Private plane? She has one? Oh, wait, yes. Maybe I *did* know that. I never really thought about it before, but she did brag about the plane over a business lunch once, ages ago. How long would it take to fly from Florida to New York?"

"Oh, say around five hours."

"There you go! That explains, no, blows her alibi!"

"It won't if you don't pipe down and keep it under that unique specimen of a hat you're wearing."

Liz blinked at his dry tone, and Leo McLaughlan returned to his dessert. He'd give that remark a little time to sink in.

"Okay, okay, I can zip my lips." When Leo's expression betrayed his doubts about her discipline, Liz asserted, "I can do it if Larry's life and nailing Evan's killer are at stake."

That Leo could buy. Yet he also knew too much temptation could topple the strongest resolve. So he needed to make his move tonight, but not before confirming certain suspicions. He queried Elizabeth, "When you and Alanna were getting all convivial, did she tell you where she lands in New York?"

"*Tell* me? She went on and on about how she was keeping this little airfield alive with *her* patronage. She loved the privacy and some quaint little restaurant nearby. What was the name of that field, now? Named after a president. McKinley?"

"Garfield."

"Sure, that's it! It was one of those guys who got himself assassinated at the turn of the century." While Leo took a sip of coffee, Liz pressed, "How did you know about it? I can't imagine she'd be advertising it *now*."

"She's too cozy for that. I only knew because I saw a photo in her apartment. I thought I recognized the field, but I wasn't 100% sure. My Dad used to take me and my brothers there when we were kids. I still keep in touch with the main security guard."

"She *showed* you the photo?"

"Not exactly. It was in the room where we had our little chat."

"I'm surprised she left it where you could see it," Liz speculated, pausing to murmur thanks to the waiter delivering her coffee and dessert.

Waiting until the man left, Leo observed, "She's sharp, but I don't think she expected anyone to notice it. I wonder if she noticed anything except herself in those pictures."

Liz berated herself, "Why didn't I make the connection with the plane before? I didn't even remember about it until you brought it up just now. Think of all the time and agony I could have saved by pointing out that hole in her alibi."

Liz Minton looked so genuinely miserable that Leo was at a loss for what to say. He didn't owe her anything, really, but ... He must be going soft. Finally, all he said was, "What's done cannot be undone."

Liz shook her head, "My sister's always saying that."

"Makes sense, an actress spouting Shakespeare. You just don't expect it from a flatfoot, though."

He was having a little fun with her now, but she didn't get upset. Instead,

Elizabeth returned, “Detective, I don’t care if you play Beethoven’s Fifth on a kazoo. I just want this case solved, with the innocent parties off the hook and the guilty ones wriggling all the way down to their peroxide roots.”

“You think Eddie Kubek has a bleach job?”

“I think I want to know what’s next on the agenda,” Liz returned.

McLaughlan’s mouth quirked. He finished his coffee, then stared Liz down when he answered, “This is police business, Miss Minton. Let’s just say it’s not policy to keep a suspect’s intended informed on everything.”

Liz raised an eyebrow but managed to bridle what Leo McLaughlan knew was a formidable temper. She wanted something from him and knew she wouldn’t get it by antagonizing him.

“Tell you what, Miss Minton. I’ll let you know something you’re after, if you’ll come clean for me–not even the whole shirt, just the collar and cuffs, so to speak.”

Liz considered, then spoke levelly, with just a trace of a gambler’s smile, “I like your metaphor. Go on.”

“I can tell you this. That anonymous tip is like a burr under my saddle. Why make that call? Why say you have the gun? Why not send us after Sanders, himself? Associating you, not just Sanders, with the murder weapon is pretty strong medicine.”

“Just what are you getting at?” Liz asked, her voice now taut.

“What do you think I’m getting at, Miss Minton?” he returned, unperturbed by her reaction.

Elizabeth Minton sat back. She could have been thinking about his question, or she could have been figuring how to answer without giving anything away. Finally, she replied, “I don’t think, I *know*, Larry did not kill Evan Blair. I *know* you’ll never find the gun he used to commit the crime because he’s innocent. I *know* Alanna Tewkesbury is no good and that she’d stop at nothing to destroy us.”

“But why you? Why claim you have the murder weapon?”

“I can’t answer that,” Liz replied tensely.

Couldn’t or wouldn’t, McLaughlan wondered. But he said, friendly-like, “How about I let you in on a theory of mine?”

“I’m all ears.” Liz folded her arms defensively before her.

“Let’s say Larry Sanders has a gun...”

“He did not murder anyone!”

“Didn’t say that he did, Miss Minton. Smoke? Oh, sorry, you’re quitting, aren’t you?”

“All this beating around the bush isn’t making it any easier.” Liz’s brow arched. “But do go on with your charming story.”

“Let’s say that Larry Sanders had a gun,” Leo proposed. “Let’s say it went missing, ended up in the hands of someone who wanted Blair, Stuyvesant, dead. It’d be mighty convenient for someone settling an old score to use that gun to bump off your partner and leave some innocent schmo holding the bag."

Elizabeth Minton gave Leo McLaughlan a pensive stare. Was she mulling the danger of confirming his story or was she just plain affronted? Her cheek twitched, but Liz Minton was tough to read. Maybe she needed another gentle nudge.

"Tell you what, Miss Minton. You give me what you know–and I mean all of it–about Larry Sanders and the gun, and I'll give you an idea about what I can do with the dope on Mrs. Tewkesbury's aeronautical peregrinations."

"Could you put that last part in English, detective?"

"Her flying."

"What I know is that Larry has no gun–and I can say that without reservation," she seemed almost relieved to state. "You should be able to check registrations to confirm."

"We both know that there are a lot of free-floating weapons."

"Owning an illegal weapon would be out of character for Larry," Elizabeth countered promptly. "Why, just the other day I saw him give a waitress the devil for offering him too much coffee."

"That's all you have to tell me?"

"You don't believe me?"

It wasn't belligerent, but she was definitely calling his bluff.

"All right." Leo shrugged and went for his wallet, pausing to say, "But remember, I didn't say Sanders was guilty. I just thought you might explain why someone could frame him. Otherwise, sending us on this wild goose chase actually works against the frame, since we didn't find anything. Heck, it almost sounds as if you or your sister cooked up the call to clear Sanders in a backhanded way."

For a minute, Leo thought Elizabeth was going to explode at his suggestion, but she held back her Vesuvius temper. Instead, she deftly proposed a different read on the fruitless search: "The more sensible deduction is that no weapon was found because there was none to find."

"Boyd believes you moved it somewhere else. See, if you don't give me more to go on, I don't have any reason to make him look at your pal Tewkesbury," the detective pointed out. "That book and the picture aren't a direct enough link to the murder itself. And it looks worse if I do find you've been holding out on me, covering up for Sanders having the gun."

"You think I'm that dishonest?" Liz's tone was tight, though not exactly indignant.

He parried this second attempt to put him on the defensive: "I think you believe in Sanders, and you'll do whatever it takes to protect him. Just remember, if you go out on a limb, you might end up sawing it off, and you won't go down alone. There's Sanders, and I'm willing to bet your sister, too. I don't see you as the kind of woman who wants to hurt the people she cares about."

Elizabeth tightened her lips, but her eyes weren't hostile anymore. She seemed to do some tall thinking before replying, "Look, I'll do whatever I can to help you, to help Larry, because he's innocent. But I can't tell you what you want to hear because you want to hear it. I'm sorry. I've said all I can. So, now what are you going to do about Alanna Tewkesbury's alibi? How do you check it out? *When* do you check it out?"

"Pretty soon. I don't want her to have time to figure out that I'm wise to the hitch in her alibi."

"You're going to the airfield tonight, then? Will there be some kind of record? Maybe I should go along and help you check it out!"

"Whoa, sister! Maybe you should just sit tight and let the police take care of police business."

"But you could use a witness, right, to back up that you found evidence against her there."

"Some corroborating witness: the suspect's girlfriend, who happens to have it in for the gal the evidence incriminates."

"Oh."

"I thought you'd say that." The bill arrived, and Leo silenced Liz's protest about his covering her coffee and dessert before he continued, "You just sit tight. Eddie Kubek's chat with your sister, this siccing a search team on you both, my being bounced off the official investigation: they're playing hardball, and it's only going to get worse. Getting in the line of fire is my job not yours."

"But..."

"No 'buts.' If you knew Eddie Kubek's rap sheet, you'd take a nosedive into a foxhole. One dead dressmaker is enough for the garment industry. Clear?"

"Crystal."

Leo regarded Elizabeth Minton speculatively. She'd given in a little too easily. He warned, "And if I were you, I'd keep an eye on your sister, too. If Eddie Kubek had one 'chat' with her, he's liable to have a rematch on his mind. Where is she right now, anyway?"

Liz had gone increasingly whiter at McLaughlan's warning. She stumbled a little in answering, "She's with some friends. After she did damage control at her apartment, they took her out to dinner. My heavens, do you think she's in danger?"

"The both of you just lay low. I intend to keep a low profile, myself, but, if I do stir up a hornets' nest tonight, I don't want you two getting stung. I can't tell you to leave town since you're involved in an ongoing investigation, and considering the jam you almost got yourself into the time you 'vacationed' in Lowell, it's probably better you don't wander too far."

"We also got you some case-breaking clues," Liz disputed.

"Don't exaggerate their importance. Just keep in mind no clues will bring a smile to your pal Sanders' face if they free him to attend your funeral."

"You really know how to cheer a girl up."

"Never mind that. Be temporarily glum rather than a corpse with an undertaker's smile fixed on your pan. I mean it. You two stay out of trouble," McLaughlan warned.

"But you *are* going to the airfield tonight? What kind of evidence would it be, a logbook? Can you just take it or what?"

"Don't worry about that, Miss Minton. You do as I told you. If you have any trouble, call me. You understand?"

Liz nodded. They left together, with Leo putting Elizabeth in a cab. All thoughts of surreptitiously trailing him to Garfield Field had gone up in smoke, smoke from the fire kindled by his warnings about people she loved. That had been exactly his plan. He didn't like the way the pressure was building. He'd better get enough goods on Alanna Tewkesbury, and fast, to neutralize her and her crew before they had a chance to strike.

Damn, if he weren't officially off the case ... He couldn't walk in on his own and seize the logbooks. He didn't even have a partner with him to confirm where he found them or what they said. There was that little item called the Sixth Amendment standing in his way. Right now, he had a snowball's chance in hell of getting any judge to issue a search warrant.

But if he were at the field as just a member of the public, that was no problem. And if he stumbled across the log, a public record, without bothering anyone, that wouldn't be a problem, either. And best of all, if he happened to come back on Monday with a Federal Agent, Jeff Hooley, as his officer in charge, that would be pay dirt. There was the likelihood that a G-man would be able to get a federal warrant to seize the books, giving him an end-run around Alanna Tewkesbury's local juice. But he had to know the books were there; he had to be able to hand this agent more than a suspicion before asking him, especially since the guy was already doing him a big favor by delivering the prints, personally.

Leo McLaughlan wasn't any crusader, but he didn't like to see a lot of dough buying someone out of a murder rap. He didn't like to see an innocent guy fry for it, either. And he was more than a little sore that Tewkesbury had put him behind the eight ball. Aaron Boyd wasn't the only one who wanted to keep his job long enough to collect his pension.

A couple of things still nagged at Leo, though. Liz Minton hadn't grabbed the out he'd given her with his scenario about her, Sanders, and the gun. Was she trying to make a patsy of him? And then there was that Lois Wong standing silently in the background. She couldn't have been happy to find the architect of her family's disaster happily running a business with one of her chums. She had an alibi, but was it legit? Could Lois Wong have slipped out without her friend knowing? Maybe her apartment was the one they should have searched. But he wasn't on the case giving directions anymore. Then again, he still had Aaron's ear, didn't he? He just had to be careful what he whispered into it.

Saturday, June 2, later in the evening

Jessica Minton knew she had only a few minutes before it was too late. She blew the mink away from her face, then offered Iris Rossetti an over-the-shoulder, knowing look to pronounce, “Iris, this is divine!”

Draped over her armchair, in black silk loungewear, Iris purred, “Too bad you have an allergy to that kind of fur.”

“Now that’s a pity,” Wes Castle joined in, standing next to Iris. “A glamour girl who can’t wear mink. There ought to be a law.”

Slipping out of the luxurious coat that had covered her fitted, black linen dress, Jessica shrugged, “I tell myself at least I’m not condemning a herd of furry beasts to death.”

“If you’re trying to make me feel guilty,” quipped Iris, unwinding her limber limbs from the chair, “it won’t work. They’re just a bunch of rodents in my book.”

“Ah,” surmised Jessica, handing over the coat, “then perhaps we should trade this in for fur of rat?”

Wes chuckled.

Iris gave Jess the evil eye, then glided off with her prized possession, saying, “I’m putting this away before either of you gets any ideas about re-clothing naked minks.”

“Can’t imagine Iris getting much use out of that glad rag in June,” Wes grinned.

Clasping her hands playfully behind her back, Jessica grinned back, “June is the only time a girl on our salary can afford a coat like that–and showing off for her pals is half the fun!”

“Ah, a little tip on the female psyche.” He winked.

From the bedroom, Jamie barked grumpily, Iris’s entrance having disturbed his snooze. Jess tensed, and Wes remarked, surprised, “I thought you liked the pup.”

“Oh, I do,” Jess returned, hoping not *too* quickly. She couldn’t exactly say it wasn’t the dog but remembering where she’d gotten him that triggered her reaction. “He just startled me; that’s all. I’ve been living with a cat too long not to jump when I unexpectedly hear a dog. Blackie sure is a playful little guy, isn’t he?”

She and Liz had come up with a pretty routine AKA for Jamie. All the better to help him blend into the woodwork–she hoped!

“Playful! You can say that again! He won’t let me stop throwing that rubber ball of his. Sometimes, I wonder if I’m going out with him or Iris.”

Jessica and Wes lounged over to the modern lines of Iris’s *faux* fireplace. Wes and Iris had taken her out this evening to get her mind off the police tossing her apartment. Jess wasn't sure whether she or they were trying harder to keep things light and gay. She wasn't even sure how she did feel. Should she be afraid because Alanna had called them on taking back the gun and raised the stakes by giving that anonymous tip to incriminate them? Or dare she feel relieved that the attempt had been thwarted when both Minton apartments came up clean?

Hiding her concerns, she smiled at Wes, "Unlike Iris, Blackie comes with his own fur coat."

"To tell you the truth, I think Iris is hoping you never find the dog's real owner."

Jessica concurred, "He's definitely better off with Iris."

"I thought you didn't know where he came from?"

"Oh, I don't, really. I just meant with all Iris's love and attention, he's a lot better off than down in Battery Park where I found him."

"Is she telling you about where she meets fellas?" Iris teased, rejoining them, Jamie at her heels.

"It's nice to see you girls get along so well," kidded Wes. To Iris, he added, "Say, here's a coincidence. Last night at the Wansteads' dinner, Alanna Tewkesbury mentioned that her prize-winning Scottie went missing."

Thank God Wes only had eyes for Iris, Jess decided because she was pretty sure every ounce of color had drained from her face. And Iris, what a trooper, her glance only briefly flickered at Jess's reaction before she smoothly commented, "Oh, she must have millions of prize-winning pooches. What's one less, more or less?"

"Quite a lot more. He's worth more than your coat," Wes explained, encircling Iris with his arm.

"There you go, Iris," Jessica managed to kid, "you could have saved yourself a battle with the other gals for that mink and just wrapped Blackie around your shoulders."

"Maybe. This dog was a pedigreed pooch: James Stuart VI," Wes laughed.

Jamie/Blackie barked at his secret identity, ending with a growl.

"Huh, he acts like he knows the name," Wes noted. "And does he ever hate it! Did you hear that growl?"

"I'll say!" Jessica chimed in. "He must have a grudge against some other Scottie with a similar name, right Iris?"

"Wha ... oh, sure."

Wes was down, wrestling away the rubber ball that "Blackie" had brought in, rubbing the critter's head, before tossing the toy across the room.

Iris, suspiciously studied her friend over Wes's head, while he played with the dog.

Jessica struggled to disguise what she was dying to ask: had Wes mentioned this dog when Alanna Tewkesbury talked about the missing Jamie? If Tewkesbury knew that Iris had the valuable Scottie from the same apartment as the now-missing-murder weapon, she might go after her friend. What Jess wouldn't give for a bromo!

As Jamie came trotting back with the ball, Iris queried, "So, when Alanna Tewkesbury was talking about her Scottie, did you say anything about my fine fellow?"

Jessica held her breath when Wes looked up and thought before answering, "About Blackie? No, why should I? Jess found him way down in the Battery. That's pretty distant from where you'd find Alanna. Those little legs wouldn't carry him that far–unless you think he hopped the subway."

"You think he snuck in under the turnstile?" Jess joked, she hoped playfully enough.

"Poor boy would end up flat as a pancake if he tried that during rush hour," Iris kidded, rubbing her pup's noggin.

Jess thanked God that Wes went off on a tangent: "Now there's something I've never done, ride the subway."

"Unless you've always wanted to feel like a canned sardine, Wes, you haven't missed anything," she assured him.

Wes smiled and tossed Jamie's ball, continuing, "Besides, Mrs. Tewkesbury lost an investment. Jessica found a pal for my girl. It's not the same thing at all."

As he stood up, Iris fastened her boyfriend in a big hug and crowed, "And you wonder why I adore this big lug."

"No," Jessica smiled. "I don't think I wonder at all."

"Aw shucks, you two will give a guy a swelled head."

Jamie-cum-Blackie barked.

"Well, on that note of familial bliss, I've got to get home." Jessica glanced down at her watch and exclaimed, "Good gosh, it's after one! It's been a long day." *They didn't know the half of it!* "I'll just call a cab."

"At this hour, Jessica?" Iris chided. "Nonsense. Wes will see you down to the lobby and take you home in his car."

"Even seeing me down to a cab would be fine," Jessica protested. To be honest, though, she'd be happier if he walked in her door and stood armed guard. No, she'd really be happier if *James* were here to stand armed guard.

"I'll step into the next room and call for my driver to come around," Wes promised.

Iris smiled her agreement then gave Jessica a "don't-you-dare-argue-with-me look."

With a playful curtsey, Jess relented, "The three of us will await your return, kind sir."

"Maybe not the three of you," Wes laughed as "Blackie" trotted after him.

With Wes out of earshot, Iris, pounced on Jessica, "So, have you made Wes and me accessories after the fact?"

Jessica shrugged, inwardly kicking herself for having to fib, "I don't get you, Iris."

She couldn't face her friend, so she moved off and pretended to enjoy the view from the picture window. They both knew it was a lame attempt at avoidance.

Iris put a hand on Jessica's shoulder and persisted, "Okay, kiddo, out with it. What am I doing with Alanna Tewkesbury's pooch?"

Their voices were low, so as not to carry into the next room. Jessica couldn't hold out on Iris any longer. "I knew that I should have given you the full story. But Liz made it seem you'd be safer if you really could claim you thought we had given you a stray. She convinced me that it was a million-to-one shot anyone would ever be the wiser. We couldn't let him stay in that apartment where God knows what they might do to him out of anger. The creep watching Jamie was violent towards him!"

"Look, Jess, you got me wrong. I don't mind. That pup is aces with me–and Mrs. T., let's just say she's a different type of dog altogether, a real bi..."

"Then you know she's not someone to mess with, Iris. But, from what Wes was saying, it doesn't look as if she'll figure out you have her dog. Still, there is something you could help me with. How close is Wes to Alanna Tewkesbury?"

"I'm not sure. Not that close. I think his parents and her husband moved in the same circles. He never gave me the impression *he* knew her well."

Jessica probed further, "Do you think he's said anything about knowing Liz and me to her?"

"Why would he? That crowd isn't so hot on us thespians, you know. It's not like she talks to him much, anyway. More like she doesn't object if he's in the same room. Anyway, I can't imagine Wes would ever agree with anything bad she would say about you," Iris insisted.

"Not a man who seems sweet on you and your dog," Jess impishly assured her pal.

"My illegal dog?"

"Remember, Iris, not unless he hopped the subway."

"No, my Blackie would grab a cab," Iris playfully concluded.

Wes rejoined them, saying, "And where are we driving you, Mademoiselle Minton?"

"The exclusive *Chez Minton*, at Damascus Place."

"Then let us be off. Joining us, Iris?"

"Ah, no. It's late to be traipsing off. I trust you to get her home safely."

After a few pleasantries and Wes's promising to call Iris while he was away on the business trip he was leaving on tomorrow, Jessica slung her bag over her shoulder, and they were on their way. Iris's building was one of those modern jobs with an automatic elevator, so Jessica and Wes were alone. For the entire ride down, Jess was dying to pry something out Wes Castle about their "mutual friend" Alanna, but after everything she'd gone through today, the right words–or was it the nerve–eluded her. Anyway, might such questions actually set him wondering about her curiosity concerning the great lady?

The elevator stopped, and they stepped out to cross the lobby, making small talk Jessica could barely keep her mind on. With any luck, Wes would chalk up her distraction to her long day.

Once outside on the still deliciously warm June evening, Jessica noted nary a car on the street. A limo approached, and as it pulled up before them, Wes announced, "Ah, here's my chariot now."

Jess allowed herself to enjoy the chauffeur stepping out to hold the door for her as much as Wes's teasing, "Fair ladies all aboard."

"On behalf of Fair Ladies Amalgamated, Local 343, I thank you, kind sir."

Her smile weakened, though, when it seemed as if someone stirred in the shadows of a doorway across and down the street.

"Everything all right, Jessica?"

"Oh, what? Yes, yes, of course. Jumpy as a cat, that's me. I'm getting too much like my four-footed roommate."

"As long as you don't start chasing mice, it's okay with me. Anyway, no reason to jump at shadows when you have me and Martin here to protect you."

"You said it!" Jess put on a cheerful expression and hopped into the car.

Once Wes was neatly ensconced in the back seat with her, the chauffer trotted around to the driver's side. Even with everything on her mind, Jessica had to admit that the limo was aces! The luxurious cushioning was quite a switch from riding in her sister's jalopy–or maybe it wasn't having to dread Liz's kamikaze driving that made the difference. This would be a treat of a ride–then again, maybe not. The engine was having trouble turning over.

"What's wrong, Martin?" Wes inquired.

"It's the starter, Sir. Right after I took your call at the garage, it began acting up. I do apologize, sir."

"Hmm," Wes considered. Then he brightened, "All right, here's what we'll do. Martin, you go back in and phone for service and a taxi. I have this young lady to escort."

"Very good, sir."

As much as she hated being a burden, tonight, Jess far more hated the thought of traveling alone. She only weakly protested, "I can't put you out anymore, Wes."

"Don't be silly, Jessica. When I make a promise, I keep it. Besides, it's no trouble at all."

Once again, she and Wes were out on the deserted, by New York standards, street. That's when Wes had his brainstorm: "Wait, Martin. Don't call a taxi, after all."

"Sir?"

"I have a great idea," Wes continued, brightly. "There's a subway stop around the corner. I remember seeing it. I've never been on one. Let's take that, Jessica. It would be a treat for me."

After braving New York subways for umpteen years, Jessica decidedly did not consider riding the underground anything remotely like a "treat." Still, maybe to a privileged guy like Wes Castle, it seemed an exciting challenge. Fortunately, he'd picked a station that would get them close to her apartment without too many stops.

"Sure, Wes. It's not a long ride. It could take us that long to get a cab. I'm game."

"Great! It's too beautiful a night to give up a stroll around the block to sit in a stuffy cab."

Jessica refrained from adding, "Instead of descending into an even stuffier underground tunnel?" Anyway, he looked like a little kid getting ready for his first roller coaster ride. Boy, would he be surprised!

"Great evening, isn't it?" Wes almost exulted as they started down to the intersection with 5th Avenue, his arm through Jessica's.

Jess nodded, then inquired, "So, Wes, you really never rode the subway?"

"Never. See something back there?"

"Uh, no. Not at all." She hadn't even realized she'd glanced back. "Nobody here but us chickens."

Wes rolled his eyes, complaining, "If I hear that song one more time, I think I'll have Phil Harris shipped off to the Pacific Theatre."

"That could be a secret weapon, broadcasting that song–or 'Three Little Fishies,'" Jess kidded.

"There's a rumor that 'Mairzy Doats' is what made Germany surrender."

Jessica shook her head and disagreed, "Probably against the Geneva Convention."

The evening actually was gorgeous, Jess had to admit. All things considered, and she had a lot to consider, it could be worse. For the moment, relief had out-gunned anxiety. But not entirely.

Wes cut into her thoughts, "Awfully quiet, Jess. Won't you like going by Bryant Park?"

"After one in the a.m.?"

"Nervous?"

"Not much. We just won't see a heck of a lot. You're sure you want to hop the subway?"

"Indulge me."

Jessica smiled at Wes's eagerness, and they strolled up a street enlivened only by an occasional bar or all-night automat.

Wes continued, "Of course, I imagine that I'm not getting the full atmosphere of the subway this time of night."

"Be grateful. A 'full atmosphere' might knock you out cold."

"What can I say, Jess? I'm a sheltered boy."

As they approached the entrance, Jessica teased, "I'll forgive you. Just don't ask for a tour of the sewer system next time."

"I don't want *that* much atmosphere."

They descended the steep, grungy, tiled stairs.

"Of course," Jessica continued, "they say the rats there are big enough to saddle and ride."

"Sounds delightful. Do you ride, Miss Minton?"

"Only horses."

"But of course. Well, at least let me treat you to a ride on this modern mechanical marvel. All for only a nickel apiece."

Fortunately, Wes had sufficient small change for the turnstile, since it was too late for anyone to be on duty in the booth.

"I hope this is worth the wait," Jess shook her head, amused.

"You bet. I can't understand why Iris would never do this, just for fun."

"Wes, you would if you'd worked the subway circuit for years like us. Believe me, the glamour wears off."

Waiting on the platform, Jess would normally have enjoyed Wes's studying his surroundings like a kid on a new adventure. Except, the platform seemed dimmer than usual, though not without an eye-aching fluorescent glare. Say, had someone just moved abruptly out of sight around the pillar to her left? Maybe, she'd just lean forward and peek ... but Wes Castle moved, grinning, into her path to enthuse, "Say, this place has real character, hasn't it?"

"And some of it's sticking to your shoe right now."

"Oh, heck. How do I get this off?"

"You *are* a babe in the tubes," Jessica teased, fishing a scrap of paper from her purse. "This ought to help you scrape it off. Had enough 'atmosphere,' yet?"

"Oh, I'm tougher than you think, Jessica." Wes finished scraping most of the gum off against the floor, continuing, "No, this is great. Just like the set of a movie."

"Yeah, *The Seventh Victim*."

"A subway scene in there?"

"You bet," Jess explained. "Kim Stanley runs away from a murder and hops the subway. She's too upset to know where to get off, and when the train circles back to her original stop, who should get on but two guys dragging the murder victim as if he were a drunk. By the time she gets some help from the conductor, they've blown."

"Sounds cheery."

"I know. What am I saying?" Jessica shook her head, once more drawn to look off to the left. Was someone trying to keep a low profile way down the platform? She must be going batty. Of course other people would be waiting for the train. That any of them would duck out of her sight was all in her mind. At last she heard the train rumbling towards them.

"Don't worry about movie murderers and corpses, Jessica. I'm here to take care of you," Wes promised gallantly, moving closer and putting one arm around her shoulder. "Iris would never let me forget it if I didn't!"

The lights of the train glared out of the tunnel's darkness, and Wes excitedly leaned forward, moving Jessica with him, ahead of him.

Instinctively, Jessica twisted to the side and back, warning, "They put that yellow line there for a reason, Wes. You don't want your adventure to end in a 'splat,' do you?"

As the cars of the tubular monster slowed past them and stopped, he agreed, "I guess you have a point. Well, here we are."

The passing first cars hosted a few passengers, oddly reassuring to Jessica. She refused to consider too closely why. Yes, there were three or so down in the first car, and Jess started in that direction, saying, "If you want a treat, let's take the lead car. You can look through the front window, almost like on an amusement park ride. It's the subway fanatics' delight."

"Oh no," Wes countered, pulling her back and onto an empty car. "I want the same flavor that the everyday guy gets. Here. Let's get in here."

Before she could joke that they'd need a few million more passengers if he really wanted that effect, she saw two men move out of the shadows and into the next car: the perfect place for waiting to make their move until the train was in motion and she couldn't get off.

"Oh my god! He's one of them!" escaped her.

"Who?"

"Those two are after me. Let's get out of here. They're dangerous. Maybe armed."

"Armed? Don't be silly. Besides, I'm right here."

Wes's hand tightened on the bare flesh of her arm. Looking at him in surprise, Jessica saw something in his eyes that put a new, frightening perspective on a felicitously failing car and this sudden, odd fascination with the subway. His unexpected knowledge of the station's location and the line's routes made horrible sense now. He certainly was more than someone Alanna Tewkesbury ignored at dinner.

The door-closing alarm clanged. Instinct took over, and, before the doors trapped her, Jess slammed her purse down on Wes's head, while one foot torpedoed his shim.

Getting off *now* was imperative! The look on Eddie Kubek's face as he'd hopped on the train told her he was ready to pay her back in spades for the library this morning.

The doors slammed shut behind her, but there was no time to waste checking if anyone was in pursuit. As Jessica hit the stairs, she could hear racing footsteps on the platform. Then there was some kind of crash. *Please God, let that buy me some time!*

The top of the stairs loomed above. Had Alanna's boys been smart enough to post someone up there to catch her? No time to hesitate. She'd just have to hold tight to her giant shoulder bag and come out swinging.

Outside. The fresh evening air hit her at the same time she realized that no hoods lurked to grab her. But neither was there anyone to help her. Breathing raggedly, Jessica hurtled down 42nd Street, recognizing too late that she was actually moving away from her best source of help, Times Square. No time to double back, past the underground entrance that might even now be disgorging her pursuers. A glance back. A movement in the darkness? In the shrubs of Bryant Park? She couldn't keep this pace up forever.

The Public Library loomed monstrously to her right. Yes, the library!

Putting on one more burst of speed, Jessica veered to her right onto 5th Avenue, her eyes fastening on the nearest of the library's famous recumbent lion statues, its base cloaked in shadows. Another glance behind before the corner separated her from her pursuers' vision, and vice-versa. Too hasty, nothing clear. And no cabs in sight to try and hop into!

Jess scrambled up the lowest, broadest portion of the stone steps leading into the library, then sank into the darkness at the statue's base. A few quick, deep breaths were all she could afford before she had to focus on making herself undetectable to the eye and ear. All that mattered was melting into the shadows. Thank God she was wearing black, except for a white lace collar. Swiftly, her hand covered it.

It was as still and dark as death. Even the echo of traffic was muffled and distant. No help there, no more than in any of the silent stores, the brooding library behind her, or the few still-open bars that glared into 42nd Street and 5th Ave. Should she have tried to go in and get help? No, any bar she popped into, her 'friends' could, too—and easily haul her off as if she were drunk.

Her eyes hadn't discerned anyone up 5th Avenue. Yes, hiding was her best bet. If she'd kept running, they would have seen her straight ahead, and she'd have run out of steam way too soon. If they didn't see her, would they come back? No, this was the best choice. The statue base, cold and rough against her cheek, beneath her hand, hid her from the street. But her knees began to feel creaky from crouching after her mad sprint. If she could just shift....

Footsteps came charging up and around the corner. Jessica couldn't even gulp. She could only make the Deity a thousand promises for spiritual reform to get her out of this jam. And there was one message from the heart sent straight to James.

Wait a minute. Only one set of footsteps dashing past, yes, past, her? Damn, now they were slowing. Looking for her? Why only one of them? Wes alone? Had she made a colossal ass of herself? But then there had been that unmistakably cruel glint in his eyes, that hard grip on her arm when she'd spotted Eddie Kubek and his playmate. No, she hadn't been wrong.

Oh God, the footsteps were coming back! With one last thought of James, Jess's hand tightened on her bag. If she could get in just one good clout....

"Jessica! Jessica Minton?"

Hearing almost the last voice she ever expected in this dark, lonely place, Jess nearly fell back on her tuffet.

"Here." It came out of her as a squeak. "I'm here."

Jessica stumbled out from behind the lion to meet, loping up the steps to her, the lanky, trench-coated form of....

"Jeff Hooley," Jessica exhaled, incredulously, leaning against the base of the Public Library Lion.

His hands on her arms steadied Jess as he asked, "Why is it every time I see you, you're in trouble?"

First, Jessica took a long drink of that youthful face with the hint of a broken nose, the eyes that might have been a soulful brown if not for the sardonic glint. Then, she gulped out, "Boy, am I glad to see you!"

"I'd like to think it's because of my winsome charm, but I'm willing to bet you've got yourself tangled up with those two mugs I tailed to this station. I saw you jump ship and take off like a bat out of hell, then my two pals. I figured I could keep an eye on them and keep you out of trouble–till someone slammed me into the wall so hard I saw stars.

Jessica shot a terrified glance past Hooley, toward the 42nd Street corner. Not realizing what she was doing, she gripped his arms and demanded, "They're not still out there?"

"Relax. My little collision must have bought you enough time to get out of sight. When I got to the top of the stairs, they were gone. I saw them and another guy being driven off toward Times Square, in the opposite direction of the library. They don't know you like I do, that you have soft spot for this place, so I followed my hunch, and here we are."

Jess gave her "rescuer" a quizzical look and asked, "You left them for me?"

That wasn't just surprising; it was almost touching, except that this was Jeff Hooley.

Hooley, not about to go all soft, remarked, "Someone had to keep you from galloping off into the night. And I didn't see Sir Galahad around to protect you. Where is your knight in shining armor, anyway?"

Dropping her hands, Jessica shot back, "In England. In a hospital."

"Oh. I didn't know." Even Hooley was a bit abashed. Awkwardly, he asked, "Is he going to pull through?"

Jessica's chin came up, and she replied, "He's on the mend. He'll be okay. That's what he wrote me. Anyway, why do you always have to be making cracks about him? Why do you have to..."

"Spoil a beautiful moment like this?"

"Look, sonny, I'm going back behind the lion to get my purse. You go over there and pick up that hat you dropped, and just remember, I already crowned one guy with my bag tonight. The warranty guarantees it against even a hard head like yours."

"You sure know how to sweet talk a guy."

"Never mind getting smart. Just collect your hat."

Hooley was standing there, surveying the street when Jessica rejoined him. His features were calm, if concentrated. It unnerved Jessica a little when he commented in a skeptical tone, "It's a rough crowd for you to run with, or should I say 'from'?"

"You know Eddie Kubek? He's been in trouble with the Feds?"

"He's been in trouble with everyone but Hitler."

"I'm sure he's just Scheicklegruber's cup of tea."

"He's not the kind of mug a nice girl like you should be dancing around with," Hooley observed. "How did you get into this mess? Or maybe I should give you credit, gearing down from Nazis to just a crime ring?"

"You know, Hooley, it's a good thing I can't afford to stay mad at you, with you coming through with the evidence to clear Larry."

Hooley's weight shifted to his right leg. Hands in pockets, he slowly tapped the other foot. Barely managing not to look sheepish, the agent admitted, "Yeah, about that; there's been a SNAFU."

A chill washed Jessica. In a measured voice, she demanded, "Exactly what *kind* of a SNAFU, Agent Hooley?"

"You know, Jessica, I just spent all day tracking a guy palling around with Eddie Kubek. That and saving your skin really works up a fella's appetite. How about we backtrack around the corner? I saw an automat there. I bet you could use a cup of coffee and a piece of pie."

"I'm not hungry."

"We could have a much better confab sitting down."

"I'm tempted to knock you down, right on your..."

"A Federal agent? Armed?"

"Hooley, this is no joke to me. We're talking about a guy's life here. Lord knows Liz and I have both put Larry Sanders through enough..."

"I know, I know." He wasn't flip anymore. "But not here." He cocked his head back toward 42nd Street. "Let's sit down. I've got a long story for you."

"With a *King Lear*-type ending?" Jessica remarked.

"I don't know the ending, yet. That's for us to work out–and I really am starved. I haven't had an actual meal since I caught a hot dog right after blowing into Penn."

Damn, he knew how to use those brown eyes to quell her temper, even in this jam.

Jessica gave in, "All right. You win, Hooley. But this better be good. A man's life is on the line."

"More than one; I have a stake of my own."

"What does that mean?" Jess demanded.

"I can explain better on a full stomach."

Jessica nodded her "okay," and they started off. Annoyed as she was, she still couldn't resist linking her arm through Hooley's. To his quizzical expression, she answered, "'Don't mind me if I'm the gregarious type. It's just the herding instinct.'"

Hooley nodded, then tilted his head and queried, "Seems I've heard that somewhere."

"Joan Bennett to Lloyd Nolan and Francis Lederer after the former got her released from the clutches of Nazis in *The Man I Married*."

"Oh sure, nice line. Who am I, Francis or Lloyd?"

"I'll let you know after we get this murder business unscrambled," she replied. Then, Jess stopped them, questioning,, "Say, Hooley, how did you manage to be here exactly when I needed you? Some funny coincidence."

"Not exactly," Hooley answered with a crooked grin. "This interstate gambling case brought me here to your big, bad city. There's this chump we've got a shot at turning against the big fish in the ring, but only if I can get him alone for a chat. The last place a guy like that would be inclined to be 'cooperative' would be with Eddie Kubek tagging along. I was trailing them all day, hoping to get him alone. So, I'm in the station, trying to lay low, and I notice those two doing the same, but from whom, I couldn't see without giving myself away. I follow them onto the train and imagine my surprise when I see Kubek get on a car, you jump off, then him and my pal hop off right after you. The rest I already told you."

For a fraction of a second, Hooley hesitated, as if he wanted to say more. He didn't. Jessica knew better than to press Jeff Hooley too hard. Instead, she said, "So, he got away–and the guy who slammed you must have been Wes Castle; he got away, too. Don't you have to go after them?"

"Not if I want to look like anything more than a gallant sap trying to help a lady in distress," Hooley explained. "I don't want to get my mark in Dutch if anyone should spot us together. And I don't want to spook him by letting him know I'm on his tail. So, around the corner? Eats?"

"Gee, Hooley, I'm heartbroken. I'd never have thought that a chum of Eddie Kubek's would replace me as the apple of your eye," Jess cracked. "Okay, let's go."

Chapter Twenty

Sunday (morning), June 3

The automat was almost glaring: too much fluorescence on white-painted walls and black-and-white diamond-tiled floor. Hooley had wryly concluded that the food couldn't be too bad if the management had the guts to expose it like this. When the glass door refused to slide back on the shepherd's pie, he'd mused it might be a divine portent to go with the Salisbury steak. On none of these witticisms did Jessica bite, until Hooley conjectured that he must be losing his touch, not getting anything out of her.

"Maybe, Hooley, there's too much at stake to get cute over steak," she coolly retorted.

"All right. I get it. Enough with the chit-chat. But allow me to get a little of this gourmet cuisine in me. I can talk better on a full stomach."

She nodded, tightly, not letting Jeff Hooley see that she did feel a twinge of guilt for being tough on him. After all, the F.B.I was supposed to be all wrapped up in taking down foreign spies and interstate crime rings. Yet here he was, going out of his way to help her.

So as her companion finished paying the cashier and was picking up the tray with his dinner and her coffee, Jess touched his arm and said, "Sorry, Hooley. I'm just worried."

For once, Hooley wasn't a wise alec. He nodded and guided her towards a table.

They sat down. While making her automat coffee drinkable with cream and sugar, Jessica softened a little more: "Why don't you dig in before you start explaining?"

She hated waiting, but even Captain America had to eat.

After a forkful of Salisbury steak and a brief but pensive course of mastication, Hooley took a slug of milk and began, "Suppose you give me the complete low down on this case, Jessica. All I know is that this Detective

McLaughlan called me on your recommendation. He gives me a summation of the Blair murder case, shoots me some questions on Blair, then asks for help expediting a request to the Identification Division's Fingerprint Bureau for not only Blair's prints but Betty Weisenthal's. So, I have a few questions for you, like why's this Evan Blair being tied to the old Weisenthal gang? That's ancient history. Beyond that, exactly whom do you suspect of being Betty and why pussy-foot around her? Does she have some kind of juice?"

Jess took a deep breath before she answered, "Where do you want me to begin?"

"Take it from the top but give me the *Reader's Digest* version. I'll ask if I need details." Another slug of milk. "Okay, how did you make the connection between Evan Blair and the Weisenthal gang?"

"Blair told Liz."

"He *told* your sister? That's sounds surprisingly cozy."

"Get your mind out of the gutter, Hooley. Evan was a backer in Liz's dress business. She didn't know about his criminal background when he bought in, obviously." Jess didn't like seeing Hooley's expression, but she went on, "No one would give a woman with no experience a chance, so when she met this gambler on a trip to California, she decided she wasn't going to ask too many questions. As always, my 'psychic' sister followed her 'instincts' and trusted Blair. Neither of us knew he was really Gabriel Stuyvesant, a member of the Wesienthal gang who'd gone state's evidence on them. Anyway, I thought it was too good to be true, but the deal was done before I could put in my two cents."

"She met him out West?"

"Right," Jessica affirmed. "Liz was taking a vacation to get away from people asking about the divorce."

"It makes sense that's where she met him. Stuyvesant had been relocated to Washington state. Go on."

"He came back East, as Liz's silent partner. Blair kept a pretty low profile, with the exception of some extracurricular activity with the models. He kept his address under wraps, too, and lived in a low low-rent district. *Now* I know why."

"So, you were saying the locals wanted to hang this rap on Larry Sanders, your sister's intended? If they thought Blair was mixed up with the last of the Weisenthal gang, why would they go that route? Or maybe I can guess. You made Blair sound like something of a skirt-chaser. Was he cutting in on Sanders' territory?"

Setting down her cup so hard coffee splashed over its rim, Jessica bit out, "Yes, Evan Blair had a penchant for the ladies, but my sister was not going to ditch Larry for him."

"Did Larry think she was?" Hooley questioned incisively.

"Get this straight. Even if Larry thought so, he wouldn't kill out of jealousy. It would take more than that."

"What if he thought he was protecting your sister?" Hooley's eyes might have been a soft hazel-brown, but they probed her mordantly.

For a moment, Jess acknowledged that possibility to herself, but she stopped and insisted, "We're getting away from the subject. I thought you were here to help us nail Betty Weisenthal."

"Just trying to cover all the angles. You've no idea just how sticky this case is."

"Well, here's an angle you'd better cover. Evan Blair told my sister several hours before he was murdered that 'Betty' had recognized him and he had to leave town before she had him killed or did it herself."

Hooley put down his fork and sat back. Finally he questioned, "But the locals didn't buy Liz's story? Why not?"

"One of them at least listened to us. That's the guy who contacted you. Didn't he say anything to you about who Betty is now? That might answer your question."

"No, McLaughlan was pretty careful not to name names. I thought he was being coy, maybe trying to keep a big collar to himself. Who is she?"

"Alanna Tewkesbury."

"Alanna ... ?"

To Hooley's quizzical expression, Jessica elaborated, "As in Mrs. Wilmington..."

"Tewkesbury." Hooley snapped his fingers. "The big industrialist. The only guy to come close to outfoxing the Truman Commission. Damn, that explains a lot."

"A lot? Like what?"

"Like how Betty Weisenthal's prints could go missing."

Jessica's eyes bulged. She stammered, "The prints? Missing?"

"You said it, Jess. The Paul Weisenthal stuff is still there–and some of the files on Gabriel Stuyvesant. But funny, what has gone missing on him concerns where he was relocated."

"Then you think the husband is in on the cover up, Hooley?" Jess questioned, surprised. "Wouldn't a man with his standing want to dump Alanna once he knew her true background?"

"Dumping a wife raises a lot of notoriety," Hooley pointed out. "Divorce with that much community property in the mix can be pretty messy. Besides, from what I've heard about Tewkesbury, he's not the kind of gent who likes to admit his mistakes–or give anyone else the chance to bring them up."

"A powerful rich guy thwarting justice? Are you putting me on? Corruption in the F.B.I.? This sounds like some kind of wild conspiracy!" Jessica protested. "You're supposed to be the good guys."

"A lot of us are. All it takes is one or two well-placed bad apples, a guy with a lot of clout like Tewkesbury, and..."

"But wait, Jeff. Wouldn't it make more sense to replace the prints with someone else's, rather than just lose hers? Doesn't losing them red flag the tampering?"

"I said the Tewkesburys had connections. I didn't say they had the most brilliant ones. People forget when they weave conspiracy plots that most humans are too flawed or lazy or short-sighted to cover all the angles."

"Then couldn't you make a big stink about this? Blow the case wide open? I'll bet Alanna would never count on *that*."

Hooley shook his head, "With a big wheel like Tewkesbury in the picture, we can't afford to play our hand yet. We need *all* the links in the chain connecting back to him."

"So, what are you saying, Hooley, that Tewkesbury has so much power you Feds can't touch him?" Jessica demanded, angry and scared at once.

Hooley weighed how best to explain before answering, "You already know a little about me: bright scholarship kid recruited straight out of Yale so he can use that fancy education and those crackerjack analytical skills to help break some tough cases. You don't know, though, that it's more than my 'winning' personality that's held me back, almost kept them from recruiting me." He paused awkwardly, then went on, "Usually having a law enforcement pedigree helps, but let's just say that when you're the kid brother of a cop whom people think went crooked, the obstacle course gets a little rougher."

"You said 'think.' He got a raw deal?"

"From the Weisenthal gang."

That put a double charge into her permanent wave. Jessica nodded knowingly: "I get the picture. That ties in with what Blair told Liz about the gang's M.O., playing a law enforcement guy for an inside track."

Hooley continued, "Mitch, my brother, let Betty think she was stringing him along. He was going to double-cross and turn them in. Quite a *coup* for a small town detective. But they got wise to him, don't ask me how, and left him wearing a crooked little frame. Not a perfect one, just good enough to ruin his life without sending him to prison. He died before he could clear himself."

"And that's why you let the Bureau recruit you? To make up for the phony aspersions, maybe even to nail what was left of the gang?"

"That's my sad story in a nutshell."

"Well, that explains why you're so cocky, even downright obnoxious, at times," Jessica granted him. "It still doesn't make your being a royal pain okay, but now I understand why."

Leaning back in his chair, arms folded, Hooley dryly returned, "Now don't get all sentimental on me, Jessica Minton."

"Don't worry about that, buster. So, would Alanna know that you're on the case? That you're gunning for her?"

"Do you really think she bothered researching my brother's family tree? She probably couldn't even remember *him*. How many of her victims do you think she could?"

"Apparently not enough," Jessica observed. "Remember the last one, the Boston case? My friend Lois does. Her brother was their patsy. He killed himself."

"Curiouser and curiouser. Then your friend has a motive, too."

"And an alibi, wise guy! But I guess it's not the best one," Jessica admitted. "I'll come clean. She saw Alanna Tewkesbury in the building where Evan, I mean Gabriel, was murdered that night."

Jeff Hooley leaned forward for, "And the locals know this?"

"No, no. She's afraid to tell them because she might have a motive, and..."

"And?"

"She saw Larry there that night, too."

"The boyfriend? Why do I have the bad feeling that the locals don't know this, either?"

Jessica couldn't look at Hooley. She just shook her head.

"You ever hear of a little term, Jessica, called 'obstruction of justice'?"

Jess faced Hooley, wounded and desperate. "Jeff, I can't talk to the police. They're all but ready to run Larry in now. Well, maybe McLaughlan isn't, but if he knew a few things, I'm afraid we'd lose him. And, damn, I can't say that I'd completely blame him."

"So, why are you telling me all this now, Jess? You seem to have me confused with a Catholic priest. The sanctity of the confessional is pretty much the opposite of the responsibilities of a Federal agent."

"I trust you, Hooley," Jessica confessed. "85% of the time I'd like to wring your neck, but I still think you're on the square. And you know the Weisenthal gang. You could clear Larry by bringing them into the picture. Don't you see that Alanna Tewkesbury's motive beats everyone's? I know that you'll give Larry a fair shake. You could use your influence here as a Fed..."

"Hold on, kid. Don't go spending money I don't have," Jeff warned. "I told you, I can't afford to make any big waves too soon. When the Director of the Fingerprints Division got the word that Betty Weisenthal's prints had gone AWOL, from the girl filling my request, he went directly to my AD. Knowing my family history, they decided I was the boy with a big enough stake in this to make good and sure to clean up the mess. They sent me here under cover of working on the gambling ring, to avoid suspicions in high places. Lucky for you, making my cover look good put me smack in the middle of your little adventure tonight. But it's a touchy situation, Jessica. The director can't afford to let word leak out that someone has infiltrated us that deeply, not in the middle of a war. If I jump the gun and blow this thing, the brass aren't only going to want my hide, but they're going to say I was on my own. My AD warned me that if I took this on, *persona*-less-than-*grata* thanks to my family background and winning charm, nobody would cover my back if the investigation went sour. Now that you've thrown someone with the clout of Wilmington Tewkesbury into the mix, I've really got to watch my step."

"They'd throw you to the wolves?" Jessica flared.

"With a little A-1 sauce for flavor," Hooley cynically answered. "So, I need to come up with something airtight. I'm not about to let Betty Weisenthal notch up another fall guy."

Jessica warred with herself over how much she dared tell Jeff Hooley about her and Liz's skating on the left side of the law. She was darned scared of how he would react, but Larry's life hung in the balance.

"Hooley, we, Liz and I, almost had something, something big."

"How big?"

"A photo of Lois's brother with Alanna when she was Betty," Jess answered, leaning forward. "It was a little fuzzy; she'd changed her appearance, but you can definitely identify her."

"You have a picture of Betty Weisenthal?"

"*Had* is the operative word, Hooley."

"*Had*?"

"Had," Jessica bitterly confirmed.

"But you don't have it anymore?" Hooley was all skepticism again.

"You don't believe me, do you?"

"*I* want to believe you, Jessica, but most people would probably say that your proof has disappeared a little too conveniently."

Jessica brooded, "I had the damn thing right in my hands. Liz saw it, too."

"Just out of curiosity, how did you manage to lose a piece of evidence that could have settled *all* our grudges?"

Jessica rolled her eyes before answering, "It's a looong story. The short version is we found it in an apartment that Evan Blair had kept secretly in Lowell. He'd told us about it in a letter that arrived after his death, as a way to get back at Alanna if she murdered him and to return the stolen jade to clear Lois's brother."

"You had all this implicating Alanna Tewkesbury, and the cops didn't even talk to her?" Hooley sat up, surprised.

"Ah, well, here's the rub." A coffee cup was so fascinating when you had something this difficult to confess. "We couldn't tell the police because Alanna Tewkesbury said she had Larry's gun. He told us it had been stolen some time before, and since it was the same caliber as the murder weapon, and this Detective Boyd was already slavering to run in Larry, she said she'd hand it over to the police if we set them after her anymore. When Liz and I received Evan's postmortem missive, we acted on it, hoping to find something that would neutralize Alanna's threat. And it kind of worked."

"'Kind of,' as in you found but couldn't keep the picture," Hooley summed up.

"Not exactly."

"Why do I get the feeling 'exactly' is going to give me gray hair?"

Jessica pressed on while she still had the nerve, "I had the picture, when we heard Alanna Tewkesbury and Eddie Kubek outside. When we rushed to hide, I tripped and dropped it. There was no time to grab it. Then we heard them find the photo and take it away, but we also heard something else..."

Hooley gave her the fisheye, but Jessica continued, "Where they were hiding the gun."

"Which you should have told the police, but I can see from that expression, you didn't."

"It's not that simple, Hooley. I wanted to, but Liz talked me out of it. It might have been Larry's gun that they used to kill Blair. And, frankly, we weren't sure the police would believe us, let alone act on our tip."

"So, why do I have the feeling you two did something cockeyed like steal the gun from Alanna Tewkesbury?"

"Sixth sense?"

"You really have a problem with grasping that obstruction concept, don't you?"

"Am I obstructing justice if I report everything to an investigating officer, like you? If I turn the gun over to you for your investigation, which could include this murder, under an anonymity deal, then we're all to the good, right?"

Hooley shook his head disbelievingly, finally saying, "How did you stumble across this gun that we're allegedly making a deal over–or will that give me a coronary?"

"There's this apartment that belongs to Alanna Tewkesbury, although it's leased under another name. I went there as a maid, under the contract the lessee had with Lois Wong's cleaning agency. The contract didn't specify *who* would be doing the cleaning. The guy in the apartment let me in, and I found it while cleaning. Am I stealing if I return something that was already stolen? What if I was returning it to the rightful owner?" Jessica pushed, struggling to squelch her anxiety over the thin logic of her argument.

"Rather than to the police investigating a capital crime," he countered disapprovingly.

"I'm turning it over to an officer of the law investigating a federal offense. Look, Hooley, I can send the gun to the locals anonymously, if that's what you want. Then I'd be off the hook, right? But where would Larry be? For all we know, this might not even be the murder weapon; Mrs. Tewkesbury could be bluffing to keep us in line. But maybe if I let you hold all the cards, you can lean on Kubek or the guy you were tracking to get the goods on Alanna. That way something decent can come of all this, for Larry's sake and your brother's."

"And I conveniently forget you brought all this up in the first place?" Again disapprovingly.

"I know you, Hooley. I know you're not a by-the-book guy. I saw you at work in San Francisco," Jessica countered. "I know you'd never frame anyone, but we both know that you aren't above bending the rules to get out the truth." Then she gambled, "Anyway, if my actions help you and your top brass nail the last of the Weisenthal gang and catch the person behind infiltrating the Bureau, wouldn't you Feds feel a little gratitude? Enough to exert some influence to keep Liz and me out of the pokey?"

"And everyone thinks you're such a Girl Scout."

Jessica dropped her eyes at his cool sarcasm. The cream had congealed on the surface of her coffee. She pushed her cup away before responding, "I wish I could be, Jeff. I wish I could trust and let the system take its course, but I'm up against people who know how to twist that system six ways from Sunday. If I don't do some fancy stepping, if I don't pull whatever strings I can, some vicious people will create more terrible tragedies. As Liz once said, 'I'd play volleyball with the Devil if he stayed on his own side of the net.'"

"Come again?"

"Well... I don't understand exactly what it means, either. Somehow it seems to apply."

Hooley was looking at her long and hard, but Jessica would not blink under his scrutiny.

"All right."

"All right, what, Hooley?" Jessica questioned uncertainly.

"All right I'll help you," he agreed, though far from cheerfully.

She beamed in response.

"I didn't say I liked it, or that it was a great idea," warned Hooley.

"I didn't say so, either Jeff." She was so grateful.

Jess could see that her earnestness was melting him, in spite of himself. Hooley's eyes were on what was left in his plate. His expression briefly seemed to reveal that he'd eaten really bad food really too fast. But only briefly. He finally opened up to Jess, "It just burns me. She or her husband must have used some clout, called in some heavy-duty favors to get in and scotch our one shred of identifying evidence on her. You ain't just whistling Dixie about them and the rules. But if we want to do any rule bending, we'd better be damned meticulous. I don't have a multimillion-dollar fortune to fall back on. How about you?"

"Not even a fox coat. But, Hooley, I don't want to go any further over the line on this. I just want to clear the suspicion away from Larry and put it back on the woman who deserves it."

"Maybe I can move you a little closer to Girl-Scout territory, after all."

Jessica wearily smiled, and Hooley added, "Raw deal that you two lost the Kodak. Did you come up with *anything* else?"

Jessica responded hopefully, "Well, maybe."

"That sounds specific."

"As a matter of fact, wise guy, I found the picture in an old copy of e. e.

cummings's poetry. The clues in Evan Blair's letter led me to that book and the phrase 'angry candy' in 'Cambridge Ladies.'"

Hooley almost brightened and questioned, "What'd you do with the book?"

"Brought it home and hid it. Detective McLaughlan was supposed to pick it up today, but let's just say it didn't pan out."

"Then what are we waiting for? Let's go. I want to take a gander at it while you still have it."

"Then here's another little tidbit for you, Hooley," Jessica offered as they both stood up. "In the apartment, I found another photo about the same vintage as the Alanna Tewkesbury one, which I still have."

"And you're just mentioning this *now*?"

"Give me a break, Hooley. I've had quite a day, okay? Anyway, in the photo was Evan, I mean Gabriel, with some other guy. I saw a detective's badge fastened to his vest, so he must have been a plainclothes cop."

"He could be Jay Kavanaugh, the detective in charge of Stuyvesant in Boston after he made his deal to turn state's evidence," Hooley reflected. "The two actually got kind of chummy, especially since Stuyvesant saved Kavanaugh's wife when she happened to be on hand when some Weisenthal pals tried to permanently silence him outside the station."

"Do you think he could identify Alanna Tewkesbury as Betty Weisenthal?" Jess hoped.

"I can't write you a guarantee. It's a touchy. Kavanaugh was injured in a later attempt on Stuyvesant, a shootout that wiped out the remainder of the Weisenthal gang not in custody. Anyway, he lost his job in Boston. Last I heard, he was in Connecticut, but whether he's still there..."

"Why didn't he come forward once he heard about Evan's murder?" Jess pondered.

"Would he have heard about it?" Hooley countered. "Even if he somehow knew Stuyvesant's new alias, odds are that a story on the murder of an obscure dress manufacturer wouldn't make his local papers, especially with a war in the Pacific."

Hopefully, Jess questioned, "So, we do have a lead, Hooley, with this picture?"

"We might. You said that McLaughlan was supposed to pick up the evidence today, but he didn't. That's mighty funny."

"Funnier than you think. Instead of McLaughlan coming back, his partner led a search of Liz's apartment, while another guy was in charge of tossing mine. They were looking for the murder weapon, based on an anonymous tip. Gee, I wonder who could have made that little ole call?"

"And you didn't volunteer what you had to his partner?" Hooley asked.

"If I had, I wouldn't be able to turn it over to you. Besides, I promised it to McLaughlan not Boyd."

"Well, don't look so glum, Jessica," Hooley told her. "I'm ready to do a little investigating on my own. But, first, I want to see that Kodak and the book."

"So, you would recognize Kavanaugh?" Jess asked.

"There's not much I don't know about that gang and anyone connected to them. My brother actually tracked down Kavanaugh, trying to clear his own name. Fortunately, I kept the picture Mitch had of him."

"But Kavanaugh couldn't help your brother, Hooley?"

"Wouldn't. I got the sense he didn't want to cooperate because he was covering for Stuyvesant. He didn't want to stir up any trouble since he owed Stuyvesant for his wife."

"And maybe if Kavanaugh would cover to protect Stuyvesant, he'd come forward to nail the guy's killers?"

"Maybe. But we won't find out hanging around here. Let's grab a cab to your place and see."

Hooley let Jessica out of the cab, first, paying the driver as she started up the steps to her apartment. Part way, she stopped and looked around nervously.

"Anything wrong?" Hooley queried.

Jess wondered if Jeff Hooley were concerned for her or on point against danger. He waited, opposite her, one step down.

"I don't know," Jessica answered uneasily. "I was wondering if we might have been followed."

"Ah." His tone just edged over from wry to sarcastic. "Don't trust me to keep you safe? Wishing your missing Prince Charming was here to protect you?"

"Cut the wise cracks, Hooley. This is serious business. I thought we were going to help each other."

Turning away to ascend the steps, denying Hooley a chance to dispute her or apologize, Jess plundered her purse for the front-door key. Unfortunately, she missed the top step, tripped, and sent herself, her purse, and her keys all over the landing. Hooley was right there.

"Are you all right?" his voice was unexpectedly concerned.

"All right?" Jessica snapped, somewhere between rage and tears. "You've got me worried about doing a stretch in a women's penitentiary; I'm going nuts trying to save an innocent guy from the chair; I just skinned my knee and ruined a beautiful pair of nylons; all my portable personal effects are scattered across this landing; I nearly got shanghaied by some hoods–which means I have to tell one of my best friends that her dreamboat is a U-boat–then you throw in my face that the guy I love is an

Atlantic Ocean away, and I can't even talk to him. So, you tell me, does that sound all right to you?!"

Sitting down next to her, Hooley deadpanned, "Don't forget. Your sister is in on this, too. They'll probably have you share a cell. She'll make you clean."

Jessica tried to narrow her eyes, but she couldn't help it. She giggled. Her hand went up over her mouth, but tears and giggles produced a few healthy snorts.

"There's the charm that makes you such a gracious lady of the stage."

"Stop it, Hooley!" Jess couldn't look at him as she continued to snort, progressing to bulldog mode.

"Okay, Minton. But how's that knee?"

"Bloody but unbowed."

"Need me to check it out?"

"What's this?" Jess demanded, tongue in cheek. "A lame attempt to take a gander at my gams?"

"Just want to see if you're ambulatory. Anyway, after straining my eyes all day watching a couple of mugs, I could use a little diversification."

Jessica faced Jeff Hooley in the street-lamp light, finally answering, "I'm okay. I ... it's just so much. Even the toughest nut has to crack, and, well, I really miss James so much right now, but I can't even tell him. Even if I could contact him, how could I trouble him with all this when he's laid up in a hospital?"

"Yeah, it's hard on a guy when he can't help the girl he cares about. I understand. I'll lay off," Hooley promised, "best I can."

Jess smiled at the addendum. It really would near kill Hooley to let the opportunity for a smart crack slip by, but, beneath it all, he *was* a good guy. She saw beyond the cynicism in his eyes that he read her thoughts, and he was leaning his face toward hers....

A car door slammed! Sending them to opposite sides of the step.

Immediately, Jessica recognized Aaron Boyd. Who was the other guy, though? A quick glance at Hooley told her that he was deeply disconcerted at not having noticed the car pull up on them.

"Not interrupting anything, am I?"

Jessica did not like Boyd's tone, at all. A glance at Hooley showed her he was sizing up Boyd.

"Where's Detective McLaughlan?" Jessica questioned bluntly.

"I'll be doing all the asking, if you don't mind, Miss Minton. Like who's this character?" A nod in Hooley's direction.

"Federal Agent Jeffrey Hooley," her companion answered, unruffled. The trace of a smile at the corners of his mouth barely betrayed that he enjoyed disconcerting Boyd. "I'll take out my badge, from my inner coat pocket, if you need to see it."

The policeman nodded, and as Hooley identified himself, Boyd's companion added, "I'm Martinelli. This is Detective Boyd."

Jess studied the new detective. His voice was gruff, but without Boyd's hostility.

"You're the Fed McLaughlan called in," Boyd concluded, not hiding his skepticism. "What're you doing here with her? Shouldn't you be looking up me or McLaughlan?"

"Where *is* McLaughlan?" Jessica interjected. "Why isn't he here with you now?"

Boyd and Martinelli exchanged looks. Boyd spoke, "For now, let's just say that he's been replaced on the case."

"Replaced?" Jessica went cold as the word escaped her. Damned good thing she had saved that evidence for Hooley.

Hooley was cool as he probed, "No one informed me."

"It only happened tonight," Boyd answered. "But we're looking for McLaughlan now. We need to talk to him."

"You're his partner? You can't find him?" Hooley's skepticism needled Boyd, even through his rhino hide.

"Why would he be here?" Jessica questioned. "Why expect I'd have any idea where he was?"

That was the final straw. Boyd flashed on her: "Because ever since he hooked up with you two dames, he hasn't been thinking right. We had the beginnings of a pretty good case against Sanders, and then you two got Leo sidetracked. First, you get him thrown off the case. Now..."

"Aar!" Martinelli cut Boyd off.

Boyd seethed but channeled his frustrated fury into a snort.

Hooley pushed, "Now *what*, Detective Boyd?"

Boyd glared and replied with a controlled, "Now, you keep your nose out of..."

"McLaughlan requested me." Cool and level.

"He's through requesting anything for a while. He's up to his neck in trouble, and he needs my help. He needs to turn himself in downtown or come with me. I'll even come and get him, myself. But he needs to turn himself in right away."

"Turn himself in? McLaughlan?" Jessica couldn't figure this out. "What in heaven's name do you think he's done?"

"It ain't what I think," Boyd sounded more tired than angry now. "It's what the evidence says–and he's not going to clear himself by taking it on the lam."

Hooley stepped in, "Maybe we can be more help if we know what's going on."

Boyd and Martinelli exchanged looks.

"Maybe you don't trust Miss Minton or her sister, but I'm a federal officer," Hooley prodded reasonably. "I can help. That's why I came here in the first place. And if these Mintons know anything, believe me, I'll get them to talk."

Jessica wasn't at all sure she liked the way Hooley put that, but if it made Boyd spill the beans....

Boyd replied, "Okay, Mr. Fed, how's this? The night watchman at Garfield Airport was found shot tonight, but someone roughed him up good, first. The bullet was a .38, policeman's special. Guess whose piece was found nearby."

Jessica blanched and cried, "McLaughlan's? You can't think for one minute McLaughlan did it! You're his partner!"

"Doesn't matter what I think, lady, just what the evidence says," Boyd retorted bitterly. "And if he doesn't come in and clear himself, it's gonna look even worse. He's my partner, so I want to bring him in before anyone else gets at him. I'm trying to give the dumb S.O.B. a break."

"Just how much of a break is that?" came Hooley's level voice.

"More than he'll get if he hooks up with those two. I'm telling you, he's not gonna take a fall for them and their pal Sanders. You see him, you send him to me."

Boyd forced his card on Jessica, growled at Hooley, and left with his partner.

The still June night, or more accurately morning, found Jessica Minton and Jeff Hooley alone and silent on her steps. The innards of Jessica's purse now gathered and stowed, Hooley broke the silence with, "Did you notice anything odd about our little encounter just now?"

Jessica raised her eyebrows and answered, "Was there anything *not* odd about it?"

"The prints. I was called in to deliver prints to identify Betty Weisenthal. Never even came up. Boyd wasn't even curious. Seem screwy to you?"

Jessica thought before finally answering, "He was worried about his partner. Even he must have a sense of loyalty. And he never did believe in Mrs. Tewkesbury's involvement or the relevance of Evan Blair's past. Leo McLaughlan was the only one who was interested in the prints. To Boyd, you're just standing in his way to railroading Larry. No, I'm not at all surprised he doesn't care about the prints, Jeff."

Hooley sighed, "Maybe you're right."

Jess added, while digging for the key she could have sworn she'd just had in hand, "But this magilla about McLaughlan. It sounds like another frame, like what they pulled on Larry. Why can't Boyd see *that*?"

"And what's Boyd's take on the first frame?" Hooley reminded Jessica,

"Oh, right. I don't know what to do, Jeff," Jessica frowned. "This spot is getting tighter every minute. Look what happens when people try to help. Is it hopeless?"

"If I have anything to say about it, your friend Larry won't be another victim, and neither will this McLaughlan. We're going to straighten this mess out. Believe me."

Jessica nodded and smiled, heartened by Hooley's intensity. She opened the door and led him in, flicking on the lights as she promised, "Well, let's get down to busi..."

A crash from behind the library doors startled them both silent.

Their eyes locked, and Hooley cut off Jessica's nascent question with a finger to his lips, as he slowly drew his gun from its shoulder holster. As soon as a swift surveillance told him she'd be safe, he jerked his head for her to hide down the corridor nearer the kitchen. Jessica refused to shake, visibly anyway, as Hooley sidled out of sight into the living room, toward whatever lurked behind the library doors.

Chapter Twenty-One

Sunday (morning), June 3

Those library door smacked open, and Jessica had all she could do not to jump. Thank God Dusty was in Connecticut! All was silent. Or had she just heard a muttered oath?

Hooley's voice cut across the apartment, "Jessica, get me some ice! Make it snappy!"

"Ice?" What was that all about? Jessica raced around the corner, across the living room, and toward the library, calling, "Hooley, what the dickens do you need ice for?"

Hooley popped his head out the one opened door, ignoring her comment, and added, "Where's the whiskey?"

"In the liquor cabinet, by the window. Say, come back!"

Hooley had disappeared back into the library. Following him, Jessica insisted as she entered the room, "Hooley, this is no time fix yourself a stiff one... Oh my God!"

Propped on one of the chairs before the fireplace was a sorely battered Leo McLaughlan.

"Nice to see you, too, Miss Minton," McLaughlan managed with an ironic smile, despite the shiners and the split lip.

"Good heavens! I've got to get some ice!"

"Good idea," Hooley commented dryly, McLaughlan's shot of whiskey in hand.

"My Lord, McLaughlan, what happened to you? Oh no, never mind, the ice–and alcohol. You need antiseptic. Anything broken?"

McLaughlan coughed, but the whiskey steadied him.

"Do you need a doctor?" Jessica pressed.

"No." McLaughlan was abrupt. "I just need to straighten out my head before I talk to Aaron." Turning to Hooley, Leo McLaughlan requested, "Give me another shot of Dr. Johnny Walker, will you? I need something to help me pull my head together."

"You don't know?" Jessica asked. "Your partner was here. They're after you for the murder of a security guard at the airport. What's going on McLaughlan?"

Beneath the black and blue, McLaughlan blanched, speechless at first. Finally, he said, "Maybe I'm punch drunk, but what did you say about me and murder?"

Jessica and Hooley exchanged tense looks, then she let Hooley take the lead: "Suppose we patch you up and then explain things, McLaughlan?"

"Suppose we get things straightened out right now," McLaughlan bristled. "I want to know exactly what kind of a jam I'm in."

"We don't know exactly," Jessica explained. "Right before we came in, your partner showed up looking for you. He told us a night watchman was killed at McKinley Airport."

"Garfield," McLaughlan corrected automatically.

"Sure, sure. The watchman was killed with your gun. Boyd wanted you to turn..." Before Jessica had finished, McLaughlan uttered a low, "Jesus, not Pop."

While Jess mastered the urge to ask why all night watchmen were old and named "Pop," Hooley took over: "Perhaps we'd better get your story before we fix you up, after all."

"I'm as curious as the next Joe, Hooley," Jessica cut in, "but I think we ought to check this guy for broken bones or internal injuries..."

"Sorry, Minton, I didn't bring my portable X-ray. But I gave him a cursory check. His eyes are okay. No concussion. No broken ribs. McLaughlan, just what does a two-bit private airport have to do with the price of tea in China?"

"There's the snag, pal, private as in belonging to Tewkesbury Estates, Inc. Say, I could use another hit."

Jessica took Leo McLaughlan's glass and went to refill it, saying, "No problem, just keep the story going. What about them owning an airport?"

To Jessica's and Hooley's impatience, McLaughlan didn't pipe up again until she returned the glass to him. He took a bracing swig, grimaced, and resumed, "I had reason to believe there was a log at the airport that would blow Alanna Tewkesbury's alibi."

"How?" Jessica questioned eagerly.

Skeptical, Hooley was more to the point: "You were able to get a warrant?"

"That's the tricky part. Tewkesbury used her husband's juice to get me pulled from the case. No judge would give me the time of day right now."

"But with people as high-placed as Tewkesbury, you can't just grab a piece of evidence without a warrant," Hooley brooded.

"Hadn't planned to grab it." McLaughlan glanced at Jessica and commented, "Your F.B.I. boy is right on the ball, isn't he?"

"So you know this is Hooley?"

"Yeah, we introduced ourselves when he was scraping me up off the floor before you came in. Sorry about jimmying open your window, then taking down your end table when I collapsed."

"Never mind that," Jeff Hooley cut in. "Back to the airport. What were you doing out there if you couldn't seize the evidence? That's just tipping your hand."

"Not exactly. I knew Pop from way back, when the airport was public. I knew he'd let me look at the log, if I asked. That's legal enough. He's the agent in charge, so he can show me the log. That's all I needed to know for now. I figured ... uh ... give me a minute here, the room's starting to pirouette. Okay, I'm okay now. I figured if I *knew* there was evidence, I could bring you out to witness it, and *you* might be able to get a warrant. Betty Weisenthal crossed state lines, so her crimes are under federal jurisdiction."

"So what went wrong?" Hooley prompted.

"Nothing, at first. Took a cab out there, just in case they were looking for my car."

"They knew you might be checking?" Jessica queried.

"Long story. Ask your sister."

"Then it'll get even longer, McLaughlan," Jessica remarked.

"Do you mind?" Hooley cut in.

Jessica shrugged, then settled into a chair while Hooley, hands in pockets, leaned against the fireplace and nodded for McLaughlan to resume.

The detective pushed on, "Pops showed the log to me, no problem. He even decided to put it away for safekeeping. Swore not to let out a peep about my being there. I thought I was on easy street when I walked out the doors of that hangar–that's when they lowered the boom."

"What happened?" Jessica breathed.

"They roughed me up good and knocked me out. I came to earlier than they expected, in a car. Played possum, but I could tell from their chatter that I was on a one-way ride. I felt for my gun when they weren't paying attention. Guess I know now that they didn't snatch it just to make me more peaceable. Damn, they got the old guy. He was probably only trying to protect me, and this is what it got him."

"But you escaped," Hooley refocused the detective.

"Yeah, yeah," McLaughlan continued. "I got away. They stopped at an intersection near Central Park."

"And you jumped out?" Jessica supplied.

"Nah, I figured they'd be on guard then. We were just pulling out, picking up a little speed. I waited till they relaxed some, but we weren't flying enough to bounce me too hard off the asphalt. That's when I took a powder out the door."

"Your judgment could use a little fine tuning, McLaughlan," Hooley observed.

"You're telling me. Anyway, there was other traffic around. I held together long enough to get away and finally grab a cab. Lucky, they didn't nab my wallet."

"Lucky," Hooley absently agreed, mulling over the story.

Jessica considered a moment before questioning, "But why come here? Why not an emergency room? Your own place? Back to the precinct?"

"My place or a hospital would be the first place those apes would go looking for me," McLaughlan answered. "I figured no one would expect me to dare come here or your sister's after your places were turned upside down. Unfortunately, I passed out right before you two came in. Since I wasn't in much shape to make a statement, I thought it'd be smart to get myself straightened out before I reported in at the station. What happened to Pops scotches that idea."

"I'll say," Jessica agreed. Then, looking at Hooley, she asked, "So, now what?"

Hooley thought it over before abruptly deciding, "Now we patch him up. Let him get a good night's rest."

"What about the murder charge?" Jessica insisted. McLaughlan nodded agreement.

"The whole situation smells to me. I don't want this guy facing the grilling they're going to give him until he's got his head back on. It makes things too easy for Betty to hang a phony rap on another guy to stay in the clear. I'm not letting her or her husband throw up a smokescreen so they can get off with everything I've told you," Hooley decided.

His voice was hard. Jess glanced at McLaughlan, who didn't know about Jeff Hooley's brother. However, McLaughlan had his wits about him, for he abruptly questioned, "Say what about the prints you were delivering? You can clear up this whole mess with that evidence, a lot of it anyway. I don't like that look on your face, Hooley. What else has been queered?"

Hooley frowned tightly before replying, "I'll give it to you straight. The prints are gone. Someone tampered with the file."

McLaughlan seemed to collapse into himself. He only muttered, "Cripes."

Jess came over and put a hand on McLaughlan's arm, saying, "There's still one shot, Detective. Hooley says he might be able to i.d. the picture that I did bring back. He thinks that guy could help us put the finger on Alanna Tewkesbury. The race isn't over yet."

"It's going to be a damned tight photo finish," McLaughlan returned almost bitterly.

"No race is over until the stewards..."

"All right! Okay!" Hooley cut in. "Enough with the horse-racing metaphors. The sooner this guy's patched up, the sooner you and I can check out the picture and make some plans."

Sometime later, Jessica wearily replaced the phone on the receiver and collapsed onto the couch. Leo McLaughlan was bandaged up, tucked in, and lost to the world in her room; Jeff Hooley was brooding over a plate of cookies and a glass of milk in the kitchen–where she'd left him after a frantically ringing phone had announced her sister's fury at Boyd's dropping in on her in the middle of the night, er, morning, to look for McLaughlan. From their conversation, Jess gathered that Liz had gone off like a firecracker and driven him away with his tail between his legs. About to spill the beans concerning her houseguest, Jess had stopped herself. If Boyd had gotten a warrant for searching their apartments so fast, he might easily have procured one for a wiretap. So, her lips remained zipped on McLaughlan's presence. She could, however, let Liz know that Hooley was in town; Boyd knew that much already. The upshot was that Liz would come over early tomorrow for a confab.

What she wouldn't give for a nuzzle from Dusty right now–better yet, one from James. Maybe she could dig out those two Browning poems he'd given her for a little romantic comfort. No time, it was back to seeing what Hooley could do for them.

Trudging back into the kitchen, Jess remarked, "I see the commotion hasn't affected your appetite, Hooley."

He paused in pouring himself another glass of milk, shrugged, and answered, "I need something to wash down those cookies. Homemade?"

Folding her arms and nodding, Jessica replied, "I'm a woman of many talents: I can act, teach, out run thugs, double-talk hostile officers of the law, and *cook*."

"How about cooking up that Kodak for me?"

"It's a snap."

Jess went to her silverware drawer and pulled out a small, sharp paring knife, all the while explaining, "I was afraid Alanna would have someone give my place a once over, never mind the cops. So, I hid the picture."

With a nod to the knife, Hooley conjectured, "In a fruit?"

"Hardly." Jess moved across to the counter and pulled out a thick cookbook. "It's a variation on Poe's 'Purloined Letter.' I know those creeps wouldn't connect a photo with *haute cuisine*, but just to be on the safe side, I hid it so that they wouldn't be able to knock it or shake it out of the book."

Deftly, Jessica separated the paper connected to the back cover and pulled out the small photo, continuing, "I slit the paper carefully, slipped the photo in, then re-glued it. Pretty nifty, huh?"

Hooley smiled. "Glad you're on our side. So, let's see what you have for me."

Jessica slapped the picture down in front of him.

Jeff Hooley stared at it, his lips tightening. Finally, he looked up at her to say, "It does look like Kavanaugh." He flipped over the photo and frowned at the smudge, musing as he read the back, "John. Jay's a nickname for John. Maybe ... so, what's the rest? Looks like some kind of an address."

"It *was* an address, until that creep Kubek stepped on it and smudged it all to blue blazes," Jessica groused, sitting down, disgusted.

Hooley picked up the picture, thinking aloud, "I'm not 100% sure it's him."

"How about 95%?"

"How about, it's worth investigating?"

"*Really*, Hooley? You're not kidding? We may have something to go on here?"

"Yeah, we might," the young man allowed. "But hold your horses. Even if it's Kavanaugh, I still have to find out for certain where he is now."

That was hitting a wall, and Jessica's tone didn't hide her frustration, "How long will that take, Jeff? Do you have any idea where to start?"

"Starting's not the problem. It's finishing that worries me. But don't get into a funk. It's not hopeless. I have some contacts on the Boston P.D., in our own local office, too. I can also track down the records through the newspapers. I have a friend who can get me into the Boston Public Library, even on a Sunday morning. I'll grab an early train this morning."

"Boston? This morning? When was the last time you slept, Hooley?"

"I'll catch forty winks on the train. Four hours is plenty of time." Returning his attention to the Kodak, he mused, "Wonder what the book is? The one they're holding."

"What? Let me see. Oh, it's funny, but you know, Hooley, the clues he sent us were all connected to e. e. cummings's poetry, and I found the photos in a book by him in the apartment."

"Do you think the book you found is the same one in the picture?"

"Well, I don't know. It's hard to judge from such a small picture."

"You have the book?"

"Of course! I wouldn't leave that behind!"

"So, maybe I should take a look at it."

"Yeah, but I've got to tell you, Hooley, Liz and I went over the book with a fine-toothed comb, and we couldn't find anything else hidden beyond the two pictures, well, the one picture now."

"So, how about letting a pro give it the once over?"

Jessica started to argue but thought, *Don't you want something more to hope for? There are more important things at stake than not letting Hooley one-up you!*

"I'll be right back, Hooley. It's in the library."

"What, no secret hideaways?"

"Hey, people know me as a well-read young lady, so they expect me to have literature. It's stacked with the rest of my poetry, filed according to era, nation of origin, and alphabetical order."

"That's not obsessive?"

"Don't get wise, wise guy," Jessica warned, getting up. "Just sit tight and I'll be right back."

And after all that–nothing. For a moment, both felt a thrill at discerning underlinings in various odd poems, but that dissipated as they realized the underlinings were accompanied by comments that seemed no more than the annotations of an amateur scholar. There were some stray lines drawn, too, vaguely familiar in appearance to Jess, but they didn't seem to follow any kind of a logic, let alone add up to a message. They were back to the photos and the smudged address, with Hooley puzzling out, "Norwell? Nowell? Lowell?"

"We thought 'Lowell' made more sense, Jeff. It's a big enough town to hide in, and if Kavanaugh had gotten chummy with Gabriel Stuyvesant, he might have wanted to keep tabs on him. Maybe even protect him."

"Or maybe he was interested in the stolen jade," Jeff Hooley cogitated. "Better yet, maybe he thought Stuyvesant might help him, directly or not, nail the last of the Weisenthal crew. Kavanaugh could have functioned as a contact to help Stuyvesant come East as Evan Blair."

"So, you think they were in contact after Blair came back East?"

"Could be. But I'll tell you one thing. I'm not going to find out anything sitting around this table shooting the breeze with you. First thing tomorrow, I'm going to do a little research in Boston."

"Do you need any help from me?" Jessica asked earnestly.

"Somebody's got to stay here and babysit."

"Oh, yikes, I forgot. Hooley, do you think the cops will be back, looking for McLaughlan?"

He considered, then shook his head, pointing out, "I think Boyd was just playing a long shot. If he'd had a real hunch, he'd have found a way to get in and take a look around. No, he was mainly warning you not to hold out on him if by some one-in-a-million chance..."

"A chance that would have paid off, since McLaughlan is now catching a few zzzs under my chintz."

"Precisely."

Jessica continued, "Well, we can't let McLaughlan turn himself in until you've got something that can clear him. I know it's not according to Hoyle, but Mrs. Tewkesbury is too dangerous. Even if his partner is trying to look out for him, no detective is strong enough to stand against the frame up she's concocted, not unless we can completely turn the tables on her."

"Once you veer off that straight and narrow, you never look back at Girl Scout Camp, do you, Minton?" he dryly noted.

"It's not funny, Hooley. I don't mind telling you I'm scared. I'm in way over my head."

"Worse than dodging Nazis? Oh, I forgot, you had James Crawford looking out for you then."

Jessica volleyed back, "You know, Hooley, for a while you almost made me forget what a fourteen-karat jackass you can be. Why don't you save that rapier wit of yours for something useful, like tracking down the guy who might clear innocent people?"

"Including my brother," he tellingly added.

"I never forgot that. You know it is possible to help people without kicking them in the pants at the same time."

"But not as much fun," he deadpanned.

"Don't forget, some of us kick back," Jessica coolly warned, before adding, "Maybe it's time you were on your merry way. In fact, the door behind you is the quickest way out."

Hooley smiled sardonically at Jessica, enjoying her barbs. She hated that from him.

He surprised her with a businesslike, "What's outside the door? Where does it lead?"

"There's an alley perpendicular to Damascus Place on one end and runs into the street behind us. Why?"

"Think I'll check it out. If the locals decide to watch your house, they might not realize the alley has access to the next street. Is the connection to the next street visible from Damascus Place?"

"No. It looks as if it just leads into my back yard," Jess answered.

"Might be a good way to get in and out without being noticed, just in case," he explained. "So, wish me luck tomorrow, I mean today. I'll contact you as soon as I get anything, but I won't call in case the line is tapped. Just make sure that your houseguest keeps a low profile. And definitely don't let him do anything until you hear from me. Tell him that's an order from the Feds. You sit tight, too, no matter what that sister of yours tries to bulldoze you into doing."

Jess had a snappy retort primed and ready, but Hooley was gone. Coward! Afraid to let her get the last word. Recalling all that had happened over the last twenty-four hours, Jess realized she needed two words: "Good luck!"

Eight o'clock Sunday morning and Jessica Minton stood in her sunny kitchen working her orange-juice squeezing contraption, an apron protecting her silk dress of white surplice top and full, soft-blue skirt. She paused, her glance falling on the white portable radio atop the counter. Music would be a wonderful distraction, but it would probably wake McLaughlan. The least she could do was see that he got plenty of shuteye after all he'd been through for Minton & Company. That and give him a decent breakfast.

Hands on hips, Jess studied the counter, musing: what did you feed a guy who'd been sapped, had jumped out of a moving car, and been framed for murder? Hmm, Dick Powell in *Murder, My Sweet* had put in for coffee made with scotch and scrambled eggs–also with a scotch chaser. Frankly, she could use that scotch herself.

A heavy clunk from somewhere in the vicinity of the front door startled Jessica. The cops back again? Eddie Kubek and a passel of goons? A glance at the clock on the wall eased her mind: right about time for the "weighty" *Times* to descend on her front stoop. Wiping her hands on her apron, untying it, and tossing it onto a chair, Jess went striding out of the room to retrieve the paper. She moved more softly while passing McLaughlan's "bower of bliss." The energetic sawing of wood emanating from thence suggested that he might be in better shape than he'd looked to be last night.

The morning on which Jessica opened her door was warm and bright, a stark contrast to the thunderheads inside her. Glances up and down the street revealed that she was not under anyone's surveillance. So why didn't she feel better? Straightening up, paper in hand, Jess checked the headlines. Nothing on Pop's murder. Then again, a guy named "Pop" wasn't exactly front-page material for the *New York Times*.

Sitting down on a dining-room chair, Jessica snapped open the paper and searched for the complete scoop on the murder rap hanging over McLaughlan. She got to page five before that story left her muttering a very unladylike, "Damn, damn, damn." Slowly, thoughtfully, Jess closed the paper.

What sounded like her bedside table and too many breakables hitting the floor snapped Jess to attention. Then there was a groan. Paper still in hand, Jessica flew down the corridor and into her bedroom.

The room was in shadows from the drawn curtains, but there, sitting up in bed, was Leo McLaughlan. Jess switched on the overhead light, and his glance went from her to the floor and back again before he offered, "Sorry about the lamp and the other stuff. I don't think anything's broken. I wasn't quite awake when I leaned over."

Jess's twinge of guilt at her concern for the state of her possessions quickly changed to relief as she recognized that McLaughlan didn't look half as bad as she'd expected–although with his bruises in full flower, he wasn't exactly a threat to Cary Grant. Absently tossing the paper on her bureau by the door, she came forward, reassuring her houseguest, "Don't worry about it. I'll take care of the mess."

But McLaughlan was already nearly finished putting back what he'd knocked over. Still, he let Jessica push him back and answered her query about how he was feeling with, "Not too bad, for a guy who fell out of an airplane the night before."

"Next time, use a parachute. Now sit back while I go and get you a cold towel for that Technicolor noggin of yours."

"That bad, huh?"

Jessica tossed over her shoulder, "I've seen worse."

In the bathroom, the door open, Jess soaked a clean towel in cold water. She was quiet, thinking about what she'd read in the paper. How much should she tell McLaughlan? *When* should she tell him? Pray God that Boyd didn't get any bright ideas and come back here before Hooley got the goods on Alanna Tewkesbury. Shoot! McLaughlan was talking to her. Wringing out the towel, Jess called without looking up, "Sorry, McLaughlan. I wasn't paying attention. Concentrating on this." Emerging from the bathroom, Jessica continued, "Now, what did you say?"

Sitting down next to McLaughlan, she put the towel over his forehead and listened as her patient repeated, "I said I've got to call in and straighten out this SNAFU about Pop and me. What time is it, anyway?"

"It's early. Eight o'clock. Not even dawn for theatre folk."

"Yeah, anyway, where's your phone?"

"Let the cloth set a bit."

"Lady, this is a murder investigation. It's not about only me. Somebody killed Pop, and I intend to make damn sure the real murderer doesn't get off."

"So get your head on straight, first. You're not up for a third-degree grilling, bud, believe me. Take a look at that pan of yours!"

Jess flipped up her hand mirror from the bedside table.

He winced at what he saw, but only for a second. "Look, I'm not in a beauty contest. I'm trying to solve *two* murders now. I've got to get in and talk to Aaron, straighten this out."

Jessica was on her feet, gnawing her lower lip.

"Okay, lady, what gives? What're you holding out on me?"

"All right, McLaughlan, I'll level with you. But it's not pretty, not for any of us. There's a story in this morning's paper that says, well, you passed third grade. Read it yourself and see if Hooley isn't right to say you need to lay low till he gets back."

Without acknowledging McLaughlan's doubting expression, Jess retrieved the paper and opened it to the story. Dropping the paper into his lap, she said simply, "Read."

McLaughlan's expression as he read made Jessica wince. But how else would he react to the story? Good old Roarke (probably glad to pay for his ineptitude with a non-fatal bullet and a little jail time rather than coffin time) spilling his guts, implicating Leo McLaughlan in corruption so tightly that all his efforts to support her and her sister's charges against Alanna Tewkesbury crumbled like Miss Havisham's wedding cake. Roarke painted himself as a low-level hood, thinking he was scaring an old security guard into faking a flight log that would implicate Mrs. Tewkesbury in a murder. Why her? Well, seems murder victim Evan Blair had quite a record of his own and was working with McLaughlan to shake her down. Unfortunately, Blair got too greedy, so McLaughlan offed him using a stolen gun. When the two Minton dames started making noises about Alanna Tewkesbury, he figured to keep the blackmail going himself. But even Roarke had scruples: putting the screws on a rich dame was one thing, but bumping off an old guy, that was way over the line. So, he claimed he took a bullet for his trouble from a rogue cop who'd latched onto the jealous fantasies of two skirts and parlayed them into a get-rich-quick scheme to shake down a ritzy dame. The rest of the story detailed how McLaughlan's partner, in order to prove he was clean, was under pressure to bring in the dirty cop, whatever it took.

"What is this bunk?!" Leo McLaughlan growled, slapping the newspaper. "The Lieutenant actually bought it? I'm telling you, lady, if they leave me alone with this clown for ten minutes, I'll crack his story wide open."

"According to the paper, McLaughlan, that attitude almost got your partner thrown off the case. It doesn't look as if he's going to be much help to you, not unless we come up with something solid to discredit this story."

"Yeah, but what gets me is this Roarke. I don't know him from Adam. What's his connection?"

"Ah, maybe he works for Alanna Tewkesbury."

"You say that as if you knew something."

"It makes perfect sense. She's got her fingers in every pie," Jessica sidestepped him. It killed her not being free to come completely clean with McLaughlan, especially after he'd taken such a working over in their cause, but how much dared she tell him just yet?

"She must have some hold on this bum for him to take a bullet and do time for her," Leo McLaughlan speculated, glaring at the paper.

"Hey, if she can disappear fingerprints from the F.B.I. who knows what kind of power she can exert over some poor schmoe."

"Damn. I really want to get these bastards now," Leo McLaughlan spat out. "Pop, Blair, even though he was no prize, you, your sister, Sanders, Aaron, and meddling with the Federal government. Is this what our guys have been fighting and dying for? So some rich jerks can play fast and loose with the law, with people's lives? I want to get this *grande dame* so bad I can taste it."

"Swell, McLaughlan," Jessica blurted sincerely. "I'm in there with you."

"Good, because if you're holding anything back..."

"What? Why would I do that? I'm on your side."

"Yeah? But you know, I was talking to your sister yesterday ... seems like twenty years ago ... and I had the distinct feeling she was holding out on me."

"Did you? Well, she was probably just nervous. You guys did ransack her apartment."

"Your sister is about as nervous as a Sherman tank. Last night, I got bounced like a basketball, and now I have a murder rap hanging over my head. A decent old man died. You'd better not be holding out on me after all that," McLaughlan warned.

The knocking on the front door cut him short. McLaughlan shot Jessica a sharp look and demanded, "You expecting Hooley this soon?"

"No, no. Do you think it's the cops, searching again?"

McLaughlan considered, before deciding, "They were just here. Twice in less than a day? It's too soon for them to hit a place that's not a primary target, unless you and Hooley acted as if you were hiding something."

Jess shook her head, wishing that she could be 100% sure. Then she gasped, "Oh my God, what if it's Eddie Kubek?"

"You think he'd knock?"

"You think Alanna would let him come crashing in and justify what we've been saying about them being dangerous?" Jessica disputed nervously.

"Tell you what. Stash me in the cellar. If it's the boys in blue, I can make it look as if I snuck in without you knowing. If it's Kubek, I can create enough of a distraction for you to get away."

"Are you out of your mind?" Jessica argued. "In your condition, he'd make mincemeat out of you!"

"Don't argue with me. I know what I'm doing. Now get a wiggle on."

McLaughlan was sprier than Jess had expected, but it still seemed to take forever to stash him behind the cellar door. The bell was ringing now. With a shudder, Jessica launched herself at the door and opened it.

Chapter Twenty-Two

Sunday (morning), June 3

"It's about time," Elizabeth snapped. "It'd take you less time to hide a man."

"Ha, ha."

A quick glance up and down the street, and Jessica hauled her sister inside and, before Liz uttered a peep, had shut the door and breathed, "Liz, you don't know how relieved I am to see you."

"So you *have* read today's paper about McLaughlan?" Liz was indignant. "How dare they pull a fast one on the only guy with nerve enough to listen to us. No one can convince me that McLaughlan killed the guard. Not in a million years! The guy may be pigheaded, but he's no cold-blooded murderer!"

"Fine, you can tell him to his face," Jessica managed to get a word in. "He's parked in the cellar right this minute."

Liz was half-way to the cellar door, tossing over her shoulder, "What on earth is he doing there?"

"Hiding out," Jess replied trotting up and stopping her sister. "After our chum Alanna had some apes work him over, kill the guard, and wrap a nifty little frame around him."

Then Jessica put a finger over her lips and beckoned Liz over to a writing pad on the dining table. Silently, she dashed off "Careful. He doesn't know about the gun–Hooley said to keep quiet about it for now."

"Okay. But Hooley is here?" Liz whispered. "He brought the prints, then, and we can ... Why are you shaking your head?"

"Sit down, Liz."

"Why don't I assume that the prints actually match Eleanor Roosevelt and faint now?"

"It's not quite that bad. Close, though. Let me give it to you fast so we can 'liberate' McLaughlan: the prints 'disappeared' from the F.B.I. Central files, but Hooley recognized the guy in the picture with Evan Blair. Hooley's on his way to Massachusetts right now, checking it out. So we're not completely behind the eight ball."

"I can't believe that woman got to the Feds," Elizabeth breathed.

"I couldn't, at first, either" Jess concurred, then urged, "So, let's rescue McLaughlan from the cellar. He could use more rest, and a good breakfast wouldn't hurt him, either."

They approached the cellar door. As a precaution, Jessica knocked and called, "It's me, Jessica, with my sister. It's okay. We're going to let you out."

No answer.

"Kind of quiet, isn't he?" Liz observed uneasily. Then she brightened and suggested, "Maybe he's playing possum! He could think Eddie Kubek or someone is forcing you to expose him. Be careful he doesn't leap out at you by mistake."

Jess opened the door, and McLaughlan corrected Liz from his seat on the second step, "At the moment, McLaughlan isn't up for leaping, *leaning* maybe."

"Good heavens!" Liz was genuinely taken aback at his battered features. "What happened to you! You look dreadful!"

"It's the unflattering light," McLaughlan dryly cracked, as he was getting up.

"Here, let me help you," Liz insisted, giving a hand.

"Thanks. Whoa take it easy, tiger!" McLaughlan protested as Liz officiously, but kindly, almost dragged him out of the cellar.

Getting a better look at McLaughlan's face in the light, Liz went solemn and silent. In fact, not a word escaped her until they got him back into bed. Elizabeth even adjusted the pillows carefully, concern and rumination clear in her features. When Jess promised McLaughlan something easy to get down for breakfast, he quipped that at least Tewkesbury's goons had done him the favor of leaving him all his teeth. That made Liz sharply inhale. Wordlessly, she followed her sister into the kitchen, so Jess knew wheels were grinding, big time, in Liz's head.

Jessica glanced briefly at her sister, standing silently at the kitchen table, then grabbed a pot and the cream of wheat. Liz or no, McLaughlan needed some fuel. As soon as she had the cereal started, Jess moved the orange-juice squeezer over to her sister and suggested, "How about making some juice for all of us?"

"What? No, you squeeze. I'll do the cream of wheat. Yours always comes out lumpy."

"Some people like the lumps."

"Not someone who got his face pushed in to protect us."

Before Jess could start to comfort her sister, Liz moved past her to preside over the cream of wheat. All that was left was for Jess to tie on an apron and consider how best to reach her big sister.

"Hey, Liz, how about I start some coffee?"

"You'll get burned, and that will be my fault, too!"

"Gee, Liz, if it makes you feel better, once it starts perking, I can always splash a little over your hand."

Liz whirled, furious, then weakened and said with remorse that broke Jess's heart, "Don't you get it, Jessica? Look what I'm responsible for. Larry could go to the chair because I got mixed up with Evan and Alanna. The security guard was murdered. That man in your room almost got killed helping us. His career is in an ash can, and he's under suspicion for murder because I drove him to make dangerous enemies. Just like I did to you, sending you into that apartment..."

"Now, hold on a minute, Elizabeth Minton. I'm a big girl. I can say no if I have to."

"The point is," Liz argued back, "I've been pushing people around, telling everyone what to do. But you've been taking all the risks. I've been sitting back on my shapely fanny..."

"Well," Jess glanced at her sister's derrière and tried to kid away her pain, "You could stand a little reducing."

"Do you think I'm joking, Jessica?"

"Elizabeth, we listened to you because you had some inspired, albeit unusual, ideas. We had a choice," Jessica countered. "You didn't *make* anyone do anything. Besides, you couldn't do what the rest of us did. I knew disguises and acting, so I was the logical choice to play cleaning girl. McLaughlan was the one with the contact at the airfield, again not you."

"Oh, I'm supposed to feel good about what happened to McLaughlan?" Liz reproached herself sarcastically.

"No. I don't. He certainly doesn't. But maybe you should feel okay that you're trying your best not to let justice be sold to the highest bidder. You're protecting Larry from that Tewkesbury viper. You're bringing justice to Evan Blair, to Lois's brother, to everyone the Weisenthal gang destroyed. Don't give up now."

Liz folded her arms, thinking.

Jess came around the table and gave her sister's shoulder a shake, "Don't go soft on me now, just when Hooley's getting us into the homestretch. He really thinks he can get somewhere if he finds this guy in the Kodak, this Jay Kavanaugh."

"If?"

"All right, *when*. Hooley's a real bulldog. And that sketchy business with the prints has only made him more tenacious. He even indicated," here her voice dropped low, to make certain that McLaughlan couldn't hear, "he can keep us out of trouble over the, well, you know."

"Scotch terrier?" Liz code-worded for "gun" with a wink.

"Close enough."

"Speaking of which," Liz stopped, her eyes flashing alarm. "We left that paper where you wrote about the 'Scottie' out in plain sight in the other room."

"Go get it, then. You were feeling guilty about making everyone else do the dirty work."

"Not very dangerous, especially with Dusty out of town."

"You might trip, Liz."

"What are the odds?"

"I could stick my foot out."

"Ha, ha." A skeptical look. "Can I trust you to finish cooking this porridge? After all, McLaughlan's suffered enough."

"I'll try my best."

"Okay. Then make the coffee while you're at it. And remember, no lumps."

"In the coffee or the cereal?" Jess queried innocently.

"You're a college graduate. Figure it out."

Elizabeth coasted out of the kitchen, but her glance lingered at the bedroom door. So did she. After a moment, she made a gentle but peremptory knock and went in.

McLaughlan was sitting up, the paper in front of him. Regarding Liz's entrance, he commented, "Lucky I'm decent."

Liz began with a surprising lack of her typical assertiveness, "May I come in?"

"Looks like you are."

Liz let that slide and closed the door quietly behind her.

McLaughlan regarded her action skeptically before remarking, "What will your sister think?"

"She's broadminded, but I can leave the door ajar if it makes you feel safer. You don't exactly look as if you're up for any monkey business." Liz's wit was back.

"So you said before." He was waiting for her to come to the point.

"You must be pretty sore with me for getting you into this jam."

"You're right about me being sore–but not at you, exactly." He slapped the newspaper. "It's this damned hatchet job. They've got me and Aaron on the hot seat, and that Tewkesbury dame is sitting pretty. The newspapers, the public, the Commissioner, they're eating it all up."

"But McLaughlan, Agent Hooley seems to think that if he digs up some guy named Kavanaugh, the one in the picture with Evan, he can put the finger on Alanna Tewkesbury. Once he does that, we can shake her claims against you, probably even expose her link to Roarke giving you the bum rap."

"If I could just talk to Aaron, he could do the legwork to help Hooley make that connection," muttered McLaughlan, frustrated.

"But you read the paper. You know Boyd's under suspicion, too," Elizabeth pointed out. "They're probably watching him to get a line on you. You've got to leave him out of the loop for now. You'll only make it worse for all of us, especially Boyd–not that I'm in a hurry to do *him* any favors."

"You don't like Aaron, do you?" McLaughlan's smile was crooked.

"Not like Aaron Boyd? Not like the guy who's trying to send someone dear to me to the chair, who ransacked my apartment–and my sister's, too–who treats everyone I care about like something head lice would sneer at? What's not to like?" Liz sarcastically queried.

"Okay, I get the picture. I'm willing to admit he might have jumped the gun a little."

"How about pole vaulted over it?"

"He's a good cop, Miss Minton. He's been a good cop close to ten years. He's been a darned good partner since when I was a college-boy rookie."

"But you're not a rookie anymore, McLaughlan."

"Maybe. But I don't want to see Aaron get taken for a ride because of my mistake."

"You think it was a mistake to listen to me?" Liz asked quietly, unable to keep a trace of guilt from her voice.

"No," McLaughlan answered, surprised at an urge to comfort her. He continued, "Let's say that I didn't anticipate how far the opposition would go to keep me quiet. I should have played my cards closer to the vest with Tewkesbury. I should have known she'd dope out my next step. The worst is that I didn't see I wasn't the only one who'd have to pay. There's Pops."

"McLaughlan, if you beat up on anyone, beat up on me," Elizabeth proposed, lifting her chin. "I encouraged you to go after that airplane log. I set you on Tewkesbury's trail, pushed you all the time. If I hadn't been trying so hard to defend Larry and bring Evan's murderers to justice..."

"I'd still have seen there was something hinky about this case. Stop beating up on yourself, Miss Minton."

"After you literally took it on the chin for me, the least I can do is tell you to call me Liz," she proposed.

"That's jake with me, Liz." He thought a moment, then began, "There is something else you can do for me."

"I'm not calling Aaron Boyd."

"No, no, not that. But it is important. When I talked to you last night, and when I talked to your sister this morning, I could see that you were both holding something back from me. I don't know if this is something you let Hooley in on, but if I'm going to get my brains beat in and my partner is going to be put on the hot seat, I think I'm entitled to the straight dope, all of it. Don't you?"

Liz leaned against the bureau. What was the right thing to do? Jess said that Hooley wanted them to keep their traps shut, but could telling McLaughlan the truth hurt now? She did owe the man. More than that, she liked and trusted him. And it wasn't as if he was in any position to haul them in.

McLaughlan must have been a mind reader, for he prodded, "It's not exactly as if I could run you in for anything now."

"Mush!"

Jessica was standing in the open doorway and staring McLaughlan down.

"Mush? You don't buy what I'm telling your sister?"

"No," Jessica returned sweetly, waltzing into the room, carrying a tray laden with cream of wheat, orange juice, and a cup of coffee. "That's what I'm serving you, mush. Easy to chew and digest. Fluff the pillow, eh, Liz?"

"Oh, um, sure," Liz stammered, rushing to comply, skeptical of both her companions.

Jessica took up the thread of conversation, "As for your claim that you couldn't arrest any of us, Detective, I'm going with the opposite conclusion. You might think arresting Liz, Larry, and me would be quite a feather in your cap. Someone could even suggest that you say one, maybe all of us, rather than Alanna, framed you."

"You believe that after everything I've been through I'd still sell you down the river?" McLaughlan demanded coldly.

"Yeah, Jess! This poor guy really looks like hell!" Liz indignantly supported him.

"Don't try to butter me up so much," McLaughlan remarked.

Unconvinced by either McLaughlan or her sister, Jessica informed him, "I think that neither Liz nor I have anything we can tell you. Furthermore, we're not going to be manipulated into saying something incriminating."

"Maybe after I have a word or two with this Hooley, I can worm the truth out of you two," the detective warned.

"Nuts."

"Don't get cute, Miss Minton."

"I just wanted to know if you'd like some pecans to make the mush a little less bland," Jess pleasantly corrected him. As McLaughlan scowled, Jessica turned to her sister, "Let's leave him to eat. I think we're bad for his digestion." Back to McLaughlan, "I'm not leading you astray. I'm just following Hooley's orders. Now eat up and rest. We'll probably all need full reserves before this game is played out. And that's the straight dope."

"Baloney."

"I've never heard of putting deli meat on cream of wheat," Liz puzzled.

"It's not what I want to eat; it's what I think about your sister's claims."

"Fine. Eat. Sulk. Rest," Jess serenely returned. "Save your complaints for Hooley. I trust him to call the shots. Come on, Liz."

Hustled out the door and down to the kitchen, Liz queried, "What did he just mutter, kid?"

"I don't know," Jessica fibbed. "Let's have us some coffee."

"You bet. I could really use a little java jive at this point!"

Jess didn't have the nerve to tell her sister that McLaughlan had grumbled how much he hated lumps in his cereal.

Before the living room's picture window, Jess had taken the couch while Liz sat in a nearby chair. The coffee table held a breakfast tray with food barely touched.

Liz broke the silence, asking hopefully, "You really think that Hooley can dig up enough on Mrs. Tewkesbury?"

Jessica contemplated her coffee and returned the cup to the low table before answering, "Lord knows we're due for a break. Besides, he's got his own stake in nailing her."

"I bet I know just what that stake is," Liz returned, knowingly. "It's plain as the nose on your face; he's sweet on you."

A car door slamming outside saved Jessica the trouble of arguing that *her* romantic interests lay across the ocean. Swiftly, she moved to the window seat and looked out, while Liz craned her neck to see. Sighing relief, Jessica turned back and said, "Relax. It's Larry."

"Larry? What's he ... ?"

"With that paper rolled up under his arm? Three guesses and the first two don't count."

Liz glanced anxiously toward the room where McLaughlan was catching forty winks. Jessica advised, "Stay cool, Liz. Just keep Larry on safe topics and out of earshot of our house guest." She slid from the window seat and moved swiftly to answer Larry's rapping.

"Right. We won't talk about the," here Liz's voice dropped, "gu–'Scotch Terrier.'"

"Fine." Jess tried not to roll her eyes.

Jess opened the door, and Larry pounced on her with, "Is Liz here? I've been a wreck trying to reach her. Right, there she is." He rushed to Liz, demanding, "You've seen the paper, about that murdered security guard, Pop? Why do they always call these chaps 'Pop'?"

"I don't know," Jess answered for her sister, she hoped calmly, "but have some coffee. Liz, take Larry over by the fireplace, where it's cozier." *And keep him from waking up McLaughlan*!

"Sure, what I need is more caffeine," Larry remarked, only briefly giving her his attention. Then back to Liz and taking her hands, he asked, "Liz, what do you know about this? It's incredible, fabulous! They're claiming Detective McLaughlan is a murderer. What have we started here?"

"Larry, Larry, calm down" Liz calmed him, taking his arm. She drew Larry across the living room to the fireplace and continued, "This will all straighten itself out. People are working to clear up this dreadful mistake."

"Mistake? You mean he's not guilty? McLaughlan *didn't* kill this chap?"

"Hardly. He's been framed. Just like you. Mrs. Tewkesbury thought he was getting too close to the truth..."

"The truth?"

"Yes, about her past. She was afraid he could break her alibi, so she had the old guy killed to put McLaughlan on the spot so he couldn't push his investigation any further."

Larry harshly berated himself, "So this is my fault, too, then, isn't it, Liz? If McLaughlan hadn't been trying to clear me..."

"He's trying to expose the truth, Larry," Liz declared. "It's not only about Evan Blair. McLaughlan's trying to bring that Tewkesbury female to justice for all her crimes. Larry, don't blame yourself. *You're* one of the good guys. In fact, if it wasn't for your case, none of Alanna's vile past would have come to light. Don't you see that if we don't get her for Evan's murder, we're not going to get her for anything? This case is the lynchpin. We owe this to Lois and her brother and all the innocent saps she helped destroy."

Larry studied her keenly before finally saying, "Is that the God's honest truth, Elizabeth?"

"So help me, Larry."

"Then this story doesn't bode well for us, does it? McLaughlan believed in you. He was the only one pursuing Tewkesbury, and if she's neutralized him..."

"They haven't caught him, yet" Liz pointed out.

"Still, it all looks rather bleak, wouldn't you say? McLaughlan on the dodge isn't much help to anyone. The only one left standing is that Detective Boyd, and we all know where *his* suspicions lie," Larry brooded.

"We're not washed up yet, Larry," Elizabeth encouraged, squeezing his hand. "Jessica's G-Man pal Jeff Hooley is on the case. He's in Massachusetts now, running down some leads."

"Massachusetts?" Larry puzzled. "Far afield, isn't it?"

"Not if you want to dig up an old cop who knew Evan Blair when he was Gabriel Stuyvesant," Liz explained. "This guy can pull the rug right out from under that tarantula in Adrian. Larry, we've caught a break here. It's just a shame McLaughlan got himself in the middle,"

Larry sighed heavily, finally agreeing, almost a little relieved, "I suppose you're right, Elizabeth. I've no right to stand in the way of bringing that woman to justice, especially after all you've done to help me."

Jessica smiled at Larry's acquiescence, but that smile died on her face when the doorbell unexpectedly rang, again. Significant looks were exchanged all around.

Larry bleakly conjectured, “I’ll wager it’s Boyd come to harass me. I’ve been wondering why he hasn’t dragged me off for a roughhouse *tête à tête* now that his partner isn’t around to hold him back.”

“Do you want to slip out the back, through the kitchen?” Jessica suggested.

Larry stiffened his spine and set her straight, “Hardly, Jessica. Whatever mistakes I’ve made so far, I’m not about to slink off like a whipped cur. I can take whatever that ‘gentleman’ dishes out. Open the door.”

Liz squared her shoulders, at battle stations to protect Larry. But she wished he weren’t so stiff upper lip, much as she admired him for it. Striding across the room, Jessica steeled herself for an encounter she dreaded.

Chapter Twenty-Three

"You look real happy to see me, Miss Minton," stated Aaron Boyd with all the charm of a cobra.

Jess coolly returned, "I've been seeing a lot of you lately, Boyd."

"Too much for comfort?"

"How about substituting 'pleasure' for 'comfort?' It takes more than a lug like you to get under my skin. What're you doing back here so soon? Am I *that* irresistible?"

Ignoring her wisecrack, or at least pretending to, Boyd nodded to the street where Liz and Larry had parked their cars and said, "I see you're not alone."

"It's not against the law to have a Sunday brunch. Did you drop by to check up on my social life?"

"Only if it includes my partner. You going to invite me in?"

"No."

That surprised him.

Jess continued, "Look, do you honestly expect me to play gracious hostess to a guy who turned my apartment upside down? Especially when it meant you were leaving the real criminal free as a bird. So then you find nothing because there's nothing here for you to find, but you keep coming back, snooping, not once but twice, including last night. It ought to be a cinch for a bright boy like you to figure out why I'm not greeting you with open arms."

"I was here then, and I'm here now because I'm looking out for my partner–"

"Why on earth would you think that I could tell you anything? I'm not the one he conferred with–"

"No, your sister was, and she's in your house right now. You know I had a search warrant–"

"That warrant was dated for yesterday and made out specifying a search for the .38 caliber pistol that killed Evan Blair–not for my sister. It doesn't hold water anymore, Detective Boyd."

"You're quite the legal eagle, aren't you? Been talking to your mouthpiece?"

"You bet. Both Liz and I had a little consultation with them yesterday, and they wouldn't like me to have this much of a chat with you without them."

"I could haul you down to the station," Boyd threatened.

"Or you could better spend your time trying to save your partner from being railroaded by Mrs. Tewkesbury."

"You never let up on her, do you?"

Angrily, Jessica fired back, "Maybe you should start up. This whole smear of Leo McLaughlan didn't happen until after he had his chat with her. Doesn't that seem fishy? Come on, you can't believe in coincidence that much!"

"It was getting mixed up with you and your sister that got him into this jam, lady," Boyd shot back, but Jess could see uneasiness in his eyes.

"Do you really buy that, Boyd? Look at the facts. McLaughlan's been listening to Liz for some time now, but, *again*, it was only after he dug up something funny about Alanna Tewkesbury's alibi..."

"Like what?"

Had she gone too far? But shouldn't she be trying to hand McLaughlan's partner the baton? Maybe she was uneasy about handing that blonde juggernaut another victim to roll over. Finally, Jessica only offered, "I don't know any details. *You're* his partner. Certainly, he'd talk to you not me."

"Never mind that. My worry is finding him before the wolf pack does. If you have any leads, maybe I can follow them for him, that is if you're not just snowing me."

The suasion was tempting, but Jessica also calculated that Boyd was way too low on the totem pole to protect Leo McLaughlan. She answered, "If I can tell him to give himself up, I will, but what are the odds that I'll be seeing him?"

"What about your sister?"

"I wouldn't expect him to seek her out, either. But, fine, I'll deliver your message, anyway."

"You do that. But don't get too cocky about your pal Sanders."

"What's that supposed to mean?"

"Maybe right now the department is more worried about the egg on its face from the possibility of a crooked cop, especially with a bigwig like Tewkesbury breathing down our necks. Maybe I am 'preoccupied' with saving my partner's skin, but, let me tell you, I'm not forgetting Sanders and the Blair murder. Sooner or later, I'll get back to him."

"Maybe, Detective Boyd, someone will dig up evidence that clears Larry *and* McLaughlan."

"Oh yeah, you mean that Junior G-Man boyfriend of yours. Where is he, anyway? Isn't he supposed to have some important dope for us, or couldn't he come up with anything linking Mrs. Tewkesbury to the case?"

"He's *not* my boyfriend." Well, didn't that sound perfectly eight-grade! "He's still digging." That wasn't a lie.

"Yeah, well, tell him not bury himself. I have to solve two murders and clear my friend. I'm not gonna let my partner hang for you and your chums. You can take that to the bank. Be seeing you around."

Jessica refrained from answering, "Not if I see you first," as Boyd moved down the walk to the street. But there was one decent thing she should tell Boyd, no matter how she felt about him: "Boyd, I hope you can clear McLaughlan. He's a square guy. He doesn't deserve this frame job."

Boyd stopped and looked back at her, surprised, but he recovered and returned with defensive harshness, "Just make sure you send him to me if you see him. That goes double for that sister of yours. I'll be talking to her sooner or later."

Closing the door on Boyd felt good. Having to face Liz and Larry by the fireplace did not. Before she did anything, though, Jess wanted to be sure Boyd was really gone. Moving to the window seat, she watched through the picture window as Boyd got into his car, but he didn't drive off.

"For the love of Mike, Jessica! What did Boyd have to say?"

Liz's inquiry cut across the room, and she, herself, followed a split second behind. Larry lingered, ruminating, by the fireplace; however, he soon joined the sisters.

Jess explained, "Essentially, Boyd's on the trail of McLaughlan."

Larry's brow furrowed and he asked, "Why look for his partner *here*?"

Liz strolled away, mercifully managing not to whistle nonchalantly. Jessica answered, "I couldn't say, but he wanted to put out the word to his partner to turn himself in."

"Your sister and McLaughlan seemed to be doing quite a bit of confabbing over the case recently," Larry reflected.

"What's that supposed to mean?" Liz demanded.

"All I meant was that you might have an idea as to where McLaughlan might go next—what he might be thinking," Larry tried to unruffle her feathers.

Realizing she'd overreacted, Liz quickly apologized, "I'm sorry, Larry. It's the strain. I don't want to quarrel with you."

Jessica moved to smooth everything out, "Well, here's something to set you on an even keel, Liz. Boyd let slip that, for now, there's more interest in nabbing McLaughlan than in pinning something on Larry. That may give Hooley time to dig up what we need on Tewkesbury. Exposing her should also clear McLaughlan."

"So, what you're saying," Larry began carefully, "is that clearing me clears McLaughlan?"

"You're the crux," Jessica agreed.

"That's a relief," Larry breathed, slowly sitting down on the couch. "I don't want that man's life on my hands, too."

"But right now, Larry," Jessica urged, "you should get away from here. Boyd might even be planning to get another warrant or haul us all in for questioning. The heat's off you temporarily. Let's keep it that way. Right now, though, he's sitting tight in his car, waiting for us to make a move."

So the three decided, as much as Larry and Liz wanted to stick together, it was better for them to separate and for Liz to lead Boyd on a nice long drive to Jersey. That would keep him away from Larry. Jess was also politic enough not to mention that she didn't trust Elizabeth not to accidentally tell Larry whom they were hiding in the apartment. He was in enough hot water without having to hold out to Boyd about McLaughlan.

After Larry left, Elizabeth gave her sister a once over, then said, "Kiddo, I've been so busy concentrating on everyone else, I've ignored you. You look like something the cat dragged in and tossed back out again."

"Thanks a lot."

"No, I mean it. You look beat. How much sleep did you get last night?"

"Sleep? What's that?"

"Okay, baby sister, enough. I'm going to tuck you in on the couch for a nap."

"But what if Hooley comes back? What if something happens?"

"Then you'll wake up and take care of it," Liz pronounced. "Now go conk out before I find something blunt and conk you out myself."

"I knew I shouldn't have let you study anesthesiology under the Three Stooges."

Brrringggg!!!!!

The impatient doorbell yanked Jessica Minton back to consciousness. Reality and dreamy memory of that cold February night James had made warm with his proposal swirled together. Then realization hit like a Joe Louis right cross. No della Mirandolla's. No James. All alone on her living room couch. Where was Liz?! Oh yes, the wild goose chase. Was McLaughlan still here? The peremptory doorbell was joined by an equally aggressive knocking. Those beautiful bittersweet thoughts of James were fading, eluding her. Cruelly, anxiety over who wanted in predominated. Boyd come back? McLaughlan's wood-sawing in the next room made clear there would be no hiding him.

Hurrying across the room, Jess slowly returned to painful reality. By the time she reached the door, the memory of her last encounter with Boyd inspired her to peek through the window curtain before opening up. *Good grief! What was he doing here, now?*

Jessica yanked the door open so abruptly that Jeff Hooley almost fell in.

She had barely closed the door before he grumbled, "Took you long enough. I was beginning to get worried. Everything all right here?"

"Just Jim Dandy, considering. I thought you were going to send me a telegram with the latest. What are you doing back here?"

"Change of plans. How fast can you get McLaughlan ready to move?"

"Move McLaughlan? Hooley, you weren't followed were you?" Jessica demanded anxiously.

"No on the last count, but we're still on borrowed time. I've got to get you both to Bridgeport."

"Bridgeport? Connecticut?"

"Connecticut."

"What the dickens is in Bridgeport?"

"Kavanaugh."

"You found him?" The wise alec drained right out of Jessica.

"In a manner of speaking."

"In a manner of ... say, what, exactly, are you giving me here, Hooley?" Jessica challenged, exasperated.

"Just help me get this show on the road." Before he had finished speaking, Hooley had taken Jessica by the elbow and propelled her towards her room. "I'll fill you in while you change, and I get McLaughlan back amongst the living."

A snore that shuddered the old brownstone's rafters prompted Hooley to correct himself, "Okay, he's still alive. I just need to bring him back from the land of Nod."

Jerking free her elbow, Jessica stopped Hooley with, "Never mind the cute talk. Nobody's doing anything until I know what's going on. I've been through way too much craziness already to jump feet first on your say-so. Are you telling me that Kavanaugh is still alive?"

"Very much so. That's why you're changing into that black satin number you wore for the play you were in when I first met you. You know, the one they broke theatre protocol for to give you as a joke gift when the show closed."

"Okay, that sinks it, mister. You want me to dress up in a floozy ensemble for a guy who's 'very much alive.' Do I look like an assault victim waiting to be, uh, assaulted? What kind of a half-baked scheme are you pushing me into, Hooley? Who do you think you are, my sister?"

"I'll explain it to you if you stop dragging your heels, Minton," Hooley impatiently promised. "But we don't have time to debate. Has Boyd or any other of the police been here today looking for Sleeping Beauty there?"

"Yes! Boyd was here earlier, but I wouldn't let him in. I said he'd had one go at the place yesterday, and he'd have to get himself a new warrant if he wanted another today. I talked to my lawyers."

"How'd he take it?" questioned Hooley intently.

"He wasn't happy," Jess answered. "Boyd was worried about his partner mostly."

"But he let it go?" Hooley asked, unconvinced Boyd wasn't up to something.

"Sort of. He sat waiting in the car, watching. So I sent Liz off, and he followed her. I think it's Liz he's really interested in. Anyway, I told her to take a tour of the Jersey shore."

"How long ago?"

Jess looked at her watch to answer, "It's after five now. Several hours ago."

Jeff Hooley speculated, "That's an awfully long Jersey tour."

"Meaning?"

"Meaning: how well can your sister hold up under a grilling?"

Jessica blanched, "No! Would they rough her up, Jeff?"

"Probably not rough her up," Hooley dryly corrected, "but they can ask questions in ways that would make a gal feel more than a little uncomfortable."

"It could backfire on them," Jess proposed. "Knowing my sister, I'd say she wouldn't crack, but they might."

"Even if they threaten Larry Sanders?"

"Oh, gosh. That might be a different story," Jessica worried. "She'd never intentionally spill anything, but when she gets steamed..."

"That's why we're going to get out of here now," Hooley finished, guiding Jessica into her room.

Shortly later, in the bedroom with the curtains drawn against prying eyes, McLaughlan was beefing about Hooley's shaking him awake. Meanwhile, Jessica was fishing the dress out of her walk-in closet across the room. Stepping out, she griped, "Look, Hooley, you still haven't explained to me why I have to wear *this* outfit. It had better be good!"

"I'll explain while you change in the bathroom. Leave the door open so we can talk to each other."

McLaughlan raised an eyebrow, and Jessica cut them both dead with, "I don't think so."

"Oh, yeah, right," Hooley acknowledged his gaffe. "I guess you can still hear me if you just crack the door. We promise not to peek. But you better get a wiggle on. I've got to get you to Bridgeport for nine."

"Bridgeport?" It was McLaughlan's turn to be perplexed. "What the hell is in Bridgeport? Sorry about the language, Miss Minton."

"Jay Kavanaugh. Our link to Alanna Tewkesbury and the crime," Hooley answered.

Puzzled, the detective questioned, "So why are *we* going up there? Why not just get some of the boys from the force in Bridgeport?"

"Because he won't talk to cops. He won't talk to me, either. It's been tried before. He won't talk to anyone but..."

"But whom?" McLaughlan pushed.

At that moment, Jessica stepped out, sleek in black satin, cut low and clinging in all the right places, heavy white-shell necklace and bracelet, and ankle-strap sandals that could intimidate Joan Crawford: an outfit that said, "I'm here and open for business."

"Her. He'll talk to her." Hooley nodded toward Jessica.

"Huh?" McLaughlan scratched his head. "What kind of a game are you running here, Hooley? He doesn't know Jessica Minton. And if he did, he probably wouldn't recognize her all tricked out like that."

Jessica nodded and quipped, "Thanks, McLaughlan, that's practically the nicest thing anyone's said to me all day. It's certainly the most sense I've heard since Hooley came through the door. I still don't know why I'm agreeing to do this, let alone *what* I've agreed to do. Hooley, this better be good, real good."

She folded her arms determinedly as she finished.

Hooley took a little too much time admiring the effect of the black satin drapery, until a glare from Jessica put him back on track, "It is good. Better than any play you've been in. But we've got to write our own happy ending. And, Jessica, you've got to play this part for everybody's life."

"Sure, Hooley, but *what* part?!"

"I'm getting to that," he tried to placate her. "Remember, Jess, I told you that Kavanaugh was the cop protecting Gabriel Stuyvesant before he went into protective custody? You know this story, McLaughlan?"

"Some of it. Keep going."

"There was an attempt on Blair and Kavanaugh when his wife accidentally happened on the scene. Blair saved her, so Kavanaugh kind of had a soft spot for him afterward."

"I know all this," Jess interjected. "Cut to the chase. Why am I in this Sadie Thompson get-up?"

"All right, all right. Kavanaugh was always trying to get Stuyvesant to go straight, even turn over the rest of the stolen jade. There was some talk he was even in touch with him when he was out West."

"So, you haven't talked to Kavanaugh, yet?" McLaughlan cut in. "You just got this stuff through..."

"My contacts in Lowell and Boston–but that's the point, McLaughlan. Kavanugh won't talk to anyone about Stuyvesant. They say he's defensive, kind of protecting the guy, giving him one last chance to square things."

"Not much chance of that now," Leo McLaughlan noted sourly.

"That's the beauty of it," Hooley countered, getting excited. "Kavanaugh doesn't know Gabriel Stuyvesant is dead. Even if he has heard of a guy called Evan Blair being murdered, it's nothing to him. He probably doesn't know that name."

"So, you think that if he finds out that it's too late for Blair, or whatever you want to call the guy, to go straight, he might talk to nail his killer," McLaughlan concluded.

"Not to us, but to her." Hooley jerked his head at Jess.

"Me? Why me?" Jessica was genuinely bewildered.

"That's where the outfit comes in," Hooley clarified.

"You're not telling us you expect her to 'vamp' it out of him?" Leo snorted.

Jessica wanted to hug him for his disapproving question.

"No, I don't expect her to try to pull something like that off. She wouldn't interest him that way."

"And why not? What's wrong with me, in any outfit?" Jessica flashed.

"I thought you were crabbing about having to play *femme fatale*," Hooley dryly explained. "Don't worry, I wasn't going to ask you to sully your honor. I'll keep you pure for James."

Looking really bewildered at yet another member added to the cast, McLaughlan demanded, "James? Who's James?"

"It's a long, and right now, irrelevant story, McLaughlan," Jess assured him patiently, before turning on Hooley with, "So, are you going to finish your yarn or are we going to stand around here beating our gums until the local gendarmes come back and haul us all in?"

"Okay, okay. Here's the lowdown. Kavanaugh shut himself off from the world a few years back when his wife was murdered. She'd been a B-girl years before when he met her and pulled her out of the business. An old 'associate' came across her; and when she wouldn't come across for him, he killed her. He had a slick mouthpiece and beat the rap because of the wife's past history. Out of disgust with the system, Kavanaugh took an early retirement and squirreled himself away in Bridgeport. Works as a night watchman at a warehouse. He has a reputation for keeping an eye out for the 'working girls' when they get in trouble. A contact put me in touch with one gal. I learned that he spilled some interesting facts about the Blair case to her. She didn't know what she had, but I did."

McLaughlan glanced at Jessica, read her uneasiness over the prospect of this acting assignment, and left her inwardly blessing him when he suggested to Hooley, "Can't we get this dame to work on him for us instead?"

"Don't think we could keep her sober long enough, but with Jessica –"

"I'll just start drinking after this misadventure," Jess interrupted. "Are you out of your mind? I mean, the idea is to play a shady lady in distress in order to lure Kavanaugh into telling me all about Evan and Alanna? And he'll be just so charmed by my womanly wiles that he'll volunteer to trot back to the Big Apple with me and i.d. Alanna Tewkesbury as Betty Weisenthal?"

Hooley shook his head, "You're not getting it. It's not your womanly wiles that will win Kavanaugh. He's drawn to the down-trodden, battered type. After last night, with those circles under your eyes, that hunted, haggard look, you're a cinch to convince him."

"McLaughlan," Jess began with menace in her voice, "it's a good thing that you lost your gun last night because if you still had it I'd be using it on him!" Then she turned on Hooley, "This has to be the most cockeyed, harebrained, Rube Goldberg scheme I've ever heard of!"

"That includes your hijinks with James Crawford?" Jeff inquired innocently.

Jessica ignored Hooley's remark to crack, "Maybe I lack your masterly imagination, but how about I just go up to Kavanaugh in my regular duds, as myself, and tell him the truth: my friend is being railroaded straight to the electric chair by the woman who had his friend killed; the police are persecuting my sister; and the only protection I have is a lame-brained F.B.I. agent?"

Jess caught McLaughlin wincing for Hooley but doing nothing to pull his fat from the fire.

"Sorry, Jessica," Jeff insisted, unfazed. "This is the only way it will work. Otherwise, Kavanaugh wouldn't even stop to listen to you. There's only one type of gal he'll give the time of day to. Can you let the only witness who can help us slip through our fingers?"

"All right," Jessica gave in, adding, "You know, Hooley, I really hate you."

"Was there ever a question?" Hooley queried easily. Then he switched gears and tried to encourage her, "Don't sweat it, Jessica. I'm going to coach you. It's a long ride up Route 15. Anyway, we'd better shake a leg. I've got the car out of sight, backed into the alley on the street running parallel to this one. We can make it out..."

"Hold it a minute, son," McLaughlan cut in. "You mean to say that you think you're just going to drive me across the Triborough Bridge? Some people want to chat with me about a murder. You don't think they'll spot me when we hit the toll booth?"

"Not with you stashed in the trunk. They're not stopping every car; only the ones with a passenger fitting your description."

"You expect me to crunch myself in a trunk the day after I got the tar whaled out of me? She's right. You are nuts," McLaughlan justifiably griped.

"Not nuts. Prepared. I've got a big car and lots of cushions. You'll be okay. Besides, you can't afford to wait for your pals on the force to get tired of circling around the wagons. They're going to come back looking for you. So, let's go. We need you to set up this scam and to keep an eye on Jessica when she's with Kavanaugh."

"And what will you be doing, Junior G-Man?" Leo McLaughlan wanted to know.

"Spinning out the rest of the web. Are you in? Because we need you. You say no, and the game plan goes completely south."

"All right. All right," McLaughlan relented. Turning to Jessica, he said, "If I still had my gun, *you* wouldn't need to use it."

Chapter Twenty-Four

Same date

Eight-thirty, Sunday night. Jessica Minton's heels clicked on pavement slick from an earlier cloudburst as she paced around the corner streetlamp, reviewing the part she'd worked out with Hooley. What had she gotten herself into? Could this harebrained scheme possibly work?

She leaned more irritably than seductively against the lamppost and coughed out her reaction to the miasma of dead fish, seaweed, and saltwater wafting up from the waterfront. Ah, the balmy ocean breezes. This had to be the worst part of Bridgeport that she'd ever seen, not that she'd actually seen that much of it. Still, if you were a burnt-out cop given to night rambles, this was the place to be.

"Say, sister, need a light?"

Jumping back, Jessica anxiously peered into the alley behind her, whence the voice had come. Someone shifted in the shadows.

"Hey, honey," the voice came again, as a figure emerged and grabbed her arm. "I asked you a question."

His breath could have anesthetized a Clydesdale.

"Get lost, bub." She knew from the old photo that this was not Kavanaugh. "I'm on my coffee break."

"Geesh, everybody's got a union these days. You're not gonna do much business that way, sister."

"I'll take my chances. Now take a hike before I report you to my shop steward."

He stumbled off, muttering some imprecations against Samuel Gompers and the AF of L, but Jessica had more pressing concerns on this humid June evening. It felt as if her flaming lipstick were melting, which her compact mirror confirmed. She repaired the damage, then snapped the compact shut. 8:45 couldn't come too soon.

Hooley's reason for going back to New York didn't sit right with her, either. It made some sense that he should smooth things over with the locals, but couldn't that wait until after they'd pulled off this little caper? Smoothing would go a heck of a lot easier if they could hand over Mrs. Wilmington Tewkesbury on a silver platter. She'd have felt a whole lot better if this plan were James's idea, if he were sitting in the shadows watching out for her.

"Gimme what's in the bag and make it snappy!"

Jessica felt herself wrenched around so abruptly she thought she'd left her head behind. A little cry escaped her before she realized that she was looking into Leo McLaughlan's face. The game was afoot, kind of. For a moment, McLaughlan hesitated, clearly concerned he'd played his part too well and might have hurt her. He said too softly for anyone but them to hear, "Sorry, didn't mean to get too rough with you."

Equally low, Jessica shot back, "I can take it. Stay in character, McLaughlan." A quick glance up the street revealed a tall figure coming toward them. Show time: "No dice, you stinker! I been working my dogs to the bone all night! Get lost! You promised we'd split it when I got home!"

For his part, McLaughlan gave Jess a good shaking and cussed her out loud enough for their intended audience of one.

After a few choice observations on her assailant's canine ancestry, Jess whispered, "He's looking. Bring it home. Fake that you're slugging me."

"I can't do that..."

"Don't actually paste me one. Fake it. I'll do the rest. Quick, he's moving."

McLaughlan managed to fake a slap, rip the purse off Jess, then shove her backwards and beat it.

Jess slowly reoriented herself, sitting up on the curb's edge. Hearing footsteps, she made it look good by working her lower jaw with one hand as if worried about permanent damage. The footsteps started past her, in pursuit of McLaughlan. That wasn't the plan.

Jess let out: "Ooo, ow!"

It worked! Her mark stopped. She could sense his hesitation.

"Jeepers, my jaw!"

She made it the almost whimper of a dame who didn't let on much, so when anything escaped her, she was hurting.

"You okay, sister?"

The voice wasn't as tough as Jess had expected, but it wasn't exactly dulcet, either.

"Yeah, I'll live, but I won't be chewing too good for a while." This without looking up.

He had her on her feet as if she were a feather, with a terse, "He poke you in the jaw?"

"That and made off with my bankroll, such as it was. Couldn't wait till I got home. Probably got a hot game going somewheres."

She was facing him now, a big guy in his forties or so. With a face that weary, it was hard to tell. Their eyes locked. His eyes had seen too much. They'd shut out a lot, too. You'd have to be a real heel to want to scam this guy. But this situation wasn't about how she felt; it was about saving the skins of people she loved. Maybe she was even giving this guy a chance to square some old scores.

"Who is that creep?" he asked. "I have some connections. Maybe I can have him tracked down. Get your bankroll back, anyway."

"Aren't you the Sir Galahad," she sarcastically pronounced.

"Tough little cookie, aren't you? How's that jaw? Let me see." His hand was on her face before she knew it, and Jess had to fight hard against the shakes. It was a strong hand, and she had a delicate jaw. "Feels okay," he concluded. "Nothing broken. Just gonna be tender. Not like you, right?"

"What's that supposed to mean?"

"It means I've seen a lot of girls like you, and not one of you is as tough as she thinks she is. You all end up the same if you don't get wise to yourselves before it's too late."

"Get wise to myself?"

"Yeah, hang up your gloves, drop your pimp boyfriends, and get into some line of work with a little less wear and tear on the chassis. It's starting in on you already, honey. You're not as young as you used to be, and you're not bringing in the lettuce like you used to. So your 'boyfriend' figures he can afford to rough you up. He's got some younger, livelier skirt he's stringing along like he did you. He's keeping her in the wings until he's squeezed the last drop out of you. Then he passes you on to somebody who's not so particular. Who'll dope or liquor you up to keep you tractable."

"So, you got it all figured out, do you, smart guy? What are you, some kind of missionary or social worker or something?"

"Yeah, something."

"Think you know so much, huh?" Jessica almost sneered. "Well, save that tune for the Salvation Army Band. Maybe he's the only guy who ever treated me like something special. Maybe he got me out of a house with a family that'd drink and eat up everything I earned. You expect me to go back to that? Not on your life!"

"From where I'm standing, doesn't look as if he sees you as anything special now, except maybe a special punching bag."

It was no fun snowing this tough guy with a heart, but Jess knew she couldn't quit. Turning away, she set her chin to trembling and began one of her best suppressed blubbers.

"Hey, dry up. Dry up."

"Well, what do you expect?" She wouldn't turn around. "He just brought me here from outa town. Now, you're telling me he wants to trade me in for a newer model. I got no way to get out of town. I got no place to go, anyway. I haven't even eaten since this morning–at least I got steak and eggs."

"Okay, okay." He tapped Jess on the shoulder, prompting her to face him again, and he handed her a handkerchief. Eying him suspiciously, she accepted and blew her nose.

He suggested, "Maybe I can help."

Projecting wariness, Jessica challenged, "Yeah? How?"

"At least I can stake you to some grub tonight. Maybe I can help you figure things out, point you to some folks who might get you straightened out. There's a place around the corner. I go there to eat when I'm off shift. You want to come with me?"

"You're being awfully swell to someone you don't even know. What's your angle?"

"My angle? Maybe my angle's that someone like you is the only one worth helping. Maybe I'm sick of the respectable types trying to get something for nothing. But you, kid, you're playing against a stacked deck. Some of those people who stacked the deck against you played the same dirty tricks on me."

So, Hooley was right. The real Jessica Minton probably wouldn't have had much luck getting Jay Kavanugh's help. But approaching him in this role, she might get him to see Hooley and McLaughlan as people who could help him even the score for his friend Gabriel Stuyvesant.

"Yeah, well, okay, I'll go with you. They have any decent coffee at this joint?"

"They do."

"Okey-doke. I got nothing to lose with Fred gone."

"Fred? Oh, the 'boyfriend.'"

"You don't need to get smart. I'm going." She added sarcastically, "Maybe I wanna see you take a crack at making me 'respectable.'"

"This way. Down the street another block. You can walk all right?"

"I don't walk on my jaw, Mr. ... ?"

"Kavanaugh."

They had started walking toward the place where Hooley said Kavanaugh always grabbed a bite when he came off-shift.

"Kid, I just asked what's your name?"

"Oh, ah, you caught me dopin'. I'm Gerry, Gerry Bennett. Short for Geraldine, but everyone calls me Gerry."

"Okay, Gerry. It's just a little ways down."

"Sounds swell to me. You know I could use a nice big hunk of cherry pie with that java, that okay with you?"

"Maybe you'd better preface that hunk of pie with a sandwich."

"Sure, whatever you say, Kavanaugh. You know, you're all right. Nothing like Fred. I only knew one other guy who talked to me like you, when Fred and me moved to Lowell."

He tensed at the city's name, and Jess pretended not to notice. You couldn't rush things with this guy.

"Yeah, he was okay–you might be, too–unless you're expecting some kinda payback." She stopped and looked at him hard.

Kavanaugh smiled bitterly at her cynicism and shot back, "I don't want any payback. There's only one payback I'd like out of life, and that's out of my league. Too bad you weren't just as careful before hooking up with your pal, Fred."

"Lay off Fred. That's spilled milk, okay? You want me to turn over a new leaf? Okay, I'm turning. So let's just hit this joint. I'm starving."

Jess glanced imperceptibly over her shoulder as they walked on. Yes, the idea of shadowing someone *was* not to be seen, but she'd have felt a darned sight better if she could have detected McLaughlan while Kavanugh loomed over her.

The restaurant was below ground level, with a big neon sign pointing you in the right direction. They descended the stairs to the door, which Kavanaugh held for Jess. So she gave him an ironic, "Thanks, Galahad."

The place was old, but no dive. The smell of hash, burgers, coffee, and eggs elicited a subtle growling in her stomach, reminding Jessica that she'd been too busy to fuel up sufficiently today.

"You got a favorite place to sit?" she questioned, as Kavanaugh waved to the guy behind the counter.

"They're all okay. Maybe a booth this time. Easier to take a load off."

"Fine, just so I get to keep my eye on the door. That's one thing I learned from the old man."

As they sat down, Kavanaugh queried, "So, what did your old man do?"

"Not much of anything, 'cept drink and smack us around."

That line of questioning was forestalled, as a waitress sauntered over and greeted, "Hiya, Jay. Got company, tonight?"

"Yeah," Jess snapped. "What's it to you?"

Kavanaugh's look shut up Jess, in and out of character.

"I'm taking her out for her charm school graduation. How about two coffees, Vera, and two ham and cheeses?"

"Don't forget my cherry pie," Jess insisted.

Vera gave Jess the once-over before remarking, "Sure you can afford it, honey? Wouldn't want to strain the seams on that dress."

Ouch! First, Kavanaugh remarked she's no kid anymore, then this gal says she's packing away the pounds.

"That's fine, Vera," Kavanaugh went on. "Bring it after we have the sandwiches. Cut me a slice of the apple pie with some cheese on it while you're at it."

"Sure thing, Jay. We aim to please."

Jessica watched the waitress walk away, then turned to Kavanaugh and commented, “Charming friends you got. Sure you won’t ruin your rep, bringing me in? Or maybe they’re used to your making like a one-man Salvation Army?”

“Where you from again, kid?”

Jess blinked and fumbled, but recovered with, “Originally? Up North. What’s it to you?”

“North’s a big place. Massachusetts? New Hampshire? Canada?”

“Let’s just say Santa Claus and I ain’t neighbors.”

The waitress brought their coffee first, and Jessica automatically thanked her. She caught Kavanaugh regarding her speculatively. Staying in character, she met his gaze boldly. He casually checked out the specials listed above the counter. Sipping her coffee, Jess took advantage of her companion’s distraction to peek out the window fronting the joint. All she could see on the sidewalk was a pair of men’s trousers, from the knees down. They looked like Hooley’s pants. Then another pair joined them, and the legs shifted as if the two were facing each other.

“Something out there?”

She nearly jumped. As it was, she knocked the sugar over.

“Better watch out. Sugar’s still like gold.”

He helped her clean up the mess, and Jessica tried to take control with, “Jeepers! You know how to give a girl the heebie-jeebies. I was just looking.”

“You’re the kind of girl who likes to keep herself busy?”

“That’s me, Kavanaugh. Always on the go.”

The sandwiches arrived, and Jessica was so hungry she plowed into hers. But she was still unnervingly aware of Kavanaugh’s studying her.

“Slow down, there. The pig’s dead. That sandwich isn’t going anywhere.”

Jessica nodded and slurped up some coffee. Better get back to working the case. Cynically she asked, “So, what makes you such a patron saint of working girls like me?”

“What’s the difference?” he replied, unperturbed. “You’re getting a sweet deal, and a ham and cheese to boot.”

“That’s just it. No one does something for nothing. Why *should* I trust you if you don’t completely level with me?” Jess countered.

“Looks like they make ’em tough *and* suspicious up North.”

“You bet your boots.” She stared him down.

“Okay, kid. If I level with you on why I’d want to help you, will level with me?”

“Deal. Spill.”

“Aah, no big story.” A sip of coffee, then, “I was a cop, ‘up North’ in Massachusetts. I got burned on a big case. Saw some decent people get the shaft and some slippery ones get away. Lost my wife and that was the end of it. Came down here to forget.”

“You like the balmy ocean breezes?”

"Something like that."

It was Jessica's turn to drink her coffee, giving her the excuse to glance quickly over Kavanaugh's shoulder. No legs out there now. Good, bad, or immaterial?

"So, tough stuff, what's the whole story on you?"

"Not much. I gave you the basics. Crummy family, a guy who promised me better, and here I am, living it up at this joint. What more could a girl ask for?"

"What's next?"

"Therein lies the rub."

He blinked at Shakespeare coming out of her not so delicate little mouth, and she smiled inside and out. Good, he was taking the bait.

"Didn't think someone like me could quote poetry, did you? I didn't drop out till I got to high school. I won a prize for memorizing that speech. That's all I remember now, but that's still better than most of the mugs I went to school with. I know some other stuff, too, like that. You'd be surprised. Listen to this one:

if sometimes in its box of
sky lavender and cornerless, the
moon rattles like a fragment of angry candy."

His eyes narrowed keenly, and Jessica went cold. But before she could decide how to work that reaction, Vera arrived with the pies and commented on Kavanaugh's expression, "Say, Jay, what's the matter?" Then the waitress turned on Jessica: "You little snip, what'd you say to him?"

"Who, me? I just quoted some poetry. I don't get this. I don't even know what it means."

"It's okay, Vera." He patted the waitress's arm. "The kid only did what she said. Don't get your ears in an uproar."

"But you looked like you seen a ghost!"

"Naw. Just hungry waiting for this pie." He took a hunk and cracked, "Still the best in the city." Turning his attention to Jessica, he added, "Eat up, kid."

Vera left them reluctantly, and Jessica put on her best sullen puss to question, "Say, what'd I do? It was just some poem. Nothing but words."

"Never mind, kid, eat up." He had an air of "she couldn't possibly know what she was saying" as he attacked his pie and coffee.

Good or bad? Kavanaugh was letting her bait float on downstream. She needed to make another move, but a deft one. This guy was no slouch. What about if she made him see the poetry as a way to pierce a troubled girl's cynical armor?

"I just like the sound of the words 'sky lavender,'" she began casually, as if she were testing whether she could let her guard down. "It's like a dress, a pretty dress. And 'angry candy,' how can candy be mad? It makes you think. It's so impossible, it makes you think."

"Thinking's good, kid. Ever consider thinking yourself away from Fred?"

"He didn't like me thinking much." Jess took some more coffee before seeming to reflect aloud, "He didn't like poetry. Said it was for dopes and sissies. But I don't know. Sometimes it puts pictures in your head, know what I mean?"

"Yeah. I know. So, you memorized that in school, too?"

"Oh no. It was when Fred had me in Lowell. This guy in our building, down by the train station, he used to talk to me about it sometimes. Even read me stuff. Not exactly the kind of gent you'd expect to meet in a dive on Cambridge Street."

Kavanaugh's voice barely betrayed an edge: "Who was this guy?"

His black eyes glinted, as if he didn't want to believe she was talking about Gabriel Stuyvesant, but he had to know for certain. Her move now. She'd better make it smooth.

"Just some guy. Nice-looking fella. He must have had money at one time, not then, though–or else what would he be doing there or talking to the likes of me? Real nice manners, though. Nicer to me than Fred. Kept to himself most of the time."

"Except for you."

"Well, Fred locked me out a couple of times. One night I was sittin' on the curb. I guess I must of done a little blubbering, and since his window was next to me, just level with the street, he heard me. Came out and talked to me. Now that I think of it, it was kind of funny, the way he did it–made sure nobody was around to see him. Like I said, he liked to keep to himself."

"Another social worker?"

"Hey, maybe. You do remind me of him a little–except he was, well, kinda lighter–Errol Flynn-like, but taller and lighter, and he never put the make on me. Like I said, a gentleman."

"That's a surprise. Well, maybe not."

"That's a funny thing for you to say about a guy you don't even know."

"I meant it's a surprise that your charms were on the blink."

"Oh, yeah, right."

She'd nearly overplayed that hand. But before Jessica could shift strategy, Kavanaugh picked up the thread again: "So, you say this guy read you poetry? Must have been tough to leave an admirer like that behind."

"More like the other way around."

"What's that mean?"

"I didn't see him for a while.'

"Maybe he had to blow town."

"No. I heard around that someone knocked him off–out of town."

This time Kavanaugh couldn't hide that the wind had been clouted out of him. Jessica pretended not to notice. "Yeah. I'd almost feel bad–if I was the type. He treated me all right, acted like I actually had something in the old noggin. Would you believe that he actually gave *me* some books for my own. Fred tried to make me leave 'em behind, but I sneaked this one book of poems. That's where I got the one I was reciting. He really thought it was something."

Kavanaugh studied her carefully over the rim of his coffee cup as he responded, "Did he? Sounds like a regular librarian."

Jess was flip, "Aren't jealous, are you?'

"No, just thinking about a friend I once had, gave me a book like that. He spent some time in Lowell, himself. What do you say to that?"

Evan gave out twin books? Wait, hadn't his coded letter said something about near twins? Near twin books? Jess pondered, but then Kavanaugh casually pressed, "Anything interesting in that book he gave you?"

Keep it cool! Jessica ordered herself. She only replied, "Like what, a bookmark?"

"Maybe. Or maybe a paper? A picture?"

"That's a funny thing to ask, Kavanaugh."

"Is it? Funny coincidences, funny questions." His words were casual, but their meaning wasn't to Jessica. "What was your buddy's name?"

Now it was Jess's turn to play cool, just naturally curious. "You think you know him, Kavanaugh? Your friend was from Lowell, too?"

"I asked you first."

"Well, that's the really screwy thing. The name on the mailbox was Bill, but he said I could call him Gabe. Can you figure that?"

Kavanaugh's lips compressed, then cracked into a strange smile.

What the devil? Why can't I read him? This is not good.

"I carry my book with me. I like to read it from time to time. You like to see it, Gerry?"

"Sure, why not?" Not letting her eagerness show, *that* took acting!

Kavanaugh went for the depths of his trench coat pocket, then stopped and smiled, saying, "What about *your* book? I'd like to have a looksee."

Is he playing right into Hooley's plan, or is this all too easy? Jessica wondered uneasily. *Well, it was time to go for broke*! She forced out a sarcastic, "Hey, Kavanaugh, you think I tote a book around on *my* job? C'mon."

"So where is it?"

"At my place. A couple of blocks away." Jess didn't mention that "her place" was where McLaughlan was supposed to tail them, where Hooley would be waiting after he'd returned.

"Let's go, then."

"Right now? Before I finish the pie?" She didn't want to sound uncharacteristically eager, and the pie was awfully good.

"You can finish the pie first, unless you're afraid of running into your pal, Fred."

"No sweat," Jess assured him. "Fred's got my bankroll. If he's not at a hot game, he'll be drinking his way through it till the morning."

"Good."

She had to say, "All this just so you can look at my book, Kavanaugh?" Giving in to such an odd whim too easily would look fishy.

"We can get your gear together for when I bring you to some people who'll give you a place to stay and help you get straightened out."

"How do I know I'm not going from the frying pan into the fire?" Jess demanded.

"From where I'm sitting, it doesn't look as if things could get much hotter for you than they are already."

Jessica scowled, but she agreed, as if she hadn't any other choice, "All right. Okay. Looks like Fred doesn't have much left to offer me but a good clobberin'. I'll check it out, but if something looks screwy, I blow. Get it?"

"Got it. I'll give you the lowdown on them while we walk."

"Fine."

Hungrily scarfing up one last chunk of pie, Jess pronounced, "Okay, let's hit the road."

Kavanaugh stood up, tossed some bills on the table, and let Jessica precede him up the stairs and out the door. Once on the street, he interrupted her attempt at unnoticed surveillance with, "You looking for someone?"

"Who me? Nah, not exactly. I just wanted to see if Fred was out here. Just to be on the safe side. Looks like the coast is clear."

"Cigarette?"

"No, I don't ... not tonight. My throat's kinda sore."

Kavanaugh's concentration while cupping the light for his cigarette reassured Jessica he hadn't noticed her lame ad lib. Still, it was mighty hard to tell what went on behind those hooded eyes.

"Ready?"

"Sure, Kavanaugh. Just a block down this way," Jess nodded in the direction, "then right."

They started off, Kavanaugh observing, "So, you live only a block away and you don't know Deke's?"

"I just blew into town. Remember? I'm not psychic. So, where are you planning to take me, anyway?"

"Told you. I have some friends who're pretty good about helping people get straightened out: getting you a place to stay and helping you find a legit job. Besides, could it be any worse than where you're shacked up now?"

"Yeah, well, just don't turn me over to no Bible thumpers. I'm not about to get religion for nobody."

She'd stopped to lay that one on with a jabbing finger. It wouldn't pay to look too credulous about getting "saved." Right now, though, the main thing was to get Kavanaugh into the room where she could go to work on him. Let him know about Blair cluing her in on Alanna Tewkesbury, about a Fed investigating Blair's murder and the jewel robberies giving her his card. Once she got Kavanaugh fired up for evening old scores and a new one of murder, he'd be ready to head straight for Jeff Hooley. But she had to make Kavanaugh not only think it was his idea, but that Hooley was his only way to right the wrongs embittering him. Jess hated this dirty business, even though she knew it was necessary for so many people's good, including Kavanaugh's. Still, she felt soiled by manipulating a man who seemed to think he was saving a girl with no options left.

"Something bothering you, kid? Second thoughts?"

"Lots of thoughts. Just nothing you need to worry about, Sigmund Freud. Turn down here. That's it. Second one on this side."

The street was flanked by rows of sorry tenements, occasionally relieved by a dilapidated liquor store or bar. Jessica started up the steps of one of the tenements.

"Nice neighborhood your boyfriend picked."

Jess stopped, looked down, and cracked, "We thought we'd work our way up to Park Avenue slowly."

Her sarcasm bounced off Kavanaugh, so Jess figured she could chance a quick look over his head, down the street. No one. Would that Leo McLaughlan weren't *quite* so good at shadowing. Shooting a glance up at the front door, she beckoned, "Up here, Kavanaugh. First floor, in the back."

"Nice of him not to make you do too much climbing, where you're on your feet all the time."

"Not all the time," she retorted in a voice harsh enough to make Kavanaugh drop his eyes. No, he was only getting rid of his cigarette, or maybe that's just what he wanted her to think.

"No use hanging around, Kavanaugh," she pushed. "The sooner I get out of here the better. We don't have all night, especially if you want to take a look at the book he left me."

"Yeah, I'd like to do that."

Hooley had read him perfectly. Except, there was something about the impassiveness in his eyes when Kavanaugh mentioned the book that didn't sit right with Jessica. She couldn't put her finger on it, but....

"C'mon. Let's get the lead out," Kavanaugh insisted, covering two steps in one stride. With a light hand on her back, he started her up the rest of the steps, through the front door, and into the ill-lit corridor.

"Keep your shirt on," she finally managed. "It's a book, not a bank roll. Let me get my key."

He was behind her, looming in the grimy darkness. His voice came from above her, too close for comfort, "What're you shaking for? You think your boyfriend's back? Don't worry. I'm here. He won't get you."

Inwardly, Jessica prayed that Leo McLaughlan was nearby somewhere, but she only mumbled about the key sticking and flipped on the lights as soon as she got the door open.

The room was just as grim as when Hooley had briefed her and McLaughlan a few hours ago. Kavanaugh ruminated aloud, "*This* was better than your family?"

"Believe it or not, yeah," Jessica replied, entering, her hands tightening on her bag the only clue how she felt when Kavanaugh closed the door behind them. A trooper, she didn't hesitate, heading for a table next to a truly unappealing bed and saying, "The book's over here. Fred used it to prop up the shaky table legs."

"Okay. I'll get your stuff out of the closet."

Jess didn't turn around but froze at those causal words. Hooley hadn't thought of everything, after all.

"I guess you like to travel light," Kavanaugh said, after opening the door on an empty closet.

The words were just this side of sarcastic. Improvising, Jessica whirled and snapped, "Why that stinker! He must have taken my stuff! Hidden it or something so all I'd have is this rag on my back, so I couldn't run out on him!"

"Old Fred must have gotten a little confused and taken his own duds, too. No men's clothes here, either. Just two empty hangers."

His eyes sliced into Jessica, but she refused to crack.

"The rat! That's why he stole all my dough! He must have come back here and then run out on me. Damn! If he's run out on me, I got nothing. You gonna run out on me, too?"

Kavanaugh was thinking it over. Jess felt like a real heel for playing him, but too much was on the line not to–including her skin!

Then he looked her straight in the eye and said, "Suppose you show me that book."

Whew. He'd bought it. It was unnerving to turn her back on Kavanaugh, but she had to get the book.

Jessica turned back and proffered the book, "Here it is, chum. Look for yourself."

He studied her then came over but stopped when he got a good look at the book. Recognizing it, Kavanaugh stared, then questioned skeptically, "He just gave this to you?"

"It's just a book, not the crown jewels."

Kavanaugh took the volume from Jess, giving her a little push as he turned to the same marked pages Hooley had dismissed as amateur scholarship. He left her fidgeting under his piercing look when he questioned, "How do you know he's dead?"

"The landlord. I went looking for the guy one time and he told me the guy was dead."

"How did he die?"

"Jeepers, I don't know. He stopped breathing. The landlord didn't have the details. How about *your* book? Can I have a peek?"

"You're awfully eager. I never thought you were such a bibliophile."

"A what?"

"Never mind. It's not important."

"So, Kavanaugh, how about your book? I let you take a look at mine. Fair's fair."

"You really think there's that much fairness going around? You sure you don't know how this guy died?"

"Sure as my name's Gerry Bennett."

Jessica did *not* like the way Kavanaugh smiled at her. *Where the hell was McLaughlan?*

Kavanaugh went on, "Too bad. I'd like to know more about your chum."

"Why?" Jess tried to sound nonchalant.

"He sounds a heck of a lot like my friend, don't you think?" Kavanaugh's words were casual, his features calm. But his eyes showed speculation, and that soured any excitement Jess might have felt that Hooley's plan seemed to be succeeding. She had the unnerving feeling that now *Kavanaugh* was leading *her*.

"Yeah, think about it, *Gerry*." An edge of sarcasm when he pronounced her name. "Sure, he sounds a lot like the buddy I mentioned before: the one who liked poetry. Funny, they're both from Lowell; they both give away books. Even the same edition, except mine has a fancy leather cover. And now you say he's dead?"

Jessica fought down her panic and managed not to sound like a tricky conniver but a sympathetic ally–or as sympathetic as her "Gerry" persona could manage, "Gee, I'm sorry if he's your pal and he's dead. He was an okay Joe. I didn't want to see him croak."

"Neither did I. I had a lot of hope for him. You sure that you don't know how he died?"

"Well, I didn't want to say this before, but if he *does* turn out to be your friend, maybe you should know. The landlord told me to keep my lip buttoned but seeing how this could be a pal of yours, I guess it's oaky. He thought there might have been something fishy about it. Seemed kind of nervous about going into details. I think someone with a little juice might have wanted to hush things up."

"Funny that landlord should be so forthcoming with *you*, huh?"

"He's the kind of a guy who'd have to say something to someone. He figured I wasn't going to tell nobody."

"Except me."

"He's dead now. It doesn't matter anymore. And, well, I guess I *kinda* trust you, after how you're getting me away from Fred."

"That's good, kid. And I'm going to trust you, too." He reached deep into his overcoat pocket, and Jessica gulped. *Good God! Is he going for a gun?*

He pulled out a book with a beautiful, thick leather cover, about the size of her own, and placed it on the table between them, next to hers.

"That's it, Kavanaugh?"

He nodded.

Jess licked her lower lip, then reached out–and as her hand came near the book, Kavanaugh's closed onto her wrist and he bit out, "Not so fast. If I find out that you're working for Betty Weisenthal, I'll snap your pretty little neck."

Jess had to brace herself against his stone-cold threat, but she managed, "Say, what's with you? Are you crazy or something?"

"Crazy like a fox." The calculation in his eyes was as painful as his lock on her wrist. Jessica hung tough, though, and played out this dangerous game for all she was worth.

"Hey! You're hurting me!"

"Drop the act, sister. You were pretty good for an amateur, but the show's over. You better level with me. It doesn't take a genius to smell a set up here. No clothes in the closet, turning down a smoke, and your just happening to know Gabe Stuyvesant and end up in my neck of the woods? You must take me for some kind of a sap. Tell me what Betty Weisenthal wants, and maybe I'll give you the benefit of the doubt. C'mon spill it and make it snappy!"

Realizing she had no choice left but to go for broke, Jess fixed Kavanaugh with her own piercing stare and let him have it: "I hate Betty Weisenthal. Work for her? I'd rather push her under a tank. I'm here because you can help me nail her, if you've got the guts."

Now Kavanaugh hesitated, trying to read her features. He released her, thinking hard but still poised to cut her off should she try to beat it.

Jessica rubbed her wrist and continued, "She killed Gabriel Stuyvesant, Evan Blair as I knew him."

"Why would *you* care about him? Girlfriend or something?"

His granite skepticism was not easy to face, but there was no backing down.

Jessica fiercely laid it all out for him, "No. He jumped the protection program and came back East to go into business with my sister, Liz, under a new identity. She got the bright idea to bring this socialite, Alanna Tewkesbury, into their business. We didn't know it at the time, but that Tewkesbury woman was Betty Weisenthal. She changed her looks, but it's the same person–except if anyone found out, all that clover she was living in would go pffft! When she found out about Evan, she had him bumped off before he could beat town."

"And you're doing all this for a business partner of your sister? What kind of partnership did they have?"

"Why don't you run that imagination of yours through the laundromat,

Kavanaugh. You better hear the whole story, about how Liz's boyfriend is being framed for the murder by Betty; how a cop, a good cop, is in a jam for trying to help us; about how an old man was killed to put this detective in that tight spot. Don't get me wrong. I know Evan Blair wasn't any angel, but he didn't deserve to be murdered, especially when he was planning on coming clean with the jade."

"Gabe was going straight? That's how you got the book and how you knew about me?"

"The book? Kind of. He sent my sister this coded letter leading us to Cambridge Street. I found this book there. He'd left two pictures in the book. One was of you and him, the other was of our favorite pin-up gal and George Wong."

"So if you had the picture, why didn't you just turn it over to the cops? What do you need me for?"

"Because we lost hold of the Alanna picture. She and her goons came into the apartment, we had to hide fast, and they found the picture where I dropped it," Jessica shot back.

"But they didn't find the book? Convenient for you, for your yarn anyway. I wasn't born yesterday, sister, and I wasn't working this town when the picture was taken. So how'd you know where to find me?"

He started around the table, but Jessica managed to stop him with an outstretched palm and a sharp, "Wait!"

"This better be good."

"I have a friend in the F.B.I., Jeff Hooley." She held back, *I also have a cop who's supposed to be keeping an eye out for me. Where in Sam Hill is he?*

The name made Kavanaugh think, but he only said, "Keep going. This is getting better than radio."

"Jeff identified you from the photo and tracked you down." Here, she hesitated. "He also determined you wouldn't help us if we tried the direct approach, so he dreamed up this scheme. The plan was to let you know where Betty Weisenthal was, what she'd done to Gabriel, and then get you fired up to go to Hooley. That way we'd have a chance to get her investigated and take the heat off the people she'd framed, maybe even square things for the Wong family. See, George Wong's sister, Lois, is my close friend. You could help so many people if..."

"You really expect me to believe this cockamamie yarn?"

"It's the truth," Jessica defied him.

"And you have some proof?"

"Here, look in this book. That's the picture of you and Evan Blair."

"Betty'd be sharp enough to hand you this to convince me. Let me guess; that guy who faked roughing you up is one of her goons and is parked outside waiting to lower the boom."

"That's the detective she set up," Jessica disabused him. "He's a good man and she's destroying him, like she did you, Kavanaugh. In fact, he was tailing us here. He's probably right outside the door, so don't try anything funny on me."

That struck home. Kavanaugh reached into his right pocket, as if he were positioning a gun, and suggested, "Suppose you open the door and see if he'd like to join our little tea party."

"Why? What do you have in mind?" Jessica questioned warily.

"Checking out this tall tale of yours. Open the door, sister, if you want this to go any further."

Jessica bit her lower lip. Hooley's plan was out the window, and she was playing it by ear. She agreed decisively, "All right. Fine. Detective McLaughlan will corroborate my story."

He seemed a little surprised when she gave in but smiled bitterly, "As if I should trust him any more than I trust you."

She couldn't afford to let that crack discourage her and turned to the door behind her. Still, what would she say to McLaughlan about this change in plans? How good was he at tap dancing? Had he heard the conversation through the door so he could adapt their plan?

The door opened under her hand. No one.

"What the heck?" Jessica blurted.

"Looks like your pal has run out on you." Kavanaugh had maneuvered out of the line of sight of anyone outside, giving himself a neat view through the crack along the hinged side of the door. "Maybe he hightailed it back to Betty to tell her you're not doing so hot with me."

Anxiety flashing into anger, Jessica wheeled on Kavanaugh, "I've had all I can take of your cynicism, Kavanaugh! I'm trying to get justice for people who died because of Betty Weisenthal. I'm trying to help my friend Lois get some real peace and to protect my friends. I'm offering you a chance to avenge what happened to your friend. If you really cared as much about him as I do about my friends, you'd help me!"

"Why should I help you?"

His words were harsh, but Jessica sensed a flicker of a chance. He was fighting her now because he was beginning to weaken, she hoped. "Listen, Kavanaugh, under the bed I stashed my purse, with my wallet. In it is Blair's letter to my sister, Liz. You ought to be able to recognize your own friend's handwriting." Then she gambled that one of Evan's interests had been a longstanding one. "If you really knew him, you'll recognize his penchant for code."

That last comment gave Kavanaugh food for thought. He questioned dubiously, "He put it in code?"

"You bet. Now, you want to see it or not?" Jessica challenged. She cocked her head toward the bed.

Kavanaugh snorted, "Wait a minute. You think I'm going to crawl under the bed, and trust you to stand here waiting? Tell it to the Marines."

"Well, it won't be ladylike, but okay, I'll do it myself if I have to," Jessica glared.

"And pull a rod out when you come back up? You think I was born yesterday, kid?"

"Then, what ... ?"

Before Jessica could finish, Kavanaugh grabbed her elbow and propelled her into the closet. The dark closet. The door slammed shut. By the time she whirled around, Jess heard a chair shoved under the outside doorknob, trapping her. What if Kavanaugh grabbed both books and scrammed?

"Kavanaugh! Let me out of here! You can't do this! Let me out!"

"Pipe down! Cut that pounding. You don't want the neighbors to complain, do you? I'll let you out in a minute."

Jess stopped in mid-pound. Making a ruckus wouldn't prevent Kavanaugh from taking off with the goods. And where the hell was McLaughlan? Had something happened to him?!

Calm down, kid. Sit tight. A moment's examination of the purse will prove you're on the square. It wasn't as if you have any other options, anyway. Damn, I've spent way too much time hiding in closets this month.

The seconds dragged on. Five seconds, five minutes, or five years?

"C'mon out, Jessica Minton," came Kavanaugh's voice.

The door opened. Jess gave her skirt an entirely unnecessary smoothing and her hair a totally necessary toss over her shoulders. Then she emerged with, "So, now you know I'm on the level."

"The letter jibes. So does the picture. I saw the Actors' Equity Card. Should I apologize about the 'amateur' crack?"

"I don't give a hoot in Hades. Are you going to help me or not?" Jessica launched into Kavanaugh. "This is your chance to really do something about all the corruption you've been complaining about. We need each other for that."

Jessica's words hit home. It took a moment for him to pull himself together, but when he did, Kavanaugh was fighting mad, though not at Jess: "She's not going to get away with killing Gabriel Stuyvesant. He wasn't like the rest of the gang. And if your Fed pal told you everything, you know that I owe Gabe."

"Yeah, I know." Jess's ire melted into sympathy. "Thanks, Kavanaugh. I also know this isn't easy. Now, the next step is to get back to my F.B.I. contact."

"No, the next step is to check out these two books. That's how we find the jade."

"What?"

"Gabe told me that if he ever decided to make amends, he'd send me a signal in a second book. It looks like that's your book. I was going through your copy and comparing it with mine. They both have words underlined in the same poems, but different words."

"Let me see." Even as she spoke, Jessica was moving to Kavanaugh's side of the table. She flipped both books open before her, explaining, "Hooley and I saw that some of the words were marked off, as if Evan were just commenting on the poems. Likely, those are the words we need to look at. Different combinations of the words could mean something, but which order? And how do we know he didn't make some phony marks, just to be misleading if the wrong person got her grubby paws on the books? It could take all night just to decipher."

"Maybe he marked off the right ones in a way we can figure out in the table of contents," Kavanaugh offered.

"It's worth taking a look. I always had this sense that I knew them from somewhere, but I couldn't concentrate enough to place them."

"Not much help, then, are they?"

"Guess that's the point," Jess remarked sourly. "Wouldn't be much of a code if it was obvious to any schmoe, let alone a smart cookie like Alanna Tewkesbury. But darn it all, I could swear I've seen these marks before. It's right on the tip of my tongue."

Kavanaugh conjectured uncertainly, "Some look like tally marks, but the others..."

"Tally? Son of a gun! Just the jog my memory needed! Mah-jongg!"

"Mah-jongg? You mean the game little old Jewish ladies play?"

"But little old Chinese ladies played first. These are numbers in Chinese, Kavanaugh. I've seen them when I played Mah-jongg with Lois's mother. They mark the number of each suit on the tiles."

"Chinese? Sure, that's right up Gabe's alley, that kind of poetic justice," Kavanaugh noted. "Jives perfectly with the *Wong* case."

"I'll say," Jess concurred, her mind already interpreting. "So wait, let me take a good look at these markings. Sure! They're the same Chinese numbers. It's just hard to recognize because they're smaller, lighter. And who would expect Evan Blair or Gabriel Stuyvesant to be able to write Chinese numbers?"

"So, sister, where do we go from here?"

"Let me think. It's a code. A code that only works when you put both volumes together. Look, the order of numbers jumps back and forth between the books. In mine, the symbol for 'one,' in yours 'two,' then back to me for 'three,' and so on."

"So, we go to the poem marked one in the first book," concluded Kavanaugh.

Jess swiftly thumbed through the pages, adding, "And see the letter marked for one. Okay, here, first line. I think we pick out each letter with the number symbols in the order they're numbered to form the first word. Go through the whole five poems and we should get the message on where to find the jade."

"Nice work you two," a voice cut into their concentration. "Mrs. Tewkesbury will be so appreciable."

Jessica and Kavanaugh looked up at the man she recognized from her stint in the Lowell closet as Alanna's flunky Mickey. The mug's malapropism might have had some chuckle value, but his .38 definitely put the kibbosh on Jessica's sense of humor. Why in blue blazes had she and Kavanaugh forgotten to close that door in their excitement? And where *was* McLaughlan?

"Betty Weisenthal's crooks crawl out from almost any woodwork," Kavanaugh remarked, one hand unobtrusively pulling Jessica back, a little behind him to his right, the gunsel's left.

"Never mind the smart talk," Mickey growled. "The only thing I want to hear out of either of you two is where to find the jade."

"Maybe you shoulda heard that we haven't figured it out yet, bud," Kavanaugh snorted. "If you had more brains than greed, you'd have waited till we did. Betty's not getting her money's worth out of you."

Jess prayed that Kavanaugh knew what he was doing because it seemed to her you ought to be nice to a guy with a gun.

"Yak, yak, yak!" Mickey griped. "My boss figured if we kept an eye on this skirt, we'd get ourselves onto something, but nothing *this* big. I'm gonna to be cuttin' myself into a hefty bonus if I can deliver the jade to her. Maybe I'll even ace out Eddie Kubek."

"Wouldn't that crack just make him sit up and smile?" Kavanaugh observed.

Jessica looked from Kavanaugh to Tewkesbury's creature and back. She really hoped that her new ally was trying to get Mickey enough off balance for him to get to his own gun.

"You know Eddie, big guy? Nah, you wouldn't, not a hick from these sticks. Never mind the stallin'. I want the jade."

"Maybe you weren't listening before, Einstein. We just said we haven't been able to figure that out yet," Kavanaugh mocked.

"What about little Mary Sunshine over there? She's been mighty quiet."

"What do you want," Jess snapped, "a recitation of Shakespeare?"

"Don't get smart with me, cutie. No wonder my boss don't like you or your sibling."

"There's a ten-dollar word," Kavanaugh grinned.

"Yeah, neither of you won't be worth a plugged nickel if you don't get to cooperating."

"Since you put it so prettily, how can we refuse?" Jessica smiled acidly.

"So get to it, girlie–or maybe you need me to shut up your friend over here, permanently, for incentive."

"I wouldn't do that. I need his help. He knows more about Chinese Mah-jongg than I do," Jessica lied.

"He don't look like no sinologist to me."

Jess and Kavanaugh both blinked over that one. Kavanaugh recovered first, warning, "Looks can be deceiving, bud. Now take a peek at this first book. The code's ingenious. Come over. You can't see the marks from there. Afraid? You got the gun. You hold all the aces. I bet your pal Eddie Kubek wouldn't be afraid. Probably why he's top dog and you're only..."

"Let me take a gander. I ain't affrighted of you two palookas."

He cautiously came forward, as Kavanaugh subtly edged Jessica further away, while turning the book to the thug. Jessica watched carefully as Kavanaugh slid the book forward on the table, one hand tapping at a line, his words promising quite a bounty at the unraveling of clues to their captor, who was greedily eating it all up. Then all hell broke loose.

The table flew up in the mug's face with nose-breaking force, and Jessica found herself hurled away to the floor with enough power to turn her world black before she could see if Kavanaugh had survived.

Chapter Twenty-Five

Same evening

The lights were low, and two feet were propped, shoeless, on the coffee table. Long legs reached up to a body collapsed on the couch. An irritated groan escaped the lips of the dark-haired woman as the clock chimed eleven p.m.

Liz Minton forced herself to sit up. She'd been back half an hour, and not a single, solitary peep from her sister or that crew of Keystone Kops supposed to be clearing Larry. Where *was* Larry, anyway?

Liz swung her feet to the floor, fishing for her shoes; then she gave up. Why bother? Her dogs were barking enough as it was. She'd certainly done her part leading Aaron Boyd 'round Robin Hood's barn until she'd lost him, but not before losing herself about eight o'clock. Of course, if he'd figured out she was leading him on a snipe hunt, he could have headed back and run in the whole kit and kaboodle of her team. That'd leave her the only one to shine the spotlight on the real killer. Not a cheery thought.

Massaging the ball of her foot, Liz speculated hopefully that if Boyd had already run in her pals, he probably would have nabbed her the minute she'd come back. What she wouldn't give to hear just one word from that old gang of hers!

Her apartment's buzzer rasped through the silence. Liz froze. Maybe she wasn't so eager for news, after all. News could be bad. The buzzer taunted her again, but the intercom relieved her a little with a familiar voice, "Liz, it's Lois with Iris. We have to see you!"

With the gangling grace of a giraffe disentangling its limbs for a run, Liz was on her feet and dashing for the intercom.

"Okay, okay. What's the scoop?"

"Not here, Liz," Lois's voice sounded. "Let us in."

Liz hurriedly buzzed her friends up. As soon as she unlocked the door, Iris burst in first. As usual, Lois's entrance was far more subdued, but Liz could detect her friend's tension.

Her black taffeta skirt swirling, Iris accosted Liz, "Thank God you're back. Larry's been looking all over for you."

"Larry?" Liz was immediately on point. "I tried to call him just half an hour ago. There was no one home, or at work." Her eyes pinned Lois now, "Is Larry all right? What's wrong?"

"We don't know," Lois answered carefully. "I was taking Iris out to get her mind off Wes being away, when Larry caught us going out the door. He was troubled, Liz."

"*Troubled*?" Iris disagreed. "I'd say he was fit to be tied."

"'Fit to be tied' angry or 'fit to be tied' worried?" Liz anxiously questioned.

"Angry." "Worried." Answered Iris and Lois, respectively, in unison.

"*Could* you two make up your minds before something happens to him?" Liz impatiently chided.

Lois clasped the neck of her mink a little tighter over her silver sheath and quelled Iris's impatience with a glance, then explained, "There's something eating Larry about the case, and he badly wants to talk to you. He wouldn't tell *us*, though."

Elizabeth conjectured, "Maybe he remembered something he'd seen at the office that night to implicate Alanna."

"Seen?" Iris puzzled. "What would Larry have seen? He wasn't even there, right?"

Swiftly plunging into damage control, Lois suggested, "He might have seen something when he visited before. Don't go trying to place Larry at the scene of the murder, Iris. He's in enough hot water as it is."

"That's right!" Iris agreed. "Anyone around the crime scene that night would be a prime suspect, especially someone with a juicy motive like Larry!"

Or like Lois, Liz silently considered, seeing her friend wince at Iris's conjecture.

Lois took charge: "Liz, your best bet is to sit tight in case Larry tries back here again. We already swung by Jessica's. No sign of Larry there. If you think it's better, we can leave you alone "

Iris interrupted. "Lois, Elizabeth looks a wreck. We should stay and give her moral support. We could play a round of mah-jongg."

Liz concurred. "Iris, you've got something there. I could use a little companionship about now."

"You're sure?" Lois questioned, doubtful.

Liz nodded.

Iris brightened, concluding, "See! I told you it would be jake. All we need is a little java, a little girl talk, and everything will be just dandy. Say Liz, have any donuts to go with that coffee?"

The ringing phone eclipsed Liz's answer.

"That must be Larry now," Lois reassured.

Liz nodded and crossed swiftly to the phone.

"Hello, Larry?"

"Not by a long shot. This is Detective Boyd."

"Swell."

"Yeah, I'm fond of you, too. You alone?"

Liz looked at her two friends, watching her curiously. It might pay to keep Boyd in the dark about her company. He might spill something if he thought she hadn't any witnesses.

"Sure, *Detective Boyd*. I'm alone."

Lois put a hand over Iris's mouth to keep her from betraying their presence. She gave Liz a nod to go on.

"What's this all about?" Liz asked carefully.

"I have something that might make you a little friendlier toward me. Interested?"

Curiosity and distrust warred inside Elizabeth. What the devil did Boyd have to say? Finally Liz answered, "I don't know what you're up to Boyd, but if you're planning to haul me in for this chat, you better make sure you put me in a room big enough for my lawyers, too."

"Hold your horses, Miss Minton. You don't need your lawyers. It kills me to admit it, but I've come up with something that makes me think maybe you weren't so far off the beam about that Tewkesbury broad."

"You agree with me? Excuse me while I faint."

He chuckled, but not much. Boyd proceeded to further flabbergast Elizabeth, "Yeah, well I guess I might have had that coming. Not that I'm promising your pal Sanders is completely in the clear. But there is something I need to check out in *your* office, on the mirror. A kind of coded message scratched on the back. It's not like I can haul that thing over to your apartment or down to the precinct."

Suspiciously, Elizabeth questioned, "None of your boys in blue noticed it when they first investigated?"

"Hey, it wasn't part of the original crime scene, but some of the stuff your sister said to me today got me thinking," he admitted reluctantly. "I had your watchman let me in to check out if we'd missed anything. So what do you say? Gonna help me?"

Liz mulled over Boyd's proposition. She'd do almost anything to clear Larry, but what if it was a trick to make her incriminate him somehow?

"Say, Boyd, you've undergone one whale of a change of heart," she began carefully. "I find it hard to believe you've suddenly come over to my side."

"I'm not on *your* side," the detective set her straight. "I'm on the side of the law and the truth." He took a breath, then admitted, "And I need your help to clear my partner of the bum rap Tewkesbury's pinned on him. McLaughlan wouldn't be in this jam if he hadn't stuck *his* neck out for *you*."

Elizabeth thought over Boyd's words. Could she afford to turn down even the longest shot to clear either Larry or a decent guy like McLaughlan?

"Okay, okay. I'm in," she announced.

"Swell. I'm at the station now. It'll be quicker if I meet you at the office. I can get there in about twenty minutes. And mum's the word. If Mrs. Tewkesbury is as dangerous as you think, you don't want any scuttlebutt about what we're up to getting back to her."

"Yes, certainly."

"Okay. See you in twenty."

The phone connection clicked off.

Liz turned back to her friends, watching her from across the room.

"What did Boyd want?" Lois questioned, from her seat on the couch..

Liz answered, "He says he has new evidence and a change of heart about Alanna Tewkesbury. He wants to meet me at the office in twenty minutes. I'm also not supposed to tell anyone."

"But that's just what you're doing now," ventured a perplexed Iris.

"You don't trust him," Lois cut to the chase.

"Should I?"

"I wouldn't. And I wouldn't meet him either," Lois warned.

"Do I have a choice, Lois? If I believe Larry's innocent, I can't pass up an opportunity like this. It could also help clear Leo McLaughlan."

"This could be a trap to get you to divulge something incriminating about Larry," Lois argued.

Liz didn't speak at first, wondering if Lois were solely concerned with *Larry's* incrimination. Finally, she promised, "I'll be wily as a fox, Lois."

Once more perplexed, Iris pointed out, "Aren't foxes sly? Coyotes are wily, Liz."

"True, Iris," Liz returned. "But *nobody* wears coyote, and fox looks just *divine*."

Iris gave her friend a quizzical look, then gave up, and said, "I think we could use some coffee about now." With that, she went off to the kitchen.

Lois turned her sharp eyes on Liz and questioned, "What if Larry calls?"

"Tell him to let me know where I can find him and to sit tight. I'll be back and tell him everything I've learned as soon as I can shake Boyd," Elizabeth directed. "Lois, I'm depending on you to hold down the fort, especially if Larry or Jessica shows. Hooley's up to something with her, but I'm not sure what. Well, I know *one* thing he's up to, but that's another kettle of mackerel. Anyway, I trust you to keep things from going to Hades in a handbag. I'll be back as soon as I can. Try to stonewall Iris if she asks too many questions. I love her, but..."

"She's Iris. Don't worry about that. You just be careful."

Liz nodded, appreciating her friend's steadfastness. So, after powering into her blazer and slapping on her hat, she was gone.

Liz pulled out the emergency brake as she parked her car in front of the office building. No Boyd anywhere. Was she walking into a set up? Had Alanna somehow gotten wind of their plans and sent her trained apes to take care of him, like they had Leo McLaughlan? She wasn't exactly a good luck charm for New York's finest.

The approach of a slowing car snapped Liz from her dark musings. The grey sedan parked behind her. The car's front door opened, but she was too nervous to turn her head. Her eyes fastened on the reflection in the side-view mirror. Then she relaxed.

Boyd's voice came quietly through her open window, "Sorry I'm late. I should have told you to park in the alley. Don't know why I didn't think of it when I had you on the line."

Liz arched an eyebrow, "Park in the alley? Why?"

"Because, lady, I'm going out on a limb here, and I don't want to chance tipping off Mrs. Tewkesbury that you and I may have come to a little understanding. What do you think will happen when she gets wise to the fact that you and I aren't at loggerheads anymore?"

"So," Liz observed, "you *do* believe me."

"I'm here, aren't I? So, let's stop wasting time. You pull your car into the alley. I'll be right behind you."

"I..."

"You want to try and clear your boyfriend and my partner, don't you? I thought you were serious about trying to nail Tewkesbury. This may be our last shot."

"Okay, okay. You win," Liz gave in, turning the key in her ignition and going for the clutch. Boyd hopped back in his own car, and, in a jiffy, the two were parked in the alley, Boyd's car last in, bumper uncomfortably nuzzling bumper in the dead-end. Even if Elizabeth didn't feel entirely confident in Boyd's change of heart, she told herself that she owed too much to Larry and McLaughlan not to play this long shot.

A few minutes later, they were in the building, going up in one of the elevators set away from the main entrance. Before she could flick on the light in the car, Boyd's hand stopped her. Pulling a flashlight from his trench coat pocket, he warned, "Don't want to draw any attention."

Liz nodded, tightlipped. She hadn't had much luck with secretive trips to this office building in the dark of night. Well, if Eddie Kubek showed up for another little tea party, at least Boyd would be better protection than Jessica had been.

"I'd give a grand to know what was going on between those ears of yours," Boyd interrupted her thoughts.

"I just bet you would," Liz retorted.

"Hey, you better not be holding out on me," he impatiently warned. "I'm trying to help you now. Make it worth my while. I aim to look out for Leo, even if he's not so hot about doing it himself." The elevator stopped and Boyd pulled the grill doors open for Liz, but he wouldn't let her off before saying, "That's why I'm willing to give this a shot. After you."

"Just as long as you don't take a shot *at* me," Liz returned, stepping off the elevator into the corridor, illuminated vaguely by Boyd's down-turned flashlight.

Elizabeth fumbled for the keys as they proceeded through the murk to the main office. Getting that key in the lock was made difficult by her trembling hands. Precisely what had Boyd found on the back of her mirror? How far would it go to saving Larry and to vindicating McLaughlan? She pushed the door open, but Boyd raised a hand to prevent her going first. He took the gun from his shoulder holster, leaving Liz more than happy to let him precede her; she was even happier when nothing happened to him. Maybe Eddie Kubek was off somewhere having a beer. Maybe he'd even choke on a pretzel–no, even Eddie wasn't that much of a dope!

Following Aaron Boyd's signal, Liz stepped into the main office. He'd put away the gun.

"Shall I turn on the lights, Boyd? I can close the blinds."

He shook his head, "Nope. We don't need them. Wait till we get into your office and can take a look at the mirror together."

Liz nodded and said, "Follow me."

Once she'd unlocked the office, they relaxed a notch. The outer office's emptiness suggested they were alone. Boyd even let Elizabeth enter first. She briskly strode ahead to her desk, pausing to switch on its lamp. A thud behind Liz startled her into whirling 'round.

Just within the edge of the lamp's aura, Aaron Boyd had crumpled to the floor in a heap. Above him, having stepped from behind the door to conk out Boyd, Eddie Kubek hulked. Even in the shadowy lighting, Elizabeth could see his shark's smile. She had nowhere to run.

Chapter Twenty-Six

Eddie Kubek moved closer, horrifying Elizabeth Minton with his vicious eyes. Instinctively, Liz grabbed a paperweight and let it fly. Kubek ducked and came back up with a gun that stopped Liz cold.

"That's it, sister. Sit tight. You ain't going nowhere."

"If you shoot me, it will confirm everything I've been saying!"

"Oooo. I'm shaking in my boots. Get over here. There's someone who wants to have a little pow-wow with you."

"I can just guess who," Liz sarcastically surmised.

"Save the jawboning for the dame what wants to talk to you."

"Where are you taking me?" Maybe if she stalled, Boyd would come around and take out this big ape.

"Look, sister, I'm not a patient guy. I warned you and your sister before, and neither of you paid any attention. I don't like to be ignored. You've ticked off Mrs. Tewkesbury, too, and she's been blaming me. It won't take much to make me blow my stack about now."

"Kubek, if you kill me, my ghost will tell her to go soak her head, not whatever she wants to know," Elizabeth snapped.

"Then put this in your pipe and smoke it, smart gal. I don't have to kill you. I can wing you and make you pretty damned sorry you weren't more cooperative."

He had her. Elizabeth knew she couldn't even threaten him with the night watchman. They could write up the Treaty of Versailles before he'd get up here–if she could wake him up.

That shark smile again, and Kubek ordered, his gun pointing the way, "Your partner's office. Cozier in there."

"Murderer returns to the scene of the crime?"

Kubek's smile deepened as if he knew something she didn't. He chuckled, "Yeah, I guess you could say that."

She'd have loved to wash that smile off with sulfuric acid. Liz also noticed that Kubek closed but didn't lock the door to the main office. Cocky creep! Pretty darn sure Boyd was down for the count, wasn't he? If she could string him and Tewkesbury along, she might buy time for Boyd to recover and call in the cavalry. Maybe.

Eddie Kubek shoved Evan's office door open to reveal Alanna Tewkesbury checking her lipstick in a gold-gleaming compact in the smoky spotlight of the desk lamp. *Did they have a key to every room here? Well, they were criminals; breaking in was right up their alley.*

The compact snapped shut, and Alanna Tewkesbury haughtily stared down her guest. Designer to the end, Liz caught herself sizing up the evening gown of midnight-blue sequins encasing her adversary up to her bust where pink chiffon took over.

"Dear me," Liz quipped sarcastically, "if I'd known this was a formal kidnapping, I'd have worn a silk number. But you know, dear, that shade of pink only flatters a girl *under* thirty."

"Think you're pretty smart, don't you, Elizabeth Minton?" Tewkesbury sneered in tones not usually displayed in public by her set. "You won't be giving me so much lip when you see my special surprise."

Leaning forward, smiling viciously, Alanna shifted the desk lamp to spotlight a corner of the room to her right.

For once, Liz was speechless, save for her painful gasp. Tied up in a chair, out cold, was Larry Sanders.

"You bi..."

"Watch your lip, Dear. I have the upper hand."

"And I have the gun," added Kubek, immensely pleased with his wit.

Liz recovered quickly and started toward Larry, but a signal from her blonde-pompadored adversary had Kubek stopping her.

"That's far enough, Miss Minton," Alanna commanded, with the smile of the cat who had not only eaten the canary but had, first, perpetrated some nasty acts of torture.

"What have you done to Larry? If you've hurt him..."

"You'll what? Eddie has you nicely under the gun. I think you'll speak only when spoken to. Don't you, Eddie?"

Liz's mouth opened, but Eddie's gun had tremendous quieting power.

"Relax, for now," Tewkesbury instructed. "Your fellow is fine. A little passive from a drugged cloth over his face when he came through the same door you just did..."

"Here? Why would he have come here?"

"Perhaps because of a call saying we wanted to work out a compromise over the murder?"

"Compromise? What kind of a compromise?" Liz spat out.

"Simply to discuss how we might leave you, your sister, and him alone, *if* he could get you to lay off digging into my background."

"It was harder to frame him after we got the gun away from you, wasn't it?" Liz triumphed.

"You are such a fool, Miss Minton. Do you think that's the *only* option I had to protect myself?" Alanna gloated. "You just had to keep pushing the issue after we warned you. Now we'll have to get rid of you both. Make it look like murder/suicide. If you'd known what was good for you..."

"I'd have let you get away with ruining my friend Lois Wong's family? Let you frame Larry? Let you frame Leo McLaughlan? Let you get away with murdering my friend, Evan Blair?"

"You really are too naïve!" the vicious woman laughed. "You want to believe too much in people's innocence, especially Gabriel Stuyvesant–oh, excuse me, Evan Blair. *He*'s worth 'avenging'? He was a crook like the rest of us."

"Evan was better than you!"

"Was he?" Alanna taunted. "Maybe you're forgetting he was just as much involved as the rest of the gang in ruining the Wong family, and all the others."

"He turned state's evidence to help convict the rest of you rats," Liz riposted.

"He got a deal when he ratted us out to save his own skin. But he couldn't stay away. He got greedy and came back. Gabe might have gotten immunity from the Feds, but he wasn't immune from *my* revenge. Someone had to even the score for the gang."

"Evan had changed," Liz countered. "He was trying to straighten out things for Lois and give back the jade."

"Give back the jade?" Alanna Tewkesbury hadn't expected that. Even in the dark shadows of the office, Liz could see the wheels turning under that perfectly coiffed blonde pompadour. Maybe she could make her knowledge about the jade, or at least what she wanted Alanna to think she knew, work for her. Larry's groan sliced through the tension.

At Liz's instinctive move toward Larry, Eddie Kubek sarcastically tsk-tsked her.

Liz turned to Alanna and pointed out, "You hold all the cards. What difference does it make if I go over and see how he is?"

It killed her to give that woman this much, but Liz was determined to help Larry and find some way to stall for time. Tewkesbury smiled, eating up the sop to her vanity, and nodded to Eddie that Liz might join Larry.

"Larry, Larry, are you all right? It's Liz." As she spoke, Liz was kneeling by his side, one hand brushing the dark hair from his brow.

Larry's eyes were bleary from the drug and the dim lighting. He tried to shift, but the ropes pinioned him. That sudden realization sheered through his mental cobwebs.

"My God! Liz! What's going on here?"

"We're having a little tête à tête, Mr. Sanders," Alanna explained, languidly perching on the desk. "I'm sure you realize we can't make this deal final until we have Elizabeth Minton here with you. I don't want any double crosses if either of you suddenly gets cold feet."

"You are evil," Larry condemned her in a voice that would have annihilated anyone but a female with a hunk of Antarctica where her heart should have been. "I understand now why Liz wanted to see you neutralized." Larry turned his face to Liz, "I can't tell you how sorry I am that I got you into this. If I'd known..."

"No, Larry. It's not your fault. If anyone's, it's mine. But these two may have overplayed their hand."

Liz's eyes challenged Alanna Tewkesbury so fiercely that the ice queen flinched and demanded suspiciously, "Meaning?"

"Meaning my sister, Detective McLaughlan, and Agent Hooley. If we turn up dead, do you think they'll ever stop digging for the truth?"

Alanna nearly straightened Liz's permanent with her throaty, triumphant laugh. The grand dame leaned forward and taunted, "You really think that McLaughlan can help you now? As for your sister, Jay Kavanaugh will take care of her."

"Kavanaugh? How you know about Kavanaugh?" Anger at Tewkesbury and fear for her sister drove Liz to her feet. "Answer me!"

Liz's nemesis wore a cruel half smile when she replied, "You ought to remember I always use an inside man to set up my pigeons–a man who could set up your sister, so she'd be at Jay Kavanaugh's tender mercies. Kavanaugh's *such* an angry man."

"Who?" Liz demanded, ready to slap the Max Factor right off Alanna Tewkesbury, Eddie Kubek or not.

"Who's our inside man?" That smile of hers was as hard and biting as a diamond drill. She leaned back to the intercom, explaining before she flipped the switch. "My man should be sitting at your desk by now. The location is superb for lookout."

Liz and Larry looked at each other tensely, as Alanna Tewkesbury queried into the speaker, "We're working on Minton and Sanders now. Still all clear out there?"

"All clear."

Liz couldn't quite place the voice, but she didn't have to. Alanna Tewkesbury's signoff left her ready to hit the floor like a bobbysoxer seeing Sinatra.

"Thanks, Hooley. Keep up the good work." She turned back to her captives and took genuine, vicious pleasure in explaining, "Charming boy, that Hooley. He knew exactly how to pique my interest, so I'd make a deal with him when he came to see me after finding out my identity."

"But my sister said he hated you?" Liz wondered, still not letting her astonishment undermine her resolve.

"Because of his older brother? He's smarter than that. When he came to me, he told me that jumping the Feds would be payback for the way they'd treated the brother."

Elizabeth snorted, "He didn't figure *you* deserved payback?"

"That's what I like about the kid, the way he thinks. He saw me as a crook, just following my instincts when I worked his brother. But the law, they should have known their man and not given him a raw deal. Hooley is a sharp customer. He'll go far. Maybe we'll make some beautiful music together."

"I'm sure Mr. Tewkesbury would appreciate those sentiments," Larry coldly observed.

Alanna Tewkesbury's darkly cordial smile and her warm tone creepily colored her words: "Nobody lives forever, Mr. Sanders, especially an old man–and a grieving widow needs some comfort."

"That grieving widow better inherit a pile of dough," Liz interjected sarcastically, "because it won't be many moons before she'll need some expensive nips and tucks if she wants to hold onto a young Turk like Hooley. Otherwise, he'll be looking for some comforting of his own when you find enough bags under your eyes to open a luggage shop."

Liz knew she'd hit a nerve because Alanna's expression moved Eddie Kubek to inquire, "Should I plug them now, Mrs. Tewkesbury?"

Tewkesbury pulled herself together and, with a dismissive wave of her hand, told him, "No, not yet, much as the prospect thrills me. There's still some business Elizabeth Minton needs to settle for me." Turning on her captive, Alanna continued, "Maybe you can still save your and Sanders' skins, if you play your cards right."

"Oh? And what cards are those?"

"Here's the deal, sweet and simple. You said that Gabe wanted to use the jade to make restitution. I think that means he probably clued you in to where the pieces are. I want that jade. Are you going to cooperate?"

"If you're such a wealthy woman, and planning to be an even wealthier widow, what do you need the jade for?" Liz stalled.

Alanna's expression darkened as she wrestled with how much to tell her enemy. In the end, the jade won out and she revealed, "My dear husband is no sap. To tell the truth, if he dies, I get a pittance. For once, I was the chump, marrying a guy who's going to take it with him. But if I have that jade, I can write my own ticket to some place nice and warm and extradition-free. I want that jade. I'll do anything for it!"

The savagery of her words silenced them all, until the phone shattered that silence.

It took a second for Alanna Tewkesbury to regain enough composure to accuse Elizabeth, "You told someone you were coming!"

Liz shook her head, pleased to see that dolled-up barracuda disconcerted.

The phone continued to insist they answer. Liz dryly observed, "It must be important. Whom did *you* tell you'd be here?"

Behind icy eyes, Tewkesbury's mind raced, until she ordered, "All right, Minton. You answer, but no funny business." With a telling glance in the direction of Eddie Kubek's gun, she warned, "if you catch my drift."

"You shoot us and whoever's calling will know..."

"You'll be too dead to squeal, and we'll be too far away to be caught by the time whoever's on the horn gets here. Answer it."

Her hand on the receiver, Liz affected *sang-froid* and quipped, "Persistent little devil," but her mind was racing like a PT boat: how could she subtly signal her and Larry's danger to the caller–if it was an ally?

"Hello, Liz Minton here."

Larry studied Liz's back. She seemed to be just listening. In the spotlight of the desk lamp, Alanna Tewkesbury strained impatiently, her sequins sparkling and casting weird reflections on her face, glinting with far more warmth than her cold, blue eyes. Eddie Kubek hovered at the periphery of the halo, a crude, vicious phantom holding a very real gun–a gun much like the one Larry had lost–the one that had killed Evan Blair. Larry looked away.

"It's for you, Alanna," came Liz's coolly cordial voice as she extended the receiver to her enemy.

The deadly glamour girl's eyes narrowed, suspicion dripped from her lips, "Who? You spent a long time listening to a call for *me*. What's the catch?"

"No catch. Just the chance to get that jade you want so much. But you won't find out how by gabbing with me," Liz replied with a maddeningly bland expression.

Zeroing in on was the word "jade," Alanna Tewkesbury whipped the receiver from Liz. Satisfied, Elizabeth stepped back to Larry, squeezing his shoulder as he looked questioningly up at her. Eddie and Alanna encircled the phone.

"Hi Alanna, I heard you were in the market for some precious stones, jade to be specific."

"Who is ... ?" The identity of the speaker clicked with Alanna Tewkesbury, and her glance fastened on Liz, with the hissed accusation, "Your sister!"

"Imagine that," Liz returned pleasantly.

"Hey, Alanna." The voice over the line drew the peroxide predator back. "I'm the one who wants to parley. I'm the only one who can."

"*You* have the Wong jade? You must be bluffing."

"Not at all. In fact, I can prove I'm not. I can give you a little show of good faith."

"Such as?"

"Such as I cracked the code Evan, sorry Gabe, set up for hiding the stones. This evening, with the help of Jay Kavanaugh, we retrieved them. But I'm willing to turn them over to you on the condition that you let my sister and Larry go and lay off McLaughlan."

"Where are you?"

"Never mind, and never mind sending anyone around to look for me, either. Here's the deal. I bring you a sample. You check it out. After you let Liz and Larry go, I send you more, one at a time. That way, you don't get greedy and double-cross me by trying to knock me off tonight. As added insurance, we both have the goods on each other–you pull any funny business, and the cops find out you have the jade; I pull anything, and you can start up on Larry and McLaughlan. Do we have a deal?"

"I'll have to see the jade first."

"Of course. I'll be over in ... well, when I get there, I get there. You're not going anywhere, and this jade really is something else. I'll try to get there as quickly as I can."

"I could send someone for you."

"Isn't that just sweet of you? And I suppose I could end up in the East River wearing cement spectator pumps. Who're you kidding, lady? Play your cards right, and you'll get all the jade–and I'll get my sister and my friends back. Then everybody will be happy."

Alanna Tewkesbury's expression would have given Goering the creeps, but she agreed, "All right. You've got a deal. We'll be waiting. But you better not try to pull anything."

She hung up and turned to inform Liz, "Your kid sister is quite the wheeler-dealer. You better hope she's not trying to pull a fast one or..."

"Hi! Anybody want some simply divine jade?"

Startled eyes flew to the doorway to the main office. Jessica Minton was draped there, mock seductively, a raincoat tucked through her bent arm. Liz rolled her eyes: a life and death situation and their only hope of rescue was a bigger ham than anything that had ever come out of Armour.

Eddie Kubek's gun was trained on Jess, but his keeper waved him down.

"Uh, uh, uh," Jessica chided with a wagging finger. "If you want *all* the jade, play nice."

Eddie telegraphed a questioning look at his boss lady. Disappointed, he obeyed her eyes' command to lower his gun, but he still kept it mighty handy.

Watching his weapon, Jess approved, "That's better; not great, but better."

"Don't push your luck, Miss Minton," Alanna threatened. "If you know what's good for you, for *them*, hand over that jade."

Liz couldn't help blurting, "For the love of Mike, Jess, don't trust them!"

Larry joined in, "Your sister is right, Jessica. These people are reprehensible."

"Pipe down," Eddie Kubek snapped, raising his gun, vaguely grasping that "reprehensible" wasn't a compliment.

"This does not sound like the nice, reasonable business deal I had in mind," Jessica disapproved, folding her arms. "Don't you want to get *all* of the jade? Not going to happen if you make me cranky."

Ignoring Jessica, Alanna Tewkesbury ordered, "Eddie, bring her over here. I want a look at that jade."

Kubek grabbed Jessica, almost shaking her shoulder bag off, and dragged her to the desk, all the while she protested, "Hey, take it easy, you big mug. Don't bruise the merchandise."

"What did you expect," Liz cut in, "tea and cookies?"

At the desk, Jessica answered Liz, while surveying the two stone-hearted captors flanking her, "I expect these two to act smart. Anything happens to me, they don't get the rest of this haul. Anything happens to me, and some letters go to the D.A., the police here and in Boston, and the Feds telling them where to get the rest of those precious stones–and Jay Kavanaugh puts the finger on Lady Astor and her pet horse over there."

"You think you're pretty smart, girlie," Eddie Kubek growled.

"Shut up, Eddie," Alanna commanded, continuing fiercely, "She is. But let me tell *you* something, Minton. If these aren't the real McCoy, if you're trying to flim-flam me, you're going to wish you'd never been born–and your friends will be in the same boat. Now where's that jade?"

Unintimidated, Jessica smiled as if she had a handful of aces when she pulled a leather-bound book from her raincoat and tossed it on the desk.

Her two antagonists were startled, but only for a heartbeat. Alanna recovered first, snapping, "It's a book? What kind of a gag is this?"

"It's a book that hid those tiny but pricey squares of jade in the padded leather covers. Look where I slit it in front and back. I left one square for you in the front."

Swiftly thinking over Jessica's words, Alanna then told Eddie, "Put her over there with the other two. If this is a con, we'll waste all three at once."

Eddie shoved Jess into Elizabeth, who only kept from snapping at him when his gun caught the desk lamp's gleam.

Alanna Tewkesbury held the book in her velvet-gloved hands, lamplight washing her wraithlike, no, demonic, face. Eyes piercing Jessica, she demanded, "In the front? What about the back?"

"That's my insurance. Don't worry, toots. You'll get what you bargained for when I get what I want."

"They'll never come through for you, Jessica," Larry argued tautly. "They'll find a way to double-cross us all."

"Shut up, Sanders!" Eddie growled, his eyes returning greedily to the book his keeper handled. He took a step toward her and the prize.

"You wouldn't be so brave if you didn't have that gun," Jessica accused, despite warning glares from Liz and Larry.

"Oh yeah?" Kubek retorted, putting the gun down on the desk and stepping toward the three. "I think I'll just show you how tough I can be with a smart-mouth dame like you."

"Eddie! We don't have time for..."

The rest of Alanna Tewkesbury's words were lost in a blur. Jessica shoved Liz into Larry's chair so the three hit the floor in a crazy jumble, while both doors to the office slammed open as McLaughlan charged through one and Hooley the other, both armed.

"Hooley! Kill him!" Alanna Tewkesbury screamed, diving for the gun, only to connect with Eddie Kubek's head, bouncing them both dazedly to the floor.

Hooley grabbed the gun on the desk and stepped back, having all of them under his surveillance. He turned to Alanna Tewkesbury and questioned, "You two all right?"

Shaking her head, Alanna managed, "Ah, yeah, okay. Eddie's out, but thank God you're here. Disarm the other cop."

"Good," Hooley smiled, "because I'd hate for something to happen to you before I got a chance to send you to the pen."

"The pen?! What?!" Alanna snarled, shocked.

"I guess you *can* con a con," Hooley smiled wickedly. He turned to McLaughlan, "And Feds and locals can coordinate, after all."

"You said it, Brother," McLaughlan concurred.

"Okay, Tewkesbury," Hooley took charge, "on your feet. You too, Kubek." But Eddie was down for the count, apparently having connected to the floor with his head when he'd gone down. Turning to Jess, Liz, and Larry, as he cuffed his former "ally," Hooley asked, "Everyone all right?"

"Aside from being scared witless," Jessica began, a warning look at Liz not to seize the straight line, "I don't have any complaints. Where's Kavanaugh?"

McLaughlan answered, while cuffing the unconscious Kubek, "I'll give him the signal to come up as soon as I call in for a limo to take Mrs. Tewkesbury downtown."

"Aren't we downtown already?" Liz contradicted.

"It's an expression, Liz," Jess said, putting an arm around her sister and giving her an affectionate squeeze.

"I know that, but why can't people use expressions that everyone else can make sense of?"

"Like 'a pretty arm and a penny' and 'he's very flat-headed'?"

Liz narrowed her eyes.

"Say, would someone mind untying me?" Larry interjected. "If you're not too busy quibbling."

"Oh, no!" both sisters blurted, scrambling to liberate the much-put-upon Larry Sanders.

McLaughlan eyed Alanna Tewkesbury hard and said, "I don't mind telling you, you're one tough cookie I'll be glad to see crumble."

There was a collective groan at that metaphor, except for Liz who countered, "Gee, I kind of liked it."

"You *would*," Jessica rolled her eyes. Still, she added, "You're on the money, McLaughlan."

Larry had turned to Liz and taken her hand with, "Thank God this is over, Liz. Now we can get back on track."

McLaughlan turned away to make his calls to Kavanaugh and the station, while Liz said, "We'll talk about it later. I just want to get out of here. But first, what the devil happened? Hooley was on our side, then he wasn't, then he was. Jess comes in wearing a floozy outfit ..."

"An attractive floozy outfit," Hooley corrected.

"Gee, you're so gallànt," Jessica returned sarcastically.

"*Anyway*," Liz reasserted control over the conversation. "What gives?"

"Okay, I'll play Charlie Chan," Jess offered. "Hooley had me put on this get up to play on Kavanaugh's better nature."

"That's *not* what *I'd* call it," Liz corrected.

"It's a long story. Let me make it short, so we can finish before Alanna comes up for trial," Jess cracked wise.

"*If* I come up."

"Don't worry, sister; we've got plenty on you," McLaughlan kindly assured her.

"Wait until my lawyers get through with..."

"Hey!" Liz thundered. Upon gaining everyone's attention, she continued calmly, "I'm trying to hear a story–all right?!"

"Okay," Jess continued, "Kavanaugh and I figured out that my book from Evan and the one he had, when put together, contained a code telling where to find the jade,

"Stowed inside the padded leather cover of Kavanaugh's book!" Liz surmised excitedly.

"Exactly. Good old Betty almost cooked our goose when two of her goons followed us to Bridgeport. One guy tried to trick McLaughlan into leaving me behind by pretending to be a cop, but McLaughlan ditched him and beat it back to help Kavanaugh take the other one out."

Liz glanced at Hooley and demanded, "And Hooley, what about Hooley? Tewkesbury said he was her inside man."

"That's what I wanted her to believe," Hooley took over. "I've been developing the bait for this trap a long time, not knowing exactly on whom I'd be springing it. When you dropped this case in my lap, all the pieces fell into place. When I got back into town, before I went to see you, Jess, I turned on the boyish charm and set Alanna up with a proposition to help her secure the jade and get out of the country. She bit." To Alanna he shrugged, "Sorry, Beautiful."

"I have nothing to say without my mouthpiece–attorney. And he'll do a number on the lot of you." She was imperious through it all.

"Careful, dear, your slip's showing," Liz smiled with sulfuric charm.

"I wouldn't be so smug," Alanna retorted with equal corrosiveness. "I'm not the only one around here in trouble, with something to hide."

The tense spell was shattered by an unexpected voice: "I couldn't sit on my hands in your apartment, Liz. I had to see the vermin who destroyed my brother."

The accusation came from the doorway to the main office, where Lois Wong's fury seemed to make her small figure tower. Iris peeked over her shoulder and explained, "Kavanaugh said we could come up now."

"Is he still down there?" asked McLaughlan.

"Said he'd be up when the paddy wagon came," Iris assured them.

Lois Wong was silent, her stare making even Alanna Tewkesbury flinch. Then Lois came into the room, halting across the desk from the woman she so loathed. "I would love to kill you. Instead, I'll just tell the police now that I saw you here that night, the night Gabriel Stuyvesant was killed."

"Don't be ridiculous. I have an alibi. I was in Florida. People saw me leave by train."

"But you could have come back because you have a private plane that flies out of Garfield Airport," McLaughlan undercut her.

"You can't prove that I used it. The logbook's gone..."

"How would you know the log's gone?" McLaughlan pressed.

"I meant to say that there wouldn't be any record in the log."

"But that's not what you said," he calmly pointed out.

"I heard it, too," Hooley concurred. "How many other people heard her say it? Let's have a hand count. Two, three, six, and me, makes seven. You lose, Mrs. Tewkesbury."

"You can talk to my lawyer about that," she snapped.

"Sure, Mrs. Tewkesbury," McLaughlan concurred. "And the D.A. will talk to you about how the night I went to look for it, the watchman was killed. Sounds like you had much more of a motive than I did to bump off Pop and make the log go 'bye-bye. Then again, Hooley also told me on the drive back that there's a log back in Florida, from when you took off, which will queer your 'alibi.' Being a Fed and all, he's already put the word out to hold it. I see by your expression you didn't think about that."

"You're forgetting something," she bargained. "Even if I was here that night, Lois Wong had to be here, too, to see me. And I have a witness to testify that when I left, Gabriel Stuyvesant was still alive."

"Eddie Kubeck?" Leo McLaughlan snorted.

"It's better than her alibi, especially if you compare motives. She hated him, wanted him dead for her brother's death."

"And I suppose you wanted to smother him in kisses for double-crossing you?" Hooley undercut her.

"I wanted the jade before anything. I wouldn't have much chance of getting it if Gabriel Stuyvesant were dead, would I? No, you have to admit, I'm the one with the least reason to want him dead that night."

McLaughlan and Hooley exchanged thoughtful glances.

"Oh, and I *almost* forgot," Alanna continued. "Lois Wong and I weren't Gabe's only callers that night. I'm *shocked* she didn't tell you about his other visitor. Getting forgetful, dear? Do you want to name names, or shall I?"

Lois's eyes widened. She couldn't see her friends hurt. Anger and anguish had driven all those concerns from her mind until Alanna Tewkesbury brutally yanked them back.

That's when Larry interposed, "Leave her alone, you witch. I'll tell them for you. Gentlemen, I was there that night, too. I went to tell off Blair, Stuyvesant, whoever he was, to get him out of Elizabeth's life. If you go after Lois Wong, you have to go after me as well."

"Larry, shh," Liz pleaded, but he went on. "I'll testify that Blair was alive when Lois left."

"So you've been lying to us all along, Sanders," McLaughlan asserted, a harsh look fastening on Liz after those words.

"Leave Liz and Jessica out of this. They didn't know I was there. They just tried to keep me clear of this woman."

"This *woman* who has far less motive than Mr. Larry Sanders or Miss Lois Wong for committing murder," Alanna smiled. "You see, Eddie and I had a spot outside where we had an eye on all the exits, so we'd wait for the coast to clear. Then we'd go back in and work Gabe over till we got what I wanted out of him. But while we were waiting, we heard gunfire. We figured if Gabe hadn't been killed, we'd nab him when he tried to escape; if someone else came out, well, I wasn't about to get mixed up in someone else's murder. If you gentlemen are willing to cut a deal that pleases me, I'll tell you which of these two was last to leave."

"Don't." Lois grabbed McLaughlan's arm. "Look at everything she's done, all the lives she's ruined."

"You still think you can make a deal with me?" Hooley sarcastically inquired of his prisoner.

"If you want to know how deep the corruption goes, I can tell you what rocks to look under–but only if I like the immunity deal. I could help you take down my husband for interfering with the bureau to save his reputation. Maybe I'll even show you how to nail some of the toadies who ruined your brother. Think about it. Now, do you want to send up me or Sanders?"

"We still have enough to hold you," McLaughlan countered.

"Hold me, but not enough to convict me," Alanna smiled sardonically, relishing her power. "And when you fail, think how I'll have dragged Lois

Wong and Sanders and the rest of them through the mud. Maybe these two sisters aren't as innocent as Sanders claims. Maybe I can draw them in as a part of the plot. How many years for conspiracy to murder?"

"Any of this malarkey true?" McLaughlan demanded of Liz.

She started to try and explain, but Larry's hand on her arm silenced her. He came forward and asserted, "Don't listen to that termagant. These two girls are innocent. But if it will save Lois Wong, if it will help you convict Alanna Tewkesbury for her other crimes and vindicate the lives she's ruined, I'll confess."

"Larry!" Liz cried.

Lois's throaty voice insisted, "Larry, please, don't try to cover for me–or her. Don't take a rap for that, that thing. She'll just be wrecking another life."

"You on the level, Sanders?" McLaughlan was skeptical. "I can't use a confession made out of false gallantry."

"Of course I'm on the level," Larry replied in a steady voice. He hesitated, then found the strength to push forward. "It was an accident. I went in after Lois left. I'd been hiding in Liz's office. We had an argument. There was a gun. We struggled. It went off. I'm afraid I panicked at first and wandered outside. I may have tossed the gun away, or I may have left it in the office, without thinking. Maybe that's how Tewkesbury and Kubeck got their hands on it. I don't know. Then, after the way your partner grilled me, I didn't trust anyone to believe me."

"Larry, don't do this," Liz pleaded. "We can get her in court. We have a chance now."

"Kavanaugh can identify her," Jessica added.

Larry ignored them all and drove on, "McLaughlan, just remember, I'm telling you that I never told Liz or Jess any of this. If you leave them alone and go after Tewkesbury for her other crimes, you can save Lois, Jessica, and Liz, while putting that vicious criminal behind bars, where she belongs. That's the only thing that made me let you people keep up this gambit, a chance to put this creature away so she could pay for her crimes and to prevent her from destroying anyone else."

"You seem to be forgetting Agent Hooley over there," Alanna Tewkesbury deftly stole control of the conversation. "He's a Fed. He can beat any of your local charges with a Federal immunity deal–and I've made him a tempting offer. Actually, I've made quite a few tempting offers this evening."

"Don't flatter yourself," Liz cracked.

"Hooley," Jessica protested, "you can't be thinking of cutting a deal with this sequined spider!"

"Dear, face it. You've been outclassed." Then Alanna turned to Hooley and queried. "What do you say, Hooley? A chance to settle old scores? A boost at the bureau?"

"Well, first I say: nice alliteration. And that is a tempting offer..."

"Say, somebody give a party and forget to invite me?"

It was Aaron Boyd, moving into the room a little weakly, holding the back of his head.

"Good Lord!" escaped Liz. "I forgot all about him. Kubek slugged him in my office."

Hooley blinked at those words and blurted, "There was no one in your..."

It was too late. Boyd had deftly relieved an unsuspecting McLaughlan of his gun and grabbed Lois as a shield. Then he commanded, "Okay, you, Hooley, drop the gat. Drop it! Or this little girl gets her nice mink all splattered with blood, hers! You, Fed, uncuff Alanna. Make it snappy."

Iris fainted; Hooley complied with both Boyd's commands.

"That's right. Nobody needs to get hurt if you all behave nice and keep quiet. Alanna, rip out that phone and take the Fed's gun. Don't want him tipping anyone off too soon. Thanks to Leo's first call, we don't have much time. Good, Alanna, now grab that jade."

She pointed out, "Jessica, she knows where the rest of it is."

As Boyd's co-conspirator moved next to him, he countered, "There's no time. We gotta blow. You have some dough stashed offshore, right? They won't be able to trace us."

"Why, Aar?" demanded a shocked Leo McLaughlan.

"I wish I had time to explain, Leo, but we gotta run. Let's just say I'm tired of worrying about my pension, and I never forgot Betty from back in Boston. Now stay put and nobody gets hurt."

That was when Lois stomped her Cuban heel down on Boyd, simultaneously chopping backward with her elbow. His gun hand went up, Lois dropped to the floor, and Alanna furiously aimed at the girl. Hooley was on Alanna in a flash, wrestling away the weapon, but not before Boyd had drawn a bead on him and pulled the trigger. It was the man nearest the fray who leaped in and took the bullet meant for Hooley.

Liz screamed. Larry collapsed to his knees, one hand on the white shirt stained with spreading red, his eyes filled with disbelief. Liz was with him, vaguely aware of Hooley cuffing Alanna Tewkesbury, McLaughlan securing Boyd, Jessica at her side.

"Larry, what were you thinking?" Liz managed in a voice cracked with agony, as Larry sank back into her arms.

"I'll call in for an ambulance," came Hooley's voice as he disappeared into the next room.

McLaughlan had pulled open the sticky shirt and was examining Larry's wound. His expression took the breaths right out of Liz and Jess. Guilt and concern pleaded from Liz's eyes for McLaughlan to change his silent diagnosis. No dice. He couldn't face her.

Larry, despite his pain, said, "I guess I'll be saving the state of New York some room and board."

"Just hold tight, fella," McLaughlan urged. "The bus will be here in a jiffy."

"I don't have a jiffy, Detective. We both know that. So, I've got to get this off my chest."

Liz looked over his head at McLaughlan, agonized. The detective's eyes quieted her. Then he said to Larry, "Don't get yourself het up. We have Tewkesbury now. You don't need to play the knight in shining armor."

"But I do need to come clean." His voice was weakening. "I'm not going to let Lois get dragged through more misery, even if it does convict Alanna Tewkesbury. You have enough on her. You don't have to take Lois down. I did kill Blair. I didn't mean to. It was an accident."

"Oh, Larry..."

"It's all right, Liz. If things had been right for us, I wouldn't have been angry or afraid. I would have trusted you. It's not your fault. It's mine. So you've got to promise me that you will never blame yourself." Liz nodded, and Larry gathered all his fading strength to finish, "But I am responsible for his death. I confronted him, then I dropped my gun on the desk and blundered off into Liz's office, but I didn't keep going. I hid there so that I could continue where I left off after Lois left. I heard her telling him off for his whole sordid life. I thought of what a man with a history like that could do to Liz, and I saw red. When she left, I charged back in, and we both went after each other. I'd brought my gun to frighten him. He got his hands on it. I don't know what happened next, just that the gun went off and he was dead."

"Then why did you let these two cover for you?" Hooley questioned.

Jessica shot Jeff a sharp look. Liz was looking anxiously from Larry to Leo McLaughlan.

"No, it wasn't like that." Larry startlingly asserted himself, then sank back against Liz. "I should have come forward, but first I panicked, and then Liz showed me that this crime was the key to bringing Alanna Tewkesbury to justice. A thousand times, I almost spilled what I knew, but then I'd think about all that woman had done, all she'd continue to do if someone didn't trip her up. This looked to be the only chance. One thing, McLaughlan, Jess and Liz knew nothing. They're completely innocent. You understand that?"

McLaughlan considered, then agreed, "I read you, Sanders. My report'll convey just what you've told us."

Larry closed his eyes and smiled. Finally, his voice much fainter, he managed, "Jess, Liz, no regrets. Whatever I did, it was my decision, nobody's fault but mine. For a while, it was a grand ride. I know we all did our best. No regrets."

His head slipped down as his soul slipped away. The moment seemed to freeze into eternity. Liz felt, no, sensed, McLaughlan's hand on her shoulder, Jessica's on her other arm. She was past feeling right now.

Epilogue

Elizabeth Minton shoved the desk drawer shut where she kept her cigarettes. Three weeks since Larry's death, and she knew she had to stop punishing herself. It wouldn't have been what Larry wanted. She pensively clasped her arms, the material of her olive sheath dress comfortingly soft beneath her fingers, but not soft enough.

A polite but strong rap on her apartment door terminated her survey of the empty room. Who would be dropping in on a Sunday afternoon? She'd seen Jessica and Dusty off to Connecticut, insisting she'd really rather be alone just now. One unnecessary pat of her upsweep and she was striding across the room, opening the door on a preoccupied Leo McLaughlan.

She queried, "Detective McLaughlan?"

Why did it actually feel a little comforting to see that strong, sincere face of his? Liz brushed that question aside and instead said, "I didn't expect to see you. I thought we wouldn't have to deal with the case again for some time?"

Ill at ease, he didn't exactly wince at the edge in her voice, but it took him a moment to force calm back into his features for, "Yes, well, I dropped by because I wanted to let you know that the case, maybe I should say the cases, are going much better than I expected. I was just coming off shift."

"Oh." Silence hung awkwardly between them. Then Liz offered, "Would you like to come in?"

"I, sure, for a moment."

Liz stepped aside, indicating the sofa, querying, not without a trace of speculation in her gracious query, "Coffee?"

"No, no thanks." McLaughlan waited for Liz to take the chair before he sat on the sofa, a little unsettled at how deeply he sank into the thing.

"They call it the quicksand model," Liz commented, pleasant but not quite at ease. "Cigarette?"

"No, no. Like I said, I was just on my way home, coming off shift, and I wanted to let you know that the D.A. is satisfied with your and your sister's testimony."

The fact that he could have phoned to tell her that, that he didn't have to come in person, hung unspoken between them. And Liz was unsettled that she felt vaguely pleased that he had. McLaughlan continued, "I wanted you to know that you won't be having any trouble from Wilmington Tewkesbury. I know he made some noises about getting even for messing up his life, but his lovely wife actually did you what I'm sure was the unintended favor of rolling on her husband to the Feds over his tampering with government files."

"She's not getting any kind of sweetheart deal, is she?" Liz exploded.

"No, no, not at all," McLaughlan assured her hastily, "She may not be getting a lethal permanent wave, but she's going to do heavy time for contracting the security guard's death and her involvement in Sanders' ... her other crimes."

He realized too late he'd gone a step too far, mentioning Larry. As Liz winced, McLaughlan offered, "Damn it, Miss Minton. I didn't mean to bring..."

Liz stopped McLaughlan: "It's not your fault. If anyone's to blame..."

"It's not yours. Sanders said that to you when he cashed out. You need to think about that. He made some bad choices ..."

"Because of me."

"Because he was a human being and he made mistakes. Give him credit for being able to make up his own mind. And give him credit for that last sacrifice. It won't mean much if you crucify yourself. A guy needs to get credit for what he did right. Give him the honor of what he did for you at the end; don't bury that in being guilty and angry at yourself. Don't take his last act away from him. If you can remember him for that, you haven't completely lost him."

Liz thought over McLaughlan's words before she turned to him sympathetically, "I'm not the only one haunted by what's happened. Your partner's selling you down the river couldn't have been any picnic for you. Working together all those years, you must have trusted him with your life. And now that's all gone."

McLaughlan shrugged uneasily, perhaps surprised how welcome her compassion for his loss felt. Or maybe not. He'd always felt, on some level, that there was something special about this gal. But it still wasn't easy to open up and say, "Ah, well, you know. He made his own choices, too. Looks like your friend, Larry, made better ones, in the end." He hesitated before finishing gruffly, "But thanks for what you said."

Then he was on his feet with, "Maybe I'd better hit the road."

Liz was up, too, and asking, "Sure you won't have a cup of coffee?"

"Better not." They were walking to the door. When they reached it, Leo McLaughlan stopped and faced Liz. "Maybe I could take a rain check sometime."

Liz thought a moment, then agreed, "Maybe you could, but not too soon."

"Sounds fair to me. Be seeing you Miss Minton."

In the sunny, ocean-side living room, Jessica Minton formed the apex of the triangle of herself and her friend Rose' two daughters, ages thirteen and nine. She straightened her silver coil of a necklace, adjusted the square neckline of her wine-colored silk dress, sprigged with cream and pale green flowers, then gave the hair bow of Kathleen, the younger, a final adjustment before saying, "Shoot, David." The ladies' mouths all formed into grins as they laughed "Cheshire," for Rose's husband, David Nyquist, trying out his new birthday present, the latest in Brownies.

"Great!" David beamed, snapping the shot, "Glamour girls present and future!"

"I hope 'past' doesn't sneak up on me too soon," Jessica laughed to Tess, her arm around Rose's other daughter.

"You'll always look good to us, Jess," David grinned. Then he added "How about one more, just for insurance?"

"As long as Rose didn't get you to buy the policy from Fred McMurray," Jessica gibed.

The girls giggled, and Jess wasn't sure if they really got the joke. *Double Indemnity* was a bit mature for kids. They were a little young to be seeing movies about adultery and murder plotted by an insurance agent under the seductive wiles of Barbara Stanwyck.

"Do us in a line, Daddy!" insisted Kathleen, the younger daughter. "Start with me, then Terry, then Jessica."

"We're going by height, not age, right?" Jess queried.

"You're not old," Kathleen assured Jessica. "You still like to help us find frogs and grasshoppers and stuff."

"So that's the secret to eternal youth," David observed.

"Okay," Jessica agreed, organizing the girls. "One more shot. David, an order of prints for my agent."

"They'll be perfect for radio," he kidded.

"Ha, ha," Jess pretended to grouse. "Okay, girls, exude glamour."

Kathleen wrinkled her nose, Theresa crossed her eyes, and Jessica did both.

"Perfect. The Jerry Colona School of Beauty," David effused. A flash and a snap and the photo shoot was over. That was when Jessica noticed Rose, dressed in a white blouse and navy slacks, hovering in the open doorway off the main corridor. She seemed to have something on her mind.

"Rose? Come to join David's photo shoot?" Jessica inquired.

"I always have room for one more," David kidded, then added, "Well, actually, no I don't. That's the end of the roll."

"That's all right, David," Rose dryly remarked. "You got quite a few of me taking the curlers out of my hair; in my exercise baggies; and let's not forget, coming in from gardening with mud on my face."

"*Au naturel*, Honey. Roughing it!"

"I'll rough you *up*, Mister!" Rose grinned.

"Please," Jess offered in mock horror, hands covering the girls' eyes. "Not in front of the children."

Rose laughed, "Those two. If anyone around here rough-houses!"

"Not that you'd have it any other way, Rose Nyquist!" Jessica teased back. "You're still quite the tomboy, yourself. Anyway, where is *my* little girl, the four-footed one?"

Rose's mouth quirked before she answered, "Oh, funny you should ask. She just went bouncing into the study."

"I think I'll go in and annoy her. I have to make up for lost time. I'm still getting the cold, albeit furry, shoulder."

"She's sitting on the window seat."

"Ah, a favorite place, especially for the great view of goldfinches dining on your cosmos seeds. Dusty gives new meaning to the concept of 'bird watching.'"

"And 'bird feeders,'" Rose added.

Jessica smiled, then strolled past Rose and David down the corridor of light-painted walls, decorated with Rose's own watercolors. This was a lovely place, bright, breezy, tangy with salt air in the summer and cozy and warm in the winter. Of course, Rose and her family's friendship was the most refreshing of all–especially after the past several weeks. If only she could have persuaded Liz to come away with her for a couple of days. But, right now, Liz seemed to see work as her best therapy. Well, she'd be back in the city tomorrow evening. And Iris and Lois were keeping an eye on Liz. Come to think of it, neither McLaughlan nor Hooley had been very far off either. All things considered, they'd both proved darned invaluable in the clinches. Maybe she'd been a little too hard on Jeff Hooley, after all.

There was the study door. Pushing it open, Jess's eyes went expectantly to the window seat across from her, overlooking the wildflower garden and ocean beyond. There was Dusty, all right, comfy on the window seat–but not alone. The backlighting of the afternoon sun reduced the form on whose lap Dusty snuggled to a silhouette, until he turned at her entrance. Jess knew that face, and she suddenly went all wobbly.

Even with the little table behind her to steady her, Jess found herself sinking with shock. He called her name, and Dusty made an affronted "brrrp" when her human seat abruptly disappeared. But he was across the room in a jiffy, even with something of a hobble, and his arms surrounded her, supporting her. A too-long-missed British voice, more of a caress than the actual words might suggest, cleared the fog from her brain: "Well, Love, I'm glad to see you haven't been going overboard on those cherry Danish."

There was a kiss that seemed to swallow both them up with joy. Then he had an arm around her and was helping her to the window seat, but not before she coolly answered his quip with, "*You* are a stinker, James Crawford."

"But I'm *your* stinker."

James's arms were around her, crushing Jessica so close she almost couldn't breathe, but who had time for respiration when there was so much lost time to make up? He finally spoke against the softness of her hair, "And you stuck with me." He pulled back suddenly serious, suddenly worried, "You still feel the same? You still want this, too?"

Jessica violently nodded her head, lovingly exasperated that he had to ask after she'd nearly gone down for the count at the joy of his being here again. She bumped her forehead to his, letting it rest there to answer, "You think this is how I greet the milkman?"

James's arms slipped back around Jess, enfolding her contentedly, "I know it's been so long. You know how I've missed you."

"I know."

He turned her so her back nestled against his chest, his arms around her, their hands locked; no one was leaving anyone.

"Brrp."

This was the ascent variation of that feline expression. Dusty settled down with them, forepaws on Jessica's thigh, a nuzzle to James's hand.

"Seems as if I've been adopted into the family. How does that sound to you, Jessica? If the cat wants us to make it legal, I don't see how we have any choice."

He turned Jessica to face him, only slightly discombobulating Dusty, and went on, "I'm assigned here now as a liaison until I'm demobbed. You don't even have to worry about starting over again in another country." To her protesting expression, James answered, "I know that wasn't an issue for you, but I've seen you making enough sacrifices for me. I may be a bit gimpy in the knees, I'm not a wealthy bloke, but I do make you laugh; and now I'll be here when you need me. Do you still think a glamour girl could marry a chap like me?"

"I don't know about a glamour girl, but I know I'd be pretty darned ecstatic. Yes, as soon as we can."

"Just one thing."

"Yes?"

"Milk deliveries–I'll do all the greeting."

Dusty blinked her approval.

Made in the USA
Middletown, DE
03 February 2023

23828000R00191